THE

CONFESSIONAL

KILLINGS

DI Gallway Investigates

D. R. BAILEY

The Confessional Killings Copyright © 2019 by D. R. Bailey

This book is a work of fiction. Names, characters, places, and incidents either
are products of the author's imagination or are used fictitiously. Any resemblance to
actual persons, living or dead, events, or locales is entirely coincidental.

Published by Twisted Tree Publications
www.twistedtreepublications.com
info@twistedtreepublications.com

Paperback ISBN: 978-1-9996169-7-7

For my sister Bizet

From the time that I was born my sister has always been there for me. With help, advice and comfort throughout all the ups and downs of my life. But above all she contributed to my love of books and literature.

She typed up the very first story about my teddy bears which I dictated at nine years old.

An accomplished and published author my sister has encouraged my own forays into authorship. My sister has always put others first and sacrificed much of her own personal life. Without her inspiration I would probably never have arrived here with my first completed crime novel.

Love you Bizet, you are the best.

VESPERS

The sting of death is sin, and the power of sin is the law.
1 Corinthians 15:56

F ather O'Flaherty entered his church at approximately seven thirty on a chilly early autumn evening in early September. The night was drawing in and he was glad to get out of the cold. Shutting the door firmly behind him he listened to the echoes die away. With a measured tread, he began to walk up the aisle towards his confessional stall. Each step sounded brittle and hollow on the stone floor just as it always did. The church was empty, just as it always was. A sign of the times, he sighed inwardly reflecting on the days when once his little church was full to bursting. It was just at the outer limit of his normal confession times. Sometimes he just liked to come and sit. Sit there, with no real purpose, just to imagine the life he once had and the bustling church.

He didn't notice the hunched figure seated in a pew until he was almost upon it. He stopped alongside and all of a sudden, a pale white face turned to up to look at him. The eyes were shaded by a hood in the dim church light, but he could just about make out what he thought was a male with what appeared to be stubble on his chin. The eyes glittered in the darkness. The person said nothing.

"Can I help you there, my son?" he enquired gently.

There was no response.

He tried again, "Do you need something from God... or me?" He laughed lightly trying to inject a little humour.

Still nothing. He waited a few moments more and then, "Well, I'll be in the confessional if you need me." He smiled and moved on, making his way up the church.

O'Flaherty paused just outside his stall before entering and looked back. The person was still there, hunched and still, but he could feel a pair of eyes penetrating through the darkness. He had a vague feeling of unease but shrugged it off. Nothing worse than a broken window had ever disturbed his peace in the parish of Ballysruth until now. He entered his compartment, sat and waited, perhaps they would come and seek the help they needed.

He did not have to wait for long. The sound of light steps was borne in through the curtain becoming louder as they approached. There was a flurry and a shadow appeared behind the grilled partition.

"Welcome, my son," said O'Flaherty. "Do you have something to confess?"

There was another minute or two of silence before the other spoke.

"Yes."

"Well? What is it, my son?"

"I... err... I." The voice was not quite manly nor womanly either, he had expected someone gruff, but the tones were quite cultured. "Forgive me, father, for I have sinned."

These lines were quite familiar to O'Flaherty and he responded, "We are here in the sight of God, don't be afraid, just tell me what is troubling you."

"I have done something very bad."

"OK."

"I... I err... I killed a man."

"I see." He had not quite been expecting that and it took him a little aback. Gathering his wits, he continued, "Who or should I say whom did you kill?"

"A... a priest."

"What!" O'Flaherty could not help the startled alarm with which he received this information. His heart was beating a little faster, but he tried to steady himself. "I mean, when, when did you commit this sin, my son?"

"Today."

"Today?" He hadn't heard of any priests being killed on the news, in fact, this was news to him. "Are you sure it was today?"

"Yes, I am sure."

"Who...?" he hesitated and began again, "Who was this priest?"

"You know him, Father," the other told him.

"I do?... err I am not sure I... err... I." O'Flaherty did not finish the sentence. He may be a priest, but he knew when he was staring down the barrel of a lethal weapon. There was an ominous silence as he took it in. "Now then... now then... don't do anything hasty," he said quietly. "You seem as if you are troubled and I want to help."

"I am sorry," said the other. There was an unmistakable sound of the hammer being drawn back on the very large service pistol now pointing at O'Flaherty's head.

"You don't want to do that now," said O'Flaherty.

"I do," was the response.

3

"But why?... why? I don't even know you? Why do you want to kill me?"

"You bastard."

"I..." began O'Flaherty but he got no further. The loud report of the gunshot reverberated in the church. Gun smoke filled the confessional. The unmistakable spatter of blood appeared where the priest was sitting only a moment ago. He sat no longer. His body was sprawled half out of his confessional amid a spreading pool of red.

The intruder stepped lightly out of the other side of the stall and stood staring for a long while at the dead priest. There was a moment while they contemplated spitting on his body and thought better of it. Spitting leaves evidence, DNA evidence.

Then as silent as a ghost, they quietly slipped away.

* * *

Seamus Gallway was not in a particularly good mood as he strode up to the crime scene. He had been interrupted in the middle of a particularly promising tinder date just over an hour ago. He had driven to what he considered the back of beyond, and now this. He stopped at a suitable distance and stood morosely looking at the dead priest, taking in the knowledge pretty rapidly this was not going to be a short investigation.

A jovial looking officer appeared out of nowhere at his elbow.

"Ah you must be the fellah from Dublin is it?"

Seamus swivelled his head and took in the Garda officer, a sergeant, who had addressed him. He was a slightly overweight individual, forty-something with greying thinning hair. Other than that, he seemed harmless enough. Seamus had, however, no good opinion of the provincial Garda. Seamus was a little taller than the sergeant and in his thirties. He was a good-looking man with black hair and brown eyes, his physique was still good for his age and he tried to keep himself well and in shape.

"Yes," Seamus confirmed. "Detective Inspector Seamus Gallway assigned to this investigation."

Gallway was from GNCBI, the Garda National Bureau of Criminal Investigation. Murder was one of their specialist areas, hence the call he had received from his boss earlier that night.

"Indeed, indeed, indeed," the other smiled back. Seamus rolled his eyes.

"Well, this is a bad business inspector, a bad business," continued the sergeant. "By the way, the name's Connor O'Rorden, Sergeant O'Rorden," he added unnecessarily.

"Thanks," returned Seamus, "so who found the body?"

"Ah well now, yes, that would be Mrs Lynch, the organist that found him." And then O'Rorden unnecessarily added, in case Seamus had not made the connection himself, "Yes, she plays the organ here in the church you see."

"Really, who would have thought it," said Seamus without a trace of irony in his voice. He sighed inwardly, this was going to be a long night.

"Yes, she came to do her usual and there he was, dead, on the floor, there, dead"

"Her usual what?" enquired Seamus.

"Well, she comes to practice of an evening, on the organ you know, hymns and so forth, and you can imagine I am sure. She wasn't expecting to find the Father you know, dead, shot in the head, lying there on the floor like that, dead."

5

"Yes, yes I see," said Seamus somewhat testily. "But how did you know he was shot?" he asked as he hadn't been close enough to see.

"Oh well, I had a closer look you know, to check if he was alive and well, if that's not a gunshot wound then my name's not O'Rorden. Nasty, you know, very nasty. A big hole right in his—"

"Sure, I get it," Seamus cut him off. "Have you called Garda Technical Bureau yet?"

"Oh, well yes, yes indeed, our other sergeant, that is Kathryn O'Flynn, or Kathy as she prefers, did that right away, right away once we ascertained it was murder and they should be here by now."

"Well, we don't know for sure it was murder now do we?" Seamus pointed out. At the moment he wasn't interested in what Sergeant O'Flynn did or did not prefer to be called.

"Well true, true... but if Father O'Flaherty had shot himself then where's the weapon?"

Seamus studied him briefly and realised perhaps he wasn't quite as stupid as he first thought.

"OK good point, well let's get down to business, then shall we? Make sure nobody comes near the body at all, we need to get the pathologist here if you haven't already, someone will need to interview this organist, and I will take a closer look at things."

"Ah to be sure," said O'Rorden. "I'll get onto it right away, yes right away just now I will." And with that, he disappeared as magically as he had arrived.

Seamus moved closer to the dead priest to get a better view but without disturbing any evidence forensics may discover. The man was in his fifties, balding with grey hair. That much he was able to gather. A circle, plainly visible, in the centre of the man's forehead clearly indicated it had been a single bullet to the head that had killed him. The murderer was either very lucky or a very good shot. Whichever it was they could certainly handle a high calibre weapon. Where did they get it and why? Why would they come all the way to this godforsaken town and kill the local priest? Unless of course, it was someone local, with a grudge? Against a priest? That was all too likely judging by the reputation of some of the clergy over the past few decades.

He glanced at the confessional, but the curtain obscured the exit hole the bullet had undoubtedly made through the wall of the confessional. He would examine it later in detail along with everything else once Garda Technical Bureau had finished their work.

"Ah, it's a bad business for sure, a bad business." It was O'Rorden, who had once again appeared at his elbow without warning. A habit Seamus was soon going to find irritating.

"Yes, so you said I believe."

"Poor Father O'Flaherty, I can't imagine who would want to harm him like this. He would never harm a fly, so he wouldn't and that's a fact."

"I suppose now you are going to tell me he led a blameless life, had no enemies and nothing to hide," said Seamus sardonically.

"Ah well now, the Father did like a drink or two for sure, but otherwise he was well liked around here. I can't think of anything to blame him for."

"And how well did you know him, Sergeant?"

"I've spent most of my life here, Inspector, so I'd say I know him well enough, just an ordinary priest going about his business, that's what he was."

"A blameless priest, who just happens to have someone come into his confessional and shoot him dead."

"Well now, I admit that's a little puzzling to be sure, not sure what to think about that one."

"No, I imagine not," Seamus continued and then in a somewhat resigned voice, "We are going to have to interview all of the people who knew him. I will probably be here for a few days. I will need an office and some sort of incident room and somewhere to stay, can you arrange it for me?"

"There's a room at the Baker's Arms, I've already taken the liberty and there's a desk you can use at the station, plus we have a sort of room you can use for the incident stuff, yes indeed."

"The Baker's Arms?"

"Yes, it's the nearest pub to the station I'm afraid, we're a bit of a small place really, now some people would call it town, but I wouldn't, no that I wouldn't."

"Don't tell me, let me guess, the pub used to be a bakery?" said Seamus with a faint smile and a poor attempt at humour.

"As a matter of fact, that's right," said O'Rorden. "I can see now why you made detective."

"Where can I get a cup of coffee?" asked Seamus, now not certain if O'Rorden was being sarcastic or if he really was a congenital idiot.

"Now, that's another story."

"Spare me the details and find me the coffee, if you wouldn't mind?"

"To be sure, I will, to be sure, won't be long, it might not be like your fancy Starbucks mind." O'Rorden disappeared towards the vestry.

"That's fine," said Seamus to his retreating back. It really was going to be a long night.

* * *

"What's the story?" Seamus' boss Brogan was terse, unsurprisingly considering it was the small wee hours of the morning.

"A priest has been shot, in the head."

"A priest? A priest you say."

"Yes," said Seamus. "A very dead priest"

"I'm sure," replied Brogan. "Oh, this is a bad business, a bad business"

"That's what O'Rorden said."

"Who the fuck is O'Rorden when he's at home?"

"Well, he's one of the sergeants here who was first on the scene."

"Oh, well, is he? Hmmm, well he's right. Priests and murder, not good, the church will get involved, shit, I'll have to think about that."

"Look, sir, I need a team down here, we've got interviews to do, house to house, all the usual stuff." Seamus ignored the bit about the Church, for the moment, he knew he would have enough on his plate without the clergy meddling in his investigation.

"OK, OK, I'll get you what I can."

"What's that mean?" said Seamus, although from his tone it was obvious he knew.

"Well we're short staffed at the moment, Seamus, you know that."

"Oh, come on, this is a murder investigation, sir, and we're always short staffed, apparently."

"Yes, and I've got budgets which aren't being met."

"Fine!" Seamus knew argument was pointless. "If you can get me some, any people, it would help."

"I will do my best and, in the meantime, use what you've got."

"Use what I've got?" Seamus looked up to see O'Rorden standing there with a cup containing some sort of steaming liquid which might potentially be coffee, or not.

"Keep me posted," Brogan disconnected.

"Your coffee, sir," said O'Rorden beaming at him.

"Thanks." Seamus took the cup and noticed it did at least smell like coffee when he put it to his lips. The liquid, however, that found its way down his throat was indeed one of, if not the worst attempts at making the beverage he had ever tasted. He tried not to grimace.

"Mmm," was all he managed trying to look pleased whilst the noxious fluid found its way to his stomach.

"See, we can make a cup of coffee down here in Ballysruth, sure we can," said O'Rorden.

"Yes, I can vouch for that." Many other things sprang to mind at this point about the coffee making abilities of Ballysruth residents, but Seamus quelled them with an effort. "Right let's see what else you can do?"

"The pathologist will be here any minute," said O'Rorden.

"Good," said Seamus. "That's something at any rate."

He stared mournfully at the dreadful coffee in his hand and wondered just how long he was going to be here for. With a lack of backup staff looming it could be a long while.

THE CONFESSIONAL KILLINGS

* * *

The woman stood, quite tall in black stilettoes, a ribbon of black hair cascading down her back. Her torso was encased in a tightly laced black leather corset contrasting with the whiteness of her skin. From one hand resplendent with bright red nails trailed a thick leather strap.

Lying bent across the end of the bed was a man, naked from the waist down. He wore a black shirt and the dog collar denoting his calling was unmistakable. His buttocks were tinged a deep shade of red, and his hands gripped tightly onto the bedspread.

"So, Father," the woman said, "do you think you've been punished enough?"

"I don't know," said the man quietly.

"Obviously not then, Father."

She raised the strap and brought it somewhat expertly down across his rear end. He winced and cried out as it struck with a resounding crack. And then again, and then four more. She paused.

"That's another six," she muttered to herself in satisfaction She liked to think in sixes, ever since that time. Memories came crowding back into her mind, her face clouded briefly and then relaxed as she mentally waved them away.

She walked away to a table and picked up a cigarette. She took a long pull and slowly let the smoke out with a sigh. She wasn't really much of a smoker, in fact, she despised it somehow, but when she was carrying out her profession or sometimes after having sex, she found it calming. Also, it probably went with the image. Outside of those times she never touched tobacco or spirits, or alcohol, or drugs. There was too much turmoil in her mind already to introduce some more.

"Well?" she asked him again.

"Yes, yes I have," he said, with what seemed quite an effort.

"Really? You don't seem very sure." She put down the cigarette in the ashtray and walked back to the bed.

"Please," he pleaded, "please I've had enough."

"Is that so?" she said sardonically. "You've had enough?"

"Yes, yes I have."

"Yes what?" she said suddenly giving him another crack across he buttocks.

"Yes... Mistress"

"Better," she told him.

"So, who is the person who decides if you have had enough now? Is it you now, is it? Is it?"

"No, no it's not."

"No... who?" she raised the strap.

"No... Mistress... it's you, you decide, you do, but please, please I am truly sorry for what I've done, I've been bad, I needed to pay the price for it, but I can't take anymore."

"Is that right? And what about the girl?" she asked him "The one you broke your vows with, what if she had asked you would you have stopped then? And what about all the others?"

He said nothing.

"I thought so," she said, "You definitely need some more of this."

The strap rose and fell again repeatedly, rhythmically, methodically, in a deliberate and unhurried sort of way, the sound of the leather on his skin cascading echoes in the dimly lit room. All the while she was smiling, almost with perverse enjoyment at his discomfort. This continued until the priest began to sob like a baby. She stopped then, lowered her arm and dropped the strap to the floor. She walked to the bed and sat down beside him.

"Well, then maybe you have, now." She smiled at him, her ruby red lips revealing perfect white teeth. Her green eyes twinkling denoted the Irish blood that ran through her veins.

He looked up at her questioningly as his sobs subsided, his face suffused with colour.

"You can get up now," she told him. "I've decided you have had enough, for now at least"

"Yes, Mistress."

"And what do you say?" she said severely.

"Thank you, thank you, Mistress."

"Get up, get dressed!"

He got himself up and stood, quite tall, middle-aged, grey thinning hair.

He wiped his face dashing away the teardrops. He walked to the mirror and surveyed his backside.

"Admiring my handiwork?" she laughed.

"You would have made a great nun, you know," he joked wincing, it seemed he had recovered his composure quite quickly from his ordeal.

"I was raised by them, I learned from the best," she said sardonically, then, "funny, though, in a way we do the same job, don't we?"

"What do you mean?" He was pulling on his underwear and trousers and starting to tie his shoes.

"Well, people come to you to confess their sins and pay a penance to be absolved. And you come to me, to confess, and pay a penance, and be absolved, ironic really when you look at it."

"I guess." He wasn't smiling now.

13

"Don't worry, your secrets are safe with me." She flashed her teeth, she looked quite charming in a way, a classic Irish beauty. But in her eyes, there was a hint of something more, of iron, steel, of depths unfathomed by anyone.

"I hope they are," said the priest.

"Oh yes, oh indeed they are, I will take them to my grave, or yours."

He looked up quickly then but saw she was smiling. He placed a wad of notes on the dressing table and moved to the door.

"Mind how you go," she told him. "I'm sure it won't be too comfortable sitting down for a while."

"You certainly made sure of that," he grimaced.

"I did my best, try not to break your vows again, or you know what will happen." She smiled again. He glanced back at her briefly, locked eyes and walked to the door.

She watched his retreating back and the closing door and her smile faded. The door shut firmly, and then she heard his footsteps down the hall and the front door open and close.

"See you soon, you stupid weak-minded bastard," she said to herself contemptuously.

* * *

The pathologist completed his preliminary examination of the body in situ. Seamus was watching him the whole time and O'Rorden also gawking in open fascination.

"Well," said Jewbry, the pathologist, "You don't need me to tell you he died of a gunshot wound to the head."

"No," said Seamus.

"He would have died instantly of course. From what I can see so far, there are no other marks on the body and so it would appear there were no signs of a struggle or anything else. I would say he wasn't expecting it to be honest."

"I doubt any priest is expecting to be killed in his own confessional," Seamus offered.

"No, most likely not."

"Time of death?" asked Seamus

"Well, judging by the state of the body, I would say several hours had passed, so I think it would be at the earliest a little before eight pm."

"OK."

The pathologist rose and started to pack up his things.

"Once Garda Technical Bureau has completed their examination, we will ship the body over to you for a PM," Seamus told him.

"Great," said Jewbry. "I'll look forward to it."

"No doubt," Seamus re-joined.

The two men looked at each other ironically and Jewbry strode away.

"Well, it's nice to see a man enjoying his work," put in O'Rorden.

"I don't think enjoyment was the first thing on his mind."

"Was it not? He seemed happy enough to me."

"Indeed." Seamus looked around and nodded to the Garda Technical Bureau team who had by now arrived and were patiently waiting. "Your turn, we'll move the body when you're done."

As the team moved in to start their examination, Seamus turned to O'Rorden.

"Maybe you can show me to my digs, so I can get some sleep in what's left of the night. Garda Technical Bureau will take a while, we don't need to be here, but I do need at least one officer minding the church and keeping public away, nobody, is to come inside, got it? Nobody, not anyone other than our officers, not even the Bishop." He was half-joking at that last remark, surely it was the last thing that could happen.

"Right to be sure, that's what we'll do, we'll lock this place up tight, don't you worry, follow me. Nobody is getting in this church now, or my name's not O'Rorden, which of course it is."

Seamus followed O'Rorden's retreating figure, shaking his head and wondering if O'Rorden ever stopped talking.

* * *

Liam lay in the bed beside Mistress Dana. One hand caressed her pale white cheek and traced a line along her red full lips. Her green eyes locked upon his pale blue ones and her hand ruffled his black hair. The bed smelled of sex, and so did the room. In one corner lay her roughly discarded leather corset along with the leather strap she had lately used with such precision.

"Have you been giving another priest a good hiding then?" he asked.

"Well, he deserved it," she laughed.

"What did this one do then?"

"Oh, the usual you know, a girl, he couldn't keep his hands to himself, broke his vows, a little bit of coercion, that sort of thing. There were several others before that too."

"Fucking priests, they're all the same, damn them to hell!"

"Now, now," she put one finger to his lips to quiet him. "That's not spoken like a good Catholic now is it?"

"I'm not a good Catholic," he retorted. "I am done with being a good Catholic, I was done with that a long time ago."

She didn't ask him why because she could see it in his eyes. Perhaps it was what drew them to each other. The secrets, the dirty little secrets meted out by the clergy on the unsuspecting. Her green eyes sparkled, and she laughed instead. She left the bed in one swift movement, lit a cigarette and stood there naked and unashamed. Surprising how she could feel unashamed after what had happened before, a long time before. Once more, just as she did every day, with an effort, she parted the clouds in her mind. The smoke drifted upwards catching in the evening rays of the sun filtered through the skylight gently playing on the floor below.

"God you're beautiful," he told her, openly admiring her.

She smiled. "Charmer."

"Charmer is it? I'm serious now, so I am."

"Yeah sure you are," she laughed. "I'm sure you say that to all the girls from here to Ballysruth."

"Ach, you know there's only you."

"And I'm the Queen of England," she teased, stubbing out her smoke and sitting on the bed.

"What's it like?" he asked her.

"What's what like?" she said.

"You know, what's it like having a priest lying there at your mercy, punishing them, what's it like?"

"Oh, it's a job you know, pays well," she was evasive.

"No, no I think it's more than that," he quizzed her watching her face.

"What do you think? It's a calling? It's my calling to be giving priests a taste of their own medicine now is it?" she teased back.

"Not a calling perhaps, but I think you possibly enjoy it."

"Maybe..." A flicker of a smile crossed her face, but she said no more.

"I'd like to watch," he said. "One time, I'd like to see it."

"Oh, would you now? Why's that then, Liam? What are you a pervert?" she joked and moved onto the bed and straddled his naked torso. "Liam wants to do some perving while I give a priest a good spanking is that it?"

"I..." said Liam. "No, I'm just curious..." he finished lamely.

"It seems you are, I can tell." Her hand was on him and he was suddenly hard. Her fingers moved expertly up and down, and he gasped.

"Curious is it? I can see just how curious you are now Liam, oh yes..."

In one swift move, he was inside her and she began to rise and fall, rhythmically. She began moving slower and then faster, becoming almost frenzied in the moment. He said nothing gasping and moaning, gripping the bedsheets. Gripping the bedsheets like the priest. She flicked the image away from her thoughts. The two of them became locked in a final almost transcendental moment of pure sex.

"Liam wants to see me give a priest the belt... is that... what... you... want!!!" At her last outburst, her climax arrived closely followed by his. She was loud, very loud, and so was he, but she didn't care. She'd had soundproofing put in long ago. It was a release. A release from the thoughts which haunted her every day unless she kept them at bay. She snaked down and kissed him gently, almost lovingly, as lovingly as she could feel, almost feel, something more than loathing towards a man.

DAY 1

Seamus awoke to the sound of birds through the flimsy windowpane of his room. It was early, he could tell by the predawn light. His head was also pounding. He had no idea how much sleep he had had, or rather how much had hadn't had. His watch told him it was just after 6:00 or thereabouts, his usual waking up time.

"Shit" he swore and sat up gingerly. He had been sweating, he had no idea why. It wasn't particularly warm. He stood up looked out of the window. There was a low mist layering on the grass and the country was bathed in the emerging light of the rising sun. He breathed a sigh and went into the bathroom. He looked in the mirror above the basin and his brown eyes stared back.

"Fuck."

He looked a mess. With an effort, he dragged himself under the shower and turned it on. He was pleasantly surprised it didn't take long to get a decent temperature and the pressure was good. Most hotels he had stayed in could have won awards for the worst showers in Ireland. The water ran gently down his body bathing him in its magical healing powers. Or at least, that is how it felt. He washed his face, attended to the rest of him and began to feel somewhat more human than before.

After ten minutes he stood once again, towel around his waist and razor in hand. With deft strokes, he neatly and precisely shaved the edges of his beard. He was quite fastidious about his appearance. Or rather, very fastidious. His mother had called him a metrosexual before now. He laughed off the term but it was true, he always liked to look tidy.

Following his ablutions, he put on a suit and tie, and normality descended. The pounding in his head had lessened somewhat but he realised he had not eaten anything for more hours than he could count. Finally, he holstered the gun all detectives in the Garda were required to carry. In truth, he hated it, that part. Uniformed officers did not carry them unless on special duties. Seamus didn't like guns, there was too much chance of someone getting killed for no reason. Brogan wouldn't hear of him not wearing one, and so he did, albeit reluctantly.

On that note and glancing at himself once more to ensure he was looking as neat as possible, and with one final adjustment of his tie, he left the room and went downstairs in search of some sort of breakfast. To his relief, there appeared to be a breakfast room or at least tables which looked like they might at some point contain food. It was very still and quiet, he sat down at the nearest seat and glanced around for a menu.

"Oh my God!"

He turned his head at this outburst to see a woman, perhaps thirty-something, blonde hair, nice eyes, smiling and holding her hand to her chest. She was dressed in jeans and a light pink blouse. She was wearing sandals and had pretty looking feet with pink nail polish. Seamus was one for detail.

"God you startled me," she continued and moved forward. "Hi, I'm Kerry. I'm, well this is my pub."

"DI Gallway." He stood up and put out his hand, she took it and shook it briefly.

"Do you have a first name?" she asked, "or are we going to be on formal terms only?"

"It's Seamus." He smiled back, disarmed, but then a pretty face usually brought out the best in him.

"Well," she said, "I'm sorry I wasn't here to welcome you last night, but I hope you got in OK and slept well."

"I don't know," he answered.

"Don't know if you slept well or if you got in OK?" she twinkled.

"Well I got in but I've no idea about sleep, it was late."

"Oh dear. Well, anyway," she continued, "what can I get you? Seamus."

"Ibuprofen would be good, I've a splitting headache if you have any."

"Goodness come on you can't just have that, you need a decent breakfast I am sure."

"Well," he admitted, "I've not eaten since God knows when so it would be nice too."

"What'll you have? Or would you like a menu?"

"No, just whatever you think," he told her. "I'll leave it in your hands."

"OK, I'll give you the Irish special, you look like a man who could use one of those," she laughed

"Sounds fine," he said doubtfully. "I guess."

"You'll love it," she reassured him with a twinkle in her eye. She turned to go.

"Oh, there is one thing I'd like."

"Yes?"

"Can you make a decent cup of coffee? I'd love that."

"I think we can manage it, detective."

With that, she left to make her preparations.

* * *

The Irish breakfast proved hearty and filling. Seamus had wolfed it down ravenously, a testament to his hunger. He stared at the remains on his plate and sipped from his coffee cup. It was very good, in fact, compared to O'Rorden's foul brew it tasted like the nectar of the Gods. He sighed with satisfaction and mused upon a world devoid of coffee and how awful it would be. A particularly abhorrent form of Armageddon. A true disaster in fact.

Kerry came up to the table, she had a packet of Ibuprofen in her hand.

"Would you still like a couple of these, for your headache?"

Seamus smiled, he had not noticed but the headache had definitely subsided if not disappeared completely.

"It's fine, I'll live for now I think, thanks."

"How was the breakfast?"

"It was very good thanks."

"And the coffee?"

"Oh, now that was magnificent."

"Really? Magnificent, well I've never had quite such an accolade before."

"It's well deserved believe me."

"Great, although I'm tempted to say you are flattering me." She flashed him another smile.

"If you had tasted my sergeant's coffee you would understand," he said, then, "Erm, would you like to sit down for a few minutes?"

"Well, I've got breakfast to prepare." She glanced at the clock nervously. "But maybe five wouldn't hurt I suppose."

Kerry sat down opposite him and looked at him expectantly.

"Is this an interview? Just so I know," she asked.

"Not formally no, but I just wondered, if you run the local pub then you must know most of the people here?"

"It's true I do."

"Do you know anything about what happened last night?" He was watching her closely without seeming to.

"You mean up at the church?"

"Yes."

"Well, not really, O'Rorden said it was something bad, something happened to Father O'Flaherty?"

"He's dead."

"Oh?" She looked genuinely shocked "Oh! But I mean how, I mean what? How?"

"I can't disclose that just now," said Seamus. "We will be making a statement in due course."

"Poor Father O'Flaherty."

"Did you know him well?" asked Seamus noting her apparently genuine reaction to the news.

"Not well, no, he came in, liked a pint of Guinness or two and an occasional Irish whisky. So, I mainly knew him from the pub."

"Mainly?" Seamus did not miss the qualification, he also remembered O'Rorden had said the same thing about O'Flaherty liking a drink.

"Well, you know I've been to confession once or twice. Like a good Catholic girl." She smiled again disarmingly.

23

"Oh, I see." Seamus was a little disappointed it wasn't something more, still getting a lead this early would be sheer luck and that probably wasn't going to occur. "So, do you know if he was well liked around here?"

"I suppose," said Kerry. "I can't say he was particularly disliked."

"But then perhaps there were people or someone who didn't get on with him?" Seamus picked up on what seemed like a small deflection.

"Well, he was known for his fire and brimstone sermons, the fires of hell and all that, not everyone liked it."

"So, you've heard his sermons then?"

"A couple of times I suppose."

She was beginning to sound evasive. Seamus had a nose for these things. First, she said she only knew him from the pub, then confession, then she'd been to church to hear his sermons. He had a feeling there was more but now was not the time to probe too deeply.

"Right," he replied not sounding as if it wasn't right at all.

"I err, I've got to get on now." She reacted to the small note of disbelief in his last response. "Sorry," she added hastily so he wouldn't feel it was because of him or what he had said.

"It's fine, I've got to get on myself," he said and smiled. She returned his smile and he thought then she was very lovely, if not downright beautiful. Seamus immediately reminded himself to be professional, suspect everyone and curb his natural eye for a pretty face.

He watched her retreating back and then returned to his room to get his briefcase. It was probably going to be a long day. He made a mental note to follow up on what she did or didn't know about the priest later.

THE CONFESSIONAL KILLINGS

✳ ✳ ✳

A makeshift incident room had been set up in the Ballysruth Garda station. It was an old redbrick building with the stamp of the nineteen fifties all over it. Metal windows, thick walls, solid. Old school is what immediately came to Seamus' mind. In fact, judging by the classroom like atmosphere and size of this room it probably was the old schoolhouse. A large whiteboard had been procured from somewhere and one wall would soon contain photographs and other important pieces of evidence to try and link the crime together. There were two or three tables in the room and a half a dozen expectant and assorted Garda were sitting on various chairs. Seamus surveyed this motley crew and wondered how he was going to get anywhere with this few people, none of whom were detectives. Ballysruth was a smallish town by all accounts so initial house to house inquiries should not take long, but what then? What if the net had to be spread wider? He brushed these thoughts aside.

"OK," said Seamus rising to his feet. "So, this is day one of the investigation of the murder of Father O'Flaherty. This is our morning briefing and we will have one of these every day until the investigation is finished or the murderer is found, whichever comes first."

Nobody said anything, so he continued.

"Here's what we know so far. Father O'Flaherty was shot through the head sometime just before eight pm last night. His body was discovered by the organist. We will need a statement from her, so someone needs to obtain it. Until we get the forensic reports coming through, we won't know anymore. We don't know if the gun had a silencer or not, or

25

anything about the type of weapon. But a shot would have made a noise, someone might have heard it. Someone might have seen something, anything and we need to find out who and what. We need to make house to house inquiries of all the houses nearby and get some preliminary statements, we will follow up on anything interesting out of that, all clear so far?"

There were murmurs of assent from the others.

"Now, we need to know everything we can about O'Flaherty. Who liked him, who hated him, who might have a reason to kill him. Anything, any small thing anyone says with a clue about him I want to know. Right. We need to search O'Flaherty's house and see what we can find there. For now, no details of this murder leave this room understood. Once we have forensics, we will release a statement to the press. O'Rorden you are with me and the rest of you get busy."

The team started to bustle about and there was an atmosphere of anticipation in the air. O'Rorden came over to Seamus.

"Well now, these are exciting times for us sir, sure they are. We've not had so much as a stolen bicycle for months and never a murder."

"Yes, well murder is not something I particularly view with excitement O'Rorden."

"No, no of course not sir but it's nice to be doing some real police work for a change. Thanks for picking me sir, I appreciate it, so I do."

"Picking you for what?"

"To be your sidekick, you know sir, your wingman."

Seamus eyed him with the same look one might reserve for a very naïve young child. Many retorts sprang to his lips and died there as he surveyed the eagerness in the other's eyes.

"You watch too much TV, O'Rorden," he said finally.

"Oh yes, I've seen all the best cop shows so I have, CI5, LAPD, True Detective."

"This is not America, O'Rorden, this is Ireland, now come on let's go."

"Roger that sir, Roger that."

Seamus rolled his eyes as O'Rorden hurried after him.

* * *

They arrived at Father's O'Flaherty's house shortly thereafter. It was a fairly substantial old stone house with a large wooden gate. A well-kept garden sat either side of a long path up to the front door.

"Would you look at that," exclaimed Seamus, "these priests have it pretty cosy, don't they? It's got to be what five or six bedrooms at least?"

"Ah it's a big house to be sure," said O'Rorden. "Yes indeed, that's right."

Seamus was becoming used to the fact O'Rorden endorsed almost everything he said three times over, like some kind of dreadful parody in an Irish sitcom. It was annoying.

They reached the front door and knocked very loudly. There was no answer.

"I thought you said he had a housekeeper?" said Seamus after a few minutes, having walked around the back and still found nobody at home.

"Well so he does, she is usually there, I can't imagine where she is, so I can't. No that's a fact I just can't imagine it at all."

"So, what do we do now?" asked Seamus.

"We'll have to go around to her house I suppose, and see if she's there, that's what I'm suggesting anyhow, sir," was the answer.

"Right in that case..." began Seamus but he was cut off by his mobile ringing. "Yes?" he answered it impatiently and then, "What?... WHAT!?... I told you nobody was to go near the body! For Christ's sake! Right sit tight I am on my way; do not move from the church do you understand?"

O'Rorden looked at him enquiringly.

"The fucking Bishop has forced his way onto the crime scene," Seamus told him with unnecessary force.

"Oh, oh that's not good, no indeed I would say that's not good at all, no it's not," said O'Rorden.

"You bet it's not good, O'Rorden, it's worse than not good, I just hope he hasn't compromised it."

"Do you want to go to the housekeeper's place?" ventured O'Rorden

"No, I do not want to go there, it will have to wait because the bloody bishop wants to jeopardise our investigation!"

O'Rorden stared him somewhat taken aback.

"Well come on," said Seamus over his shoulder, heading for the car. "Let's go and handle this before it becomes any more of a fucking disaster"

"Right, sir, I'm coming, sir, be right there so I will, yes indeed." O'Rorden scurried after him.

* * *

Seamus slammed open the church door with a resounding bang. The reverberation of the sound startled the present occupants who looked up. Without a pause, he strode up the aisle to where the body of O'Flaherty lay. Another grey-haired individual was squatting down and leaning over him. As he obviously wasn't wearing his full regalia you couldn't tell him apart from a normal priest, but Seamus knew it was the Bishop.

"Who the fuck are you?" he demanded towering over the prone figure, although he knew the answer already.

The man looked up and surveyed him with cold grey eyes. He stood up and matched height with Seamus. A stocky man with an obvious air of self-importance.

"I might ask you the same question," said the Bishop.

"I'm DI Gallway the investigating officer for this murder inquiry and you are on my crime scene." Seamus wasn't in the least intimidated and showed him his badge.

"And I am the Bishop of this diocese and you are in my church, so perhaps you could moderate your language."

"I don't care if you are the fucking Pope himself," Seamus was in full cry. "You've potentially contaminated my crime scene with your DNA and prints, whilst my officers are still undertaking a forensic investigation."

"I will not be spoken to in this fashion," began the Bishop.

"Now you listen to me," said Seamus evenly. "I could take a view that what you've done is an obstruction of justice and is an arrestable offence whether you are the Bishop or not. I suggest you remove yourself from here and on the way out perhaps you wouldn't mind giving my Garda Technical Bureau team a DNA sample and fingerprints to make sure we eliminate you from the inquiry."

"I will do no such thing," said the Bishop heatedly. "I am not a criminal to be treated this way. I am a high-ranking member of the church.

"Do you want us to find the person who murdered Father O'Flaherty or not?" Seamus' voice went up a few decibels. "Because if you do, then I suggest you cooperate."

The Bishop locked eyes with him trying to stare him down, but it was to no avail. Seamus had an icy gaze when he wanted to and one that had quelled many a hardened criminal in the interview room.

"You'll be hearing more about this," said the Bishop finally. "That you will."

He strode away, closely followed by a member of the Garda Technical Bureau team to get the necessary samples.

"Bejesus, you've got some balls, I'll say that for you." O'Rorden was magically at his side again.

"I'm not being talked down to by the fucking clergy." Seamus was still fuming.

"Bishop Mullen's not one to cross though, I admire your pluck." O'Rorden seemed as if he genuinely meant it.

"These people don't intimidate me," said Seamus defiantly, although with hindsight he wondered if he had been wise to allow his temper to get the better of him. It was one of his faults, for sure. His hot Irish temper. It had certainly cost him one or two potential relationships arguing or rather, shouting matches, over trivial things. Discretion was sometimes the better part of valour he reflected. Up to now, he had never managed to exercise any such restraint.

He turned to the Garda Technical Bureau officer at his side. The man was evidently suppressing a grin.

"What's the news, Jim?" he said ignoring the other's obvious amusement.

"Well we'd pretty much done anyway, you'll have my report in the morning. We found the bullet and a few other interesting things. We found a long black hair in the confessional stall. That's interesting but considering how many people must have gone in and out of there, it's probably a red herring."

"Hmmm, run the DNA anyway," said Seamus. "We might get lucky."

"OK," replied Jim O'Grady. He had worked with Seamus before and was familiar with his temperament. "You should go easy with the clergy, Seamus," he advised.

"Ah they just wind me up, Jim, I can't help it."

"It could damage your career one of these days if you aren't careful."

Seamus studied the older man, he was talking sense and he knew it.

"Yeah, well, I guess one of these days I will learn to keep my temper."

"There's always anger management," the other teased.

"Go on with you now, anger management, before I lose my temper again," but Seamus was smiling at the irony of what he said.

"OK, but don't say I didn't warn you, you can get the body over to the pathologist we're done."

"Thanks," said Seamus.

He turned to O'Rorden who had been somehow at his elbow during this exchange.

"Make sure this remains a crime scene for now until we release it. I want to take a look around it first. Let's take a closer at the body in situ and then you can organise its removal for a PM. Then we can get back to O'Flaherty's house, assuming I'm still on the case."

31

"Ah come on now, you're joking, sure you are," said O'Rorden.

"Only half," said Seamus. "Come on let's take a proper look."

* * *

Following a careful examination of the crime scene and arriving back at O'Flaherty's residence Seamus and O'Rorden were surprised to find the front door open.

"What the...?" said Seamus and he signalled to O'Rorden to enter the house with caution.

In the hallway, an elderly woman was standing with a brush and dustpan, which she dropped onto the tiled stone floor with a clatter.

"Good gracious, mother of Mary," she exclaimed. "You gave me a fright, so you did."

"Don't be alarmed, we are Garda officers, DI Gallway and Sergeant O'Rorden," replied Seamus.

"Well now, that was quick. I've only just reported the break-in."

"Break in? What break in?" asked Seamus. "We are here about Father O'Flaherty."

"Someone's broken into the house at the back, they've left a mess, I was trying to clear it up," she said and then paused. "Where is the Father by the way? I haven't seen him since last night."

Seamus and O'Rorden exchanged glances.

"I think you'd best come inside and sit down there now, Mrs Flynt," said O'Rorden. He led her off into what appeared to be the living room. He seemed to know his way around. Gently he pressed her into a chair. They sat down opposite.

"Why? What's happened, what's the matter, oh no, oh no, something terrible, it's the Father isn't it, I knew it, I saw it in the tea leaves last night."

"I'm afraid he's dead," said Seamus quietly and without preamble, "I'm sorry."

"Dead? Dead! Oh no, oh no no no, oh nooooo, noooo." Mrs Flynt began to sob uncontrollably. Seamus looked discomfited although he'd seen such reactions before. O'Rorden got up and sat beside her putting his arm around her.

"Now, now, Mrs Flynt, don't take on so, there, he was a good man, a good man so he was."

She put her head gratefully into his shoulder and cried it out. The men patiently waited until the sobs had subsided.

"Thank you," she said smiling faintly and sitting up. O'Rorden patted her hand comfortingly.

"How, how did he die?" she asked finally.

"He was murdered," said Seamus bluntly.

A look of horror passed over her face at this news.

"Murdered? Murdered! Oh no, oh no no no, not the Father, not murdered, oh no, no nooooo, murdered oh no, nooooo." Her face crumpled once again, and she collapsed once more onto the shoulder of O'Rorden whose jacket had, by now, quite a visible tear stained patch.

Seamus empathised with her evident distress but reflected to himself this was going to take some time if every piece of news was greeted with the same response.

She finally regained her composure once more. She looked gratefully at O'Rorden and squeezed his hand, possibly a little longer than was necessary. Seamus surveyed her more critically on seeing this. She was after all quite an attractive woman, with grey hair and soft eyes, now he looked at her closely. She was well groomed and nicely dressed for a housekeeper. Probably had long service with O'Flaherty also. He raised his eyebrows quizzically at O'Rorden who gave an imperceptible shrug. Ah well, thought Seamus, it's none of my business, though he mentally filed it for later study.

"How, how did it happen?" asked Mrs Flynt.

Seamus and O'Rorden looked at each other and it was obvious they both had the same thought.

"We can't reveal that at the moment," said Seamus. "We are still investigating you understand."

"Still, I hope he didn't suffer the poor Father, such a good man, such a kind man, I wouldn't like to think he had been stabbed, or, or hit on the head, such a terrible thing if he had, or, or maybe attacked with an axe... he could have been decapitated God forbid such a terrible thing, poor Father O'Flaherty... or strangled perhaps with a long piece of thick rope..."

"Mrs Flynt," said Seamus deliberately interrupting her as the potential methods of Father O'Flaherty's demise became ever more lurid in her imagination. "You said there had been a break in?"

"Yes, that's right, someone must have been in here, made a bit of mess in places, knocking stuff over and the like."

"Can you show us please?" he asked her.

"Yes, yes to be sure, this way."

She led them down a stone hallway to a large room lined with endless shelves of books, this was evidently the library, one which would probably be envied by any bibliophile. Some of the shelves were empty or in disarray. A very big desk stood in the centre of the room, books were discarded all over it and strewn all over the floor. By the window a large vase had been knocked off the table it was standing on and shattered on the floor, spilling flowers and water onto the parquet flooring. There was a picture on the floor which bore a similarity to Father O'Flaherty. An oil painting. Seamus noted the Father's face appeared to have been stabbed multiple times, a letter opener lay discarded nearby as a testimony to that.

"I assume this is not how the room normally looks," said Seamus.

"No, no, Father likes it neat and tidy, never a book out of place, never a flower, and his painting, oh his painting was his pride and joy, and look at it now, lying there on the floor discarded, and stabbed and him, dead, oh no, oh no no no no."

"Now, Mrs Flynt," said O'Rorden trying to prevent another paroxysm of tears. "What time do you think this happened?"

"Well, I went out this morning for my walk. I like to stroll across the fields, and when I came back about half an hour ago, I found this."

"So, you were gone how long?" he persisted.

"Oh, maybe an hour or more," she replied.

"And you knew nothing about the Father's demise until just now?" continued O'Rorden.

"Well, no, no I didn't it came as a big shock I can tell you, I went to bed early last night you see, I had a bit of a headache, you know the Father comes in late sometimes, often and so I left him his usual tipple on the kitchen worktop and a snack in the refrigerator. I came down this morning and found it was still there. I thought that was unusual but anyway I went for my walk then you see."

"And you saw or heard nothing between going to bed and the morning?"

"No, nothing at all."

"We'll need you to come down to the station later and make a statement if you don't mind," said O'Rorden gently.

She nodded in assent biting her lip, her eyes once again moist with tears.

"Mrs Flynt," said Seamus. "I am afraid you can't clean any of this up, we have to get our technical team down to investigate. We are going to need a DNA sample and fingerprints from you, for elimination purposes. And I am sorry, about the bad news, I can see you were fond of the Father."

"Yes, yes I was." She was wistful and then her brow cleared, and she asked brightly, "Well, you boys must be thirsty, can I get you a cup of tea?"

"Tea, that's great," said O'Rorden.

"I'll have coffee, if you can, please," said Seamus. "With milk, no sugar."

"I can give you a hand if you like," began O'Rorden. "Make sure you are OK."

"I am sure she can manage, O'Rorden," Seamus quelled him with a look.

"Right you are, the one tea and one coffee it is," she breezed out, perhaps glad to feel useful.

"She didn't ask you how you liked it," observed Seamus.

"How I like what, sir?"

"Your tea, she didn't..." He caught a look in O'Rorden's eyes and said no more. His suspicions were confirmed.

"So, what do you think?" he asked O'Rorden, "about this?" He gestured at the scene.

"I don't know, seems like the person was interested in books?" O'Rorden ventured.

36

"So, what, the intruder thought they would do a little light reading whilst they were here, did they?" flashed back Seamus.

"If that's so they must be a fast reader, so they must," mused O'Rorden.

"Come on, think man. They didn't break in here to read the bloody books, did they!"

"Ah well, yes I see, well I guess they were looking for something then."

"Bingo, O'Rorden, we'll make a detective of you yet."

O'Rorden smiled at this and Seamus guessed he didn't get paid many compliments in his career if a semi-sarcastic one would elicit that kind of reaction.

"Whoever they were also didn't like the Father very much at all by the looks of the picture," continued Seamus indicating the defaced portrait.

"No, no indeed, they didn't to be sure, a bad business, a bad business indeed," O'Rorden agreed.

"Ok, well get the tech team down here then," Seamus told O'Rorden. "We need to place dusted for prints, and so on. And then we need to figure out what the person breaking in was looking for."

Seamus' phone buzzed. He looked at it in annoyance, it was Brogan.

He signalled to O'Rorden he had to take it.

"Big Boss," he said and left the room.

✳ ✳ ✳

"Seamus, what the fuck are you doing?" Brogan was shouting down the phone.

"Sir?" Seamus had a feeling this was coming.

"I've just had the fucking Archbishop on the phone for half an hour complaining you insulted and swore at one of his Bishops, what the fuck are you playing at for God's sake? I can't leave you on a case for half a day before all hell breaks loose, what's the matter with you, Seamus? Honestly, you'll be the fucking death of me, so you will."

"Sir, he was at the crime scene, without asking, strides in without so much as a by your leave while our tech team was working and then there he is bending over the body, putting his bloody great hoofs and prints all over the damn place."

"So, you lost your temper, did you?" said Brogan with resignation, his voice assuming a note of calm as if he understood the frustration Seamus had felt.

"Yes, I might have, just a tad."

"Seamus, Seamus, for God's sake you can't go around saying 'fuck' to Bishops it's just not protocol. No matter the provocation."

"Yes sir, I hear you, Boss."

"You hear me, but will you actually do what I'm asking? Please, for pity's sake try to control your temper, I don't need any more of these phone calls from the damn clergy, they are a pain in the arse, so they are. Next thing it'll be the Pope breathing down my neck if this carries on. I'll have the place crawling with fucking Cardinals and all sorts, you have no idea, Seamus, you really don't."

"OK, is that all sir? We've got an investigation here and all that, you know with insufficient resources as I am sure you are aware," responded Seamus tersely hoping to get rid of him.

"So, how's it going?" asked Brogan conversationally.

Seamus was immediately on the alert, there was something in his tone he recognised and it wasn't good.

When Brogan started asking questions this early in an investigation something was up.

"It's early days. Tech just finished, and we should have forensic reports today, at least preliminary ones. The team is out doing house to house and preliminary interviews," he tried to make his answer as vague as he could.

"OK, well wrap this up as soon as you can."

"Boss, this is a murder, we've hardly got started on it" replied Seamus testily.

"I know but it's most likely a sectarian killing, you know it has all the hallmarks." Brogan's conversational tone disguised the evident agenda of his statement.

And there it was, Seamus had suspected something like this was coming from the sudden familiar change in tone of his Boss' voice.

"Oh, it does, does it?" Seamus felt his hackles rising and continued with some belligerence, "and what hallmarks are those?"

"Well, you know, a gunshot wound close up, unknown assailant, that sort of thing." Brogan was still trying to be quite casual about the whole thing trying not to appear to be pushing Seamus in the direction he wanted.

"Sir, with all due respect..." began Seamus.

"Seamus, come on, this is the church we are dealing with they don't want us hanging around too long. The Archbishop is very worried about it and he... well you know, he's been around a while and he thinks it probably is the kind of thing the provost used to do in the '70s."

"Oh, he does, does he?" said Seamus with a dangerous note in his voice. He was immediately infuriated and saw it all. The church meddling once again in his investigation to their own ends, well this time he wasn't having it.

"Now, Seamus..." Brogan was trying to sound conciliatory, but Seamus was off.

"So, the church is undertaking our investigations, now are they? The church who have no detective training whatsoever and a track record of neglect and abuse. The Archbishop who hasn't been near the crime scene, has no clue about the forensics, is qualified to give an opinion about the probable murderer is he?" Seamus was holding back his temper with difficulty.

"Well, you know he was just giving his opinion, Seamus, I mean the Bishop told him what he'd seen himself."

"Oh, the Bishop is it? So, the Bishop comes waltzing in, does his own little investigation and passes his findings on to the Archbishop, why didn't I think of that? Why am I wasting my time getting forensics, interviews when it's all so simple?" Seamus told him not without some bitterness.

"Seamus, calm down now, will you calm down, it was only a suggestion, of course, it's up to you, of course, it's up to you to find out the truth." Brogan was attempting to sooth his Inspector's ruffled feathers.

"Oh, it is, is it? Well, now that's very magnanimous of you, sir. Thanks a lot. I've only spent half my career at the bureau and solved some difficult murder cases, so what would I know? You know, compared to the fucking Archbishop. Well give my respects to the Archbishop for his opinion which I'll thank him to keep to himself, now if you don't mind, I've got a murder to solve and I'm not having the fucking clergy engaging in a pissing contest and fucking it up like last time."

"Seamus, now, Seamus, don't get all hot under the collar. I wasn't suggesting you, well you know, it was just an idea, you do what you think is best."

"Catch you later sir, I will call you when I have some cold hard fact-based evidence, as opposed to conjecture from the fucking clergy." Seamus completed the sentence in icy tones and disconnected the line. He smiled with grim satisfaction. Brogan knew only too well what had happened the last time the church was involved in a murder case with Seamus and knew he couldn't push it with him. After all, Brogan had been partly to blame when things had gone pear-shaped. Seamus had salvaged the case and covered up for Brogan's mistake. Seamus knew retirement was looming for Brogan and he wanted an unblemished record. He was on a pretty loose reign from his boss as a result.

"Well that's telling him, so it is now," O'Rorden piped up appearing at his side.

Seamus jumped. "Christ, O'Rorden, will you stop doing that, you scared the bejesus out of me."

"Tech are on their way sir," said O'Rorden.

"Great!"

Mrs Flynt appeared with two cups.

"Coffee for you, Inspector," she said handing it to him. "Tea for you, Connor," she smiled at him affectionately, "just how you always like it."

O'Rorden blushed under Seamus' sardonic gaze. He was definitely going to pursue this further at some point, even if just for some perverse amusement.

"So, Mrs Flynt," said Seamus sipping his coffee. He paused and took in the excellent aroma and taste. It was actually very good by his exacting coffee standards. "Very nice coffee by the way."

"Thank you," she replied.

"Mrs Flynt, you said there was a break in, so where exactly did the intruder break in? Was it a window, or something? Can you show us?"

"Oh no, it was nothing like that, when I said break-in, what I meant was someone came into the house without asking, but they used a key for sure."

Seamus and O'Rorden looked at each other.

"How do you know they used a key?" asked Seamus.

"Well they must have left in a hurry because the back door was left open and I know I had locked it before I went out, I always do."

"You are sure, sure you locked it?" said Seamus wanting to be certain.

"Oh yes, I checked it twice, I always check twice, I remember it well, I have a great memory for things like that."

"That she has," piped up O'Rorden. "That she has indeed."

Seamus ignored this interjection.

"So, Mrs Flynt, I have to ask, apart from you and presumably Father O'Flaherty, who has a key?" he continued.

"Oh well that's easy to answer, there's only one other set of keys to this place so there is."

"And who has those?"

"Why, that's the Bishop, Bishop Mullen, he has the other keys to be sure," she smiled at Seamus whose brow suddenly looked like thunder.

"I see," said Seamus. "Mrs Flynt, if you don't mind now, I just need to talk to O'Rorden here if that's OK, our tech team is on its way."

"Of course, of course, I'll be in the kitchen if you need me."

She bustled off and after she had gone, Seamus turned to O'Rorden.

"The fucking Bishop," he said bitterly. "I might have bloody guessed"

* * *

Jim O'Grady appeared shortly afterwards with a couple of his other team members in tow.

"Well, Seamus, you certainly know how to keep us busy now don't you," he smiled.

"Don't blame me," said Seamus testily. "Blame the stupid bastard who decided to break into the Father's house."

"Oh dear," O'Grady replied. "I guess we'd better get to work."

"Before you go." Seamus stopped him, "Did you find anything in the Father's pockets?"

"Like what?" the other asked.

"Like a set of keys, house keys most likely."

"Yes, there was a set of keys, in fact, they are in the van with the other evidence."

"Can I have a look at them?" Seamus said.

"Sure." Jim disappeared and reappeared shortly with an evidence bag. There was a fairly heavy set of keys in it. Seamus took them and studied them briefly then handed them to O'Rorden.

"O'Rorden, go and ask Mrs Flynt if these are Father's keys for the house, would you?"

"What, now?" O'Rorden asked.

"No, next week will be fine." Seamus couldn't help his sarcastic retort and then more gently, "Now would be good, yes, O'Rorden, if you don't mind."

O'Rorden disappeared down the corridor with the bag in his hand.

"You shouldn't be so hard on him," said Jim.

"Shouldn't I?" Seamus responded.

"Give him a break, this is a big case for these provincial boys, he's happy as a pig in shit, you can see it."

Seamus laughed, in his mind, the idea of O'Rorden rolling in a pile of manure was quite funny.

"I guess you are right," he conceded. "I'll try harder to be nice. Anyway, come this way I'll show you the next crime scene."

"It's beginning to sound like that board game Cluedo," remarked Jim. "In the library with Mrs Plum and the candlestick."

"Fuck, I wish it was so simple." Seamus shook his head and headed for the actual library with O'Grady.

He was standing watching the tech team start work when O'Rorden materialised beside him. He didn't jump this time, perhaps he was becoming inured to his sudden appearances.

"I've asked Mrs Flynt about the keys, sir."

"And?" said Seamus.

"And she said they are definitely all there, and they are definitely are the only other set of keys and they are Father O'Flaherty's. I'd recognise those keys anywhere so I would, that's what she said."

"Fuck," exclaimed Seamus.

"Sir."

"I was hoping they wouldn't be, that somehow it was someone else that did all this, but now, we know it's the Bishop or one of his minions perhaps trying to interfere in our investigation. Damn it."

"A bad business..." began O'Rorden.

"Yes, yes, it is. But what are they trying to hide, O'Rorden? That's what we need to know," he paused then continued, "we'll have to think carefully about what we say to the others. I need to know how loyal they are to the Garda or the church."

"Yes, yes I see," said O'Rorden his brow furrowed. "A bad, bad business."

✳ ✳ ✳

With the tech team busy inside the house, Seamus decided to take a look around the grounds. The garden was large, as one might expect for a church property. The house itself was stone and very likely 15th century or 16th century originally, although it looked as if it had been modified several times in its life. It was in good repair with smallish windows but certainly did not lack comfort or the trappings of an evident well to do living.

He scoffed, the Catholic church wasn't short of a Euro or two and that was a fact. The gardens were well kept and most likely the church had employed a gardener. At the back of the house was a kitchen style garden with neat beds, vegetables and herbs. He doubted the Father cared for all of this himself. In the centre of this was a stone flagged area with some wooden seats. As it had turned out quite warm for the time of year, and surprisingly dry, Seamus sat down for a few moments, to think.

It was not long before the familiar figure of O'Rorden hove into view across the lawn from behind the house.

"There you are, sir," said O'Rorden once he was in speaking distance.

"As you perceive," replied Seamus with a little asperity. He could see it was going to be impossible to have some quiet time with his new sidekick but all the same, there was something about O'Rorden he had started to like. He was a provincial sergeant for sure, but Seamus suspected he wasn't as stupid as he first appeared and apart from his complete lack of coffee making skills, he could turn out to be an asset. Following on that last thought, O'Rorden loomed over him, breathing slightly heavily from the exertion.

"Sit down, O'Rorden, you are making me nervous up there, and also you are blocking out the sun."

"Oops." O'Rorden sat down with some alacrity, then continued, "It's all going well there, sir, with the tech team, indeed so it is."

"Great."

"What's next on the agenda, sir?" O'Rorden looked as if there was something bothering him in spite of the assumed nonchalance.

"That's what I came out here to think about."

"Oh, oh well..."

"Yes, O'Rorden, spit it out." It was obvious the man was dying to say something.

"Well, it's just, you know, you don't think Mrs Flynt had anything to do with this, do you, sir?"

"Oh, and why's that? "answered Seamus.

"Well, you know, she's an old lady and she's known the Father for years. Why would she possibly want to kill him?"

"You seem extraordinarily interested in Mrs Flynt, O'Rorden," remarked Seamus.

"Well, it's just, you see sir, I..."

"O'Rorden," interrupted Seamus. "The first rule of being a detective is to believe nobody and suspect everybody."

"Am I a detective then sir?" asked O'Rorden momentarily diverted.

"Well, you're working for me, aren't you?" shrugged Seamus. "At least for now."

"True enough, that's true enough." O'Rorden smiled at the thought. "But sir, you know Mrs Flynt..."

"O'Rorden, I know there's something between you and Mrs Flynt, I am not an idiot, but I don't want to know more, no details. And it's better if I don't." He looked meaningfully at O'Rorden. "But, if it turns out for any reason she is mixed up in this, then I am afraid you will be off the case."

"Oh!" O'Rorden looked crestfallen.

"It would be a conflict of interest."

O'Rorden looked just like someone had come over and stolen his favourite dessert.

"Look. For any suspect in a crime, and at the moment everyone is still potentially a suspect. We have to establish if they had the means, motive and opportunity to commit it, do you see?"

"Oh," said O'Rorden as if this was definitely news to him.

"Really, O'Rorden, have you not read the classic 'The Handbook of Criminal Investigation', now? Surely you've heard of it?" Seamus was surprised.

"No, no I can't say I have, sir, to be honest." He looked completely crestfallen now as if he had committed the most dreadful solecism known to policing.

"Ach, well maybe it's only when you go to detective school," said Seamus trying to reassure him.

"Maybe." O'Rorden looked doubtful and his woebegone expression was a picture. Seamus refrained from laughing with an effort.

"OK, look at it like this. Mrs Flynt. Well, she certainly had the opportunity. She went to bed early so she says and got up and nobody saw her or can vouch for her whereabouts during the time O'Flaherty was killed," he paused and noted O'Rorden was deep in thought, "However, we don't know if she had the means, I mean we have no idea if she had a gun or access to a gun, and so far we don't have any particular motive for her killing him. At least not as yet although one may still emerge. We don't know. But based on what we do know, there is less of a probability of her being the murderer, at least not at the moment."

He stopped hoping this might have reassured O'Rorden somewhat. In his own mind, he had very little expectation she was the murderer but at the end of the day she couldn't be ruled out either.

"Well," began O'Rorden. "Well, yes I see how that would work, most certainly I do sir. There is one thing though, it might be, well it might be that, if needed, there could be someone who would vouch for where she was that night if needed."

Seamus gave him a very hard stare and O'Rorden turned a bright colour of red.

"Is that so?" said Seamus.

"Well, it might be sir, yes," replied O'Rorden somewhat lamely.

"Well, if and I do mean if, she does become a credible suspect then and only then might we have to explore who that person might be, who might vouch for her on the night, do I make myself clear?"

"Yes sir, very clear indeed, yes indeed you have, sir, thank you, sir." It was certainly actually crystal clear to O'Rorden Seamus knew exactly what he was talking about and had somehow diplomatically avoided saying anything.

"Right," continued Seamus. "In that case, we will go and take a careful look around the back door, just in case there is anything interesting to be found."

The two of them approached the back entrance cautiously. It was a typical glass panelled door, easily broken into if needed. However, there was, indeed, no sign of damage. Seamus scanned the ground around it and something shiny caught his eye.

"Well, well, well, what have we here?" he exclaimed bending down for a closer look. There was a shiny set of keys lying in the flowers which ran either side of the back wall.

"Well I never, that's a sharp eye you've got and no mistake, sir." O'Rorden was by his side also peering down at the objects.

"OK," said Seamus, "tell Jim to bag these up and test them for fingerprints, and check the area for anything else, maybe a footprint or two. I've a suspicion if there are any prints on there, whose they are going to be."

"You don't think?" O'Rorden looked appalled.

"Suspect everybody, O'Rorden, believe nobody," Seamus said this last sentence over his shoulder as he walked back round to the front of the house. O'Rorden stared after him and then back to the keys, unable to believe anything quite as shocking as it appeared to be.

* * *

The forensic reports arrived later in the evening by courier. Seamus had requested urgent sight of them. He was back in the office going over the preliminary interview reports and from that compiling a list of suspects. O'Rorden had brought the report in looking like a kid to whom Christmas had come early. Seamus supposed this investigation must be somehow exciting for someone who had never been involved in a murder inquiry.

This was opposed to his own slightly jaded view of the proceedings and the inevitable pain in the arse it could often be. He enjoyed the chase however, it wasn't exactly the thrill of it, but solving puzzles was definitely his thing. From a young age, he was immersed in crosswords and other puzzle books, graduating to computer-based mysteries. He also liked jigsaws and it was perhaps the piecing together of disparate but somehow related things which interested him most.

"Well?" said O'Rorden eagerly, while Seamus perused the pages.

"Give us a chance!"

O'Rorden sat down but couldn't quite contain himself and started fidgeting. Seamus tried to ignore him.

The report was straightforward. The priest was shot through the forehead and the shot had passed through the back of his skull and lodged itself in the stout oak side of the confessional. The priest had bled profusely but died instantly. There were few traces in the other box from where the shot was evidently fired. There were smoke traces inside and various fibres but they could have been from anyone so were not a huge amount of use. It is doubtful the priest cleaned out the confessional every day for example.

There was one long strand of black or brownish hair that seemed odd to be found there but had no DNA match and Seamus was inclined to dismiss it for now, as once again it could have belonged to anyone going to confession. The report said it looked like a recently shed hair so perhaps it was from someone in the last two to three days or so. He made a mental note to follow up although it was doubtful

O'Flaherty kept records of who went to confession. It wouldn't be confidential else.

According to the ballistics report, the bullet appeared to come from a service type revolver similar to those used in the army over forty plus years ago. Seamus rolled his eyes at that because it was exactly the sort of thing the provost might use. The idea of it being a sectarian killing didn't really resonate and there would have been plenty of these guns hanging around after the war and beyond, so it was probably not hard to get hold of them. Other than that, there was nothing concrete at all. A thorough search of the area had not elicited anything of forensic value, which was somewhat annoying and was going to make the job much harder.

"Well, O'Rorden," he said handing over the papers, "read this over and pin up any relevant photos on the wall. Also, write up any interesting notes or facts from it on the whiteboard. Just remember not to put anything up about the Bishop's keys, until we get the forensic report."

"Thank you, sir, thank you." O'Rorden almost tore the sheaf of papers out his hand and set to work, happy as a sandboy.

"Doesn't seem they gleaned too much from the crime scene." O'Rorden was disappointed surveying his handiwork. There were some gruesome photos of the dead priest on the wall and a few other notes.

"That's the way it goes sometimes I am afraid. We're going to have to do this the old-fashioned way."

"What way is that, sir?"

"By leg work and asking the right questions of the right people," replied Seamus.

"But, how will we know who the right people are?"

"That, O'Rorden, is what we need to find out."

The other pursed his lips. Seamus got up from his chair and patted him on the shoulder.

"Don't worry, it's early days, very early days, I need some dinner and some sleep, and I'm sure you do too."

"Yes, yes to be sure sir," O'Rorden hesitated. "Do you mind, sir, if I stay a bit longer, I'll look through those interview notes so I will, from the house to house they did today, see if I can find something."

"Go ahead, be my guest," said Seamus. "I've scanned them, and nothing particularly stood out, but I could have missed something, don't stay up too late though."

"I won't, sir, that I won't," O'Rorden sat down at his desk.

"Night," said Seamus as he left the room. He was impressed in spite of his misgivings. O'Rorden was certainly keen and that was good.

* * *

Seamus ate dinner alone in what apparently was the dining-parlour of the pub. There were people in the public bar, but this was obviously the posher part and it was otherwise empty. The pub fare was remarkably good and wholesome. He looked down at the empty plate which had previously contained a goodly portion of steak and kidney pie, peas and mash. He picked up his glass of ginger ale and took another swig to wash down the last of the very delicious pie.

Seamus wasn't much of a drinker, except on special occasions. He liked to keep a clear head when working on a case and it had stood him in good stead on more than one occasion involving late-night chases of a suspect. Beer and spirits tended to go to his head and the few times he had imbibed too much had not turned out well. The dressing down he had received when a Garda dance had got out of hand, was etched in his memory. He could not remember if it had been his idea to handcuff the Chief Superintendent to the table, but he had nearly lost his badge the next day. Fortunately, Brogan had intervened on his behalf, that time at least. He most certainly wasn't going to chance it a second time.

"Penny for your thoughts." A voice broke into his reverie. It was Kerry.

She stood across from the table. Her blond hair fell a little in disarray and a few strands wafted across the side of her face. She moved them away with a swift movement of her hand with its perfectly painted pink nails. She looked a little flushed as if she'd been somewhere very hot, and Seamus concluded it was the kitchen. Her eyes, he now noticed, were quite a striking shade of blue, and she had the classic Brigitte Bardot pout. She was, he realised, exceptionally attractive, and the thing she had just done with her hair he found incredibly cute.

"Well?" She smiled since he had not replied.

"I err, I was just thinking you know about things."

"Things?" Without being asked she slid into the chair opposite. Her gaze was disconcertingly direct.

"Nothing particular," he responded.

"So, how's the investigation going?" she asked him conspiratorially.

"It's early days, we've got a lot of groundwork to do." He was being vague, and he knew it.

"So, no prime suspects then?" she teased.

"That would be fortunate were it the case," he said. "But I think it's going to take a little time to get to the bottom of this."

53

"All the same." She looked away then. "Poor old Father O'Flaherty, being shot like that, in cold blood."

Seamus shot her an enquiring look. "How do you know?" he asked her.

"Oh, you know, people talking." She was being evasive.

"Which people? We haven't even made a statement yet."

"Well, Mrs Lynch, the organist, she found the body, you know she was particularly upset, we got to talking and..." she trailed off looking at him to see if he believed her.

"Yes, yes I see." Seamus thought about it. It could be true. Mrs Lynch might have been able to see he was shot. It was also a small town and people did talk. Kerry knowing something like this didn't necessarily mean anything at all in a place like this, particularly as she owned the pub.

"You know..." she continued.

"Have you been asked for a statement yet?" he interrupted.

"No," she told him.

"Well maybe contact O'Rorden so you can come down the station in the next couple of days and we'll take one if it's OK?"

"Sure," she shrugged. "Of course."

"The pie was great." Seamus changed the subject.

"Really?" She seemed genuinely pleased and had, he noticed a beautiful smile with a row of almost perfect white teeth. "It's erm, it's one of my specialities."

"Oh, you are the cook as well?" he sounded surprised.

"For my sins." She looked embarrassed. "I have a chef too, at weekends or when it's busy in the week, but I like to keep my hand in with cooking and other things..." The undertone of this last statement was somewhat unmistakable.

"I'm sure you do," Seamus replied not giving away any of the slightly turbulent thoughts she inspired in him. Their eyes locked, for just a moment too long and then Seamus broke the spell.

"I need to get some shut-eye," he told her.

"OK." She got up and turned to go, then thought better of it. "If you, you know, need anything else, at all, at any time, just let me know." She looked at him somewhat meaningfully before picking up the empty plate.

"I'll be sure to do that," Seamus told her in a non-committal tone.

"Good." She smiled and this time she left with the plate in her hand.

"Thanks for the dinner," he called after her retreating back and saw her hand raised in acknowledgement.

Kerry entered the kitchen with the plate in her hand. She was smiling about her encounter with Seamus and not really paying attention. The next moment she walked slap bang into someone and the plate fell from her hand smashing on the tiled floor.

"Oh, for feck's sake," she cried. "Why don't you..." she stopped.

A young man with a shock of black hair stood in front of her. He was fresh-faced even though he was just into his twenties and was dressed from head to foot in tight black clothing. He had boots with fancy silver buckles and studs, and a silver necklace with a skull around his neck. On his fingers were an assortment of heavy rings, also silver, and bracelets on his wrists. His eyes had heavy eye shadow and liner. He was the epitome of a Goth. He smiled.

"Liam!" she exclaimed.

"Ma!" His smiled broadened and he gathered her up into a bear hug which was deceptively strong for his seemingly light frame.

"What are you doing here? Why didn't you tell me you were coming?" The joy in her voice was unmistakable.

"Oh, you know, I just wanted some of that home cooking of yours Ma." He looked at her with his black eyes which always melted her heart.

She laughed and tousled his hair. Then she drew her hand back and looked at it.

"Oh my God, Liam, how much bloody styling cream have you put in this?"

"I should have warned you about it, Ma," he chuckled as she frantically wiped her hand with some paper towel.

"I just don't understand why you have to grease yourself up like a..." She stopped at her son's expression. "Ah well, you're old enough now, you can do what you want."

"I am glad you finally realise it, Ma," he grinned.

"Don't get cocky," she warned him, but she was smiling. "Sit." She motioned him to a table in a small dining room off the kitchen. He lounged in a chair watching her put a goodly slice of pie and mash on his plate. She slid it across the table and sat watching him for a moment with satisfaction.

"Slow down, speedy," she said. "There's plenty more, I've got to go and check up on the bar, I'll be back, don't you move."

"I can help out," he told her, "at the bar."

"No," she replied firmly. "Colleen can manage, I won't be long."

She was gone for a few minutes and Liam helped himself to another slice of pie. Then he cleaned up the broken plate and put it in the bin. He always had had a good appetite in spite of being thin as a rake. His mother told him it was all the nervous energy. She probably wasn't wrong.

When Kerry returned, he said to her, "Do you mind if I smoke, Ma?"

"Oh, Liam, for God's sake," she tutted but then seeing the look on his face. "Fine, but outside, I'll come with you."

They sat on the kitchen steps on the dry night. It was slightly cold with a hint of frost. Liam took a long draw on his roll-up and let it out, the smoke hung in the air on the still night.

"When did you start smoking?" she asked him.

"Ach it's just on and off. I don't smoke all the time, and I only started since I was seeing..." then he stopped embarrassed.

"Seeing who? Who is it, a girl? What's her name come on, who is she, tell me everything..."

"Later, Ma, later, I promise." She cocked a disbelieving eyebrow at him but let it go. He would tell her in his own sweet time or otherwise, she would find a way to get it out of him.

"As much as I love you, Liam, you should have told me you were coming."

"Why? You've never asked me to let you know before?" he asked.

"It's different this time." Her voice sounded serious.

"Why?"

"Do you not know about Father O'Flaherty?" There was a note of surprise.

"What about him?" His brow clouded at the mention of the priest's name.

57

"He's dead," she told him.

"And what? Am I supposed to be sad? Good, I say, good he's dead, fucking bastard."

"Liam!"

"Sorry, Ma, but you know how much I hated him, after what he did to me, the bastard, good riddance." His voice dripped with venom, real hatred.

"Yes," she replied. "I know, and that's why you shouldn't be here."

"What?"

"Because," she continued emphatically, "he's been murdered."

"What?!" He looked at her slightly shocked and then, "What? Do you think I did it now? Is that it?"

"No!" She shook her head but stopped and looked at him directly suddenly doubtful, her blue eyes holding his dark ones in her gaze. "You didn't kill him, did you, Liam?"

"What? NO! What you can't think...," he faltered.

"Do you own a gun, Liam?" She didn't take her eyes off his.

"What kind of a question is that?"

"Well do you? Or know someone who has one?" Still looking at him intently.

"NO! Jesus, Ma! What do you take me for? Why are you asking me about guns all of a sudden?"

"Because he was shot!"

"You're kidding? And you think I...? What do you take me for? I'm not a murderer, really, Ma! Come on." He seemed annoyed.

She relaxed, let out a long breath and did not realise she had been holding it.

"I'm sorry, I had to ask, I don't know what to think. Don't you know if the Garda find out you hated him so much it gives you a motive."

"Oh, oh I see, yeah, well but they don't have to, do they?" An understanding of her concern was starting to dawn on him.

"If you weren't around it would be easier," she shrugged.

"You're not going to say anything are you." It was a statement, not a question.

"No, well, I don't know. I'm not going to lie if I am asked directly." She didn't seem too sure.

"Fine." He seemed disappointed. "But you don't have to volunteer it, right?"

"Well, I guess not," she said but there was no tone of certainty in her voice.

"Come on, Ma! Stop worrying it will be fine!" He tried to coax her a little.

"That's what your father said," she reminded him, "and look where he ended up."

"Ah you're not going to bring that up again," he complained.

"Your Dad was a member of the paramilitary, it's why he's now in prison, for the bombing, isn't he?"

"Then he couldn't have done it could he?" Liam tried to lighten the mood.

"Well, I never told him about the priest, thank God, or probably Father O'Flaherty would have been dead a lot sooner."

"Oh, but anyway how does it affect me?"

"Oh my God, Liam, your father was in the paramilitary, he had access to guns if you can't see where the Garda might go with this, then I can."

"OK, OK! But, Ma, you are exaggerating, there's no reason for them to make any of these connections, stop worrying." Liam was trying to sound confident but inside he was starting to feel far from it.

"OK." She didn't seem convinced. "I'll try, you can stay but keep out of trouble and out of the way of the cops."

"Thanks a lot," he said sarcastically.

"It's for your own good." She smiled disarmingly. He never could resist her smile. From the time he could recognise her face, her smile had pulled him through all of the times he was sad or upset or in pain. Even after Father O'Flaherty had taken his belt to him, his mother's smile had somehow magically erased the hurt.

"Come inside I'm getting cold," she said. He acquiesced, and they sat together in the small room with the table on two easy chairs. She had made them both a coffee and they sat sipping it together.

"There's something else," she said to him. "Something you don't know."

"What?" he was curious.

"When you came back that day, the day when you were fifteen and told me about the Father. When you told me how you had been working for him all that time, and then you took the church collection money." She held up her hand as he tried to speak, her eyes lost their focus as she began to recall it. "I know, I know it's because you were being bullied by the O'Sullivan boys. I know you didn't mean to do it. I know they were extorting money from you, though God knows why you just didn't tell me, but never mind.

"And then you told me you had confessed it to the Father, in his confessional, what you had done. The sanctity of the confessional! Sanctity my arse! Then, the bastard, he gave you a choice, his choice, the Garda or take his punishment. You were so ashamed you said you'd take his punishment." Her voice began to crack. "And then when you told me how he had bent you over his dining room table and taken his belt to you. You can't imagine how I felt. I saw the bruises. I was angry, I was beyond angry, I was a mother lion whose cub had been mauled by a hyena. And that man was, a fecking hyena." Her voice was harsh, rasping, full of emotion, of remembered and rekindled anger.

"I know all this, Ma," said Liam testily not wanting to remember.

"Yes, but what you don't know is I went to Father O'Flaherty. I went there that night and I told him what I thought of him."

"Yes, yes you said, you already told me, what's the point of bringing all this up again?"

"I know, but I said something else, I told him if he EVER, if he EVER touched you again, I would kill him." Her voice had suddenly changed, to icy steel, hard as nails, her eyes narrowed into slits.

"Fuck!" exclaimed Liam. "What the Fuck, Ma!"

"Yes." Her eyes were wet, and her voice had softened. "Now do you understand?" she asked him.

"Yes, but yes but, Ma..." he stopped.

"What?"

"There's something I never told you, something more, you might as well know it now, now you've told me."

"What?" she said. "What? Tell me, tell me now," her voice was shaking wondering what else could be worse than what she already knew.

"Well, after he finished the beating, I was bent there over the table, you know with my trousers down, with bare arse and he..." his voice broke and he fought to compose himself. Kerry's face was drawn into a tight mask as if she had already anticipated what he was going to say. He went on with difficulty, "He, sodomised me, Ma! He... I can't say it, I can't say it..." his voice caught on a sob. "He said it was God's punishment and God had told him to punish me like that. He said if I ever told anyone then God would strike me dead."

"SHITTTT!!" she shouted, loudly and pushed herself angrily from the chair. "Jesus fecking Christ!"

She flung her cup onto kitchen floor tiles and it shattered into pieces. She ignored it and walked over to the table and then stood there looking at him, but without seeing anything, her hands gripping the edge until her knuckles were white. There was a murderous expression in her eyes, tears were running down her face and her body was racked by sobs. The sobs of a mother for her wounded son.

Liam watched her in terrified fascination and wondered if his mother was perhaps capable of killing a priest after all.

DAY 2

"OK, this is day two of the murder inquiry into the Murder of Father O'Flaherty" Seamus was giving the morning briefing. "Let's go over what we know so far. He was shot in the head at virtually point-blank range using a military or military style service revolver. Now we know those types of weapons usually originate from the war or at least up to the 1960s. So, it would have to be something someone had stashed away for a long time or perhaps they may have got it from a friend, relative, who knows. We have very little or no forensic evidence to go on, one long strand of black or brown hair with no DNA match, it could be anybody who had been in the confessional and not necessarily the murderer. Then, we've got some other strands of cloth, etc. but nothing really we can go on.

"The murderer was obviously very clever and very careful, so they left nothing for us to identify them. We are relying on our own resources, from interviews and keeping your eyes and ears open to get a crack in this case. But believe me we will crack it, I am confident of that. I am going to give a statement to the press today about the murder and you can expect fucking journalists to be all over this. I cannot stress enough you don't talk to them, you don't make any statements, it's just no comment. Everything goes through me got it?" he paused while the assembled officers nodded in assent.

"OK so we've had some preliminary interviews so far, has anyone found anything interesting, anything at all no matter how small?" He waited and there was an uncomfortable silence. "Oh, come on now, don't be shy, I cannot believe nobody saw anything, heard anything or knows anything."

"O'Rorden," Seamus said finally, "anything from the interviews you looked over last night?"

"Well sir," he began.

"Yes?" Seamus looked at him expectantly.

"I am sorry to say no." O'Rorden looked sheepish.

Seamus did not look happy, in fact, he was far from happy and was trying desperately not to explode with wrath when Sergeant Kathryn O'Flynn raised her hand.

"Yes?" Seamus sighed.

"DI Gallway, there is one thing," she said quietly.

"Which is?" he demanded testily.

"Well, a woman we questioned yesterday said she was out walking her dog near the church on the night of the murder around the time it happened. She said she heard some sort of bang just as she was walking past the gate. Then she saw someone slip out of the main doors and brush past her. She said she didn't think she'd ever seen them before. Do you think it could be something important, sir?"

Seamus stared at her in disbelief. "Do I what?" he asked incredulously.

"Well, I was wondering if this was the kind of information you were talking about you might want to know, sir?" she repeated.

"I..." he began, "you are asking me if I might want to know it, is that what you are asking?" he continued, his voice dangerously calm.

"Well, yes to be sure, it's what I am asking, sir, yes indeed."

"Jesus Christ!" he suddenly shouted and brought his hand down on the table with such a bang everything on it jumped. The assembled officers were also startled out of their seats.

"Do I want to know if someone might have seen the fucking murderer coming out of the church? Do I want to know? YES! YES! And fucking YES!" He punctuated each 'yes' by pounding on the desk. "That, Sergeant O'Flynn, is exactly the sort of important information we need to know, and we need to know it straight away in future, do I make myself clear?"

O'Flynn looked somewhat taken aback at his unexpected reaction and seemed unable to speak.

With a visible effort Seamus forced himself to calm down and spoke again in a somewhat more normal tone. "Sergeant O'Flynn, in future I want to know anything, anything which seems like it might be important right away, do I make myself clear?"

"Yes, yes sir, very clear, sir, crystal in fact, so it is," she finally managed to say.

"Thank you," said Seamus breathing deeply. "And thank you for bringing it to our attention. And that goes for the rest of you now. Now if there is anything else anyone hasn't told me that might be important, now is the time to say it."

It was as if the floodgates were opened by magic and apparently several people had said they had heard a noise which they thought was a car backfiring about the time the gun was fired. Nobody else seemed to have seen anything though but it was at least a start.

"Right," said Seamus when they had all finished. "Thank you, thanks for all of this information and well done. We are actually starting to look like a team. Now we must write down everything, and I do mean *everything* important in future but also tell me or O'Rorden as well if you think it is important and even if you don't.

"So, O'Flynn, can you arrange to get the eyewitness down here for an interview please? Everyone else, what we need now is information on Father O'Flaherty. I want to know what his habits were, who liked him, who didn't like him, where he spent his time and when, I want to build up a full picture of this man, his friends and his enemies, and believe me he will have enemies. This information will hopefully lead us closer to his killer. We also need to know about anyone who might possess a firearm particularly the type of revolver we think was used in the crime. So, let's get busy!"

The assembled officers started to hustle around and there seemed to be more of a buzz in the air. Somehow Seamus had managed to galvanise them into action. He looked quite pleased at this activity and beckoned to O'Rorden.

"O'Rorden, was the stuff about the witness in any of these reports?" he asked.

"No sir, nothing like it at all, no there wasn't."

"Jesus!" exclaimed Seamus. "What have these guys been doing all this time? How did they not learn this stuff?"

"Well sir, it's like this, we just don't have a lot of crime here sir and there's nothing to report..."

"So, they don't learn to use the skills they learned in college..." Seamus finished it for him and O'Rorden nodded.

"By the way, sir," ventured O'Rorden. "I was wondering, are you planning to bang on the table very often sir? Just by the way of asking, sir, if you don't mind."

"I don't know," Seamus answered. "Why?"

"Well the thing is, sir, it's a very old table, and I don't think it can take much more punishment, that's all I'm saying, sir, if you see what I mean, sir."

Seamus looked at the table, which was one of those temporary tables similar to those used for wallpapering and noticed it looked a bit worse for wear and was sagging in the middle.

"Yes, yes I see," he mused contritely. "Well, O'Rorden, I'll do my best not to bang it in future, how's that?"

"That's great, so it is sir, thank you, it's just we don't have much of a budget here and if it breaks, I don't know if we can get another one."

"Your table is safe," said Seamus laughing. "Now let's get the interview room ready for the witness."

* * *

In the fairly small but adequate interview room in the Garda station, Seamus and O'Rorden sat opposite Shona McCarthy, the witness who had apparently seen the murderer on the night Father O'Flaherty was killed. She was a small woman in her forties with a pale complexion. Her hair, streaked with grey, was tied back in a ponytail. Her petite nose was pinched in at the tip, and her small mouth looked permanently pursed in an expression of disapproval.

Seamus turned on the recorder and gave the preamble regarding the witness, date and time, then he turned to Shona.

"So," he said to her, "may I call you Shona?"

"Yes, yes to be sure, Inspector, yes indeed," she assured him.

"Can you tell us, in your own words, what you told Sergeant O'Flynn you saw on the night Father O'Flaherty was murdered?"

"Well," she began, "well now, it was a cold night I remember, so I said to my husband, so I did, I'll be up and walk the dog now Michael. Then I put my coat on because it was cold, got the lead and then I..."

Seamus and O'Rorden exchanged glances, both of them were thinking the same thing, this was probably going to take some time. They sat listening to her ramble on with her preparations for the walk, hoping she would get to the point sometime soon.

Shona was continuing to talk and finally seemed to be getting somewhere near to the murder scene, "So, there I was walking out towards the church, and it was a little bit dark, I would say, yes though there was a street light of course you know. Anyway, there I was walking along, and I got past the church and then there was a kind of bang, you know."

"What did it sound like? What sort of bang?" interrupted Seamus.

"Ah well, now it's difficult to say, yes indeed. But I suppose, yes, the nearest I could describe it would be a car you know backfiring," said Shona.

"Is that what you thought it was?" asked Seamus.

"I don't really know, I didn't think it had come from the church in any case. I stopped though to see if I could find

68

out where it came from. I was right by the gate at the time you see. Also, you know, the dog was doing his business. Don't tell the Father though, he doesn't like it." She put her hand up to her mouth.

Seamus smiled. "It's OK, I don't think he's going to be likely to find out."

"Oh goodness, I can't get used to him being dead, and murdered to boot, poor old Father, it can't have been pleasant for him, no indeed."

"I am sure not, but you were telling us about what happened at the church..." said Seamus gently.

"Oh yes, yes sorry," Shona continued. "Well there I was at the church, the dog doing his business when all of sudden the church door opens, so it does."

"How long was this after the bang?" asked Seamus.

"Couldn't have been more than two or three minutes I would say," she replied, "well I saw this figure coming out."

"Can you describe the figure for us?"

"I couldn't really see clearly but he, I think it was a he, he was wearing one of those black hoodies you know, pulled right over his face so I couldn't really see it. He had, now let me see, black, no, no I think it was blue jeans yes and a pair of trainers." Shona's expression on her face was one of concentration as she was recalling the night's events.

"What colour were the trainers?" asked Seamus

"I think they were black, yes black to be honest, yes that they were," she told him after a fairly long pause.

"And then what happened?" he probed gently.

"Well, he saw me and stopped, as if he wasn't expecting me, and then just started walking, towards me."

"Started walking?" Seamus queried.

"Yes, very fast, through the gate and past me and down the road."

"And you were standing there the whole time?"

"Oh yes, yes that I was, that I was indeed. Well, I was, curious to be honest, as to who the person might be."

"Did you get a close look at him?" Seamus was looking at her intently now.

"Not really, no to be honest. He did come quite close and I was standing there, at the gate and he brushed past me."

"Did the person speak?"

"No, no he didn't, not that no."

"What about the face, did you see anything of his face?"

"Well it was hard to tell, it was so quick, that it was. His eyes were shaded by their hoodie, so I couldn't really see."

"Can you just try and think, Shona, think really hard anything, anything could be helpful," urged Seamus gently.

"Well, he didn't have a beard or anything from what I could see his skin was quite smooth, quite sort of pale I'd say, yes that's it pale. And there was something else, a sort of smell."

"What kind of smell?" He glanced at O'Rorden who was also listening to this with great interest.

"It was sort of, you know, sort of fragrant," remembered Shona.

"You mean like aftershave?"

"No, it was a more feminine smell, it was more like... perfume, that's it, perfume that's what it was." An expression of realisation came over her face.

"Perfume?"

"Oh yes. I would recognise it anywhere. I quite like a drop of perfume myself, so I spend a fair bit of time choosing them. I have smelled a lot of perfumes, detective, you wouldn't believe it. But this one, I can't quite place it, but it might something," she thought hard, "something like Chanel, that's it most likely Chanel."

"Number 5?" interjected Seamus.

"No more like another one." She knitted her brow trying to recall the exactness of the scent. "I think It's one called Mademoiselle. Yes, that's probably it, I would know it if I smelt it again that's for sure, quite distinct it was."

"Great, you're doing really well, Shona, it's fantastic information. Now can you tell me how tall this person was?"

"Well, you know I'm not a tall person, but they were taller than me, but probably not as tall as you Inspector."

"Good, good, so it gives us an idea at least." Seamus sounded pleased and then, "so, anything else you can say about this person? Anything else at all?"

"Well, and this is going to sound stupid." Shona looked embarrassed.

"It's fine, just tell us and don't worry we won't think it's stupid, everything you have told us is incredibly useful and important," Seamus went out of his way to reassure her. This was very important information and he knew it.

"Well it's just the way he walked, carried himself, the perfume, it just felt like he was actually a female, not a man like I first thought perhaps, that's what it was, she was a female. Definitely not a man at all, it was the impression I got. You know the pale smooth skin, the mouth too, she had quite a feminine sort of mouth."

Not for the first time, Seamus and O'Rorden looked at each other. This was quite a revelation for sure and they both knew it.

"So, you think she was a woman after all?"

"Yes, yes I do now I think about it."

"But you are not a hundred percent certain though, is it fair to say?"

"Yes, yes, I can't be totally sure and of course some men do wear lady's perfumes and all sorts, don't they?"

"Yes, yes, quite," Seamus assured her and then continued after a few moments of taking it all in, "thank you, Shona, is there anything else you can tell us?"

"No, that's it really, sorry I can't think of anything." She shook her head.

"OK, thank you again, Shona, I can't tell you how useful it has been and if there is anything, anything at all you can think of please let me or Sergeant O'Rorden know. We'd like to get you to perhaps help us with a photofit, it that's OK, one of the team will go through it with you, just to get a visual picture of what the murder looked like." Seamus smiled at her and she smiled back. He noticed how her face changed then, the pursed lips were gone.

"Yes, to be sure, Inspector, I would be happy to help."

They terminated the interview on the recorder, thanked Shona one more time and Seamus said goodbye. O'Rorden went with her to organise the photofit and after a while, he returned to the interview room where Seamus was still sitting, lost in thought.

"Well," said Seamus, "that wasn't what I was expecting at all."

"Me neither, I'll definitely say that, me neither, I wasn't expecting that at all."

Seamus ignored the fact O'Rorden had just repeated exactly what he had said and continued, "So, our murderer might not be a man, after all, she might be a woman."

"Yes, indeed, that's quite a turn up for the books, so it is."

"You are right about that, O'Rorden, very right about it. This changes things quite a bit, so it does, yes indeed." Seamus winced listening to himself, he was turning into O'Rorden, he hoped he wouldn't be here too much longer, or he might become a complete provincial. God forbid.

THE CONFESSIONAL KILLINGS

✳ ✳ ✳

The press statement was made outside the front of the Garda Station. A couple of local news hacks had turned up and a regional crew from *RTÉ News*. Seamus knew this wouldn't last and pretty soon the place would be full of journalists. The local news would send their reports up to the nationals and they would also see the news broadcast and bingo. He brought his attention back to the task in hand. O'Rorden stood slightly behind him and Seamus took centre stage.

"Two days ago, and late in the evening, Father O'Flaherty was found dead in his church," Seamus began. "We are currently treating his death as a murder inquiry. Garda investigations are ongoing, and we would like anyone who might have any information at all they think might be useful to come forward. You may have a friend or a member of your family who may have been acting differently or out of the ordinary. You may have seen or heard something unusual or suspicious. Anything, anything big or small please come forward and speak to us here at Ballysruth Garda station."

"Inspector Gallway, can you give us any information on how Father O'Flaherty was killed?" It was one of the local hacks.

"I am afraid we can't release those details at the moment." They didn't want to clue up the killer too much on what they did or didn't know.

"Is it true he was shot?" He kept a straight face at this, typical journalists already on the gossip trail.

"Where did you hear that?"

"Answer the question, Inspector."

They were obviously not giving up this easily.

"No comment at this time."

"So, we'll take it a yes then?"

"I said no comment, that isn't an affirmation or a denial of your question, It's a no comment. When it's appropriate to release the information we will release it, you know that." Seamus was becoming slightly irritated.

"Who would try to kill him then, Inspector, do you know?"

"As I said our enquiries are ongoing, we are not charging anyone at this stage."

"So, it means you have a suspect then, Inspector." He had not been paying attention to the local hack but now noticed they were quite a bit younger than they sounded. He took in the reddish hair and youthful face of a young man probably mid-twenties. He was obviously out there trying to make his mark. They were all the same.

"Seriously? No comment." His annoyance was starting to get the better of him.

"Who are they, what are their names?"

"OK, that's enough, thank you for coming and we will be making a further statement when we have more information, thank you, thank you." Seamus turned away before he said something he might regret. His track record with the press wasn't great and he had lost his temper a couple of times in interviews which had earned him a well-deserved bollocking from Brogan. He knew when to quit, so he turned away and started to walk back inside.

"If you won't tell us, you know we are going to find out anyway," the newshound shouted after him.

He ignored it and carried on back through the station doors with O'Rorden beside him.

"They're a bit keen aren't they, sir?" said O'Rorden.

"You could say that, the press is a fucking nuisance, so they are, and they will become more so now the news is out." Seamus sounded frustrated.

"Well, I suppose they are only doing their job," mused O'Rorden.

"Oh yeah, I just wish they'd let us do ours," snapped Seamus.

O'Rorden went quiet sensing Seamus was potentially at the edge of his temper threshold and didn't want to catch the fallout.

"Right." Seamus stopped and turned to him. "Now, if RTB has finished at O'Flaherty's place I want you to go and take a proper look around. See what you can snoop out. Just see if there are any clues to him and his life. I want to know what sort of man he really was."

"What me, sir?" O'Rorden was surprised.

"Yes, you. I've got something I need to do in the meantime. So, you go and do that and then meet me back here. Come on, you're on my team, you're keen on detecting, so now's your chance to go and detect something." Seamus smiled and softened his tone. "Besides, I thought you might like this particular assignment." He looked at O'Rorden somewhat teasingly.

"Oh, ooohhh, oh yes right, sir, yes indeed, sir. Right away, sir," said O'Rorden cottoning on to his superior's inference about Mrs Flynt. He headed off out of the door.

"Don't talk to those reporters," Seamus called after him, "and don't spend all the time at O'Flaherty's fraternising with the staff!" He could not resist the last part.

"No sir, that I won't, sir, that I won't," he heard O'Rorden say as he disappeared from view.

Chuckling to himself he went over to the main desk. Kathy O'Flynn was manning it.

"Sergeant," he said to her when she looked up. "Is there a library in this Godforsaken town?"

She looked at him not sure if he was joking or not, but he had a slight twinkle in his eye, so she relaxed. She had recently borne the brunt of his temper and didn't want to upset him again.

"Why yes, sir, there is one indeed," she replied.

"Really?" his tone was sardonic. "Would you be so kind as to tell me how to get there?"

* * *

The library, if it was possible to term it as such, turned out to be an old brick building which looked as if it had seen better days. It bore a faded sign announcing the fact over the glass door. Surprisingly the glass door opened as he approached it. Seamus had begun to expect everything in this town to be twenty years old or more, if not dating back to the war. The idea of an automatic door seemed incongruous to him.

On entering he noted it was, in fact, a reasonably spacious building with many rows of bookshelves sporting labels denoting their subject matter. In the centre of all of this was a long desk with a couple of computers on it and behind this appeared to be the librarian.

She was of average height, he noticed, with black hair tightly done up into a bun. Her plain beige dress seemed unusually well fitting, almost curvaceous in fact and she wore a yellow cardigan. A pair of green eyes watched him approach the desk and her somewhat voluptuous lips curved into a smile. The ruby red lipstick seemed somewhat out of place in a library and hinted at something much more sensual under the prim exterior.

"Can I help you?" she asked him as he reached the counter.

"DI Seamus Gallway," he replied showing her his badge.

"Oh," she spoke quite melodically. "A detective is it? Are you here to ask me some questions perhaps?"

There was a tease in her voice which he noted was almost quite flirtatious. He put the thought from his mind and spoke.

"Actually, I am not really here on official business, I am here after a book."

"A book is it?" she laughed. "Well as you can see you have come to the right place, detective."

"Yes." he acknowledged. "Yes indeed, but it's perhaps not one you would carry on the shelves."

"An unusual book is it, Inspector?" she flashed back.

"Let's say probably not a popular one at least."

"Well, if we don't have it, we can usually get it for you in a few days." She was reassuring.

"Really?" he said it with a pleased tone.

"Oh yes." She leaned a little further over the counter and looking at him under her lashes.

"It's erm, the name of the book is 'The Handbook of Criminal Investigation' by Tim Newburn," he told her. He was a little disconcerted by her seeming familiarity and wondered if this was how provincial librarians usually behaved.

"Brushing up on your detective skills is it?" she laughed, moving to the computer and expertly tapping on the keys.

"No," he replied. "No, it's for someone else."

"That's what they all say, detective." Her eyes twinkled playfully. "Hmmm, let's see, yes sure here it is. Would you like me to order it for you?"

"Yes please." He realised he was blushing slightly; her manner was somewhat disconcerting.

"You know," she told him. "You usually have to be a member for me to let you borrow a book."

"Oh," he said. "Oh, well in that case..."

"Don't worry, detective, seeing as it's you, I'll make an exception. I am sure you are not going anywhere now are you, and if you do, well I am sure I will be able to find you."

"Um, yes, thanks... erm, what did you say your name was?"

"I didn't." She smiled at him.

It felt so much like she was flirting with him, but why? Not that he was immune to this kind of banter but in a library? It was all very strange.

"It's Diana, Diana O'Malley, Head Librarian, at your service." She held out her hand to him to shake it.

He took her hand and shook it briefly, and it was soft, her nails immaculately manicured. He clocked the fact that her cardigan was Dior, by the little logo. She had expensive tastes that was for sure, for a librarian. And then there was something else, some kind of scent or perfume, he could smell just a faint undertone. It was quite distinctive.

"Is that, err, is it Chanel you are wearing?" he asked her casually.

"Why yes, Inspector, how did you know?" her eyes locked on his, and her lips curled ever so seductively.

"Just a lucky guess," he shrugged.

"Why?" she asked him.

"Why what?" He was evasive.

"Why do you want to know about my perfume? Are you thinking of buying some... for someone?" It seemed to Seamus almost as if everything she said was loaded with another meaning, although seemingly at first innocuous.

"It's just my inquisitive nature, you know being a detective." He wanted to ask her the brand but made a mental note to visit a perfume shop sometime soon. Not that he particularly suspected the town librarian, but it was those little details often led to something more.

"Sure," she said lightly and then, "is there anything else I can do for you?" There was a look in her eyes, just for a moment, a promise of something, something more, if he was interested.

"No, no that's all thank you." He set those thoughts aside, this was neither the time nor the place.

"Well then, come back in a couple of days and we will probably have the book for you then." She was suddenly matter of fact. The teasing tone was gone.

"We?" He picked up on it. "Does anyone else work here then?"

"Oh no, Inspector, it's just little old me, I mean 'we' as in the library service." And there it was again that tone. He couldn't make it out at all.

"I see, OK. Anyway, thanks for that, I will see you later then."

"I'll be here, detective."

Seamus couldn't be sure, but he could swear she had winked at him just then. He hadn't spent much time in libraries since his University days, but she seemed a little unusual for a librarian that was for sure. Perhaps she would bear closer examination when he came to retrieve the book. He turned and left, while Diana watched him, a small smile playing on her lips almost like a spider assessing her prey.

* * *

When he got back to the station, O'Rorden had returned and was at his desk in the inquiry room.

"Well?" Seamus asked him. "Did you find anything?"

"I had a good look around sir, everywhere, and I do mean everywhere," O'Rorden answered.

"And?"

"There wasn't anything too out of the ordinary sir. He liked a drink that's for sure, his cabinet was filled with booze and the bottles weren't full that's all I'm saying." O'Rorden laughed.

"Go on, what else?"

"Well, he was a neat and tidy man, everything in its place you know. A few family pictures, I am guessing of the mother and father, and so on."

"Was he an only son?" Seamus interjected.

"It seems so, yes, I don't think he had any siblings anyway. As I said there was nothing particularly out of place."

"You didn't find anything perhaps, like a diary? Letters, anything like that?"

"I err, well no diary, sir, no, there were letters from parishioners asking him to bless them, arrange their weddings and so forth."

"So, nothing you found which might be incongruous or out of the ordinary?" persisted Seamus.

"Well, sir, well there was one thing, and I thought it was a bit strange. I found something in his... the top drawer of his bedroom chest of drawers."

"And that was?"

"This, sir." O'Rorden placed an evidence bag on the table containing a packet of 12 condoms. It had evidently been opened. Seamus stared at it somewhat disbelievingly.

"Were any of them used?" he asked O'Rorden.

"Yes, sir, there's the thing, half of the packet was missing."

"And what do you make of it?"

"Well, my first thought was he was dispensing contraception," O'Rorden mused.

"And surely that would be followed by a second thought being a Catholic priest it would be unlikely."

"Yes, sir," continued O'Rorden. "Yes, for sure, that's true, contraception is forbidden or at least frowned upon by the Church."

"So?"

"Well," said O'Rorden, "I am not sure what to make of it no, sir, no I'm not."

"O'Rorden." Seamus, who had been sitting on the desk, stood up and began to pace the room. "Did I not tell you the golden rule?"

"Yes, sir, and it's already etched on my soul, so it is, suspect everybody believe nobody, yes, sir, that it is," O'Rorden told him fervently.

"So, in that case, and what follows is the second rule, people are capable of anything and I do mean anything."

"Yes, sir, I see, sir, but I don't really follow where this is going."

"Because you don't want to follow, O'Rorden, because you don't want to see what the evidence is telling you, because you are looking at a priest and not a man and thinking a priest couldn't do what a normal man would do. But the only real difference is he wears a collar, and he's supposed to follow his vows. What follows, O'Rorden, is the assumption that the person who used the condoms was Father O'Flaherty, and until we know otherwise, that's what we have to think, now do you get it?"

"Well, yes, but, well, yes, but..." O'Rorden was taking this in. "Oh my, that's well that's terrible so it is, and him a priest and all, oh my goodness."

"Exactly!" said Seamus triumphantly. "Not the Godly man everyone thought he was perhaps? Hmmm? And what did he do with those condoms and who knew about it?"

O'Rorden and Seamus were sitting there looking at each other and both thinking the same thing.

"Mrs Flynt," Seamus framed the thought.

"Yes, sir." O'Rorden looked far from happy at this realisation.

"We will get her in here tomorrow and question her further." Seamus looked a little grim and O'Rorden could see Mrs Flynt wasn't about to get an easy ride.

✳ ✳ ✳

After another hearty supper at the pub, Seamus decided to retire early. He had not been sleeping well of late and he thought perhaps he might catch up on some shut-eye.

He headed upstairs and was about to enter his room when Kerry appeared from down the corridor walking towards him.

"Hello, Inspector," she said smiling. "I was just checking on one of the empty rooms, we've got some journalists arriving tomorrow."

"Really?" Seamus sighed. "Already?"

"Oh, don't sigh so much, I am sure they'll be no bother." She was still smiling.

"They'll be plenty of bother, believe me, they will," he said with resignation.

"Surely not, Inspector. Or can I call you, Seamus?" Without him realising it, she was now incredibly close, his back was to the corridor wall and she was in front of him, her face only inches from his. He could feel her breath on his cheeks.

And she breathed deeply saying, "You know, Seamus, you are not an easy man to read."

"Is that right?" he replied uneasily.

"But the thing is, Seamus, I on the other hand, I am incredibly easy to read if you know what signals to look for."

Her mouth was only a fraction from his and she was pressing close into him. He didn't know how this had happened or how he had let it happen. It was almost as if he was mesmerised by her blue eyes staring into his, framed by her blonde hair. He could feel the heat from her lips now and from her body.

"They are?" was all he managed.

"Oh yes, Seamus, they are so easy to read, when you know how." The last sentence was more of a purr than anything else, like a cat.

Before he realised what was going on her lips had locked onto his and they kissed. It was a powerful kiss, deep and dizzy. He felt her hand snake under his shirt and onto his naked skin. It was like an electric shock when she touched him. A powerful force took hold and he couldn't help himself kissing her back, hard unreservedly. It was almost as if he was drowning, drowning in her senses. And then somewhere in his consciousness, there came a smell. It was the smell of perfume and he mused still kissing her all the while, where he had smelt it before and then it hit him, the library. His eyes which had been closed flew open and met

83

hers looking at him. She broke away and looked at him half smiling and half inquisitive.

"Why, Seamus, I would almost say your heart isn't quite in it," she said with mock hurt.

"Your perfume, what is the perfume you are wearing?" he asked her.

This time she did look taken aback and moved away a touch to better see his face.

"My perfume?"

"Yes," he said, "sorry, it's quite distinctive, what is it?"

"Well it wasn't quite what I was expecting but," she shrugged, "it's Chanel Mademoiselle if you must know, would you like to see the bottle too?" She flashed her eyes at him a little then, in mock anger but it wasn't real.

"No, no it's fine, thank you," he said feeling and looking flustered.

"Well," she purred again, "if you've finished discussing my perfume, then perhaps we could turn to more important matters... in your room?"

She moved in for another kiss but this time he stopped her. The perfume had broken the spell and brought him back to his senses.

"Tut, Seamus," she looked surprised. "And there I was thinking you had enjoyed our little moment of passion."

"I did, I was," he tried to get the words out in a way which didn't demean her or sound hurtful, though why it would be important he couldn't really say. "It's just that..."

"Just what, Seamus? Mmm?" She was teasing, her mouth was close again tempting him for another kiss, and more.

"Look, it's not that, it's just I am conducting a murder inquiry and well, I can't do anything to compromise the investigation," he said, but it sounded lame.

"And you think I might be the killer?" She looked at him a little disbelievingly pulling back again.

"It's not that." He tried to mitigate what he had said. "Look until I can categorically rule out you or any number of other people had nothing to do with it then they have to be potential suspects."

"Oh," she replied but didn't seem hurt. "Oh, I see, well, in that case, I guess this will just have to wait then won't it, until you're convinced I'm not the killer." She planted a kiss on his lips then before he had time to react. "You see, Seamus, I'm not easily deterred when there's something I want."

"No, no I bet you're not," he said ruefully.

"Until later then." She laughed and put a finger playfully on his lips before disappearing down the stairs.

Seamus opened the door to his room and sat gratefully inside trying to compose his feelings. It was a reaction he hadn't been expecting from himself. He had had plenty of experience with women, so it wasn't that. This was different, it was somehow kind of visceral, and real, and he found himself hoping very much, Kerry wasn't the murderer.

DAY 3

The morning brought Seamus down to breakfast quite early, he was hoping perhaps he wouldn't see Kerry. His mind was still somewhat in turmoil over what had happened, the recollection of the kiss was still etched vividly in his memory. The shame of it, if it was a shame, was something inside of him was, urging, craving almost, to experience the kiss again, and more like it. Women came and went in Seamus' life but none of them ever really stayed. He had tried to get serious with one or two, but something was never right for him and he couldn't understand why. Tinder had become his weapon of choice, to satisfy some of his more primal urges. But if he thought about it too much, he realised he wasn't satisfied, really, ever, not deep down. That is until now. A cliché in itself to say it.

The first time for a long time something so simple as a kiss had felt like a beating pulse as if an electrical current had run between them. It was weird. And on top of all of that, she might turn out to be the murderer, he couldn't rule it out, not after the perfume. It was the classic dichotomy of love, the heart says yes, and the head says no. Love, now, this was a word he had never used in the context of a woman. Except the once, years ago in his first teenage flush of youth, his first crush, his first consuming passion.

He pushed the image away, of the girl who stole his heart, and whose life was cruelly stolen from her. She was murdered, a famous case, in fact, the talk of Ireland at the time. It was probably then he decided to become a Garda officer. An act of vengeance? He didn't know.

He glanced idly at the daily paper, The Irish Sun, they always had one in the dining room, but he tended to ignore them as they irritated him beyond belief. The Sun was a rag in his opinion printed complete drivel on a daily basis. He read the front page and realised today was going to be no exception.

'Priest shot dead in suspected sectarian killing,' screamed the headline, the article went on, 'The Garda in Ballysruth is investigating the brutal murder of the local priest Father O'Flaherty. He was shot dead in what appears to be a crime with all the hallmarks of a sectarian style murder. Gunned down in cold blood Father O'Flaherty was cruelly murdered while taking confession. At the moment the Garda have little comment to make, but the Sun says the evidence is clear and asks if sectarian killings are back...'

"Fuck!" exclaimed Seamus angrily tossing the paper aside infuriated by the story. "Where the fuck do they get this fucking bogus information from, Jesus!"

"Having a bad morning, there are we?" It was a voice he didn't recognise. He looked up to see a young man standing in front of him with black hair and dressed predominantly in black apart from a white serving jacket. He was smiling and had obviously entered the room while Seamus was absorbed in the paper.

"Just the fucking bullshit they print in the excuse for a paper they call the Sun," Seamus replied. "Unbelievable. Un-fucking-believable."

"To be sure I never read it myself." The young man nodded sympathetically and then, "I'm Liam, by the way."

"Oh," said Seamus diverted. "Are you new here?" He had not seen the young man before, as far as he could remember, and he had a good memory for faces.

"No, not new," Liam laughed. "Perhaps I should explain, I'm Kerry's son."

"Oh." Seamus tried to hide his surprise. "She never mentioned you."

"Well, I'm usually up in Dublin," Liam explained. "I'm still studying, at Uni, I just came down for a visit and I like to help out if I can."

"I see, is your mum, erm, OK this morning?"

"Ach she's fine, fine so she is, she's just busy this morning you know we've got a few journalists arriving today."

"Journalists!" Seamus said with some annoyance.

"I can see they'll not be your favourite people." Liam smiled.

"No, I have always hoped there was a special place in hell reserved for them." Seamus sounded bitter.

"Are you a religious man then, is it?"

"No, not particularly, but I was brought up a Catholic, it's ingrained in us from birth, you know, heaven, hell, all that jazz." Seamus laughed then.

"All that jazz, I know what you mean," said Liam with feeling and then, "Anyway what'll it be, for breakfast, what would you like?"

"Oh, the usual," Seamus replied without thinking.

"And that is?" Liam smiled.

"Oh, sorry, it'll be the full Irish and white coffee please." Seamus returned the smile realising of course, Liam wouldn't know and also realising how in a very short space of time Kerry had become a familiar face. Then something invaded his nostrils. That damned scent, there it was again. Perfume.

"Is that, erm aftershave you are wearing?" he asked Liam suddenly, just as the other was about to go.

Liam looked at him slightly puzzled but then said: "No, no not aftershave." He laughed and continued "If you must know, it's my Ma's perfume, I kind of like it, suits my personality." His eyes twinkled. "I'll be off and sort your breakfast if that's all, or maybe you'd like to know what brand of toothpaste I use as well?"

"No, no, thanks, it's fine thank you."

Seamus watched Liam walk away and was perturbed. How many more people were going to be using that perfume? This was getting ridiculous. You thought you had a good clue and then it started to look like half the town was wearing it. He shook his head in disbelief.

* * *

Kerry returned to the kitchen to find Liam preparing some breakfast.

"What are you doing?" she asked unnecessarily.

"Making breakfast... for the detective," he responded keeping a weather eye on the contents of the frying pan.

"Liam! I said to keep away from the cops!" She didn't sound happy.

"Oh, come on, Ma! I was curious, no harm done." Liam was dismissive.

She sighed. "No, I suppose not, at least he doesn't know you are my son."

"Um, well..."

"You told him? Liam! For feck's sake!" Kerry was annoyed, and it showed.

"Ma! Come on it's not so bad."

"Don't you Ma me, Liam O'Shea, why did you have to go and do it? He didn't have to know, at least, not yet." She was peeved Seamus knew she had a son, she wanted to find the right time to tell him, preferably after the investigation was over. Now the cat was out the bag. Men often didn't take kindly to women with children.

Liam looked up sharply then and exclaimed, "Oh, oh I know that look." He waved his spatula her.

"What look? I don't know what you mean." Kerry tried to look innocent, but a sly smile crept into her lips.

"That look, Ma! I'm not stupid, you like him, here we go, that's why you don't want him to know isn't it, go on tell me the truth now." Liam was facing her accusingly but with a teasing expression on his face.

"What if I do?" she prevaricated, pouting at him.

"I knew it! I knew it!" He smiled. "A Garda for God's sake though, Ma!"

"OK, I admit it, I do like him, but it is also because I wanted to protect you," she said defensively.

Liam turned back to the pan and started to put Seamus' breakfast on a plate. "Yes, I'll believe you, Ma! Thousands wouldn't though, that they wouldn't."

"Liam!" she said playfully. "It's a shame you are too old for the naughty step."

He laughed. They both did. She had been the most indulgent and lenient parent imaginable. There never had been a naughty step, nor had she ever laid a hand on him.

"Whatever makes you happy, Ma." He hugged her. "It's alright with me."

"Well at least you've learned something," she said looking at the well turned out breakfast plate.

"It's all from you, Ma, it's all from you."

Liam whisked the plate out of the kitchen. Kerry put a finger up to her lips and bit it lightly. She smiled a secret smile thinking of Seamus and that kiss. She was certainly going to make sure it wasn't the last kiss she got from him, not by a long chalk. DI Seamus Gallway had better watch out, her eyes twinkled.

* * *

Seamus was on the phone to his boss whilst he walked to the Garda station from the pub.

"Brogan," came the familiar voice.

"It's Gallway, sir, I was wondering have you seen the Irish Sun this morning?"

"I've seen it," replied Brogan. "The usual rubbish that's for sure."

"I never gave them any of the information, sir, you must have seen the press conference"

"Yes, I saw it, it was very, reserved, most unlike you I have to say," Brogan said.

"No need to be sarcastic." Seamus laughed in spite of himself. "Anyway, sir, so I was wondering where they got it from." He was on the attack.

"Well not from me, if that's what you mean," Brogan said testily.

"Then where? I bet they rang you, though didn't they?" Seamus was persistent.

"They rang, I told them where to go, well not in so many words." Brogan was sounding a little evasive once again.

"Not in so many words?" Seamus wasn't going to let it go and Brogan could see that.

"Look, I said we had no comment to make at this time, the investigation was ongoing, and if they wanted to know about Father O'Flaherty then they'd best speak to the church about it"

There was a fairly long silence while Seamus digested this information.

"Seamus?" said Brogan at length when he didn't speak.

"They went to the Archbishop didn't they!" Seamus began to sound annoyed.

"Well, well they may have of course I don't know." Brogan rolled his eyes, he wished Seamus wasn't so perceptive.

"I think so, yes indeed I do," said Seamus. "How else would they get the sectarian killing idea? The fucking Archbishop."

"Now, now, Seamus.... Well, that's a possibility I suppose." Brogan was beginning to prevaricate, and Seamus could tell.

"Couldn't you just have told the Archbishop to keep his mouth shut?" Seamus was exasperated.

"I can't tell the church what to do, Seamus, you know that."

"Yes, yes, I know. It's always the same. I knew the bloody clergy would interfere one way or another. They always fucking do," Seamus said caustically.

"Well, just find the killer and we'll be all right and tight, and all this nonsense will go away," Brogan responded brightly.

"If only I could share your optimism," Seamus told him and decided to put his ire to one side, for now, it wouldn't do any good, the damage was already done, and he had other fish to fry. He continued, "well, anyway, sir, there's a favour you can do me if you would."

"Oh?" Brogan sounded suspicious.

"Come on, Boss, you owe me at least one favour, if not more," Seamus said slyly.

"Don't push your luck, Seamus," Brogan told him and then, "Go on, what is it you want?"

Brogan knew he actually owed Seamus a lot, and so usually went out of his way to assist when he could. As it turned out this particular favour was well within his remit once he knew what it was. He set to work rapidly putting the wheels in motion and pulling a few strings. One of the benefits of being Detective Chief Superintendent.

✳ ✳ ✳

Seamus arrived at the Garda station and headed for the incident room. It was Day three of the investigation. O'Rorden was already there and looked up glumly from the pages of the Irish Sun.

"Get used to it, O'Rorden, there is plenty more bullshit where that came from, don't you worry, we'll be knee deep in it in a couple of days," Seamus spoke kindly but firmly, like a doctor to a patient suffering from an incurable ailment.

"But, sir, none of this makes any sense. You didn't tell them anything at the press conference and now look at it, where did they get it all from?" O'Rorden sounded genuinely chagrined the press had printed such nonsense.

"Listen, O'Rorden, this is what they do. They have their fucking noses in the gutter all day, they feed off the bottom like fucking scavengers. Besides, they just keep on relentlessly until someone says something and then they make a story out of it."

"But, but it's not true is it, sir. I mean you don't think it really is a sectarian killing do you, sir?" O'Rorden's voice was full of concern.

Seamus snorted at the suggestion and sat down opposite his sidekick.

"You are beginning to sound like the DCS, O'Rorden. No, it's not, I don't think it is and believe me if I thought it was, I would be looking in the right places and it wouldn't be here. We'd have the anti-terror squad on our backs before you could whistle Danny Boy. I know exactly where they fucking got this idea and it's from the fucking Archbishop, so it fucking is!" Seamus was emphatic.

"But why? Why would the Archbishop? ..." O'Rorden tailed off at a loss for words.

"Because the church doesn't want us snooping around their business, O'Rorden. They want a quick clean explanation and get us out their hair. Believe me, I know, I've dealt with the clergy on other cases. They don't want the truth, they just want us gone, as fast as possible. They have got too much to fucking hide, and that's a fact."

O'Rorden subsided looking somewhat taken aback at this revelation.

"Don't kid yourself, O'Rorden. The clergy aren't the clean-living men of God you think they are. They've got a lot of dirty little secrets. It doesn't suit their purposes to have us looking at their affairs too closely. Which reminds me, has the report come back on the keys? If it's positive, we'll be paying the Bishop a little visit very soon." He gave a grim laugh.

"Well," said O'Rorden finally. "If all this is true then I am genuinely shocked and that's a fact. So, I am."

"Then you better prepare yourself, because if I am not mistaken things are going get a lot more shocking very soon." Seamus stood up because the investigation team was filing in for the morning briefing.

"OK," Seamus began. "Well, here we are again, three days in on the investigation into the murder of Father O'Flaherty. I am sure you've all read the papers by now and I'm only going to say this once. This is not a sectarian killing, I don't believe it is likely at all. You can also see the dangers of talking to the press. This is only going to get worse, they will be all over this town like a rash. Or more like the bubonic plague."

There was a ripple of amusement at this remark.

"You can tell journalists are not my favourite people. So, let's stick to the no comment policy. There are things we know we don't want out in the general public at the moment, and we don't want to alert the killer we might be on their tail. When... we do finally get to be on their tail."

He paused and then held up a photofit of the possible murderer Shona had helped put together. It wasn't much, a hooded figure with a shaded face and a feminine sort of mouth. There was something familiar about the mouth, but he couldn't really place it. It could be anyone.

"This is the only likeness we have for now of the only person who has seen the murderer. It's not much to go on but take a good look at it and see if it jogs anything in your mind. We have one other piece of evidence come to light but before I go onto that, is there anything useful that has come out of yesterday's investigations?"

He waited for some response, hoping there would be at least something of interest.

"Sir, we've got a list of all the people with firearms licenses in the area," piped up one of the Garda officers.

"Good, good," said Seamus. "It's Patrick Doyle, isn't it?" He made a point of trying to remember people's names, especially those who worked for him.

"Paddy, sir, is fine thanks." The man smiled pleased to have been recognised. Seamus knew just how important it was and how it felt when people didn't remember your name. As a young raw Garda officer, there had been one particular sergeant who never remembered who he was. In fact, he even seemed to make a point of getting his name wrong, calling him 'Sean' and even 'Simon' on one occasion. As a result, he absolutely loathed the man, just because of one simple thing, forgetting his name. The sergeant had been on the take, with some local criminals. Seamus had taken great pleasure in bringing him down and his little gang with him. He smiled at the thought.

"Great!" Seamus continued. "OK, so I need you to go and see each one of these people and examine their guns. If any have a pistol of some kind particularly one similar to a service revolver then you need to take it to be checked by ballistics. They will get it back once we're done with it, you can tell them. That way we can eliminate those, we might strike lucky and or if not then we know the murder weapon is probably an illegal weapon, or it comes from somewhere else."

"OK sir, I'll get on it right after this briefing, so I will," Paddy told him.

"That's a good start, well done, anything else?" He hoped perhaps for at least something positive.

"Sir." It was Kathy O'Flynn.

"Yes, O'Flynn?"

"Well, we've questioned quite a few people about Father O'Flaherty and it seems he wasn't universally liked by the townsfolk."

"Is that so?" But Seamus wasn't surprised. "Is there anyone in particular who said something which might stand out?"

"To be sure, there were a few people who just said he was an 'arse' and a slacker. Another one said he was a self-seeking bastard not worthy of the priesthood."

"OK," Seamus said, "but doesn't sound like any potential murderers so far, plenty of people think their priest is an arse I imagine."

"That's true, sir, that is," O'Flynn continued, "But there was one guy. He seemed quite happy Father O'Flaherty was dead, sir. He said it was a good job well done, sir. He said if he only had the balls, he'd have shot him himself, sir."

"Did he say why?" Seamus interjected interested now.

"He wouldn't tell us, sir, but I could tell he wasn't joking about Father O'Flaherty, no he wasn't."

"Get him in here for questioning," Seamus said, "and one other thing, has Mrs Lynch been interviewed yet, as she was the one who found the body?"

"Sir, sorry about that she was a bit difficult to get hold of, but I've got her interview here we did it yesterday." It was Kathy O'Flynn again and she looked a little apprehensive as if Seamus might go off on one.

"OK, not a problem, we've all been busy," Seamus told her, "anyway was there anything useful from her?"

O'Flynn looked relieved and said "No, sir, not really. She just told us how shocked, upset, surprised she was and really had nothing more to say. She couldn't think of any reason why anyone would want to kill the Father and she's got an alibi, so she can't be a suspect."

"OK, no problem, I thought she probably wouldn't reveal much, to be honest." Seamus smiled. "So, anything more from anyone at all?"

Nobody responded so Seamus decided it was time to drop the bombshell.

"Right, now what I am about to tell you doesn't leave this room, am I clear? If it gets out or into the press, I'll know it's someone from this team. I don't want this getting out until we've got a lot more evidence and we don't want anyone going to ground. Is that understood?"

He looked around and everyone was nodding in affirmation.

Picking up the evidence bag with the condoms from Father O'Flaherty's house he spoke.

"This was found in Father O'Flaherty's bedroom in his set of drawers. Six of them were missing."

If he didn't have their attention before, he certainly had it now. There was a hushed awed silence in the room.

"O'Rorden found this while searching the house, and all credit to him for doing a good job."

O'Rorden blushed and tried to demur.

"Credit where it's due," said Seamus. "Now I don't need to tell you a Catholic priest with a set of used condoms in his bedroom is not a good look."

"Sir," offered one young officer. "What if he was just keeping them or had, had confiscated them from the choir boys or something?"

"I don't think they would be in his bedroom though, do you?" Seamus told him.

"Well, no I guess not," admitted the officer.

"Listen, nobody is above suspicion, not even the victim. He wasn't killed for no reason, I don't believe it. There will be a motive and we have to find it. We all know the Catholic Church is not as pure as they'd like us to think. There are good priests and not so good priests. Father O'Flaherty obviously had his weaknesses and these condoms look like the key to finding out what those weaknesses are. However, bad they may turn out to be. So, we just need to probe a little deeper. Go back through any records of abuse, child abuse, domestic abuse, any reports whether they were acted on or not. Find out if there was anything, anything at all reported about the Father. Because everything we discover gets us another step closer to the killer. And that is our job, it's to get to the truth, no matter how difficult it may be and no matter what it may expose. Get to the truth and catch this murderer is our number one objective. Are we all with me?"

There was a resounding chorus of "Yes, sir" after this stirring speech. O'Rorden was staring at him in open-mouthed admiration.

"What?" Seamus asked him embarrassed.

"Well, and I had heard Winston Churchill was a great speaker but by God that was some speech, sir, so it was."

"Thanks." Seamus blushed a little self-consciously. "I appreciate the compliment, but I don't I think am quite up to Churchill's standards."

"Well, I think it was pretty close, I would say, yes indeed I would, pretty damn close, sir, so I think."

Seamus smiled and nodded and decided to change the subject.

"Where's the nearest Boots, O'Rorden?" he asked.

"Do you need a chemist, sir? Because we've got one right here in Ballysruth if you need anything."

"No, no I need a Boots, a reasonably big one too, I need to ask them something."

"Well, there's one in the next town, sir, if you fancy the drive," O'Rorden replied.

"Great, then let's go." Seamus started for the door.

"Do you need me to come along then, sir?" O'Rorden was doubtful

"Yes, yes it's Garda business we're going on, come on." Seamus was impatient.

"Do you mind telling me what the business is then, sir, if you would be so kind?" O'Rorden asked him while hurrying to catch up.

"We're going to find out about some perfume." Seamus smiled as they left the building.

"Perfume? Perfume sir?" O'Rorden's brow knotted in thought and then it cleared as he suddenly cottoned on. "Perfume!!! Ohhhh right, right indeed!!! Yes, sir, on we go, yes indeed."

* * *

The Boots was a reasonably sized shop Seamus noted. It was good because they should have a good selection of perfume. Boots wasn't just a chemist, they sold all sorts of cosmetics, toiletries and other things. It was a popular high street store found in every reasonably big town. If anywhere would sell a fair amount of perfume it would be them.

They entered the shop and Seamus looked around for the perfume counter. It wasn't difficult to spot, just running along the side wall. He was pleased to see there seemed to be a large selection of perfumes on display. Surely, they would know about the Chanel one in that case.

He and O'Rorden approached the counter. A woman looked up. She was in her thirties and quite heavily made up. Of course, she would be, Seamus thought, selling cosmetics. She had dyed blonde hair, the kind which was showing dark roots and in need of another rinse of colour. Everything on her face was immaculate however from the blue eyeshadow to the pink lipstick. She smiled at them.

"Can I help you, gentlemen?" she asked.

"DI Gallway and Sergeant O'Rorden." They flashed their badges

Her smile didn't fade, obviously, long years of training left her unfazed.

"Oh," she said brightly. "Garda officers is it perfume you are wanting or something else?"

"Actually it's a few minutes of your valuable time, and your expertise," Seamus answered smoothly.

Her smile deepened. He had an effect on women. It wasn't lost on O'Rorden, who was fast becoming something of a Seamus acolyte.

"And what is it you might need, my expertise on?" Her hazel eyes locked onto Seamus.

"Well, I was wondering, do you have a perfume, it's called Chanel Mademoiselle I think."

"Yes, yes we certainly do." She reached expertly into a cabinet and produced a bottle to show him.

It was a square shaped bottle with bevelled edges and a simulated cut crystal top. Had Seamus known more about perfumes he would have known this was typical Chanel branding. The perfume itself was a very pale shade of peach.

"It's a spray bottle," she told Seamus. "Would you like to smell it?"

"I would if it's not too much trouble," Seamus replied.

"Certainly." If he was expecting her to provide him with a sample stick, he was mistaken. Instead, she sprayed a liberal amount onto her wrist and held her extremely well-manicured hand up, so he could have a sniff. Seamus didn't flinch however and gently moved her wrist towards his nose and took a deep sniff. The perfume was strong and unmistakable. It was definitely the one he had now smelled on three different people. She smiled again, leaving her wrist in his hand quite comfortably it seemed.

"Strong isn't it?" she said.

"Yes, very." Seamus beckoned O'Rorden to have a sniff himself, which he did.

"Oh my," said O'Rorden. "Oh, my that's certainly a scent alright, that it is."

"Quite distinctive it is," Seamus told her.

"Yes," she replied gently withdrawing her wrist. She smiled again.

"Do you, erm, sell this particular perfume very often?" Seamus asked.

"Oh yes, we sell a lot of it. This is one of the top five selling perfumes in Ireland," she laughed.

"Oh, oh I see." Seamus looked slightly crestfallen.

"Why are you so interested in this perfume if you don't mind me asking?" she asked with interest.

"We're just following up on an inquiry that's all." Seamus was non-committal.

"Wait a minute." Her eyes widened in recognition. "You're the detective who was on the news, you're investigating the murder that's right isn't it?" She clicked her fingers. "The priest who was murdered that's right, isn't it?"

"Yes, that's right... for my sins." Seamus smiled.

"I'm his partner," piped up O'Rorden.

"Oh, yes, yes I see," she said. "So, you must be following up on a lead then." She was eager for more information.

"Something like it, yes." Seamus tried not to frown, why did everyone always want to know everything as soon as they knew he was investigating a murder.

"And this perfume, I bet this is some kind of clue, isn't it, am I right? That's right, isn't it?" The assistant was by now sounding very excited.

"I can't really say any more," Seamus replied.

"Oh!" She sounded disappointed and then made a conspiratorial face. "Oh right, right I see, mum's the word, yes indeed, detective." She tapped her finger on the side of her nose.

"Thank you," Seamus said to her. "This is a very important piece of evidence and I hope we can rely on your discretion." He locked eyes with her.

"Oh yes of course, don't you worry, oh my gosh, thank you, you can rely on me absolutely."

O'Rorden looked at him with great admiration.

"How much is a bottle by the way?" Seamus asked her.

"Oh, oh you'll be wanting one for evidence," she said catching on. "Well now, don't you worry, take that one, it's only a sample, we always have to replace them anyway."

"I couldn't possibly," he said trying to demur.

"No, no, go on, go on now, go on with you, it's fine, just take it, only too happy to help, with a real-life murder, goodness me." She almost squeaked out the last part.

"Well thanks, I appreciate it very much, in fact, the Garda thanks you for your help," said Seamus as she put the bottle in a little bag and handed it to him.

"Now remember." He was smiling. "Mum's the word! I am sure I can count on you."

"Oh yes, oh..." She seemed to have lost the power of speech and watched him and O'Rorden leave pressing her hand to her heart.

"You handled it amazingly, sir, amazingly if I might say so," O'Rorden told him.

"Thanks," Seamus replied. "Come on, let's get a coffee, a proper coffee, now we're here."

Shortly they were sat at a table in a coffee shop nearby. Seamus was sipping a cappuccino and O'Rorden a latte which Seamus had recommended.

"Do you think she's going to keep quiet, sir? About the perfume?" O'Rorden asked him.

"I hope so. But you never can tell with these people. They get fame hungry. But it doesn't really matter if she does talk anyway."

"Oh? Why's that, sir?" O'Rorden looked puzzled.

"Well you heard her it's one of the five top-selling perfumes in Ireland. On which basis it makes half the women in Ireland suspects," Seamus told him wryly.

"Oh, oh yes I see." O'Rorden digested this.

"Besides, I've already smelt the same perfume on three people in the last 24 hours," Seamus told O'Rorden what had happened omitting only the actual details of his corridor encounter with Kerry.

"Hmmm," said O'Rorden when Seamus had finished. "Not a great clue then, after all, is it? Not at all, that it isn't."

"No, no it's not, but let's look on the bright side, we know at least the killer wears perfume and what kind, you never know it might come in handy."

"What now then, sir?"

"Back to the station, hopefully, O'Flynn has brought in her man for us to question."

"Oh, yes right you are, sir." O'Rorden drained his coffee expecting they would be going right away.

"O'Rorden, really!" Seamus admonished him. "That's no way to treat good coffee, no indeed it's not."

He picked up his own cup and sipped it delicately, then smiled.

"Now that, that, O'Rorden, is how you drink coffee, it's there to be savoured not gulped down like a pint of Guinness."

"Sir!" said O'Rorden in shocked tones. "I would never, ever gulp down a pint of Guinness, now that I wouldn't, no indeed.

"Well then, it's the same with coffee," Seamus told him.

"I'll remember it next time," O'Rorden assured him. Seamus was fast becoming his equivalent of a superhero and he hung on every pronouncement Seamus made as if it was the gospel itself. Seamus may have been a little embarrassed by this adulation but fortunately, he was a little too involved in thinking about the case to notice.

✳ ✳ ✳

Returning to the Garda station they found Kathy O'Flynn eager to see them.

"I've got the suspect in the interview room, sir, waiting for you to question him," she told Seamus.

"Thanks, O'Flynn, although he's not officially a suspect, at least not yet, let's see what transpires. What's his name?"

"It's Ronan Maguire, sir, that's his name."

"Ronan Maguire, right, come on, O'Rorden, and you might as well sit in on this, O'Flynn, learn the ropes a bit, OK?"

"Thank you, sir." She looked at him as if he had just bestowed a tremendous honour on her. Seamus didn't know it, but he was becoming quite the superstar among the officers of Ballysruth Garda. Since he was quite a modest and retiring man in many ways it was probably just as well.

They entered the interview room and the occupant looked up somewhat startled jumping to his feet. Seamus could see right away he was very unlikely to be the murderer. For a start, he was a big bluff man probably over six feet three. He was almost as wide as he was tall, and he had the weathered face of someone who spent a good deal of time out of doors. He had dark hair, hazel eyes and a rim of stubble on his face. By all accounts, he was probably a farmer or worked on the land.

"Ronan Maguire, is it?" Seamus asked him and smiled in reassurance. "I am DI Gallway, this is Sergeant O'Rorden and Sergeant O'Flynn, who I am sure you probably know."

"That I do, indeed, yes that I do," nodded the other. He wasn't particularly old, looked around thirty to forty. He was wearing jeans with work boots which had seen better days and one of those green wax jackets over a brown herringbone jumper.

"Sit down, Ronan, if you don't mind me calling you that?" He motioned the other back to his seat.

Seamus and O'Rorden took up position opposite and Kathy O'Flynn sat a little off to the side so as not to crowd their interviewee too much.

Seamus put on the recorder and after the preamble, he began, "So myself and O'Rorden here just want to ask you some questions if it's OK, about what you told Sergeant O'Flynn the other day, about Father O'Flaherty."

At the mention of the Father, a scowl developed on Ronan's face. This did not go unnoticed by Seamus. He and

O'Rorden glanced at each other. O'Flaherty definitely wasn't on Ronan's Christmas list that was for certain.

"Tell me about Father O'Flaherty, Ronan, how did you come to know him?" asked Seamus gently.

"I've known him a few years," rumbled Ronan. "I was in the choir up until I was about sixteen or so up until..." he stopped and look uncomfortable.

"Up until what? Did O'Flaherty do something to upset you or concern you?" interjected Seamus.

"Upset me? Up-fucking-set me?! I'll say he fucking upset me, that bastard, that fucking bastard, he's fucking bastard, so he is," erupted Ronan.

"Was," corrected Seamus.

"Well was, yes for sure he's dead and not that he didn't deserve it the bastard," Ronan continued.

"So, what happened, Ronan, what did Father O'Flaherty do to make you feel this way?"

"I..." Ronan hesitated, "I... I would rather not say..."

"Ronan." Seamus softened his tone. "Ronan, the thing is there has been a murder and whether or not O'Flaherty was deserving of it as you say isn't the point. It's our job to catch the person who did it and everything you can tell us about the Father can help us do that."

"I would give them a medal, so I would," Ronan fired back.

"You are not helping yourself here, Ronan," said Seamus a little more sternly. "The way you are talking we might start to think you killed him yourself."

"I killed him?" Ronan looked dumbfounded. "I killed him? I never did, no I didn't, I never killed him at all, I swear."

Seamus sighed and was pondering his next move when O'Rorden piped up.

"Come on, Ronan, lad," he said as if he was talking to a child. "You know me, and you know Kathy here. We wouldn't steer you wrong, now would we? You need to tell us, Ronan. Just think, Ronan, if the Father has done something bad, wouldn't it be better we know, get it out into the open, that way eventually people will know the real Father O'Flaherty now, won't they? What do you think?"

Seamus looked at him with some surprise. O'Rorden was catching on fast, thinking on his feet. It was a great strategy. One which hadn't occurred to Seamus. Having local knowledge was quite helpful he mused.

Ronan seemed quite struck by what O'Rorden had said and after pondering for a moment, he started to speak.

"Well, I suppose you're right, that you are, might as well get it out in the open like you say. Nail the bastard, like Jesus."

Seamus wasn't sure if it was a great analogy for a Catholic and in fact, it was probably bordering on blasphemy he thought with some amusement. But Ronan was still talking.

"I was in the church choir," Ronan told them and taking in their disbelieving faces he laughed. "Ach I know you wouldn't think it to look at me now but it's true. I was quite a singer then and that's a fact. O'Flaherty was pleased to have me in the choir, he said I was special, real special; yes, indeed he got that right, the bastard." He paused for a moment scowling ferociously again and continued.

"I was in the choir for quite a few years, you know from the time I was about 8 or 9 right up until I was about 16. I used to sing solos and everything. Of course, by then I was a bit tall and starting to build a bit of muscle. Working on a farm does that. Anyway, I didn't realise it, but O'Flaherty had started to pay me a bit more attention by then. He would be nice to me, spend time talking to me, about girls and all sorts. I thought he was my friend. Fine fucking friend he turned out to be that lying scumbag fucking bastard." His face had now taken on an angry mask as he recalled something that was obviously stuck fast in his psyche.

"What happened?" Seamus coaxed him gently.

"It was one day, I remember it well. I had not long turned sixteen. It was a Sunday after communion. I used to help the Father put everything away and then I would get changed you know in the vestry. Well, that particular summer's day it had been very hot. The church was empty, all the others had gone home. It was just me and the Father there. It had been so hot I only had my boxers on under my vestments, well nobody could tell, and those garments were fucking hot, so they were."

Seamus, O'Rorden and O'Flynn were listening intently now, not daring to interrupt, they knew something potentially shocking was about to be revealed. Ronan was lost in his reverie and didn't notice.

"I took off the vestments you know, I was standing there, in my boxers and all. I never thought anything of it, so I didn't. I was just going to put my clothes on, you know my day clothes, when I saw the Father looking at me. Up until then, I'd never thought anything of being unclothed in front of him, I just thought of the Father as one of the lads. You know you don't think. But he was just looking, staring at me and I stood there half naked not knowing what to do. Then he came up to me closer and I could see it in his eyes. It was a look, a terrible look, lustful it was, sinful."

Seamus heard the catch in Ronan's voice and noticed his eyes were wet.

"Go on," Seamus said quietly.

Ronan didn't really seem to hear him, but he started speaking again, "He started saying, things. How good looking I was, handsome. What nice muscles I had for a boy my age. I didn't know what to do or say. I was just standing there I felt like I was hypnotised. He reached out and touched my arms, felt my muscles, asked me if I didn't mind. I couldn't speak. I could hear him breathing, really heavy it was. All the while he was moving closer to me, running his hands up and down my skin. I was stood there in shock in total shock not knowing what to do. He said this was just between us, and God wouldn't mind, that it wasn't a sin. He said I was the only one, the chosen one. Chosen by God. And then, and then..."

Tears began to roll down his face. Seamus glanced at O'Flynn and O'Rorden, their eyes were also wet.

"Then his hand went down and touched my schlong. He said I know what you want. You know what I want. I've seen the way you look at me. I know this is what you want, Ronan, he said. Don't be shy now. And then he touched my fucking schlong. It was the last thing I was expecting so it was. Not from him, not from anyone. Well then I couldn't help it, I just reacted, so I punched him, I punched him hard in the face and he went down." Ronan's fist went into a ball at the memory.

"What happened then?" asked Seamus.

"Well I ran, so I did, I grabbed my clothes and I ran, and I never went back. Not to his fucking church. Not to his fucking choir." He stopped and looked at Seamus. "I'm not gay," he said emphatically.

"Nobody is suggesting you are," Seamus told him.

"Yes, but that's why I punched him because he had no right to do that, I didn't say he could do it. I didn't want him to do it." Somehow Ronan felt he had to explain himself.

"I understand," said Seamus. "And what he did was wrong, firstly because he was a priest and secondly because it was without your consent. It's not illegal to be gay, Ronan, you know, that, right? Not for a moment am I suggesting you might be."

"Yes, yes I know," said Ronan. "But I'm not, he had no right. I didn't want it, not from him. That fucker, all the time I thought he was my friend."

"So, did Father O'Flaherty do anything else? Did you see him again? Talk to him?" asked Seamus.

"No," said Ronan. "I saw him alright, from a distance, but that's all, I never set foot in that bastard's church again. He had a black eye for days, so I heard. He told people he'd fallen down in the church and hit in on a pew. That's what the gossip was. Well, he did fall down in a manner of speaking."

"How did it make you feel, Ronan, when he did what he did?" Seamus said.

"I felt, dirty, defiled, I felt like he was raping me with his eyes, he didn't touch me, you know there, because I wouldn't let him, but I felt like he had, somehow violated me. I still think about it, I hated him for it, because he betrayed me, I thought he was my friend, he betrayed me." Ronan dashed his sleeve across his eyes to wipe away the tears, he retrieved a large and none too clean handkerchief from his pocket and sneezed very loudly.

"Does anyone else know about this?"

"I told my Ma," said Ronan. "She knew something was wrong and she made me tell her. Then she told me never to talk about it, but she never went to the church again either."

"Did your father know?"

"I don't know, he never said." Ronan paused. "They've both passed on anyway, it's my farm now."

"Do you know if Father O'Flaherty did anything like this to anyone else? Any other choir boys or someone else?"

"I don't know for sure, but I started to remember the way I saw him looking at the others. It was like a... like a hunter stalking his prey, biding his time, waiting for them to grow up, I never thought anything of it then but thinking back, I'd seen the look before on his face when he thought nobody was looking. I think he must have done though. Now I think about it. The bastard..." Ronan tailed off.

"Thank you, Ronan, thank you very much, you've been very helpful and incredibly brave to tell us all this. Now is there anything else you can think of about Father O'Flaherty, anything at all?" Seamus wanted to be sure he had told them everything.

"Well not really, well yeah, there was one thing, I remember once I found something in the vestry, I didn't think much of it at the time, thought it was probably young lovers getting their kicks you know."

"What was it?" enquired Seamus.

"It was a used condom, in a corner, like you would never have seen it if you hadn't looked. There was a torn packet as well."

"What did you do with it?"

"I threw it away before the Father saw, I wanted to protect him from such things. That bastard! Protect him my arse. He didn't need protecting. Now I am pretty sure it was probably his. I am pretty sure he must have used it, on someone like me, someone who didn't have the courage to stop him."

The officers all exchanged glances then. It didn't seem as if Ronan had more to say at this juncture. Seamus thanked him profusely and Ronan promised to come back and tell

Kathy if he remembered anything else. He and O'Rorden watched him lumber out the room escorted by O'Flynn.

"I told you, O'Rorden, I told you to prepare yourself."

"Well, you did that, sir, indeed you did, but this, this has taken me by surprise I can tell you that now, a very big shock so it is. It's one thing to find some condoms and it's quite another, to hear something like... this." He gestured at the chair Ronan had lately occupied as if he was still there.

"Get used to it, O'Rorden, this is only the start, there will be more for certain," Seamus said in a matter of fact tone.

O'Rorden blinked and looked disappointed. The idea there were going to be further revelations of this sort about the Father wasn't something which filled him with any pleasure.

"You know what we have to do now don't you?" said Seamus looking at him meaningfully.

O'Rorden nodded very glumly, he looked as if everything he once thought was up, was now down. His whole world turned over in an instant. Seamus knew how it felt. It came to every Garda officer at one or other moment in their career. The day you plumbed the depths humans could fall to.

"Go on and bring her in then," Seamus told him.

O'Rorden knew exactly who Seamus meant and it didn't make him very happy at all. He headed for the door to fetch Mrs Flynt in for questioning, his lack of enthusiasm for this task was evident all over his face.

* * *

It wasn't long before Seamus and O'Rorden were sitting opposite Mrs Flynt in the interview room.

With the recorder running Seamus opened up his questioning fairly mildly.

"So how are you doing, Mrs Flynt?" he said conversationally.

"Well, not too bad, Inspector, all things considered now. I've got the Father's house all back right and tight after the burglary but it's not the same without him there. I don't know what to do with myself and that's a fact, I don't know what's going to happen." She looked suddenly quite sad at the prospect of a life devoid of service to a man she had obviously been devoted to.

"I wouldn't worry too much about it at this point, Mrs Flynt, we still have an inquiry ongoing and until it's completed, I don't think the church is going to be sending a replacement for Father O'Flaherty. Besides, I am sorry to say at this moment his body can't even be released for a funeral." Seamus explained.

"It's an awful business and no mistake, it is indeed," said Mrs Flynt a little tearfully.

"Mrs Flynt, I understand this is difficult for you, but we need to ask you a few questions about Father O'Flaherty."

"Of course, Inspector, I do understand to be sure I do," she nodded.

"Would you say you knew Father O'Flaherty well?" asked Seamus.

"Why yes, yes I've been serving him, been his housekeeper for more than thirty years so I have."

"So, you of all people would know some very personal things about him I would imagine." Seamus' tone was deceptively mild.

"Well, yes I suppose so, but I am not sure what you might be meaning there, Inspector." Her voice sounded a little evasive and she wouldn't meet his eyes.

115

"Are you aware of anyone who might not like the Father very much, Mrs Flynt?"

"Well, honestly I'm sure everybody has people who don't like them, don't they?" It was becoming obvious to Seamus the indirect approach wasn't going to work and so he decided to change tack.

"Mrs Flynt, let me be quite straight with you, we already know Father O'Flaherty had enemies, we've already spoken to one of them today. So I am going to have to ask you again if you are aware of anyone who might have disliked Father O'Flaherty." The mild tone had gone.

"Well I know there were a few people who used to come to church and they stopped coming, and they wouldn't even talk to the Father."

"Can you give us their names?"

"I could I suppose, yes, but I would have to think about it for a while," said Mrs Flynt with resignation.

"Good, thank you, when this interview is over you can go over the list with O'Rorden here."

"Oh, oh OK, is there something else then, Inspector?"

"Just a few more questions, Mrs Flynt," replied Seamus.

"Goodness I am wondering if you think I'm the murderer or something," she said defensively.

"Mrs Flynt, a man has died, been murdered, you were one of the people who knew him well, we need to find his killer, but we can't do it without your help. We need to know everything we can about him to find the person responsible."

"I'll try my best, Inspector, that I will," she assured him.

He wasn't convinced but was trying hard not to lean on her more than he had to.

"Mrs Flynt, I need to ask what may, to you, be some possibly distressing questions."

"I can't imagine what those might be." She looked flustered.

"Did Father O'Flaherty ever break his vows to your knowledge?"

"He liked a drink if that's what you're meaning though I'm not sure priests are meant to be teetotal, I've never met one that is." She laughed but stopped when she saw Seamus wasn't laughing with her. Seamus decided to try to another approach.

"Father O'Flaherty had a choir at the church, didn't he?"

"Oh yes, a very good one at that, yes indeed, they sounded beautiful, so they did, beautiful." She looked wistful at the recollection.

"Did the Father ever have or attempt to have a relationship with any of the choir boys, Mrs Flynt?"

"I don't know what you're saying, what are you trying to say Inspector?" She started to look worried.

O'Rorden looked as if he was about the lean forward and say something, Seamus put a gently restraining hand on his arm.

"I am asking you, Mrs Flynt, if Father O'Flaherty ever molested or attempted to molest any of the choir boys?" Seamus decided he had to be direct.

"Oh my God, God strike me down if it was true, I would never, never believe it of him, no I don't believe it."

"Don't believe it or you weren't aware of it?" he pressed her a bit harder.

"I certainly was not aware of any such thing and I don't believe it for one second, who would make such terrible accusations against the poor Father?"

"Did you ever find any used prophylactics or condoms in the house, Mrs Flynt?"

"What? No! This is outrageous, I won't listen to this one second more." She stood up as if to go.

"Sit down, Mrs Flynt, we haven't finished," Seamus spoke more firmly than O'Rorden had heard from him before. It was almost like an order. The tone of his voice stopped Mrs Flynt in her tracks. She tossed her hair and tutted loudly but meekly sat down again in her chair.

Seamus placed the evidence bag with the condoms on the desk.

"Do you know what these are, Mrs Flynt?"

She peered at them and made a face of disgust.

"Of course, I've been about enough in the world to know what those are, Inspector, why are you asking?"

"Because, Mrs Flynt, they were found in Father O'Flaherty's bedroom drawers."

"What, no, surely not, they can't be." She looked up at O'Rorden for confirmation this was wrong, but he nodded briefly indicating it was true.

"There are six of them missing from a packet of twelve, how do you account for that?" Seamus was keeping up the pressure on her.

"I don't know, Inspector, I've never seen them before, I can't imagine how they got there." She tried to sound dismissive.

"Really!" said Seamus his voice sounding as if he didn't believe it at all.

"Can you recall an incident where the Father had a black eye, some years ago?"

"Well now." She thought for a moment. "Yes, yes, I remember he fell in the church and hit it on a church pew."

"What if I said to you it wasn't what happened, and someone punched him?"

"I can't imagine why, if that's the case, why someone would do it?"

"So, you know nothing about it?"

"No, Inspector."

"Mrs Flynt, I just want you to think about how this looks to us. You lived in Father O'Flaherty's house, you spent over thirty years with him as his housekeeper. There can't be many things you don't know about him and you are sitting there telling us he led a blameless life. Frankly, based on the evidence we already have, we don't believe you."

Mrs Flynt pursed her lips and said nothing. It was obvious to Seamus she was lying.

"Mrs Flynt, it would be a lot easier if you tell us what you know. We are going to find out anyway I can assure you of that."

"If I knew anything, I would tell you, Inspector, but I don't." She shrugged and looked at him defiantly.

Seamus sighed.

"OK, Mrs Flynt, you can go," Seamus said. "For now. But I urge you to think about what you are doing, there are some things you are not telling us which could be vital to this investigation, you could be the difference between a killer getting caught or walking away scot-free. Have a think about it over the next few days and we'll talk to you again soon."

He motioned to O'Rorden to show her out. She didn't say goodbye, but he could almost see the cogwheels turning over in her head.

"Oh, Mrs Flynt," he called after her as she reached the door.

She stopped and turned to look at him.

"We'll have the list of names you promised us earlier, thank you, O'Rorden will see to it."

She nodded slightly and left the room with O'Rorden.

O'Rorden returned in short order.

"Well," he said with some dissatisfaction, "well." It was clear he wasn't happy about Mrs Flynt's lack of truthfulness.

"Did you get the list of names?" Seamus asked him.

"She's giving it to Kathy," said O'Rorden. It was obvious the interview hadn't done anything to promote whatever the relationship was between him and Mrs Flynt.

"She's lying, O'Rorden, that's for certain and we need to get her to talk."

"Would you like me to..." O'Rorden began hopefully, "You know... off the record."

"No," said Seamus. "Absolutely not, not at all, do not discuss anything with her off or on the record is that clear?"

"Crystal sir, yes indeed," O'Rorden replied. "There's not much chance of it anyway not at the moment."

Seamus took this cryptic utterance to mean they hadn't parted on good terms. If it was the case then it wasn't a bad thing, it might protect O'Rorden from his own folly. And folly over a woman, who might be a suspect or otherwise was something he was all too painfully aware of from his own past.

* * *

O'Rorden was fairly morose for the rest of the afternoon. Moodily leafing through notes and interview transcripts. Seamus wisely left him to it and concentrated on catching up on emails and other paperwork which inevitably accompanied the investigation.

Two things he had been expecting arrived at the same time. The first was the forensic report on the 'break-in' at

Father O'Flaherty's house. This confirmed pretty much what they knew, the Bishop's prints were all over everything including the set of keys. It was pretty conclusive he had been the one in the house. The second was from Brogan letting him know the favour he had asked for was all sorted out and the paperwork was attached. He printed it off and signed it where he needed to.

"O'Rorden." Seamus broke into the other's thoughts. O'Rorden looked up from the report he had been reading for the sixth time without taking any of it in.

"Do you happen to possess a suit, O'Rorden?" he asked him.

"Well, sir, I've one or two I suppose, but I don't wear them much, you know I've got my uniform and I wear it every day." The look on his face indicated he was quite proud of it too.

"You're going to be needing a suit, O'Rorden," Seamus told him firmly.

"Are we going somewhere particular, sir?" O'Rorden looked puzzled as to why his senior was quizzing him in this fashion about his attire.

"Well, for one thing, we will be going to visit the Bishop in the next day or two and ask him some questions about the shenanigans at O'Flaherty's place, his prints are everywhere."

"But, but, sir, can't I just wear my uniform?" he said to Seamus.

"Well, no not really, O'Rorden, not if you're going to be my acting Detective Sergeant, no that you can't, you've got to look the part you see." Seamus waited for this information to sink in.

"Your acting... Detective... Sergeant?" O'Rorden looked at him strangely. "I am not sure I am following you here, sir, now that I'm not."

"It's only a temporary appointment but I got the DCS to arrange it." He tossed the paperwork which confirmed the appointment onto the desk for O'Rorden to read.

There was a stunned silence while O'Rorden digested the information and slowly leafed through the paperwork. A dawning realisation began to show on his face.

"Sir, I... I don't know what to say," he began.

"Just sign it and we'll whizz it back and it's done." Seamus smiled.

"Sir, thank you, sir, I don't know how to thank you...."

Seamus cut him short, "Don't mention it, just do a good job and let's see if we can't make it permanent shall we, after we solve this case?"

"Oh yes, sir, that I will, that I will indeed, I won't let you down, sir, no that I won't." O'Rorden was smiling as if Christmas had arrived early. "A suit you say, sir. I wonder if I might..."

"Go on, get off and get yourself a suit, O'Rorden, nothing too flash mind, dark colours are best. Just sign it before you go." Seamus laughed.

Never had he seen quite such a transformation. O'Rorden signed the papers in double quick time and almost floated out of the office. It was amazing how a small thing could have such a profound effect mused Seamus as he watched his junior sail through the door. He laughed to himself but inwardly was pleased. He liked O'Rorden in spite of himself and was pleased to have so comprehensively made the man's day.

THE CONFESSIONAL KILLINGS

* * *

Returning to the pub for dinner Seamus could hear there was more of a buzz than usual coming from the public bar. He walked past the door and headed for the dining room which was usually much quieter. Though not, it seemed this evening. Several people were sitting loudly chatting to each other with plates of food. He remembered the journalists were arriving today and so these must be them, and probably more at the bar, they liked a drink that was for sure. He mentally rolled his eyes at the thought. Journalists. As a rule, he couldn't stand them.

He took a table on its own and hoped they would stay down their end of the room. His hopes were not going to be fulfilled, he had hardly taken a seat when a man detached himself from the group and wandered across.

"Ah, Detective Inspector Gallway, if I'm not mistaken." The man, who he thought he recognised, was medium build, blonde hair, a beard and wearing nondescript clothing. Jeans, an open shirt and trainers. He had a London accent.

"And who might you be?" Seamus asked him gruffly.

"Mathew Jameson, Irish Sun, at your service." He held out his hand for a moment. Seamus looked at him declining to shake it. After about thirty seconds Jameson withdrew it, he sat down opposite Seamus.

"That's not very friendly now is it, Inspector," Jameson said smiling.

"Did I invite you to sit there? I don't think I did," Seamus told him.

"Oh, come now, Inspector, you must remember me, we worked on a case together a while back, you know the one with the missing girl."

"Firstly, no I don't and secondly, I don't work together with the press on anything," said Seamus firmly trying to keep his temper.

"No? Oh well," said the other but he didn't move. "So, come on, Inspector, what's the scoop? Is this or isn't this a sectarian murder?"

"I don't talk to the press outside of briefings and we had one yesterday, weren't you at it?" Seamus asked him.

"Come on, you can tell me off the record, what's the deal, who are the main suspects, was Father O'Flaherty the pious man everyone thinks?" Jameson wasn't giving up.

"Did you not hear me now? It's no comment to all of that, there is not going to be any off the record statements, at least not from me." Seamus glared wishing he would go away.

"Now what sort of reporter would I be if I took no for an answer, a pretty poor one I'd say."

"I just want to eat my dinner in peace, so I do, will you please stop bugging me?"

"I'll stop bugging you when you give me something to write about, I've already spoken to your Chief Super, so you might as well tell me what you know, we're going to print it anyway," retorted Jameson undeterred. This last statement was of course bullshit and Seamus knew it. Nevertheless, he was getting somewhat riled.

"Now look here..." began Seamus who was ready to launch himself into the fray, he didn't finish because a familiar voice pre-empted his impending rant.

"Ah, there you are, DI Gallway." It was Kerry. "I was just looking for you, I've got your private table prepared for you just come this way."

"How come he gets a private table?" complained the hack pretending to look offended.

"Well, he's a VIP around here, so he is, don't you know he's in charge of the very important investigation?" Kerry told him smiling.

"And I'm in charge of getting him to give us a statement," James riposted.

"Oh, hush now, give the man some air he's had a hard day, can you not see that?" Her eyes twinkled, and she beckoned to Seamus. He looked at her gratefully and left his chair without needing second bidding.

"I still don't understand why he gets the VIP treatment!" Jameson shouted after them.

Kerry stopped then and turned around.

"Well now that's the other thing, he's a lot better looking than you are." She laughed and led Seamus through the doors to the kitchen.

"It's a matter of opinion!" said Jameson loudly, laughing at his own joke. Having been so amicably thwarted he returned to his table and his compatriots.

Once through the double doors, Kerry led him down the corridor towards the kitchen.

"Thanks," Seamus told her gratefully.

"That's OK, I could see you needed rescuing and besides..." She smiled.

"Besides what?" he queried.

"Besides... it was the only way I could get you alone." Her voice had dropped very low and sounded husky. Seamus' eyes widened.

Suddenly and without warning, Kerry pulled him into an alcove. Before he knew what was happening her arms snaked around his body and she was kissing him, hard and passionately.

"Oh God Seamus," she whispered. "I don't know what it is about you... but..."

Seamus didn't find out what the 'but' was nor was he able to answer because she kissed him again and the same electric feeling was pulsing through his body, he felt the first time her lips touched his and he was unable to resist it. Somewhere in his consciousness, he felt he shouldn't be doing this, but he quenched the thought. He leaned into her kiss returning it with just as much passion, lost in the feeling.

Seamus finally let go and allowed himself to savour this moment with Kerry, the touch of her lips, feel the sweetness of her taste, the softness of her body folding into his. It felt good and safe. He really, really liked it and he could tell Kerry liked it too. She was making soft noises of appreciation as her hands ran through his hair and ruffled his locks. The kiss seemed to last forever although it was probably no more than a couple of minutes, in reality. When she finally pulled away, they were both breathing heavily.

"Bejesus," Seamus said. "Could you give me some warning next time you are going to do that."

"Hmmm, would you have let me if I had?" she purred, her eyes were dancing.

"Um well..." he began.

"Exactly," she replied. "I didn't want to take the chance."

"You planned this didn't you?" he teased.

"Well, not exactly planned but let's just say I seized the moment."

"You're incorrigible, so you are," he laughed.

"I've never been called that before."

"It means..."

"I know what it means, Seamus, I just said I hadn't been called it before."

"If the cap fits," he told her.

"I really want to kiss you again," she said suddenly serious.

"Ach, fine." He shrugged, in for a penny, in for a pound, wasn't it the saying he thought... and leaned in to meet her lips.

The next kiss was equally as long and probably more passionate than the last. Seamus felt as if his feet were leaving the ground and he thought to himself Kerry gave him the sweetest kisses he'd probably ever had, and he had many with which to compare it. After some time had passed and they just stood face to face with lips touching.

Seamus broke the silence. "So, are we going to stand here all night, or could I maybe get some dinner?"

"Well, maybe," she teased. "If I can get another kiss afterwards."

"You might." He kissed her lips lightly. "But don't be expecting any more than that."

"I know, I know." She pouted at him. "I know... because I'm a suspect."

"Sorry..." He shrugged ruefully, she was teasing but unfortunately, he meant it. He had probably already overstepped the line.

"Don't be," she smiled. "All good things are worth waiting for." She winked at him playfully.

"Is that right?"

"Oh yes, Seamus, and I can assure you, there are some very good things waiting for you on that account, that I can."

He raised an eyebrow at this and she slipped under his arm and lead him into the kitchen and to her private dining area. He wasn't used to such assertiveness in a woman and he was finding it incredibly attractive, and Kerry was, he thought, quite intoxicating so far. What would happen if they ever got into bed together he didn't know. He acknowledged quietly to himself it was something he would dearly like to discover.

Kerry sat him down at her private dining table, on a padded bench and bustled about in her kitchen. In a matter of moments, she had placed a lasagne on the table in front of him and salad. He looked at her and smiled.

"Well go on," she told him. "That's my speciality, eat it while it's hot."

Seamus picked up a fork and took a mouthful. It was perfectly cooked, melted in the mouth and very tasty. He nodded at her in appreciation.

"I told you." She winked and then, "Would you like a glass of wine with it? You look as though you need it."

He swallowed his food and then he said, "No thanks. I'm not really a drinking man, ginger ale is my tipple or water would be fine."

She laughed. "An Irishman who doesn't drink, and a Garda to boot? Wonders will never cease."

"I used to, once," he told her. "It wasn't my best look, to be honest. So now I don't, except every now and then."

She placed a glass of ginger beer next to his plate and sat down opposite to watch him eat. He did so with evident satisfaction and she was pleased. She liked a man who could enjoy his food and appreciate good cooking. She reflected it had been a long while since she had simply taken pleasure in a man's company at her dinner table. It felt comforting, she liked the feeling.

"So," began Seamus, "how come I get the VIP treatment?"

"Because you're special," she said simply. "Because I like you, really... like you." It wasn't her way to beat about the bush, not often anyway.

"You hardly know me, though." He was trying to be fair to her, trying to be sure she wasn't just trying to get on his good side. He felt she was completely genuine but the detective in him never seemed to sleep. It was the voice of his conscience and sometimes he wished he really could silence it, just for a while.

"But I like what I do know." She was undeterred. "And I'm a pretty shrewd judge of character, so I am. Running a pub an' all, you get to know how to read people pretty quickly."

"And am I that easy to read?" he asked her.

"Like a book, detective, like a book."

"I'll have to try a bit harder in that case," he joked.

"I know what you're thinking, Seamus Gallway," she continued. "You're thinking what if she's the murderer and she's just trying to get around me, what if none of this is real..."

A crack of laughter escaped him.

"Are you a mind reader as well?" he asked her with a smile.

"I told you," she teased. "I have mysterious powers, and no, for the record, I am not the murderer, Seamus." He looked into her eyes and she didn't seem to be lying.

He had finished his food and she got up and snuggled beside him on the bench. He obligingly put his arm around her and felt quite at peace with the world. There were not enough of these moments in his life he mused, not nearly enough.

Kerry sighed. "Do you believe in fate?" she asked him softly.

"You're asking the wrong guy." He was serious for once. "I don't know what I believe in, and sometimes in this job, it's hard to believe in anything."

He sounded quite sad to Kerry and she looked up at him, her eyes were soft and melting, she felt for him somehow. He looked down at her face and felt drawn to her, she was like some kind of irresistible force to him, he didn't quite know what to make of it.

"Go on and kiss me then, like you promised." Her voice was still soft and low, almost a whisper. He sensed her vulnerability, underneath all her seemingly jovial exterior.

Seamus obliged and for once his conscience remained quiet.

DAY 4

Seamus arrived early in the dining room for breakfast. He had gone to bed quite late. He and Kerry had sat talking and, to be fair, kissing, for some time before he retired. It had taken a supreme act of will not to drag her up to his room with him and he felt sure she wouldn't have resisted were he to have done so.

He had discovered a little more about her, she had been married before, although she didn't really say too much about her ex-husband, it seemed he was firmly out of the picture. Liam, her son, was absent for the night not it was really any business of Seamus' where he was. Kerry said he was visiting a friend. They talked about everything and nothing in a way. There were things neither of them was giving away just yet. But she was certainly growing on him very quickly, almost too quickly for his liking. He was normally a cautious man in relationships and was surprised at just how fast he was throwing caution to the winds.

Still musing on his conversation with Kerry, he idly picked up the Irish Sun.

"Oh, for fuck's sake," he said loudly in exasperation.

The headline said everything he needed to know.

'How I was Molested by Father O'Flaherty, The Priest of Evil' screamed the headline. 'The Sun can reveal the exclusive story of Ronan Maguire and the secret he had kept for all these years. Father O'Flaherty tried to molest me when I was fifteen and I punched him in the face, Maguire told me with tears in his eyes. O'Flaherty was seemingly a pious man of God, now shown to have a face of evil beneath the mask...'

"How do you like the story, Inspector? I thought it was pretty top notch myself." It was Mathew Jameson the journalist he had given short shrift to the night before.

Seamus scowled at him. "Where the fuck did you get this information?" he demanded.

"Oh, well, I can't reveal my sources you know," Jameson tried to deflect him.

"Don't give me that bullshit, you went and spoke to what might turn out to be a key fucking witness, so how did you get to know about it?" Seamus countered wrathfully.

"Oh well, it's amazing what a few pints in the public bar will do, Inspector, amazing how alcohol loosens the tongue." Jameson was completely unrepentant.

Seamus saw at once how it was. Ronan having carried his guilt for years had gone to the pub, had a few drinks, opened his mouth and Jameson had been there to lap it all up. He snorted in disgust.

"You people have no fucking morals," he said evenly. "None at all. You don't care how you trample over a very delicate investigation, what fucking details you reveal that might contain key information to the inquiry, it doesn't fucking well matter to you does it? As long as you get your fucking story to boost your fucking circulation."

Jameson shrugged. "Just doing my job, Inspector, and if you won't tell me what I want to know, then I'll get it elsewhere, you know how it works."

Like most tabloid journalists he had a thick skin and a sense of self-righteousness which angered Seamus to the very core of his being. If nothing else Seamus was a fair man, he hoped also a just man, at least he tried to be, and one who tried to respect the privacy of the people whose lives he had to examine, at least until he had concrete facts and evidence to charge someone with a crime. Journalists had no such filter, they didn't care whose lives they trampled on and destroyed, and he hated them with a passion.

"Doing your fucking job, my arse, you journalists are nothing but a fucking pack of rabid..." he didn't finish. Kerry was beckoning him to come to her and calling his name in a stage whisper.

Jameson saw her and remarked, "Oh oh, saved by the bell." He laughed.

"Stay the fuck out of my way," was Seamus' parting shot as he went over to Kerry.

"VIP treatment again is it?" Jameson said with a feigned hurt in his voice. But the truth was he didn't care. He was everything Seamus thought of him and more. Only the story mattered to him, and as for the people who were hurt as a consequence, he didn't give a shit.

Kerry pulled Seamus through the double doors and into her arms.

"Hello, mister," she smiled.

"Hi, and thanks, once again, for the rescue." Her lips were so inviting he bent down and kissed her as if it was the most natural thing in the world.

"Come and have some breakfast," she told him catching her breath and leading him to the parlour. "I'm not sure if it was you I was rescuing or him," she said over her shoulder.

He followed her without hesitation. He had secretly hoped for another invitation to her private parlour but did not want to presume.

She sat him down in the same place as the night before and set purposely about the frying pan.

"I could get used to this," he grinned.

"Could you now?" She grinned back and then, "anyway, what's wrong now, you don't seem to like those journalists very much at all."

Seamus favoured her quite volubly with his low opinion of those working in the journalistic profession and particularly the ones who worked for the tabloids, and even more particularly those working for the Irish Sun, and especially at the moment, Matthew Jameson. She laughed when he had finished his rant. Putting the finishing touches on his breakfast she brought it over along with his coffee. She sat down opposite him once more, leant her elbows on the table and put her chin in her hands watching him.

"Aren't you eating?" he asked her.

"I will presently," she replied. "But you know, just now, I am taking great pleasure in watching you eat instead."

"Oh," he said digesting this. She was so different, so very different from the other women he had been with.

"Go on then, what is it Matthew Jameson has done that got you so riled up this morning?" she enquired.

Seamus told her about Ronan Maguire. There seemed little point in not doing so since the Irish Sun had seen fit to splash the story all over the front page of their national paper. No doubt very soon there would be more questions from other media and he was already forming the idea they would probably have to hold a press conference. After he finished the story, Kerry was unusually quiet for some moments.

"Something bothering you about that story?" Seamus asked at length when she didn't speak.

"No, no..." She sounded a little distant.

"Then what?" he continued. "It seems to have got your attention if nothing else."

In her mind, Kerry was turning over the fact Father O'Flaherty had now been exposed and whether or not she should tell Seamus about Liam. One part of her desperately wanted to, did not want to keep anything secret from him. The other part knew she would have to ask Liam if she could and he still might not want her to. After all, it furnished him with a motive and she was also afraid. Afraid the Garda would turn his life over as a result and she didn't want that.

"Ach, I was just thinking, how people aren't always what you think they are. I mean look at Father O'Flaherty, everyone thought he was a paragon of virtue," she said lightly.

"Did they? Did they though?" Seamus seemed to be penetrating her thoughts with his gaze. "I wonder, I wonder what other dark secrets about the Father are lurking now we've discovered this."

Kerry smiled but she shifted uncomfortably in her seat. The remark was far too close to home for her liking. She turned the conversation to safer topics, like what Seamus might like for dinner and he laughed saying he obviously really was a VIP guest. She agreed, stood up and leaned across the table to kiss him and endorse the point.

* * *

Walking to the Garda station Seamus reflected on the fact Ballysruth wasn't quite the godforsaken place he thought it was after all, in fact, it was turning out to be quite pleasant in many ways, apart from the murder of course. He walked into the incident room, now becoming all too familiar and saw O'Rorden scowling at the front page of The Irish Sun and the picture of Father O'Flaherty next to one of Ronan Maguire. What Seamus also noticed was O'Rorden was sporting a rather natty looking dark blue suit, a crisp white shirt and blue tie.

"Well, O'Rorden, you certainly scrub up well, so you do," he said by way of appreciation.

O'Rorden jumped to his feet and his chair clattered to the floor.

"Easy now there, O'Rorden, I didn't mean to make you jump."

"Sorry there, sir, I was lost in thought, that I was." O'Rorden sounded apologetic and then as if he just registered what Seamus had said, "Oh, do you like it, sir? I was quite pleased with it, what do you think?"

He moved into full view so Seamus could see the full effect. He'd obviously been splashing out a little and the black brogues were also obviously new too.

"Well." There was definite approval in his voice. "Excellent job, O'Rorden, you certainly look the part of a Detective Sergeant and no mistake."

"Acting Detective Sergeant," O'Rorden corrected him modestly.

"Just a detail, O'Rorden, like I said let's see if we can't make it permanent." Seamus smiled. He had every reason to think he could fulfil the promise by working around his boss.

"I don't buy clothes that often, sir," O'Rorden told him. "So, I might have indulged myself a little you know." Seamus could see he was secretly extremely proud.

"Is that a fact?" Seamus smiled at him.

"Well, you know I thought, why not, I got myself a nice charcoal suit as well, and a few shirts, ties, you know."

"Indeed?" Seamus replied. "Well and why not, O'Rorden, why not. In fact, you'll probably show me up and I'll have to go out and buy another suit myself."

O'Rorden immediately tried to assure him this would not be necessary and in fact, Seamus was always the picture of sartorial elegance, and if he, O'Rorden could live up those standards then he would certainly be doing well. Seamus was flattered but told O'Rorden he was just joking with him and congratulated him again on his natty attire.

Seamus then lamented the fact he was unable to issue O'Rorden with a gun, as he ought to have now being a detective, but that could only be obtained from Dublin HQ. O'Rorden said being a detective was more than enough and the gun could certainly wait. Seamus said he would do his best to get him one at the next opportunity. When it would arise, of course, he did not know. However, Seamus didn't feel a gun would be particularly necessary during this investigation and held a low opinion of firearms in general.

With a discussion of his clothing complete O'Rorden turned to the matter of the paper. "How did they get it, sir? I just don't understand it."

"O'Rorden, there's nothing to understand. You are dealing with a bunch of fucking snakes who will stop at nothing to get hold of information. A journalist just bought him enough drinks to loosen his tongue that's all that happened. It's not too damaging to the case since his testimony if needed isn't going to be against the murderer."

"Well, even so, I feel like having a word with young Ronan and telling him the error of his ways," said O'Rorden with feeling.

"Well, don't let me stop you there," Seamus told him. "In fact, let's pay him a visit this morning, shall we?"

He was interested to see O'Rorden in action. It seemed somehow O'Rorden was growing into his role in a very short space of time, and the suit had definitely boosted O'Rorden's confidence. Seamus was glad to see his hunch was actually paying off.

The rest of the team was now arriving. There were definitely some curious and perhaps admiring glances at O'Rorden's new outfit.

Seamus stood up when everyone was present and began the morning briefing. "Right, this is day four of the Investigation into the murder of Father O'Flaherty. Before I go any further and to forestall any speculation let me ask you to congratulate O'Rorden here on being promoted to Acting Detective Sergeant. O'Rorden has been doing a great job as my number two on this case and it's only right good work is rewarded, plus it's usual to have a detective as my number two. If you do a good job, I'll try to find a way to show proper appreciation, though I can't promise everyone a promotion of course. Anyway, as you can see O'Rorden has stepped up the challenge with a smart looking new suit. Come on O'Rorden stand up so we can all admire it."

O'Rorden blushed modestly but stood up and gave a twirl. The other officers clapped and made congratulatory noises and said, 'well done'. He drew some particularly nice comments from Kathy O'Flynn who said he looked very handsome, making O'Rorden blush even further. Seamus had certainly brought a breath of fresh air to the mundane existence of Ballysruth Garda station, and some of the officers might be pardoned for secretly being glad they'd had a murder in their town.

"Well now we've got the pleasantries out of the way," Seamus continued once everyone had subsided. "Let's get down to business. First off, the journalists have done the dirty on us once again, and no surprises there to be sure. You see how these people operate, and why we have to be so careful with our information. In future let's learn from this and try to stop any more witnesses talking to the press, that's the first thing. Or at the very least we can advise them not to. Difficult as it may seem, for some people who perhaps see this as an opportunity for their fifteen minutes of fame. OK, so is there any progress on historical cases and reports on Father O'Flaherty? And also, any progress on the firearm investigation?"

He paused expecting and hoping for some news. He was not disappointed.

"Sir." It was Paddy O'Doyle.

"Yes, O'Doyle," said Seamus.

"I've recovered six service revolvers sir and they've gone up for ballistics checks, sir," he announced.

"Well done, Doyle, let me know if anything interesting comes back from those." Seamus wasn't expecting anything out of the exercise, but you never knew.

"Sir, we've been looking into the records for anything on Father O'Flaherty, me and Brin White that is, sir." It was Kathy O'Flynn.

"And?" asked Seamus hopefully.

"Well, we've found quite a bit as it happens."

"Go on."

"We've found several reports and complaints that were filed against Father O'Flaherty."

"What kind of complaints?"

"Molesting, attempted molesting, sexual assault, that kind of thing, sir."

"And were these minors or what?" asked Seamus.

"They were mainly over the age of 15 and 16 sir, it seems he was careful not to try to get them too young."

"Or maybe it's the age he preferred," Seamus said with some acidity in his voice.

"I've got all the paperwork here, sir, all the reports and the like." O'Flynn brought them up to the table and Seamus spread them out. The whole team came up to look them over and examine them, picking them up reading them and putting them down.

"So, what was done about these reports O'Flynn? What happened to them, any idea?"

"Nothing, sir," she replied. "At least nothing I know of."

She showed him the bottom of one report about sexual assault on a sixteen-year-old girl. It said case closed, handed over to church for investigation. He looked through a number of others, they were all the same.

"Why does that not fucking surprise me?" Seamus exclaimed. "It's just one long fucking cover-up that's what it is as far as the church is concerned. Anyway, well done O'Flynn and White, that's good work. OK, let's just finish off this briefing.

"Right, so see if can track down every one of these people and find out where they are, if they are alive, and let's see if we can talk to them, at least on the phone. One of them could be the murderer or be connected to the murderer in some way. It could be a child or relative seeking revenge, we just don't know. There looks to be at least twenty to thirty cases here, it's quite a bit of work to be getting on with. O'Rorden and I will get Mrs Flynt in here again and confront her with this latest information. But first, we've got to pay a visit to Ronan Maguire who has been blabbing his mouth off to the press. When we get back then, O'Flynn, best you get her in, I think. Tomorrow we will have another press briefing somehow, not sure where but we'll sort it out."

"Yes sir," O'Flynn said, "and the town hall is probably the best place for the press conference."

"Great," Seamus told her. "Get onto the Dublin HQ press office to set it up, will you?"

O'Flynn nodded her assent.

"Right, unless there are any questions, there's a lot of work to do and that's for sure." Seamus finished off the briefing and turned to O'Rorden. "We'll head off to see Ronan shortly but there is something I've got to do first."

"Do you want me to come with you?" asked O'Rorden.

"No, it's fine, I won't be long. Why don't you look over these cases, compile a list, tomorrow we'll pay the Bishop a little visit I think, and we'll need to confront him with this evidence."

O'Rorden looked disappointed, it seemed he felt he and Seamus should be joined at the hip. Seamus felt guilty, but it was actually on O'Rorden's account he wanted to go alone.

✳ ✳ ✳

As he reached the library, he was surprised to see Diana O'Malley locking front the door and looking as if she was about to leave. He quickened his pace hoping to catch her before she did so. Diana turned around at his approach and her mouth broke out into a sensual smile.

"Why, Detective Inspector Gallway again is it not?"

"The same," he responded with an answering smile.

"How can I help?" she asked him.

"I was going to ask if you've maybe got the book I ordered, but I see you are about to leave. I should have checked the library hours before I came, I'm sorry."

"Oh, oh it's no trouble at all, Inspector, not in the least, as it happens, I have received your book in this morning's delivery in fact. I'll just open up and we can get it." She began to unlock the door again.

"Well, if you're sure it would be no trouble," he caught himself saying. What was it about this girl, it was almost as if he felt he had to explain himself to her. It was very odd.

"Inspector, I've already told you, it's no trouble." She smiled again. "I'm completely at your service."

He caught the look in her eye and there was no mistaking the hint of lasciviousness behind it.

"That's very kind of you," he offered blandly.

Diana held the door open for him and he passed through into the library interior. He noticed she had a very curvaceous figure and she was wearing six-inch-high red stiletto heels. The fishnet stockings were somewhat incongruous for a librarian and the black pencil skirt fitted her tightly as if it was moulded to her body. She wore a tight white blouse and a coat which was well cut and evidently expensive, with a scarf that looked so soft it was most likely merino wool. Then there came a whiff of perfume to his nostrils, unmistakeable now he had smelt the sample from Boots.

The door slid closed behind him.

"Surprising," he said conversationally. "The automatic door, I didn't quite expect such modernity."

"What here in Ballysruth?" she laughed. "Are we so backward here, Inspector?"

"I didn't mean that," he amended.

"It's alright, this is not a modern place for sure, I had quite a fight to get the door put in I can tell you, anyway, this way." She beckoned him to follow.

She walked ahead of him to the counter or more correctly glided. She walked putting one foot in front of the other with her back perfectly straight as if she had been to a very expensive finishing school. He hips swayed in the rhythm of the walk and was accentuated by the heels. The undersides of the shoes were red leather, and although Seamus wasn't a connoisseur of women's clothing by any means, he knew this was a trademark of the designer shoes by Christian Louboutin. It meant they cost a packet, to say the least. He wondered once again how the town librarian was able to be kitted out in the latest designer fashion and resolved to enquire further about Diana. She looked around to make sure he was following her, but he also felt as if somehow, she wanted to know he was looking at her, as if this was a show she was putting on, just for him.

They reached the counter and she eased behind it, reached down and picked up a book. She placed 'The Handbook of Criminal Investigation' by Tim Newburn on the counter with her perfectly manicured nails on the ends of elegant lily-white fingers.

"Here we are, Inspector, just like you ordered." A lazy smile played across her lips, it was seductive, her whole manner oozed sensuality. Seamus wasn't so immune that he would be unable to appreciate it.

"Thanks, that's very fast and very efficient, thank you."

"Oh, I always try to be fast and efficient," she replied, "it's what I am good at, Inspector."

"Don't I need to sign something fill in a form?" he asked.

"No, not in the least, just bring it back when you've finished, I know where to find you if I need to after all now don't I?" Her eyes held his just for a moment too long.

"I was wondering?" asked Seamus.

"Yes? Inspector." The way she said inspector, was almost as if she savoured every syllable of the word. She said it slowly and it rolled off her tongue smooth as silk.

"Did you know Father O'Flaherty very well by any chance, or even at all?" he asked the question casually watching her face carefully.

"No," she said simply. "You see, Inspector, I'm not religious, not at all, that I'm not. I don't have anything to do with the church, so you see I wouldn't know him."

"Right." Her answer was too easy, it was too off pat for Seamus. It seemed ridiculous to him she'd never been in contact with the Father. She looked at him blandly and he could discern nothing behind her eyes. It was almost as if there was a wall, now he thought about it. There was what she wanted the world to see and what she didn't. Seamus was nothing if not perceptive when it came to people, it's what made him a good detective. He was just contemplating perhaps probing a little further when the automatic doors opened. He looked up and there was Liam, who hesitated when he saw Seamus at the counter.

"Liam," said Diana turning her eyes towards him.

"Diana," Liam replied. "Inspector."

"Well," said Seamus. "Thanks for the book, I'd best be off and leave you to it, sorry again for holding you up."

"It's fine, Inspector." He noticed her tone had changed, the seductive drawl was gone, and she had become much more business-like since Liam had entered the library. It was curiouser and curiouser, as Alice in Wonderland would have said.

"Keep the book until you've finished, there's no rush," she told him.

"Thanks again, sorry to have made you open the library again, though."

"Ah well," she sighed. "I was just going to visit my aunt, she's sick you know, cancer"

"I'm sorry," said Seamus.

"Don't be," Diana replied brightly. "Anyway, perhaps I'll stay open after all this afternoon, now I've got another customer." She looked at Liam who was standing at the counter and back at Seamus.

"Goodbye, Diana." Seamus smiled.

"Inspector." She inclined her head, graciously, almost like a queen with whom an audience had come to an end.

Seamus walked away towards the door, he could hear lowered voices and laughter behind him. As the automatic door opened, he looked back, just for a moment. The two of them were leaning on the counter still talking almost in whispers, they were obviously very good friends, or something more, it was hard to tell.

He went through the door and it slid shut behind him. As he left the building behind him, he noticed a very expensive car in the car park. It was a sleek black Jaguar with not a speck of dirt on it, from the plates he could tell it was pretty new. He wondered if it was somehow Diana's, it would fit in with her image, but he shrugged it off, how could she possibly afford something like that? He mentally filed the thought away for another day. There were more pressing things on his mind than the librarian.

* * *

The door slid shut and Diana and Liam watched Seamus disappear from view. Diana turned back to Liam and pouted.

"Where have you been?" she asked him.

"Nowhere, studying." Liam shrugged noncommittally.

"Have you got a girl, up there, in Dublin?" she said quietly, watching him all the time.

"Ach, Diana, don't start," he protested.

"I don't mind if you have," she said looking very much as if she felt the opposite. "It's not as if we're a thing or even anything." But her eyes told a different story.

"Oh, come on, Diana, we agreed didn't we, after last time we're not going to talk about this stuff again." Liam looked at her sharply.

Last time she had lost her temper. He had told her he'd slept with a couple of girls at Uni. He was a typical young man in many ways, very much like his father. Unable to resist a pretty face and there were just so many of them at university, so hard to choose. She had slapped him, hard on the face, thrown things, broken dishes, it was quite an amazing tantrum he thought afterwards. They had not spoken for days until finally, she begged his forgiveness. It was embarrassing too, she got down on her knees like a supplicant. She offered to let him punish her. He declined, told her not to be so stupid. He said this was not Fifty Shades of Grey. She had laughed. They agreed to be friends, with benefits. She agreed not to ask him about his love life. But underneath he could see she wasn't happy.

"I know, I'm sorry." She looked instantly penitent.

"It's OK," he told her and smiled.

She smiled back and took his hand, started to lead him through the myriad of bookshelves until they reached a quiet spot at the back.

"What are you doing?" he asked her, although he could certainly guess.

"Well," she told him, her lips very close to his and her body unbearably close. "I really have got to go, but I want to remind you what you've been missing these last few days."

"Your aunt, is it?" he replied.

"Oh yes," she breathed and winked at him. "It's very important."

He knew very well it wasn't her aunt she was going to see, but Diana also had her secrets, he knew that too.

Before he could say anything more, her hand slid without preamble into the front of his jeans. He was instantly hard. She made him feel like that every time. Her hand started to move gently up and down his shaft, pulling gently.

"Oh God," he moaned.

"You like that? Hmmm..." her voice was low, lustful. "I know how you like it"

Liam's head was jerked back, and his eyes were closed, he was breathing heavily. Her right arm was moving slowly and deliberately, up and down. With her left hand, she expertly undid his buckle and unzipped his pants. Using deft movements, she freed him and began to work him a little harder and faster. Liam opened his eyes and saw Diana, looking at him, with just her eyes, watching him, watching her, the tip of her tongue appeared and slid slowly across her lips as she watched him all the while. All the while her hand worked its magic.

"Christ," he told her, now she had him where she wanted him. "Don't stop... please don't stop."

"Oh, why's that?" and she did stop then. Teasing him, teasing him like she always did.

"Diana..." he pleaded.

"It's alright... sshhhhh..." She put a finger briefly to his lips to quiet him. Then she put both hands upon Liam's shoulders. Never taking her eyes off him, she slowly dropped lower and to her knees, elegantly she took him in her mouth. This was met by a long drawn out hiss from Liam as he felt her lips surrounding him. Holding him with one hand, her head began to move rhythmically faster and stronger. Liam's hands were unclenching and clenching as he surrendered himself to the sensation. He could feel his orgasm brewing and Diana kept going inexorably taking him to the brink. He came, shortly afterwards, unable to hold it, in one long loud drawn out gasping groan, it reverberated around the empty library. Diana kept him in her mouth feeling him pulse and savouring the taste. Once he subsided, she finally let go of him, he was limp and flaccid.

She smiled like the cat who had got the cream and stood up gracefully. Not a hair was out of place, she looked just as if nothing had happened.

Liam opened his eyes and looked at her, still in the afterglow of his orgasm. She carefully reached down and put him away, tidied him up and redid his buckle.

"Do you remember now, why you keep coming back?" she asked him gently.

"Yes, yes I do," he whispered.

"Good." She kissed him then, longingly and softly. She smiled inwardly. When she had finished kissing him, she straightened up. He looked at her dreamily, as if he was bewitched.

"Come on," she said. "I've got to get going, or I'll be late."

He caught her hand.

"Will you? Do you have to? Couldn't we..." he tailed off.

"No," she said firmly. "Not today, I really do have to go."

"Fine."

"I'll see you soon." She smiled at him. "Next time... you can take me, as hard as you like, and I know you like it, Liam."

He laughed, Diana was nothing if not direct, always. Liam followed her to the door and she locked it behind her. She pulled her car keys from her pocket and pressed the stud. There was a chirrup of acknowledgement from her vehicle.

"Bye then," she said to Liam.

"Bye." He smiled at her.

"Be good, or at least... try." It was her parting shot. He laughed but said nothing. She turned away and walked across the car park. Liam. He could sleep with whomever he wanted, but Liam belonged to her. Sex was sex and she was willing to share. But love, now that was different. She wasn't going to let him share with anyone else. He just didn't know it. But woe betide him if he did... fall in love with another woman, she thought grimly.

Liam stood at the door, watching her get into her car. He liked Diana, but he also was full of mixed emotions. Diana drew him in, inexorably to her web, like a spider with a fly. She intoxicated him. No other girl had ever done that, and there were many. Could he say he loved her? Or even wanted to? He didn't know. All he knew was he kept coming back to her, and the darkness of her world, no matter how much it threatened to smother him. Lost in his thoughts, internalised and unseeing, he hardly noticed as the sleek black car drove away.

* * *

D. R. BAILEY

O'Rorden looked up from the reports he was reading with obvious pleasure at seeing Seamus.

"There you are now, sir, good to see you back." O'Rorden smiled.

"I wasn't gone that long, O'Rorden, it's not like I've been an arctic expedition now is it," Seamus chided him.

"Ah but just nice to have you around, sir, so it is." O'Rorden was unabashed.

"I got you a little light reading, O'Rorden, that's where I've been in case you want to know, to the library." He put the book on O'Rorden's desk and the other took it. O'Rorden's face broke out into wreaths of smiles as he read the title.

"For me sir? Really? You got this for me?" He sounded as if he could hardly believe anyone would be quite so thoughtful on his account.

"I borrowed it," corrected Seamus. "So, once you've finished with it, it has to go back to the library."

"Yes, yes indeed for sure, but how long can I keep it, sir? I mean there's a lot to this for sure," O'Rorden asked him.

"As long as you want apparently. Just read it, digest it, learn it, until it becomes your bible, and you won't go far wrong."

"That I will." O'Rorden was anxious to reassure him. "You can be sure of that, so you can, I'll be reading this every chance I get, I will indeed."

He looked as if he wanted to start now but Seamus, reluctantly, had to stop him.

"Well, I'm afraid it's going to have to be later, O'Rorden, we've got to go and see Ronan Maguire."

"Oh yes, yes, sir, we do." O'Rorden placed the book reverently in his desk drawer patted it and closed the

150

drawer. He picked up the newspaper with Ronan's story in it and the two of them headed out to the car.

O'Rorden drove and Seamus thought perhaps now was a good time to quiz him about Diana.

"Do you know much about the girl, Diana O'Malley I think it is, the one who runs the library?" Seamus asked.

"Well, now she's an interesting character, so she is," replied O'Rorden.

"In what way?" Seamus was curious.

"Nobody really knows much about her to be sure, she wasn't brought up around here as far as we know. In fact, nobody does know."

"So, we don't know her story then?" Seamus said.

"There are many stories." O'Rorden snorted. "I can't tell you if any are factual. One day she just appeared, they had been looking for someone to run the library and she was it apparently. Rumour has it she might have been an orphan, or I've heard her parents died and she used to live abroad, the thing is nobody really knows."

"Don't you find it odd?" Seamus was puzzled.

"Odd, yes to be sure it is. But only other hand there's a lot of odd folks around here and no mistake, oh yes indeed. Probably they've a lot more to hide than she might have too." O'Rorden was dismissive. "In any case, she did wonders for the library."

"Is that a fact?"

"Oh yes, she modernised it, got in lots of books, even got that automatic door, now there's a miracle for starters, we can't even get a replacement door for the Garda station. She upgraded the computer systems, and she certainly revived and catalogued the parish records. She's done the library proud, to be honest, and nobody really bothers her and vice versa."

"But she can't earn very much even so, as a librarian, she seems to wear the most expensive clothes." Seamus wasn't ready to drop it, he was curious.

"Well, again we don't know, but some say she inherited money from her parents, others say she has a rich relative, who's to know the real story?"

"I guess." Seamus subsided. The rich relative might be an explanation. It was obviously common knowledge she was well to do, and she had mentioned she was visiting an aunt with cancer. Perhaps the aunt was her source of extra funds. He dropped the subject since it didn't seem as important as other avenues they were following up on.

The car drew up at a farmhouse. They stepped out and Seamus took in the typical look of a smallholding. There were barns, the sounds of animals, a couple of tractors and a combine. The farm was surrounded by what he took to be its fields and they were obviously being ploughed in for the winter. Otherwise, it looked to be in good repair, the paint was in good condition and it seemed Ronan kept the place pretty ship shape.

As they approached the front door, it swung open and the bluff figure of Ronan Maguire stood there to greet them.

"Ronan," said O'Rorden taking the lead. "We just need to ask you a few more questions."

"Sure, sure, come on in." Ronan led them inside to a cosy kitchen and stood there expectantly.

"What is it I can do for you now?" he asked them.

O'Rorden produced the Irish Sun and slammed it onto the table.

"What have you got to say about this, Ronan? That's what we'd like to know," O'Rorden said sternly.

Seamus stood back and watched this with some admiration. O'Rorden was certainly finding his feet.

"Fuck" swore Ronan and sat in a chair suddenly. "I didn't mean to, it wasn't meant to come out like that…"

"Well it has and a pretty mess it's stirred up, so it has," O'Rorden told him, he picked up the paper and read from it, "Father O'Flaherty deserved what was coming to him and no mistake said Ronan Maguire after tearfully spilling his tragic story. I punched him hard and he went down, and I don't regret it. He's a scumbag, I am pretty sure he molested other boys in the choir although I never saw it… what kind of talk is that Ronan?"

"I… I … never said those things…" complained Ronan, "well not like that. They twisted everything I said, they made it sound bad, different to what I said."

"I'll say they did alright," O'Rorden continued reading, "To my mind the clergy are lying scum, molesting young people in the name of God, but they are the most ungodly men to walk this earth, not worthy of the name priest, not one of them I say, they are not priests, they are not men of God, they are the devil… and what the bastard O'Flaherty did, it was the work of the devil… What were you thinking Ronan?"

"I… I wasn't… I didn't." Ronan looked so miserable Seamus took pity on him.

"Ronan, come on now, Ronan, just tell us what happened." He motioned to O'Rorden to sit down and he did the same. He put a reassuring hand on Ronan's shoulder.

"I don't know what happened. I was so, so relieved after, you know, after carrying the guilt, you know for all these years, I thought I would celebrate with a drink. The next thing there's this guy said he was a journalist, we just got to talking and then it just came out…" Ronan explained.

"Just came out? I'll say it just came out..." O'Rorden interjected.

Seamus quelled him with a look. "And then what happened?" he asked Ronan.

"He just kept buying me drinks, I was drunk, I didn't know what I was saying, he told me it was good to get it all out in the open, priests needed to be exposed, I was a hero for saying it all, and then he, then he..." Ronan put his hand into his pocket and put down a sheaf of notes. "He said that was to thank me compensate me for my time and for being so honest, he asked me if I didn't mind them printing what I said, I was so drunk I just agreed, and I took the money. I didn't know they were going to write that."

O'Rorden made some loud tutting noises to express his displeasure.

"It's OK," said Seamus when he had finished. "These journalists are tricky fucking bastards, so they are. And we've all been where you are now, had too many drinks and regretted it afterwards."

Ronan's head went up at this. "But you're a Garda officer!" he sounded shocked.

"And what?" laughed Seamus. "Do you think we don't fucking drink? Do you think the Garda are paragons of virtue? You'll be sadly mistaken in that case, so you will."

"Oh, oh I see." Ronan sounded deflated.

"Come on lad, don't take it so hard, it's just like the inspector said, we're only human, we all make mistakes." O'Rorden had softened his tone.

"Thanks, I guess so." Ronan didn't seem convinced. "I'm sorry, I didn't mean to mess up your investigation."

"It's OK, Ronan, if you were an actual witness to the murder and you blabbed it all to the media, then it might be different, it would very likely prejudice the whole case. But because the Father is dead and the victim, it's not quite as bad. Also, this stuff would come out anyway at some point, we just preferred it not be now, but it can't be helped, what's done is done," Seamus explained.

"That's for sure, that it is," echoed O'Rorden.

Ronan picked up the money. "What do I do with this? I hardly like to keep it after messing things up the way I have."

"No, you keep it, spend it, buy yourself something nice with it and don't you worry, the damage is done, no need for you to wear a hair shirt," Seamus reassured him.

"Hmmm, ok, thanks... thank you, I will, I'll buy something for my girl." Ronan brightened up considerably.

"Oh?" O'Rorden perked up.

"Not a lady friend, I should be so lucky." Ronan laughed guessing what O'Rorden was thinking. "No, this one here, come on girl." He clicked his fingers and a black Labrador appeared wagging her tail. She came up to Seamus and nuzzled him wanting to be patted. Seamus obliged.

"She's my girl, the best kind, she needs a new bed and winter coat, it's cold out here." Ronan looked affectionately at his dog who came and sat by his chair and put her head on his knee.

"Well, we'd best be off," said Seamus now their business had been concluded.

"Really?" Ronan looked very disappointed. "You've come all this way; won't you have a cup of tea?... I... I don't get many visitors, you see."

Seamus and O'Rorden looked at each other, they had a busy schedule but on the other hand, perhaps this could be their good deed for the day. It seemed churlish not to spend a few more minutes.

"Sure, OK." Seamus shrugged. "But make mine a coffee please."

"Yes, of course, sure I will, yes indeed." Ronan looked genuinely pleased and started to bustle about filling the kettle.

* * *

Mistress Dana heard the doorbell go downstairs. It opened, then shut, and she heard voices. Her housekeeper would be letting in her client and telling him the way upstairs. Bella was a godsend. She was young and had been a single mother. Her father was a devout Catholic. Her mother was dead. He had dramatically thrown her out of the house and disowned her. Mistress Dana had found her on the street, not far from her home. Destitute and with a screaming child. She took pity on her and took her in. The baby died shortly afterwards from exposure. Bella had spent three nights in the freezing cold desperately trying to care for it. Bella was distraught.

Bella became her housekeeper. She had the run of the house and was fiercely loyal. She knew exactly what went on in Mistress Dana's house and all of her secrets. But Bella understandably was not a huge fan of the church. The local priest had refused to take her in, when her father threw her out, wouldn't even let her sleep on the floor in the church. He told her she was a mortal sinner in thunderous tones. He was old school, old school like many of her clients. The church was changing, she knew, but these old men had too many secrets to hide. Mistress Dana felt they deserved a little pain.

She heard footsteps coming up the stairs. She went across to her door and opened it. A clergyman stood outside, he was a Bishop. Bishop Michael Mullen.

"Come on in, Bishop," she spoke as if she was inviting him in for tea, smiling at him with her full lips shining from the scarlet red lip gloss she favoured.

She noticed he hesitated on the threshold, looking her up and down and taking in her dress, unsure. Mistress Dana let him look. These were her work clothes and, although she had many different outfits, this was one of her favourites. A leather corset, tight and curve revealing. Bella had done the laces up for her earlier in preparation. The thinnest of black panties, also so tight he could easily see her mound pressing against the fabric. She wanted him to. Wanted him to see what he couldn't have. Her legs were bare, white and smooth. Her hands white, smooth and soft, with deep red nail polish. On her shapely feet a pair of shiny black high stiletto mules, her toes with the same red polish peeped out at the front. She liked the mules, they slapped against her heels as she walked, reminding the client of things to come. She liked her feet, they were one of her best features she thought, well shaped.

"Come on now, Bishop, don't be shy," she coaxed him in when it seemed he had had his fill of the sight of her. "I won't bite, at least not yet."

She motioned him to a seat at a table in the corner, it was a big room. This was what she called her 'punishment room', but she also slept here sometimes too. It was where she liked to have sex, surrounded by her toys. The Bishop looked around him somewhat nervously. There were several things which didn't belong in a bedroom. A basket in one corner contained a number of long lengths of bamboo. On the wall from a series of pegs, hung a wide leather strap, riding

157

crops, paddles and other similar instruments. There was what appeared to be a low vaulting horse standing on its own in an empty space.

"Like what you see?" laughed Mistress Dana, taking in his discomfort.

"I err... well, it's unusual I'll give you that." He tried to regain his composure a little, make light of it.

"It's always difficult, the first time," she assured him. "We'll have a little talk first then shall we before we start?"

She liked to put the clients at their ease before they got into it. Also, they needed to know what they were letting themselves in for. Give them a chance to back out if they wanted to because once she had begun, they would no longer have a choice.

"OK," the Bishop agreed.

"Tell me again how you got my number?" she asked.

"It was a Father in my diocese, he erm, recommended your services," he replied.

"And which Father was that? We've no secrets here, so you'll find."

The Bishop told her, and she recognised the name as a priest who had recently visited her.

"Oh, yes, I remember him well," she told him. "I gave him a good hiding, with the belt, one he won't forget for few weeks that's for sure."

"You sound as if you enjoyed it." He looked surprised.

"Oh, should I not then? I don't just do this for business, is that what you think, is it?" She laughed "Oh yes I enjoyed it, in fact, I took a great deal of pleasure in it, I always do."

He looked quite unsettled by this remark.

"What were you expecting?" she said softly, her voice was low, full of feeling. "Something cold, clinical, like a hospital, is that it? I can assure you it's not, no it isn't. Not cold, not clinical, quite the opposite, in here we get down to the raw emotion, oh yes indeed we do, Bishop. That's what you are signing up for isn't it? To purge your sins. Purging your sins here doesn't come cheap, oh no. It requires pain and often tears, raw, red raw and without mercy. Do you see that, Bishop?"

Then just like that, her tone changed, and she sounded much more matter of fact. "You don't have to go through with this if you don't want to, you can walk away now if you like? If you want? Do you? Speak now, or forever hold your peace, that's what they say isn't it, Bishop?" .

She offered him an out, if he wasn't here to give himself to it completely then she wasn't interested in having him as a client.

"No, no, I won't back out, I can't, I have to do this, I need to." He sounded resolute.

"Oh goodness, it does sound serious then. Sounds like you've got quite a lot on your mind, let's see if we can't relieve it a little bit, shall we?"

He nodded and said nothing, swallowing nervously.

"Well then to business. First things first, did you bring the cash? I always take the first payment up front, after, if you want to come back, you can pay at the end."

The Bishop frowned and pulled out a thick envelope from his inside pocket.

"One thousand Euro just as you said. It's a lot of money you know." He held the envelope out to her.

"Oh, to be sure it is," said Mistress Dana taking it and counting it carefully. "But it's probably only a week's collection for one of your churches now isn't it." She laughed. "And besides, I give very good value for money, this isn't a discount warehouse, this is the Rolls Royce... of discipline... and no mistake, as you'll soon discover, indeed you will."

She carried the envelope across to her dressing table. Reaching inside her bosom she retrieved a key. Unlocked a drawer with it and put the money inside. Then she replaced the key in her cleavage.

"Safest place," she winked at him and resumed her seat. "Now let's just go over the rules, so you understand them."

"OK," he agreed.

"Once we begin then I am completely in control. I decide what you do, when you do it and how, is that understood?"

"Completely," he nodded.

"You will address me as Mistress or Mistress Dana, anything else will render you liable to further punishment. You will speak when spoken to and do exactly what I tell you at all times. I will decide how you are punished for what you've done, for how long and what with. When I decide the punishment is over it's over and not until then. Is it all clear?"

"Yes, yes I understand." He started to look as if it was dawning on him what he was letting himself in for.

"Everything that goes on in this room is between us. It's like the confessional, your secrets are safe with me and believe me I have many, many dark secrets I have kept for other priests and clients. Oh, and you can make as much noise as you want, I've had this room soundproofed long ago. Nobody can hear you. When the session is over, I will tell you and then things can go back to normal. But until then, you are mine, mine completely, do you really understand that, Bishop?" she finished her little speech and looked at him directly.

The Bishop felt almost as if she was looking into his soul and reflected perhaps this was what it was like to stare into the eyes of the devil.

"I do," and with those words, he felt as if his pact with the devil was complete, but something drove him, the need to confess, the burden of sin he carried for himself and the others, and he needed to be cleansed, cleansed with the fire and the scourge of hell.

"Great!" she said cheerfully. "If you don't remember, don't worry I will soon remind you."

He nodded again.

"Shouldn't there be a safe word?" he asked anxiously.

"We don't do safe words in here, Bishop, once we start this, there's no stopping it."

He swallowed quite hard when he heard this.

"Are you ready then?" she asked him sweetly.

"Yes, yes I'm ready." He had the feeling, somehow, he had bitten off more than he could chew but wasn't able to back out of it now.

"Well then, let us begin..."

✳ ✳ ✳

"If I need us to do the good cop, bad cop routine, you'll be perfect for the bad cop, O'Rorden," Seamus told him as they walked to the car and began the journey back to the station.

"Thank you, sir," O'Rorden said. "Though, you're not so bad at the bad cop yourself, sir."

"Ha!" Seamus laughed at that." I've had a lot of practice."

"I bet," O'Rorden replied.

"It's my Irish temper, always got me into trouble when I was younger. The boss is always telling me to curb it. And I try, O'Rorden, I do try."

"Yes, sir." O'Rorden sounded unconvinced.

"Ach I'm not that bad, am I?" Seamus stopped and looked at him.

"Let's just say none of the team wants to get on your bad side, sir, that's all."

"Sheesh, I didn't know I was so bad," Seamus complained.

"Sir, the team all like you otherwise, they think you've done a lot for us, a few of us are very grateful, so we are," O'Rorden said seriously.

"Otherwise?... I look after my own, O'Rorden, it's how I work." Seamus was secretly pleased.

"Yes, sir."

The two men were quiet for the few minutes it took to return to Ballysruth station. The case was not at all straightforward, in fact far from it. The deeper they went into it the more convoluted it seemed to get thought Seamus. The underbelly of the church was never a good place to be and yet somehow, Seamus always seemed to end up there. The car came to a stop.

"Let's get O'Flynn to fetch in Mrs Flynt," said Seamus.

"Sir." O'Rorden looked very glum.

Seamus paused for a moment and put his hand reassuringly on O'Rorden's shoulder. "Life's a bitch, sometimes." Then he continued to the incident room.

"Yes, sir, that it is, to be sure, sir, that it is," O'Rorden called after him.

It was not long before they were once again in the interview room with Mrs Flynt.

This time she looked at them both extremely warily almost like a hunted animal.

"Do you know why you are here, Mrs Flynt?" Seamus asked her.

She shook her head and said nothing.

"I think you do, I think you know very well," Seamus continued.

She pursed her lips and looked from one to the other in open rebellion.

Seamus sighed and put the Irish Sun on the desk with the front-page story about Ronan Maguire.

"You do! You know exactly why! Don't you!" Seamus was emphatic.

It looked as though Mrs Flynt was still going to say nothing, but there was evidently a war of emotions going on inside her, and they could see it her face.

"I don't care what the story said, he didn't do it, he didn't do it, Father O'Flaherty didn't do it, it's all lies, he's a liar that Ronan, he never punched the Father, so he didn't, the Father never did it, never!" she burst out.

"So, you are saying you know nothing about it?" Seamus said when she had finished.

"I know nothing about it because it never happened, he's a liar I tell you, a liar!" Her voice started to sound quite shrill.

"Is that so? You think Ronan Maguire, and I've met him, is going to make a story up like that about the Father? The man he worshipped by all accounts, a man he looked up to, a man who he said made him special, you think he would make that up? Come on, Mrs Flynt, you know it's true don't you, stop covering up for the Father, the man you say was such a good man, he wasn't though was he, Mrs Flynt? He was a molester of young people in his care, wasn't he, Mrs

Flynt!" Seamus was pressing her hard trying to get her to crack.

"It's not true!" she shouted. "He didn't do it, he never molested anyone, he was a good man he so he was. That little bastard Ronan, he always was a nasty piece of work, he was taking money from the collection, the Father confronted him and that's why Ronan punched him, the little bastard, by God if he'd been a bit smaller I'd have given him such a hiding so I would..." She stopped, her eyes were suddenly wide open, her hand flew up to her mouth as she realised what she had just said.

"Really?" said Seamus with satisfaction. "So, Ronan did punch the Father, after all, something you just told us never happened only two minutes before. So, who's the liar now, Mrs Flynt?"

"I... I..." It seemed as if Mrs Flynt was lost for words.

"What do you know about these?" O'Rorden suddenly chimed in, his voice was hard. He banged a sheaf of papers onto the table. They were copies of reports of allegations of abuse and molestation against Father O'Flaherty. He carefully laid them out one by one in front of her, slowly and deliberately, each report with a picture of the youth attached.

A look of horror spread over her features.

"You know what these are, Mrs Flynt?" Seamus asked her.

"No... I... no... no," but it didn't seem like an answer, it seemed more like denial, denial of the evidence in front of her.

"These are young people, reported to the Garda alleging Father O'Flaherty tried to molest them or had sexually assaulted them," O'Rorden told her.

"I don't know, I don't know anything..." she began.

"You're lying," said Seamus. "And we know you're lying because you just admitted to lying to us about Ronan. So, think very carefully, Mrs Flynt, we've caught you lying once already, it's time for you to tell the truth."

She didn't answer.

"Come on now, just tell us the truth, it's better for all of us all round." O'Rorden tried a softer approach.

There was another long pause while Mrs Flynt fought a further internal battle, so it seemed. Then she spoke.

"OK, I do know, I know about some of these allegations, I do."

"How did you find out about them?" asked Seamus.

"The Father, he told me, each time. He said there might be some terrible things said against him, and they weren't true. And sometimes I was questioned by the Garda about it, I told them I didn't know anything."

"And was it true? You didn't know anything?" O'Rorden said to her.

"Yes, I'm not lying, I didn't know. The Father told me to pray to God and God would show me the truth. The Bishop came, he talked to me, said the church was going to deal with it, if the Father was guilty then he would be taken away from here, he would be punished for his sins. But they never came, they never took him away, so I thought it wasn't true, I didn't want to think the Father, the Father would do... such... things..." She started to cry softly, weeping openly.

"Mrs Flynt, there are twenty to thirty cases here at least, how could you possibly think so many young people had lied, young people in the Father's care?" Seamus was genuinely curious.

"Because I put it out of my mind. I didn't want it to be true. I didn't want it to be true. I'm not lying, I'm not." She looked desperately at Seamus and O'Rorden.

165

"I am going to have to ask you again, did you ever see Father O'Flaherty do anything to any of these young people? If you did then you need to tell us." Seamus demanded.

"No, I keep telling you no..."

"And are you sticking to the story about Ronan stealing from the collection?" Seamus continued.

"Yes, yes."

"Even though you didn't see him do it and you were simply taking Father O'Flaherty's word for it?"

"Yes." Her resolve seemed stronger now.

"Even though you lied in the first interview when you told us Father O'Flaherty had got a black eye from falling on a pew. When you knew he had been punched by Ronan?"

"I... err... I" Mrs Flynt stumbled over her words because Seamus had put her on the back foot once again.

"I am going to be straight with you, Mrs Flynt," Seamus told her. "We don't believe you are telling the truth. You have already lied to us and we don't think you are being straight with us now and that's a fact."

Mrs Flynt looked at O'Rorden who nodded to confirm he agreed, and he thought she was lying.

She lowered her eyes and said nothing.

"Mrs Flynt, do you understand what an accessory is, in the legal sense?" Seamus asked her.

She shook her head.

"It means a person knowing about a crime does nothing to prevent it, report it or tries to cover it up, is treated as if they had committed the crime itself. It means if you knew about O'Flaherty's crimes and did nothing about them, you are also guilty of the same offence," Seamus said to her.

"But the Father was murdered," she protested.

"Whether he is dead or not," said Seamus, "is not the point, if the crimes were committed and you knew about it, then you are still part of it."

"I don't know anything, I swear," Mrs Flynt retorted.

"Whoever conceals his transgressions will not prosper, but he who confesses and forsakes them will obtain mercy. Proverbs 28:13," O'Rorden told her suddenly. "You're a godly woman, Mrs Flynt, are you not? Surely the words of the Bible can show you the way, would you not think?"

Seamus looked at him impressed.

Mrs Flynt pursed her lips. It was obvious she wasn't going to admit to anything more.

"Alright, Mrs Flynt, you can go, for now, but I want you to think about what we've said, and about those young people." Seamus gestured at the table of reports. "You know something, and we know you know, make no mistake about it."

He motioned to O'Rorden who escorted her out of the interview room and handed her over to O'Flynn.

"I didn't know you were such an expert on the Bible," laughed Seamus when O'Rorden came back in.

"Oh, I'm not, believe me, sir, I'm not, but I did have to go to Sunday school and Bible class, so I did. I do remember something, sometimes, comes in handy on occasion."

"Well you know more of the bible than me and that's a fact."

"She's still lying isn't she, sir?" O'Rorden said sadly.

"Yes, yes I am afraid she is, I'm sorry, she's protecting O'Flaherty and it's not helping us."

"No, sir."

"Sorry it's turned out this way." Seamus was sympathetic to the fact there had been something between O'Rorden and Mrs Flynt, probably for a long time.

"It's OK, sir, sometimes people turn out not to be what you thought they were, so they don't."

"You are right there, O'Rorden, you are so very right."

The two men looked at each other with understanding. Seamus for the past errors of judgement and O'Rorden for the present. Each was quiet for a few moments, lost in their own thoughts.

"What now, sir?" O'Rorden broke the silence.

"We carry on, O'Rorden, we carry on, and we don't stop, until we find the killer."

* * *

It was a pleasant if cold afternoon outside in Dublin. Inside the bedroom, her punishment room, in Mistress Dana's house it was warm, the central heating keeping things a pleasant temperature. But the blinds were drawn on the triple glazed windows, and the skylight, so there was no hint of the presently sunny aspect for the current occupants of the room.

Mistress Dana sat straddling a chair gazing at the Bishop on his knees in front of her, a smile playing on her lips.

"This is how I usually like my men you know, Bishop," she mused. "On their knees, submissive."

She smiled, smiled like a predator and its prey. A black widow spider, her hair cascading down her sides, glittering emerald eyes in the half-light, the shiny leather of her black corset like the carapace of the deadly insect. Deadly but beautiful, alluring, the Bishop was mesmerised.

"Now then, Bishop, what is it you want to confess, hmmm?"

THE CONFESSIONAL KILLINGS

The Bishop began haltingly, quietly and then as the lies were revealed, and the things he had done, the things he knew other priests had done came out, he got bolder, more voluble. It was almost as if a suppurating boil had been burst and all the sins, the vile stinking pus of those dark deeds came streaming from it.

She listened, saying nothing, not a flicker or trace of any feeling passed across her face. For her, this part was the worst. As she listened to the horrible things perpetrated on others, she began to relive all those terrible moments of her teenage years and beyond. All those times when the Father... and his nuns... all those things they had done. Several times she made an effort to clear her mind, a trick she had learned out of necessity, and yet the memories would still eventually come crowding back. In a way, the memories were the fuel, the fuel that fired her, for when it came to the time to exact retribution. Though she couldn't punish those who had wronged her, she could punish by proxy, others who had done equally wrong, and it felt good.

The Bishop's confession was particularly bad, even by her standards. There were many things he had done personally, including sodomy and rape. He had successfully covered up his sins and crimes and those of other priests in his care. People would be shocked if they knew, but Mistress Dana was not. She had learned first-hand the evils of years of abuse and neglect at the hands of the Catholic Church.

When the Bishop finally finished, he was crying like a baby. She let him cry, he would soon be crying even more, and from a different cause, she smiled grimly.

"Does it make you feel sorry? Remorseful? Telling me all this?" she enquired, her voice was stern now, harsh.

"Yes," he said, "and somehow no, not completely."

"Really? So, it doesn't and you're not totally sorry? Is that it?"

The Bishop shook his head, there was something in him that couldn't feel sorry unless he had paid; paid some kind of price for it.

"Why did you want to tell me all this now? You've kept it to yourself all these years, now haven't you?"

"I, well in case anything happened to me, I wanted to know I had confessed it to someone. I needed to."

"Really? So why not confess it to another priest? Why come to me?" she pressed him.

"I can't, I couldn't and besides..."

"Besides they wouldn't give you what you want, is that it?"

He nodded. She sat and watched him for a while. Thinking about what he'd said, in no hurry to begin, making him sweat.

"It's the priest, isn't it, the one that was shot, you're afraid you might be next maybe? And if so then you won't have confessed, is that it?" Now it made sense to her.

"Yes," he said simply. "Yes, that's it."

"Well, think about it this way, he's the lucky one, but you... you've got something coming to you for sure... and what do you think should happen to you now?" She wanted him to say it, ask for it, she liked to hear it.

"You know what I need, you know what I came here for," he said quietly.

"Oh, I do but I want to hear you say it, so say it."

He was silent.

"Say it! Say it, go on ask for it, that's an order." Her eyes flashed at him, she could do mock anger quite well. In reality, this part was usually an act. One she enjoyed.

"I need to be punished," he spoke reluctantly.

170

"That's better. So, ask me, ask me to punish you," she pushed harder.

"Punish me, I want you to punish me." This time it seemed easier to say it.

She got up from the chair and squatted down in front of him, her face very close to his.

"Now, say please," she told him.

"Please, please punish me." It was clear already he wasn't enjoying this, but for her, this was the start, the start of his humiliation and his punishment.

"Please who?" she asked him. "How did I say you were to address me?"

"Please," he said with an effort. "Please punish me, Mistress."

She smiled at that, he was going to be quite easy she could see. Sometimes, the first time, she had to work them a lot harder. But every one of them, submitted to her, in the end. Every one of them was made to submit, to grovel, feel what it was like to be at someone's mercy. Because she knew, exactly how it felt, it was etched in her memory for all time.

"Well, since you asked so nicely."

She rose from her squatting position. There she stood, tall and proud, every inch a mistress in her stilettoes looking down on him. The power of it was like a drug, she craved it, loved it, it made her feel suddenly better as if the years of hurt and pain had dropped away. That's why she kept doing it, she needed it, just as much as they needed her to do it to them.

"Get up!" It was an order, low and peremptory. She knew how to use her voice; long practice had taught her.

His head jerked up surprised, but he complied and stood up facing her, waiting, watching her wondering what happened next. She walked over to the vaulting horse. Slowly, deliberately, using her heels, wanting him to feel the anticipation, wanting to tantalise him with something he could never have. It was quite a low vaulting horse about waist height for her. It was perfect for her uses. She moved the horse more into the centre of the open space in the room. She could have done it earlier before he came, but again it was about the game, she was playing with him, toying with him.

"Take your clothes off," she barked another order at him.

"But, but," he protested. "Can't I just take my trousers down?"

"No!" she said flatly. "No, I want you naked, humiliated, it's a part of your punishment, an essential part, and you didn't call me Mistress and you weren't polite. How dare you!"

She walked over to him quickly and slapped him hard across the face, once, twice. This was how she broke them down. This was how she made them obey her, completely and without question. He winced.

"Sorry, Mistress," he whispered, slightly in shock.

Slowly he removed his garments and left them in a pile on the floor. Mistress Dana watched him with a smile playing on her lips. She could tell he felt vulnerable naked, standing there in front of her. He looked somehow sad, a quite thin, grey man, without the illusion of armour his priest's clothing gave him. He had lost some of his dignity and she wanted that. She wanted him to feel how it feels to be nothing, to feel like nobody.

"Get over here, now!" She pointed to the horse.

He walked over slowly.

"Now stand in front of it."

He obeyed and waited wondering what was going to happen next, wishing he hadn't come, realising it was now too late to stop.

Mistress Dana sauntered over the basket in the corner and drew out a cane. It was similar to the ones they used to use in schools with a crook handle. She walked back until she was directly in front of him flexing it in both hands making it bend and straighten, her eyes upon him the whole time, watching his reaction, watching him squirm.

"I am sure you've seen one of these before," she remarked. "Probably used one even, on other people, children in your care no doubt, in fact, if I remember it was part of your confession."

He said nothing transfixed by the instrument in her hand, what she had said was true, but now he was afraid, of how it was going to feel, on him.

"Usually I save these for later sessions," she told him. "But I'm going to make an exception in your case, Bishop. Because you've been a very, very, very naughty boy, haven't you now."

She let go of the business end and swished the cane experimentally in the air a few times. He drew a sharp intake of breath.

"Oh yes, oh yes, Bishop, this is exactly what you came here for." Her voice was pitched low and vibrant filled with the promise of what was to come.

She tapped the end of the cane on the top of the horse.

"Come on, Bishop, bend over," she said lightly.

He obliged and automatically found the legs of the horse with his hands and then gripped them. Perhaps he unconsciously realised he was going to need some support.

"Best you hold on tight now, Bishop, and don't you get up until I say you can."

She walked slowly round to his left side and stood legs apart in a position which was to her, by now, very familiar from long practice. Carefully she placed the cane across the centre of his naked buttocks.

"You know, Bishop, you're very lucky, a very lucky man because this happens to be one of my specialities. You're in for a treat, or at least I am. Have you ever had a good whipping, now have you, Bishop?" she asked. This was all part of prolonging the suspense, she liked to take her time, build up to it, make it last. She was in no hurry that was for certain.

"I... no, not for a long time," he replied. "Not since I was very young... Mistress"

"Hmmm, you're learning, very good. Well," she breathed her voice full and almost sensual, "you're about to experience one my very best whippings and then you'll know."

She waited a little longer, lifted the cane and put it back a few times marking her place but also, so he wouldn't be sure when the first blow would come.

"Let's start with six, shall we? I like the number six," she said, finally.

This time she pulled the cane back until it was vertical, and her arm was out at one side. The sound of the cane flying through the air was unmistakable, followed by the smack of it into his bare flesh. Almost immediately she lifted it off, to increase the sting. It left a satisfying red line across his arse, she thought, appreciating the result.

For the first split second the Bishop felt nothing and all he heard was the swish of the cane falling. There is always a delay as the sensation travels up the central nervous system. As the sharp pain of the first cut registered, he screamed.

THE CONFESSIONAL KILLINGS

✳ ✳ ✳

Seamus rang Brogan to update him on the latest events and progress on the case. Brogan seemed happy with things and for once they seemed in accord. They got onto the discussion about the newspaper article and also the allegations against O'Flaherty.

"Yes, well don't worry about it, Seamus, I know what these newspapers are like, so I do, especially the Irish Sun, the bane of our lives that rag," Brogan was saying.

"It's maddening, sir, and no mistake," Seamus said with feeling. "I suppose the Archbishop got onto you about it?" He expected nothing less and waited for some further piece of ecclesiastical advice about his investigation to be forthcoming but was pleasantly surprised there wasn't any.

Brogan continued, "Yes, I had him on the phone right away ranting and raving at me about church privilege and privacy and all that stuff, I've heard it a million times before. I was right out of patience with him I can tell you that for nothing, so I can."

Seamus laughed. "Well, it's something if he's pissed you off that much."

"I've had enough of it with this case, and I told him straight," said Brogan frankly. "I said well if your fucking priests, well I didn't quite say fuck, but I said if your priests could have kept their hands to themselves and off the young people in their charge and kept their bloody vows then we wouldn't be having stories like this in the press, so we wouldn't."

"I bet he didn't like it," chortled Seamus enjoying the fact for once his boss had given the Archbishop a flea in his ear.

"I'll say he didn't." Brogan sounded amused. "He went awfully quiet and then suddenly remembered he had an appointment somewhere he'd forgotten about. I was never more glad when he put the phone down I can tell you. He won't be back in a hurry now that's for sure."

Seamus imagined some frantic phone calls probably involving Cardinals to try and mitigate the damage.

"Anyway, Boss, we've now found twenty or thirty cold cases of allegations against Father O'Flaherty," Seamus told Brogan.

Brogan gave a low whistle. "Well fuck me sideways that's quite a lot of cases."

"You're telling me," said Seamus, "and the Bishop was supposedly investigating them, they were all handed over to the church. As you can imagine nothing happened."

"I'm not surprised at all," Brogan responded to this news.

"We're checking up if any of these people are still alive and where they are, one of them could be our killer perhaps."

"Good thinking, Seamus, and if you don't mind maybe you could get a copy of those sent up here, they'll come in handy as ammunition for the next time the Archbishop gets in touch." Brogan chuckled.

"I'll get onto to it, sir."

Having got the revelation out of the way they discussed the press conference arranged for the next day and Brogan said he might come down for it. He cleared Seamus' plan to talk about the alleged abuse since it was now public knowledge and people might just come forward.

Potential views on the possible murderer and the fact it might be a woman were also thrown around. He told Brogan about the perfume but explained it was a very common make. He neglected to mention the three people he had smelt it on so far. This was partly because Brogan was often a shoot first kind of guy and might insist he brought them in and questioned them. Seamus didn't want to do it just yet, he wanted to be sure of his ground first. He waited a little longer to strike usually and the policy had paid off. If you broke too early you often missed your target, that was his experience. They ended off the phone call with some pleasantries.

"How's the new DS working out for you?" Brogan asked him. "I had to call in a few favours for it you know, so I hope it was worth it."

"He's doing well. He's an asset to the team. When this is done maybe we can make it permanent?"

"Don't jump the gun, Seamus, let's see how he does and then we'll talk, but I am glad to hear he's living up to expectations."

"Totally, sir, totally, he's a great number two."

"Great! Well, I must dash, but possibly see you tomorrow, if I am not there just carry on without me, I am sure you will be fine, you've done enough of these by now."

Brogan disconnected. Seamus fervently hoped something would come up to prevent Brogan coming down. His boss made him nervous because he would keep on poking into stuff and interfering whilst all the time professing not to be doing so. It was irritating and stressful and Seamus would rather he stayed as far away from Ballysruth as possible.

He went to find Kathy O'Flynn to find out if everything was set up for the conference, and she assured him it was. Major press and networks would probably be there. He would have to be very sure of his ground. He would take O'Flynn and O'Rorden with him, and a couple of others as observers. O'Rorden would be up on the podium and might get asked some questions. Seamus decided to brief everyone tomorrow morning on what to do.

✳ ✳ ✳

Almost an hour had now passed, and the Bishop was still lying bent across the horse. His backside was bright red, and a deeper shade of red in parts. A series of pink and red stripes crossed his cheeks. Mistress Dana stood watching him. She had made the session last particularly long. Deliberately, because for some reason she felt he had deserved special treatment, and not in a good way.

She had laid down a pattern of strokes in groups of six. Used every trick in the book, including putting a timer on a chair in front of him and setting it to intervals of six minutes so he could see exactly when the next six stokes were coming. She had lost count of the number he'd had. In fact, she thought to herself, she didn't care. She was an expert at prolonging these sessions, stretching them out, making them last. Enjoying the discomfort of her client. At the same time not hurting them too much they couldn't endure it. It was a fine line and one in which she was extremely expert.

At first, the Bishop had screamed, a lot, with each stroke. Then presently he had taken it stoically and silently. Perhaps that is why she had continued it, trying to break him, make him cry or sob, but he did neither.

She walked around in front of him again and spoke.

"Well, Bishop, have you had enough do you think now?" she asked him.

"If you think I have, Mistress, it's up to you," he replied quietly, submissively.

"That's the right answer," she smiled. "Do you feel purged, Bishop, of your sins?"

"Perhaps I do, Mistress, for now," he told her quite honestly.

"Perhaps I should give you some more then," she pondered aloud. His face twisted into a grimace at the thought. It seemed to be a sign he was probably cooked for the moment. But she wasn't quite satisfied, there had to be something more. She thought about it for a while and then brought a chair and put it fairly close, so he could see her. She sat on it and leaned back opening her legs. She felt like she needed to make him suffer just a bit more.

"You know, Bishop, I'm actually pretty wet down here," she teased him, "I bet you'd like to touch it, wouldn't you? Hmmm."

Her finger began to move pressing hard against herself through her pants and she started to moan. She could see he was looking at her with a tortured expression on his face. She knew he was aroused.

"What's it like, Bishop, knowing you can look but you can't touch?" Her finger slipped under the crotch of her panties and found her wet and weak spot. She moaned again and breathed more deeply. "Oh, Bishop, it makes me quite horny, you know, watching you squirm, caning your fucking arse, you fucking pervert." Her finger moved faster harder, it didn't take long at all, she was close "Next time and there will be a next time, you'll be getting the belt, how do you like that? Hmmm... hmmmm... ahhhhhhhh." She orgasmed heavily and loudly, bucking in the chair until everything had subsided. It was true, there was something dreadfully sexual about what she did and sometimes she couldn't hold it in.

She sat there for a long while and looked at him, tears were rolling down his cheeks silently. She had got to him, broken him, she was pleased.

"Thank you," he said. "Mistress"

"For what?" she asked suddenly angry, it wasn't supposed to happen. He wasn't meant to thank her. Something wasn't right. She shouted at him. "What? For my little show? That wasn't for you, that was for me. You bastard!"

Something inside her snapped, images crowding her mind, of times before, another face, after he had raped her, the Father, saying thank you. It had brought it all back, whatever the Bishop had meant, it had brought it all back. She was angry, she walked to her dressing table and grabbed some leather straps. Quickly and deftly she tied his wrists to the legs of the horse.

"What are you doing?" he cried in alarm. "This wasn't in the contract. What are you doing? Please..."

"I'm giving you what you deserve," she spat venomously, in a voice he had not yet heard. "It was a mistake giving you that show, you didn't deserve that show but I know what you do deserve, to feel what you did to those others, that's what you deserve."

Without another word, she fetched something from another drawer. He watched in horrified fascination as she strapped on a large dildo and began to grease it with Vaseline.

"No, please, no," he cried.

"Oh yes," she said. "Oh yes!"

The red mist had descended.

* * *

Seamus walked into Kerry's private parlour hoping for some dinner. She had given him an open invitation. Kerry wasn't there, but Liam was, bending down to peer in the oven. He stood up.

"Can I help you?" he asked with a little hostility in his voice.

"I err, I was hoping for some dinner," Seamus told him sounding a little uncertain.

"Well, the dining room is back there if you find a seat I'll come over and take your order. This is a private dining area," Liam said.

"Where he's welcome any time, Liam!" Kerry arrived putting her arms around Seamus and smiling at him.

"Sorry," Liam said to Seamus and then to Kerry, "you never told me, Ma! How was I supposed to know?"

"Oh, put your hackles down, Liam," she teased him. "This is what I have to put up with, Seamus, when he's here, my overprotective son." She laughed.

"Oh, Ma!" protested Liam

"Well to be fair he probably didn't realise." Seamus tried to mitigate the situation.

"Don't you take his side now," she warned, her eyes twinkling.

Liam rolled his eyes, and Kerry kissed Seamus full on the lips.

"Ma! Do you have to?" Liam objected.

"See, this is what kids are like." Kerry laughed, she pulled Seamus over to the table. "Come on, sit down, tell me about your day."

"Well," began Seamus. "There's only so much I can tell you, you know, some of it I can't."

He caught Liam eyeing him apprehensively and wondered if he was worried Seamus would mention Diana. Perhaps Kerry didn't know.

"Oh you," she pouted. "Well tell me about the things you can tell me then."

"Fine, but then you tell me about your day," he shot back.

"OK," she agreed.

Liam made an irritated noise at this exchange.

"I'm off so I am and leave you lovebirds to it," he said crossly.

"Hey, don't be like that, and what about the dinner service?" Kerry protested.

"I've done most of it, I'll deliver those last plates on my way out," Liam told her.

"Thanks a lot!" Kerry sounded irritated. "Where are you going?"

"Just out," said Liam. "See you, Ma!"

He bent down and kissed his mother and then he was gone carrying a couple of plates.

"Feck it!" Kerry exclaimed. "I'm sorry, about Liam, he's not used to me having a man in my life, not really."

"It's OK," Seamus told her. "It's understandable, I mean I don't have kids myself but it's understandable."

"Thanks," she said gratefully.

"So, is that what I am?" he asked her, "the man in your life?"

She looked at him quizzically, but he was being serious.

"Yes," she said. "Yes, you are, if you want to be, do you want to be?"

"I..." he began.

"I'm not the murderer, Seamus," she told him emphatically.

He took hold of her hands and looked her in the eyes.

"I'm not used to being cared for," he told her, "by someone so fucking beautiful, I'm not used to things happening so quickly."

"Are you scared?" she asked him.

"Of what?" he asked.

"Of commitment, of me, of... this..." She indicated the general direction of the pub.

"No," he told her. "I'm not scared. You're just so different, Kerry. So different and already, I am out of my depth, the depth I'm used to, and thing is this is where I might usually run. I don't, because you keep bringing me back, and so to answer your question, I wouldn't be averse to being your man, if I could be, if I can be."

She squeezed his hands realising she was pushing him too hard. The fact she was already certain about what she wanted didn't mean he had come up to her speed. She was starting to fall and that was a fact. And she liked it.

"It's OK." She smiled at him. "Thank you, for being honest with me. I'm sorry I don't mean to push you."

"You're not," he protested.

"Anyway, yes as far as I am concerned you are the man in my life, and hopefully soon I'll get to be the woman in yours." She smiled.

"OK," he smiled gently at her and as he was still holding her hands pulled her close to him and kissed her lightly. "So, if I am the man in your life, then can the man in your life please have something to eat?"

She laughed. "Maybe, if the man in my life kisses me nicely."

"Is that what I've got to do now, kiss you every time I want something?" he joked.

"Pretty much, yes," she laughed.

"Well then, best you come this side of the table." His eyes twinkled, and Kerry's were dancing. She tripped lightly round to the bench to where Seamus was sitting and sank into his arms.

Mistress Dana sat alone in her bedroom. The Bishop had gone, she had sent him on his way. The cane was discarded, flung into a corner, the dildo she had latterly used in another. Her hair was in disarray and her mascara had run from shedding tears.

She had got carried away and now she deeply regretted it. Self-control was everything, never to allow the images in her head to take over, never to allow the primal urges to override her common sense. She had taken revenge on the Bishop. She had used the dildo on him while he cried in shame, and he had cried for a very long time afterwards. Perhaps it was cathartic, for him, but not for her. She hated the fact she had lost it. Mad as fire with herself.

The Bishop had been very quiet when he left, he had thanked her, he sounded as if he really meant it. She had not said too much too him at all once it was over. Holding it all in, the emotional storm in her head. She had watched him get dressed and said she hoped he had got what he wanted from the session. He said he had, he told her he felt as if God had wanted him to suffer that day, to repent and pay for his sins. He told her perhaps he might see her again. Well, she smiled wryly, he certainly had done, he had paid for his sins, she had seen to it.

When the Bishop left, she had cried, sobbed her guts out. Somehow, this episode had brought out the very worst in her. It had been too close, too close to home. Perhaps she should stop for a while she thought. She had plenty of money in her various accounts. A week or two, a break might do her good.

She felt so alone though. Liam, where was he? She wanted Liam. For some reason, he gave her comfort in the depth of his skinny arms. She had tried calling him, texted him to no avail. Fuck him! She thought. Selfish arsehole. This was not good. There was more rage in her building inside and she could feel it. If only Liam would come, even just for one night. All would be well.

There was a soft knock at the door, it broke into Mistress Dana's reverie. When she didn't reply immediately it was opened very gently and she saw Bella's smiling face. She was carrying a tray with a cup of tea and some biscuits. Bella's smile became one of instant concern noting her Mistress' tear-streaked face. She came in and placing the tray on the bed, sat beside her employer.

"Mistress, what's wrong? You've been crying."

"Yes, yes I have," sniffed Mistress Dana, "but it's nothing, nothing for you to worry about, Bella, I'm OK."

"But why, why were you crying?" Bella persisted, and her hand gently touched her Mistress' bare shoulder. Her hand was soft, the touch was almost a caress but not quite.

"Oh, it's just the memories, of things, sometimes they overwhelm me," Mistress Dana absently reached up to take Bella's hand and held in hers. "You mustn't worry about me, Bella, really."

"Well, I brought you a cup of tea, Mistress, and your favourite biscuits, I thought you might be a bit worn out after the Bishop, it seemed like a long session."

"You're a darling and yes it was." She took Bella's hand and kissed it. This made Bella smile again and she took the mug and put it into both of her Mistress' hands.

"Thanks," said Mistress Dana gratefully.

"It's OK, you know I'll do anything for you, Mistress." Bella's eyes betrayed a fondness for her employer and perhaps a little more. Mistress Dana didn't notice but took a sip of the tea and ran a hand through her hair distractedly.

"That's nice, you always make a nice cup of tea, Bella."

"I know what you like," Bella said simply.

She offered the plate of biscuits to Mistress Dana, who took one, dipped it into her tea and ate it.

"Nothing like a chocolate digestive to make you feel better," she mused with satisfaction.

"When you're ready, I've got some dinner made, Mistress, please come down and eat, it will do you good."

"Oh, Bella, you're my rock do you know that? Always there, always know exactly what I need." she smiled at Bella now starting to feel much restored.

"I do my best," was all Bella said, but the truth was she did much more. She went over and above to make sure her Mistress was looked after and cared for. She carefully took note of her likes, and her dislikes and ran her house like clockwork. And all this for a smile, or a pleased look from the woman she had come to adore.

"I bet my mascara has run all over the place," Mistress Dana chuckled.

"I am afraid it has. Would you like me to help you fix it?"

Diana caught Bella's eyes, the softness in them, the caring expression. It unsettled her a little. She wasn't used to having someone caring for her so much, catering to her every whim and need without question. Or, to be truthful, she was now used to it and she liked it. Bella was always there. She sensed perhaps Bella wanted to be closer to her, perhaps emotionally, but Mistress Dana found it hard to let anyone in.

"It's OK, I can do it, you go and set the table if you would, I am quite hungry."

If Bella was disappointed her Mistress wouldn't let her help with her makeup, she did not betray anything in her expression. Instead, she stood up instantly and declared she would have the table and supper ready as soon as her Mistress wanted it.

"Thank you, Bella."

Mistress Dana watched her leave the room with an affectionate smile on her face.

* * *

Mistress Dana came down to dinner dressed in one of her favourite robes. She often wandered about her house in this fashion. It was black satin and hugged her figure well, she wore nothing underneath it and it left little to the imagination. However, with Bella around, she wasn't particularly concerned about how revealing her appearance might be. Her preference for casual bedroom footwear was some fluffy black slippers with only a small heel. She liked her stilettos but not particularly for comfort.

Bella had laid the dining room table for one, as she usually did and dimmed the lighting. She tucked Mistress into her place and proceeded to ladle a portion of Irish stew onto her plate, plus some mash and green beans. Mistress Dana liked wholesome food and Bella was a very good cook. She had adapted herself completely to her Mistress' tastes. She poured a glass of Merlot into her

Mistress' glass and was about to leave when Mistress Dana spoke.

"No, don't leave me, I don't want to eat alone tonight, sit and eat with me, Bella, please?" she smiled weakly. The session with the Bishop had taken its toll on her mentally as much as anything. Being a dominatrix was also surprisingly occasionally physically draining.

It would be unusual for Bella to stay; she was used to leaving her Mistress to eat on her own. Mistress Dana seemed to prefer it that way. Though, she never treated Bella as if she was a servant. Nevertheless, Bella was pleased, laid another place and served herself a plate of food. She poured water into a glass and sat down.

"Don't you want some wine?" Mistress Dana enquired.

"No, Mistress, I'm not a big drinker, to be honest."

"OK, well this is lovely as usual, Bella, beautifully cooked, delicious in fact."

"Thank you, Mistress." Bella's eyes shone under the compliment. Her red hair glinted softly in the dim light and Mistress Dana couldn't help noticing how pretty she looked. Bella certainly was a pretty girl and she kept herself well trying to look her best. Bella always wanted to look her best for her Mistress.

"Tell, me some stories, Bella, what's going on in the world?"

Bella kept up with the news and current affairs. Her Mistress was liable to ask her at any time because she wasn't a great TV watcher herself. Mostly Mistress Dana liked to read, she had a comprehensive library.

Bella filled her in on the latest gossip, politics and the like. Her Mistress was diverted and was soon in a much sunnier mood. The Bishop was forgotten as she laughed over some political anecdote.

When dinner was over Mistress Dana announced, she was tired. She asked Bella to come up and read to her. Above all this was one of her favourite things. Her mother used to read to her. Then nobody ever did so again until Bella came into her life. When she was ready for bed, she allowed Bella to tuck her in and then draw up a chair.

Bella opened the pages of 'Sense and Sensibility' and began,

"The family of Dashwood had long been settled in Sussex. Their estate was large, and their residence was at Norland Park..."

Mistress Dana smiled and her face relaxed. She closed her eyes. Bella sat there reading, watching her and admiring just how beautiful her Mistress really was. The book was one Mistress Dana was particularly fond of; it was possibly the tenth time they had read it. As the words flowed with Bella's soft melodious voice, Mistress Dana drifted off. When Bella was sure she was fully asleep, she closed the book and put it aside. Then leaning down, she placed the lightest of kisses on her Mistress' full lips.

"Goodnight my beautiful darling sweet Mistress," she whispered.

Mistress Dana stirred, smiled in her sleep and rolled over. Bella turned out the light and quietly left the room.

DAY 5

At breakfast, Seamus seemed preoccupied. Kerry watched him a little anxiously, wondering if he was having second thoughts after their heart to heart the night before. This concern was however at odds with the passion with which he had kissed her that morning on entering her private kitchen. There was nothing to suggest any feelings he might have developed for her were reduced in any way. She put her doubts aside and sat, watching him eat his breakfast as she was becoming accustomed to doing.

Seamus found this strange, she wouldn't eat with him, but he didn't demur. He teased her a little about it though.

"I'm beginning to think you might a vampire on the quiet," he suddenly said.

"What!?" Her eyes flew open. "Now why on earth would you be thinking that, Seamus Gallway?"

"Well, I've never actually seen you eat anything so far," he laughed. "And I've never seen you outside in the light to be honest, not I can recall, so I'm just beginning to wonder."

"Now just you listen here, DI Gallway," she giggled.

"Perhaps I should be paying more attention to the guests here, maybe some of them never leave," he continued his eyes dancing with humour.

"Oh, just you wait, wait until you finish breakfast."

"And then you'll drink your fill, is that it?"

Kerry shook her head, her shoulders shaking with laughter. "Oh, Seamus, you're the one that's incorrigible, not me."

Seamus polished off the last piece of toast and washed it down with a sip of coffee.

"Come over here..." he said gently.

"Are you telling me what to do?" she said playfully.

"I wouldn't dare do that," he shot back smiling.

She let out a crack of laughter but then she obliged him, came around to his side of the table and stood over him.

"What now, DI Gallway?" she asked him.

He stood up too and took her hands.

"Stop worrying," he said to her. "I'm just fretting about the press conference today that's all, you've nothing to worry, about you and me."

"And I thought I was supposed to be the mind reader," she said in mock indignation.

He pulled her in for a kiss, and she obliged by returning it with fervour, putting her concerns to one side.

* * *

At the morning briefing, Seamus kept it short.

"Here we are at day five of the investigation into the murder of Father O'Flaherty," he said. "In reality, we don't seem much closer to identifying a credible suspect and the best we can say is we are following up some leads. It's not great but I'd rather nail the right person than spend time chasing up the wrong ones. At the press conference, I will, of course, be sounding a lot more positive."

The officers laughed.

"I will do the talking at the conference. Mainly. However, O'Rorden, you will be with me on the podium and you might be asked some questions."

"Me, sir?" O'Rorden looked alarmed.

"Yes, O'Rorden, you." Seamus tried to sound reassuring. "Don't worry it's not so bad, just keep your answers short, to the point and don't be phased by anything you get asked. If you don't feel you should answer something say no comment."

O'Rorden still looked doubtful.

"Come on, O'Rorden, it's all good experience. It's all part of your role in this investigation, better get used to it."

"OK, sir, I'll do my best, that I will."

"Give it your best shot there, Connor." It was Kathy O'Flynn.

"That's the spirit, O'Flynn," Seamus said with approval. "You hear that, O'Rorden, she's got your back."

Everyone laughed again including Seamus.

"O'Flynn and White, I want you there as observers and to ensure we can keep order. Everyone else keep on with the lines of investigation you are on at the moment. It's also possible DCS Brogan, my boss, our big boss, might be joining us." He paused looking around him. "So, we've all got to be on our best behaviour if it happens." He smiled.

There was some discussion on the location of past cases, and some had been located, some had died. The ones they could find were going to be interviewed first by the Garda officers and then if there was anything of interest they would be questioned further. Normally this type of work was the job of detectives, but Brogan hadn't given Seamus any and so he was working with what he had. Most of it appeared to be down to him and O'Rorden who was, now, his only other detective on the team.

The ballistics investigation had drawn a blank, none of the weapons which were checked matched the bullets from the murder, so it was obvious the gun used to kill Father O'Flaherty was not a local one and probably obtained illegally. Paddy was tasked with returning the guns to their owners.

"So, is the DCS really going to come down?" O'Rorden asked him afterwards.

"If we're very unlucky, yes he will," Seamus replied.

"It can't be that bad surely," O'Rorden said seriously.

"Believe me, it will be a pain in the arse, asking questions, poking into this and that, trying to force lines of inquiry, yes it will be that bad. Me and the boss get on fine, as long he stays in his office," Seamus said grimly.

"Right, I see." O'Rorden frowned.

"Ah come on, O'Rorden, I'm sure I'm a pain in the arse to you sometimes," joked Seamus.

"No sir, that you're not, not at all," O'Rorden told him earnestly.

"Is that right? Well, I'm flattered, and I don't mind telling you, most people hate their bosses in my experience and I'm not always popular when I'm running the show," Seamus spoke honestly.

"Well, I think I can speak for everyone here, sir, you're very popular with us, sir, and that's a fact."

"Thanks, I appreciate it, I really do, put it there." Seamus was genuinely touched and meant it. He held out his right hand and O'Rorden shook it warmly, the two men smiled at each other.

"OK, that's enough sentimentality for one day, O'Rorden, let's get ready for the conference."

* * *

The press team from Dublin had done their usual professional job. The hall was set up nicely, a podium on the stage, sound system, the works. The media was arriving, local and national TV, all the main daily rags, and local ones as well. There were some faces in the crowd from Ballysruth, curious locals wanting to know more, some Seamus recognised, some O'Rorden pointed out to him. Right at the back, Seamus saw Kerry slide in, she gave him a reassuring smile.

They were almost ready to start. O'Rorden leaned over to Seamus and said, "looks like your Boss didn't make it, after all, sir." He was smiling.

"You spoke too soon," Seamus replied with a sinking feeling as the familiar figure of Brogan entered the hall. He was a fairly thickset big man, his grey hair betrayed his age, he was pushing on to retirement, but nevertheless, he still cut an imposing figure, and he had obviously decided to wear his uniform today. He was neatly attired and, on his chest, sported several medals earned over his seemingly illustrious career in the Garda.

Brogan climbed the stairs to the podium and took his place next to Seamus.

"You made it, sir," Seamus said.

"I didn't want to miss this, Seamus, I even cancelled some meetings just to be here," Brogan smiled, "but you'll be glad to know I can't stay long."

"Well, I don't know why you would say that, sir," Seamus demurred. "We're happy to have you here, of course."

"Cut the bullshit, Seamus, I know you think I'm a pain in the arse, but I'm here to support you not rain on your parade." Brogan was still smiling.

"Well," Seamus shrugged. "You got me there, sir, but... thanks."

"Oh, by the way," Seamus continued, "can I introduce you to DS O'Rorden, sir?" He indicated O'Rorden at his side.

"Yes, sure, absolutely you can." Brogan leaned over and shook O'Rorden's hand. "Nice to meet you, O'Rorden, I've heard a lot of good things about you, so I have."

"Thank you, thank you, sir," said O'Rorden gratefully.

"Well, keep it up and we'll see if can't make your appointment permanent, O'Rorden," Brogan continued.

"Thank you, thank you indeed, sir, I won't let you down." He looked genuinely pleased. Brogan nodded in assent. Seamus thought it was typical of Brogan to come out with it as if it was his own idea.

"Anyway, Seamus, this is your show," Brogan said.

"Well, let's do it then," Seamus replied.

He spoke into the mike, "I think we're all here, so we'll start the press conference now."

The room fell silent and all eyes were on him.

"First of all, thank you for coming. I am DI Seamus Gallway and I am leading this investigation into the murder of Father O'Flaherty, on my right is DS Connor O'Rorden, my second in command, and on my left, DCS Jack Brogan."

"I have a question, Inspector," a news hack stood up interrupting him.

"If you can wait until the end, there'll be plenty of time for questions then," Seamus replied. The reporter sat down, and Seamus continued, "First of all I'll recap on the investigation to date and then there are some specific pieces of information we'd like to share, which we hope might help assist with our enquiries." He paused and glanced at Brogan who nodded in approval.

Seamus reiterated the circumstances of the murder, how it was carried out, the weapon they thought was used and various other details. Having completed the preamble, he started on the specifics.

"Now, there's been some speculation in the press regarding Father O'Flaherty and allegations from a witness Father O'Flaherty had attempted to molest him. We can confirm we believe these allegations to be true, not only that, we have uncovered a large number of previous allegations which were made against Father O'Flaherty. Most of these date back more than ten years. For reasons we can't speculate on at this moment, these cases were not followed up on. We are, however, treating them very seriously. We would urge anyone who has knowledge of these allegations, or who may have been molested or sexually assaulted by Father O'Flaherty to contact us right away. Anything you have to say will be taken seriously and treated with the utmost confidence and care."

A hush had fallen over the room as this information was digested.

"We also have an eyewitness who may have seen the person we believe to be the murderer leaving the church, after killing Father O'Flaherty. She didn't get a very good look at the suspect but what we do have is a photofit and we will be releasing this to the press for circulation. At this point in time, we do not know if the killer was male or female, and we are looking for any further information anyone might have, no matter how small, to help us in our enquiries. Now, my team and I will be happy to answer any questions you may have."

The photofit of the suspect was handed round whilst this was going on.

"Inspector, are you saying O'Flaherty was a child molester?"

"As I said these are allegations at this time, and they all appear to have been made by girls or boys of 15 years or older," Seamus answered.

"So, he liked teenage girls and boys is that it?" It was a woman from the Evening Echo.

There was some general laughter in the room at this wisecrack.

"I can't speculate on Father O'Flaherty's preferences, I can only tell you what information we currently have," Seamus responded as smoothly as he could.

"Why didn't the Garda take any of these allegations further?" It was Jameson of the Irish Sun.

"I can't say, I am sorry, all I can say is we are sorry to have found out this wasn't done."

"Not as sorry as those people making the allegations I'll bet," Jameson responded with sarcasm.

"I am sure you are right," Seamus said.

"So, are you saying there was a cover-up, Inspector?" It was the turn of a reporter from the Irish News of the World.

"I am saying we do not know why these investigations were not pursued. We are here to investigate a murder, I have no prior knowledge of these reports up until now."

"We believe some of these allegations were investigated by the church," Brogan butted in, wanting to deflect the fire from the Garda.

"Well, we all know how much good it would have done then, don't we?" the reporter said with some acidity.

"You could always ask the Bishop," suggested Brogan.

"Oh, we'll be asking him and no mistake, don't you worry, and we'll be asking the Archbishop as well for good measure," the reporter said with some resolution.

Brogan smiled to himself and Seamus noticed the very self-satisfied look on Brogan's face. However, the ploy seemed to have killed that line of questioning at least to Seamus' relief.

"Inspector, is it true you don't actually have any specific suspects as yet?" It was a reporter from the Irish Independent.

"I can't answer that."

"It's been five days and you haven't even got a lead isn't that right?" the reporter tried to pursue their point.

"We are following up on a number of leads I can't say more than that." Seamus was stonewalling, he'd had plenty of experience with probing reporters to handle these types of questions.

"Come on, give us a bit more than that, who do you think killed the Father? Wasn't it really a sectarian murder?" It was the Irish Mirror this time.

"You can't expect us to reveal our lines of inquiry at the moment, and we don't speculate, we wait until we have the evidence to charge someone, you know that. To answer your other question, no, we don't believe this was sectarian, particularly in light of recent evidence we have uncovered. We think it's more likely an act of revenge."

"So, you're saying this was something like the Masked Revenger is that it?" The Irish Daily Star.

Typical thought Seamus to himself.

"I did not say the murderer wore a mask at any time."

"No, but it sure looks like it from this photograph." There was general amusement at this remark and Seamus could see what would be printed in tomorrow's headlines. There were then a few more questions of a general nature and then Seamus tried to see if could wrap the conference up.

"Any other questions at this time?" He asked hoping there wouldn't be.

"Yes, I've one for DS O'Rorden." It was a reporter from RTE.

"Go on."

"DS O'Rorden, how are you finding things now you have been promoted to detective, you were a uniformed sergeant before isn't that right?" This was obviously the human-interest angle Seamus reflected.

"Absolutely fine, yes indeed," O'Rorden replied.

"Don't you think you are a bit inexperienced to take this on?" the same reporter was asking.

"I'll answer it," Seamus said. "DS O'Rorden is doing a sterling job as my number two, he's an asset to the team, and I have a very good and competent team. I have every confidence in his ability."

"How did he get to be a DS?"

Seamus was irritated, sometimes they wouldn't give up.

"I recommended him for promotion based on his performance. Now, are there any other questions about the actual inquiry?" He hoped he had managed to shut the reporter down.

"Yes, I have a couple for DCS Brogan." It was Matthew Jameson again, of the Irish Sun.

"Sure, how can I help?" Brogan replied.

"Do you think DI Gallway is the right man for this job? After all, he's not come up with anything so, far has he?" Jameson asked him with a cheeky grin.

"I have absolute confidence in DI Gallway, he's a very experienced officer who has solved several very difficult cases. DI Gallway is an exceptional officer and an asset to any investigation including this one," Brogan spoke in measured tones.

"Yes, but even if it's true like you say it is, do you think he's got all the right resources to solve such an important case, DCS Brogan? Two detectives and a few inexperienced Garda officers don't seem to me as if they will cut it." Jameson was as pushy as expected.

"DI Gallway has a very good team some of whom are long serving officers and well respected. And of course, should he need any more resources to solve this case they will obviously be provided."

Brogan was nothing if not a consummate politician when it came to speaking to the press thought Seamus. He shot Brogan a look and received an urbane expression in return.

"Well, if there are no more questions, I'd like to thank you for coming. We will keep you abreast of any important developments when we are able to release them." Seamus breathed a sigh of relief when nobody else put their hand up. These events were always nerve-wracking no matter how prepared you were or how many you had done before.

The formalities were over, people began to leave talking and murmuring. The various media were packing up their gear. He saw Kerry briefly in the distance and she shot him a sly wink as she left.

"Well done," Brogan told Seamus. "Good conference, you fielded some difficult questions there."

"Journalists," Seamus said with feeling, "and thanks for your confidence, I appreciate what you said up there, sir."

"It's OK, Seamus, just make sure you live up to it," Brogan ribbed him. "Anyway, I need to make a move shortly, I have meetings, and then more meetings, followed by meetings." He sighed.

"Can you just spare a few minutes to come and meet the team, sir? It would mean a lot to them," Seamus asked him.

"Sure, of course," Brogan replied.

Seamus felt he should take advantage of Brogan's presence now he had actually turned up. It might boost their confidence. Seamus introduced him to Sergeant O'Flynn and Garda White. Then he took Brogan across to the Garda station and showed him around, presenting the other officers on his team. They seemed quite honoured the DCS had favoured them with a visit treating him with a fair bit of deference.

"Hmm, you do seem a little light on resources there, Seamus," Brogan said as Seamus walked him to his car.

"Well, if you're offering, you know, like you told the reporter, we could use a bit more help, so we could sir," Seamus said solemnly.

"Don't push your luck, Seamus, budgets, Seamus, budgets and meetings, welcome to my life," Brogan replied.

"I thought so," Seamus gave a hollow laugh.

"Keep me up to date," Brogan told him and drove away.

* * *

With Brogan out of his hair, Seamus decided it was time to see the Bishop. He collected O'Rorden and copies of the allegations that were made against Father O'Flaherty. The Bishop's residence was several kilometres away in the town of Ballykinley. They made good time and soon found themselves outside the front of an imposing building.

They had driven through massive stone gate posts on either side of the entrance and up a long driveway lined with trees just to get there. The white painted stone edifice was a mansion, not a house, thought Seamus. The driveway ended in a turning circle in the centre of which was a fountain, there were statues of cherubs holding up a large dish. The driveway was surfaced with crushed gravel which crunched beneath their feet as they got out of the car. Jets of water tinkled softly and melodically in the fountain.

O'Rorden whistled as he took it all in. "Well, will you look at that?" he said with awe.

"Welcome to the Bishop's palace," Seamus said with a hint of sarcasm in his voice.

"You got that right, sir, indeed, so you have, it looks like a palace alright and no mistake."

"Yes, O'Rorden, how the other half lives, come on stop admiring the Bishop's fountain and let's get down to business."

"Yes, but did you ever see the like of it?" O'Rorden was mightily impressed.

"That's what living off the fat of the land does for you." Seamus was cynical.

The two of them mounted the curved stone steps which led up to the front door. It was a massive piece of oak and iron, with an enormous knocker on it shaped like a dragon's claw. Seamus lifted up the heavy knocker and knocked. It seemed to him almost as if they were pounding on the very gates of hell as they listened to the echoes die away.

After a few moments, the door creaked open loudly revealing a very ancient looking priest in a cassock. He peered at them through a pair of round gold wire-framed glasses. Behind him was a hallway decorated with what Seamus considered to be excessive opulence. The floor was tiled in a black and white chequerboard pattern and on the walls were old but expensive looking paintings. The ceiling was arched and painted with a series of Renaissance styled biblical scenes by all accounts. He could also see some white marble statues on a series of plinths.

"Can I help you?" the old priest enquired in a quavering voice.

"DI Gallway and DS O'Rorden here to see Bishop Mullen if you please." They flashed their badges.

"Do you have an appointment?" the priest asked them hopefully.

"No." Seamus fixed him with a determined eye which defied the priest to attempt to prevent them from seeing the Bishop.

"Come in, come in gentlemen," said the priest, deciding perhaps it would be best not to argue with Seamus.

They entered a long hallway at the end of which was apparently a black and white rippled marble staircase leading up to a landing. Gilded rails lined the stairway and there were large columns and statues making an incongruous mixture of styles. The pictures turned out to be paintings of previous Bishops who had evidently previously occupied the position in the Diocese, some of whom were likely now Archbishops or Cardinals thought Seamus. O'Rorden didn't know where to look, there was so much to see, and he seemed almost like a child let loose in a sweetshop.

After a painfully slow ascent due to the decrepit nature of the priest who was accompanying them, and his inability to walk any faster, they arrived on a large semi-circular landing. The priest motioned them to sit in two gilded chairs upholstered in red velvet.

"I'll tell the Bishop you are here," the priest told them. "Can I tell him what it's concerning?"

"We are investigating the murder of Father O'Flaherty, we are here to ask the Bishop some questions," Seamus replied.

"Very good," the priest replied without a flicker of reaction at this information and made his way across to an ornate looking door that was most likely the Bishop's office. They watched him carefully perambulate slowly across the landing and slip quietly through the doorway, opening it just a crack.

"Well..." O'Rorden said in hushed tones.

"Well indeed," Seamus replied, although he wasn't quite so overcome as his sidekick by the extravagant surroundings. He, like many others, shared the opinion that perhaps the church could spend its money in more charitable ways than elevating the living standards of their clergy. However, these issues stretched back over hundreds of years, and he knew it was hard to change an institution. There had been some changes, he knew the present Pope was trying to address many problems and modernise the Church, it must be a difficult job.

They had only waited a few moments before the priest reappeared at the gilt-edged doorway and beckoned them forward. O'Rorden and Seamus entered the Bishop's domain and the priest quietly shut the door behind him. It was, even Seamus had to acknowledge, a magnificent room. It was large and very spacious, a set of floor to ceiling windows opened out onto what appeared to be quite a vista beyond, well-kept ornamental gardens stretched away. Inside, it was extremely ornately decorated in rococo style. The entire sense of the room was flamboyant, and the very high ceiling held what looked to be perhaps a poor imitation of the one in the Sistine Chapel. Seamus had seen the original and this was not even close.

The wooden floor was covered in parts with Moroccan style rugs and in the centre stood a large gilded desk, obviously where the Bishop spent some of his working day. The Bishop, however, was standing instead by the very large and decorative marble fireplace, above which was a large gilded mirror.

"Ah officers, officers, come in, come in, come in," he began in an over-friendly manner.

Seamus wasn't fooled, he at once detected a wariness in the other's eyes at odds with the faux smile which didn't quite reach them. He also noticed the Bishop was moving somewhat stiffly and with seeming difficulty as he came over to greet them. It was almost, Seamus thought with some amusement as if he had something rather large stuck up his backside and was finding it difficult to walk. He pushed the thought from his mind as the temptation to laugh at this idea was strong. Seamus glanced at O'Rorden and saw from the look on his face he had noticed it too. Perhaps it was old age creeping up on the Bishop thought Seamus.

They both shook the Bishop's hand it was proffered. Might as well start in a cordial manner Seamus decided.

"Di Gallway and DS O'Rorden, Bishop, we'd like to ask you a few questions if you don't mind. In connection with Father O'Flaherty's murder," Seamus told him.

"Ah yes, yes, of course," the Bishop replied. "About the business the other day, I apologise if I was perhaps a little overzealous, it's a distressing thing you know, so it is, to see one's long-time friend and a well-respected priest like that, dead on the floor." He was obviously trying to make amends and lay the groundwork in case perhaps they were going to ask some awkward questions Seamus assumed and was unconvinced by this speech.

"I'm sure," replied Seamus noncommittally.

"Please, take a seat there both of you," the Bishop continued, motioning them towards some more ornate and gilded chairs. "Now can I offer you some refreshment?"

"We're fine," Seamus said and then noticing the look of grave disappointment on O'Rorden's face amended his answer. "Well perhaps if it's not too much trouble, I'll take a cup of coffee and my partner would like tea, thank you."

The Bishop inclined his head and walked stiffly to his desk. He rang a small bell quite loudly. The priest appeared very shortly at this summons and the Bishop asked him to procure the beverages. O'Rorden looked relieved.

"Now then, now then, now then, what can I do for you gentlemen?" asked the Bishop cordially.

"Aren't you going to sit down, Bishop?" Seamus tried to be solicitous.

"No, no, no thanks, I'll stand if it's OK with you, I spend too much time sitting all day, it's nice to get up and have a walk around," the Bishop said trying to sound jovial. The way the Bishop was moving around, Seamus felt, seemed at odds with this speech, but he did not demur.

"It's perfectly OK with us," Seamus assured him.

The Bishop smiled briefly and went to resume his place by the fireplace, leaning on it and wincing slightly every now and then.

Seamus decided the Bishop's potential ailments had had enough attention and they should get on with the business in hand.

"How well did you know Father O'Flaherty?" he enquired.

"Oh well, now that's an easy question, pretty much all my life I did. We grew up together went to the same school, entered the priesthood, I eventually became a Bishop and he stayed in my Diocese."

"Did the Father not want to become a Bishop too?" Seamus was curious.

"Ah well you know, there's not many openings for Bishop's, there aren't," the Bishop answered, "It's kind of dead man shoes."

"Indeed," Seamus said, glossing over what was probably an unintended faux pas on the Bishop's part. He continued, "were you aware of any impropriety engaged in by Father O'Flaherty."

"Impropriety? Now, of course, it depends what you mean by impropriety, Inspector."

"I think you know very well what I mean, Bishop," Seamus said evenly, "I take it you've seen the newspapers?"

"Ach the newspapers, now there's a thing, the newspapers, we know what kind of stuff they print now, don't we?" The Bishop was trying to pass it off and Seamus wasn't having it.

"What kind of stuff is that?"

"Well you know, lies, fabrications, exaggerations, all that kind of thing." The wary expression was back in the Bishop's eyes.

"Except in this case, we happen to believe to be true, we have interviewed a witness, Ronan Maguire, who says Father O'Flaherty attempted to molest him when he was fifteen years old."

"Ach, well, you know it sounds like it was a long time ago if it happened at all." It was becoming obvious the Bishop wasn't going to admit to anything very easily.

Seamus said nothing, waiting for the Bishop to say something more, which he did.

"Anyway, and why did he wait so long to come forward?" the Bishop continued

What Seamus thought about this had to wait for a few moments, whilst the priest returned with a silver tray carrying a teapot, coffee pot, teacups, milk, sugar and a plate with some slices of cake. The tea set appeared to be fine bone china, very delicately patterned and probably hand painted. The priest laid the tray on a low table in front of them and slowly exited the room. O'Rorden looked at Seamus and then began to pour the tea and coffee.

"Perhaps because he was carrying the guilt, Bishop. You know, how people carry guilt I am sure, and how sometimes it takes them years for the guilt to surface," Seamus said very pointedly.

"Well, to be sure it was a long time ago," the Bishop rejoined.

"So, you are saying you know nothing about it?" demanded Seamus. Out of the corner of his eye, he noticed O'Rorden was delicately sipping his tea, but his attention also appeared to be fully on the conversation in hand.

"It's hard to remember these things." The Bishop was obviously prevaricating.

"And is it hard to remember around twenty to thirty cases of allegations of sexual assault and molestation that were filed against Father O'Flaherty too?" Seamus said.

"Well, I really don't know, where did you get this information?" the Bishop began.

"We have it all here, reports, complaints, all filed and most of them were marked passed over to the Church for investigation." Seamus produced a sheaf of papers from a file they had brought with them.

"Well, I..." The Bishop was starting to look very disconcerted.

"I am pretty sure you remember these very well, Bishop," Seamus said pushing home his advantage, "don't you!" It was a statement and not a question.

The Bishop was silent for a moment, probably considering his options and then he spoke.

"OK, OK, I do remember them, it's true they came to my attention and we certainly talked to many of those who had complained."

"And they said what?" asked Seamus feeling as if perhaps now they might be getting somewhere.

"I, I can't discuss it, it's part of church confidentiality"

"Church confidentiality?" Seamus was astounded at this brazen prevarication.

"The seal of the confessional." The Bishop played his trump card. "It's sacrosanct and cannot be discussed."

"A man has been murdered!" Seamus' exasperation was showing, the Bishop's attitude was getting under his skin.

"I know and I'm sorry for that, and I wish I could help." The Bishop shrugged as if to say his hands were tied.

Seamus rose from his chair and paced the room a couple of times. He turned to the Bishop to make one final plea for cooperation. In the meantime, O'Rorden had munched his way through several slices of cake whilst taking in this exchange like a spectator at a particularly entertaining theatrical drama. Or more like a farce, Seamus reflected bitterly.

"Bishop, I am not here to criticise your handling of these matters, although God knows there's a lot that could be said about it. But, putting that aside, one of those people could be a potential murderer and your silence could be protecting them. We need to know what you know, we need your help. Will you not help us, and help us catch Father

O'Flaherty's murderer?" He was trying, with a considerable effort, to be conciliatory and holding his temper in check.

The Bishop spread his hands wide in a gesture of seeming helplessness. "I wish I could Inspector, really I do, but I just can't break the sanctity of the church."

Seamus had had enough, he had reached his limit.

"Sanctity my arse," he exploded. He walked up to the Bishop and stood directly in front of him. "You know something and no mistake, and we know, because we know after the Father was killed you went into his house and you were looking for something, what was it?"

"What?!" the Bishop expostulated "That's an outrageous accusation. How dare you, you've got no proof. Coming here, making accusations..." he tailed off somewhat lamely. Seamus had produced an evidence bag from his pocket containing the keys to Father O'Flaherty's house.

"These," said Seamus triumphantly walking away from him apace and turning back, "have your prints all over them, they were found discarded outside of the Father's back door."

"Well and I probably dropped them, the last time I was there, I have been looking for those and of course they would have my prints on them, they're my keys," the Bishop said thinking perhaps he had come up with a clinching argument.

"Bishop, I am sorry to tell you that is absolute bullshit and you know it." Seamus threw back at him.

The Bishop looked very taken aback at being spoken to in this fashion.

Seamus carried on his attack. "We know it's bullshit because inside the house and particularly the library was in complete disarray, books everywhere, a smashed vase, a defaced picture of the Father and guess whose prints were all over everything, yours!"

O'Rorden was absolutely transfixed. He'd seen his superior in action a few times now, but this was absolutely masterly. He poured himself another cup of tea taking it all in.

The Bishop's shoulders drooped, and he looked deflated, caught out in a lie.

"I think it's time for you to come clean, don't you?" Seamus asked him, his voice much softer now, now he thought he had got the Bishop where he wanted him.

"OK," said the Bishop finally. "OK, I admit it, I was in the house, it's true, I was looking for something."

"Why make such a mess?" asked Seamus.

"I wanted to make it look like a burglary I suppose, I didn't want anyone to know I had been there," replied the Bishop.

"You defaced the Father's picture, why did you do that?"

"I thought people might think it was perhaps the murderer, you know, make it more realistic," explained the Bishop in a helpless voice.

"It must have been important to deface Father O'Flaherty's painting, to go to all that trouble, what was it you were looking for, Bishop?" insisted Seamus.

"I can't tell you." The Bishop was adamant.

"Can't or won't?" Seamus shot back at him.

"I can't it's confidential." The Bishop dropped his gaze, not wanting to look at Seamus.

"Don't try to pull the sanctity nonsense on me again, it's not going to wash with me," Seamus told him.

"But it's true, it is confidential, it was something the Father wanted me to have, in the event of his death, I had to respect his wishes."

"What was it?" demanded Seamus.

"I can't tell you that," said the Bishop. He was obviously refusing to budge.

"Jesus Christ!" Seamus was infuriated. "We are going round in circles here, you have information which could be very relevant to this inquiry and you need to tell us what it is."

The Bishop shrugged, he obviously wasn't going to volunteer anything more.

Seamus went up to him and stood very close looking him in the face. "Now you listen to me, Bishop. You are potentially impeding this investigation, and this isn't the last you are going to hear of it. I advise you to think very carefully about your attitude because the next time we come back here, it will be a search warrant."

"Don't you threaten me," the Bishop retorted nettled.

"It's not a threat, Bishop, believe me." Seamus held his gaze determined to make the Bishop understand the seriousness of the situation.

Seamus returned to the centre of the room and spoke again, "I'll give you a bit of time to come to your senses Bishop, you may be in the church, but you are not above the law, that you're not."

He turned to O'Rorden who was stuffing the last piece of cake into his mouth.

"Come on O'Rorden." He jerked his head.

O'Rorden got up quickly and the two of them headed for the door. The Bishop stood there watching them making no move.

"We'll see ourselves out, Bishop, thanks for your hospitality, good day to you." Seamus nodded at him affably and the two of them left the room.

"Did you enjoy the show there, O'Rorden?"

"Oh yes, sir."

"You certainly enjoyed the refreshments at any rate," Seamus teased him.

"They were very good, nice cake," O'Rorden replied. "You didn't drink your coffee there, sir"

"No," said Seamus with feeling. "It would have most likely stuck in my throat."

They got back into car and Seamus said, "Let's find ourselves a decent coffee house while we're here, I could use a cappuccino, so I could. Wash down the taste of the fucking Bishop and his fucking lying arse."

"Sounds good to me," O'Rorden said brightly. "We could have some cake."

"Have you not had enough now, O'Rorden?" joked Seamus.

"Ach, you can never have enough cake, sir, that you can't," O'Rorden said seriously.

"Talking of arses, did you notice how the Bishop was walking funny sir?" O'Rorden enquired as they headed down the drive.

"Yes, very odd that, very odd indeed," Seamus said thoughtfully.

"Maybe he's got a dose of the piles, do you think?" O'Rorden ventured.

"Yes, yes, it was probably the piles, you may be right now I come to think about it." Seamus reflected.

"Poor chap," O'Rorden said with feeling, "It must be very painful."

"I fucking hope so," said Seamus bitterly. They pulled out of the gates and headed into town.

VESPERS TWO

The one who sins is the one who will die.
The child will not share the guilt of the
parent, nor will the parent share the guilt of
the child.
Ezekiel 18:20

F
ather Cooney had tended his flock in the parish of Ballygilly for more years than he could count. He was a stout man, overweight and rotund, finding it hard to get around, but still managing to run his church and attend to the services. He had some help from Mother Joan Margaret whom he had known for years. At one time she had worked at and finally run the local orphanage, becoming known as the Mother, a title which stuck. Eventually, she became Cooney's helper and his companion, his friend. Father Cooney also had a maid, a youngish girl, Deidre Flanagan, he liked her, and she was very obliging in the matters of helping keep the house.

With everything apparently at peace in Father Cooney's world, he entered his church, it was time for confession. Hardly anyone ever came to confession these days, but he carried out his duty nevertheless, which most of the time consisted of him falling asleep alone in the confessional.

The church was empty which came as no surprise to him at all. In fact, he didn't mind, some of his clerical duties he found quite onerous of late. He ambled up to the confessional and taking one last look around at the empty pews entered it and sat himself down. He put on the necessary vestments and waited.

After quite some time his eyes began to close, just like they always did. Sleep was just about the claim him when he heard the door of the church open and shut gently. Light footsteps sounded, walking up the aisle, getting louder. He wondered if it was Mother Joan Margaret coming to see if he was alright, as she sometimes did. The footsteps stopped just outside his confessional box and he waited. If it was the Mother, she would say something by now, but there was silence.

The curtain on the other side of the confessional was pulled aside and someone entered it and sat down. Through the dim light and the grill, he could see a person, but their face was obscured because they were wearing a hood. He couldn't tell if it was a man or a woman. The person observed him for a few moments before speaking.

"Bless me, Father, for I have sinned." The voice was definitely female, and she continued, "will you hear my confession?"

"You are in the presence of God now my child, what is it you want to confess?" Father Cooney replied.

"I've done something very bad," the woman said softly.

"And what is it you have done?" said Father Cooney gently.

"I've committed a murder, Father," she told him.

"Murder is it?" He knew there were often people who made exaggerated and outrageous sins just perhaps for attention, but he played along thinking nothing of it. "Whom did you murder, my child?"

"Father O'Flaherty."

He was quiet for a moment, wondering if she was lying or if it was actually true. The idea made him nervous. He knew by now Father O'Flaherty had been shot and he didn't want to join him. "Are you sure?" he asked her. "Are you sure you murdered him?"

"Yes, yes I am." She sounded quite certain.

He played for time, thinking what to do, what if she had done it? "But what, what makes you so certain?" he asked again.

"This is what makes me so certain, Father."

Without warning he was staring at the barrel of a large black revolver, it was pointing directly at him.

"Now, now don't be hasty, I didn't say I didn't believe you, you know it's quite a thing to confess, I needed to know if you were serious." He realised he was babbling, fear began to take hold.

"Oh, I'm serious alright, Father, deadly serious, and you know what?" she said almost conversationally.

"What?" he said knowing he wasn't going to like the answer. He didn't.

"You're next, Father, I came here to kill you."

"But why? Why, what have I done to you? I haven't done anything I don't even know you," he protested.

"Don't you? Don't you really know me?" She sounded incredulous, annoyed. She pulled back her hood. "What about now?"

217

He stared at her face, trying to take it in, in the dim light, there was indeed something familiar about it he couldn't place. Something was stirring in the back of his mind.

"I, err, I don't really, I can't really see," he said, his voice sounded afraid. "How about we just stay here a while, think on it, you can tell me your whole confession, why don't we do that?"

She was exasperated, suddenly angry. Last night thinking of the murder had been a bad night, she couldn't sleep, images of what she did and what had happened were haunting her. This wasn't how things were meant to go but she felt she wanted him to really know. Who she was. What he had done. Know why he was going to die.

"Get out, get out of the confessional you fucking arsehole and don't make any sudden moves, don't try anything. Or you're dead." She motioned to him to get up with the barrel of the pistol and he cautiously did. Sweat began to run down his face as he eased out of the stall. She kept pace with him, also leaving the confessional on her side, keeping the pistol trained on him the whole while. He wondered if he could run but knew he wasn't capable of it and even if he were, she would probably gun him down before he was even just a few steps away. His only hope was to perhaps keep her talking, perhaps someone would come in, distract her, make her leave before killing him.

She was standing there now, in front of him. Now he looked at her, he did think perhaps he recognised her, but he still wasn't sure.

"Still don't know?" she demanded.

He shook his head.

"How about this?" Keeping the gun levelled at his body, with her other hand she fumbled in her pocket, then she held up a small black and white picture. He peered at the photograph and back at her. It was of a young girl, about fifteen or so, smiling, full of life, pretty, beautiful, one of the prettiest girls he had ever seen. The image of the face came flooding back suddenly to his mind, that beautiful smiling girl, how could he forget, except he couldn't remember her name. She saw the recognition finally, in his face.

"You do know, don't you? You remember now, don't you?" She carefully put the photograph back in her pocket with one gloved hand.

He nodded, "Yes, yes I remember you, but you had black hair, then, didn't you?"

"I prefer blonde now," she said. "It helps me to forget, the things, the things that you did."

"What, what did I do that's got you so upset?" he asked. "And why, why did you come back? Why would you want to come back like this?"

"Don't talk fucking shite," she flashed back at him. "You can't forget those things, Father, no you can't, I certainly can't."

Images crowded into her mind. Father Cooney, his stupid fat face, on top of her, raping her, over and over again. Father Cooney taking off his belt. The pain of the leather against her bare skin. Father Cooney, cursing her, calling her a whore, the devil, a witch who had bewitched him. The devil who tempted him and afterwards must be punished.

"You fucking bastard," she said through gritted teeth. "Don't tell me you don't remember, all the times you raped me, fucked me against my will, even though I pleaded with you, begged you stop. All the times you beat me with your big fat leather belt. You dare to tell me you don't fucking remember!"

Father Cooney did remember. She could see it in his eyes. See it in his face. Tears began to roll down his face. Remorse? She couldn't tell.

"Oh yes, you remember don't you, Father, you remember it now well enough, so you do."

"I'm sorry," he whispered. "So sorry for what I've done. How can I make it up to you?"

"Make it up to me? Make it up to me is that it? Fuck you, Father, we're time and past the making up stage, today is the day you fucking die."

"Please, please, don't kill me, I know I've done some terrible things, but I don't deserve to die, I'm a good man, those terrible days are far behind me, I'm a..."

She had had enough.

"Get on your knees," she said.

He looked at her struck dumb, there didn't seem like any way out.

"Get on your fucking knees!" Her voice was almost a shout, echoing around the church.

Father Cooney obeyed, at last, sobbing openly, sinking to his knees, praying God would save him, and realising God probably wasn't going to.

"That's right, Father, say your fucking prayers, pray to God, he's not going to help you now, no he's not!" all the time she was saying this, she had moved behind him and now she placed the muzzle of the pistol against the back of his head.

"Please," Father Cooney begged her one last time.

"Oh, Father." She was once again in control, clinical and composed. "You asked me why I came back. Well, this is why I came back. I've been planning this for a long time, yes, Father, so I have. First Father O'Flaherty and now you. He deserved to die and so do you."

220

"Please, please, don't kill me." It was a pointless plea and he knew it.

"This isn't a killing, Father, this an execution."

She didn't know how long she waited before pulling the trigger, maybe thirty seconds, maybe a minute. Listening to Father Cooney quietly saying his prayers almost in a whisper. The moment when he realised it really was game over, he was almost calm, waiting for the bullet that would end his life.

"Goodbye, Father Cooney."

She pulled the trigger and the gun thundered out its deadly message with a loud report which echoed through the vaulted arches of the church. The smoke cleared, and Father Cooney lay dead on the floor, blood streaming from his damaged head. Somehow though, it didn't seem to be enough. He had done so much, hurt her so badly. She hated him, hated him with a passion. It was too easy, she thought too fucking easy.

Without thinking clearly, she pointed the gun at his body. She fired once, twice, three, four, five times until the gun was empty. Each shot slammed into the Father's lifeless body jerking it up and letting it fall again. She was breathing, heavily and tears now streaked her face. She was struggling internally, to regain some sense of self-possession, but she had gone too far, this was too much. This wasn't how she had planned things. It wasn't how she did things. She was cold, calculating, clinical, composed, not like this...

"Shit!" she said out loud.

Just then, she heard the door of the church open and close, there were quick steps coming up the aisle towards her. She spun around with the gun still in her hand. A sister, quite old, in a nun's habit and cowl, was standing there her face frozen in shock as she took in the scene. The sister's hand went up to her mouth and she looked as if she was going to scream or run.

"Don't you fucking move."

The sister nodded eyes wide and staring, staring at the deadly barrel now levelled at her chest.

"What, what are you doing? What have you done to Father Cooney?" the nun asked although the answer was plainly obvious.

"He's dead," was the response and then a pause. "Wait a minute, wait a minute I know you, it's Sister Joan Margaret isn't it."

The nun nodded. "Mother Margaret," she corrected the title automatically without thinking.

"Mother Joan fucking Margaret is it, well whatever did you do to deserve that you fucking bitch?" came the retort.

"Do, do I know you?" asked Mother Margaret.

"Oh, yes, oh yes you know me, you bitch. I came to you, a small wee child. To the fucking torture house, you called an orphanage. I came to you hoping for comfort, love, help. Well, no chance of that was there? Mother, you call yourself, you're no fucking mother, you are a bitch from hell and that's a fact."

"What, what did I ever do to you?" asked Mother Margaret, her voice rising to a thin screech, the fear plainly showing in her face.

"What did you do? Is that what you're asking? What the fuck didn't you do more like? Don't you remember, the time you wouldn't let me go to the toilet and I wet myself in front of all the children? Well, I do. Don't you remember the first time you used the belt and every other time, the cane and every other instrument of pain you could inflict on me? Well, I do. Don't you remember how you groomed me for

Father Cooney, so he could have his way with me, don't you remember, Mother Margaret? Because I fucking well do!"

"I... I..." Mother Margaret seemed bereft of speech.

The intruder moved closer and reached out with one gloved hand grabbing the nun by the throat. She thrust her face into Mother Margaret's who looked at her and suddenly a look of recognition spread over her face.

"You!" the nun said fearfully, her voice was strangled by the throat hold. "You! You're the devil, the devil child, I tried to beat it out of you, I tried but I couldn't."

"Oh yes." She let Mother Margaret go. "Oh yes you do remember don't you, the devil was I? Well, I'll show you how much of a fucking devil I am now and fuck you, fuck you, you bitch."

The gun came up again pointing at Mother Margaret. It was enough. So much she wanted to say to her but there wasn't time. The bitch had to die. She pulled the trigger, once, twice, but the gun just clicked. She had forgotten. She had used up all the bullets.

"Fuck, fuck it." She moved forward again and took hold of Mother Margaret's throat once again. "I want you to look at my face because that's the last thing you're going to see before I fucking extinguish your fucking miserable life."

"No, please..." pleaded Mother Margaret.

But the gun came down, hard across the nun's temple, she fell silent at the blow. The gun fell again and again. Blood began to stream from the open wound made by the metal barrel. Mother Margaret went limp. She dropped the dead sister to the ground and looked around in panic. This had gone too far, far too far, it was supposed to be simple and it had turned to shit. She frantically looked to see if there was anything which might give away her DNA, but she had been very careful about it, it was probably OK. Gloves, everything tucked in and tucked away. She would get rid of these clothes too, just in case.

With one final look at the two murdered bodies, she fled the church, hurrying from the door glancing this way and that. There was nobody about, she hurried quickly down the path and through the gate. Last time had not been good, last time she had been seen by a person walking their dog. There seemed to be nobody about, she put back the hood and carried on to her car, she would be glad to get away from here, relieved. The engine sprang to life and she breathed a sigh of relief as her car gathered speed. Looking in the mirror as she drove, she noticed blood streaks across her face. It wasn't good. She pulled over and cleaned up. Threw the paper towels into the verge.

✳ ✳ ✳

When Seamus got back to the Baker's Arms, he went to Kerry's parlour but she wasn't there and nor was Liam. This seemed very odd. He went to find someone at the bar.

"Oh, Inspector." It was Colleen Clarke, one of the staff. "Kerry said you might be back for dinner. She told me to tell you she is sorry, she is running late, apparently, her car broke down on the way home."

"Where did she go? Is she OK? Does she need help?" Seamus was immediately concerned.

"I don't know, Inspector, and yes she's fine and no the breakdown company is sorting it out, I am sure she won't be long." Colleen laughed. "If you tell me what you want for dinner, I'll serve it up to you in Kerry's parlour."

"Fine, thank you, I would," said Seamus. He ordered the pie and made his way to the kitchen. He sat in what was now his usual spot and felt a little lost. He was becoming used to Kerry being there, when he ate, chatting, flirting with her clear blue eyes, smiling with those incredibly kissable lips. It seemed unusual she would go out without an explanation but if she had meant to be back before he returned then he understood she might not mention it. After all, it wasn't as if they were married. In fact, he didn't really know what they were at the moment but whatever it was, it felt really nice.

Collen bustled in with his pie, mash and a glass of ginger ale. Seamus tucked into it hoping Kerry would be back soon. He had just swallowed the last mouthful when his phone rang.

"Gallway," said Seamus when he answered, it was O'Rorden

"Sir, we've just been relayed a 999 call, units are already on their way, but I thought you'd like to know," O'Rorden said.

"What is it, O'Rorden, what's happened?" Seamus asked him.

"There's been a murder, sir, another priest at Ballygilly. I think he's been shot."

"You're fucking joking!"

"No sir, unfortunately, I'm not," O'Rorden said seriously.

"Right, pick me up from the Baker's Arms and let's get ourselves over there." Seamus was decisive.

"OK sir, I'll be there in about five then."

"See you shortly." Seamus clicked off the phone and put on his outdoor jacket.

"Tell Kerry I've had to go out," he told Colleen rushing out on his way past the bar.

"What already?" she laughed "that was quick."

"Something's come up," he answered over his shoulder.

O'Rorden arrived just as he headed through the front door of the pub. He jumped in the passenger seat and his DS started to drive.

Seamus looked at him for a moment and then said, "Well, come on, O'Rorden, let's not hang around, put on the blue fucking light and hit the fucking gas."

"Oh, oh right sir, right you are." O'Rorden pulled out a magnetic blue light and stuck it on the roof. The next moment O'Rorden was driving like a man possessed, and Seamus was regretting having invited him to do so.

*   *   *

When they arrived at the murder scene Seamus breathed a sigh of relief. It had certainly been a hairy ride. They had flashed round the narrow roads in double quick time with tires screaming all the way through the bends. Seamus had his heart in his mouth at the manner O'Rorden had taken some of the corners. At least, Seamus reflected gladly, they had arrived in one piece.

"Did you actually attend advanced Garda driver training?" Seamus enquired getting out of the car.

"Oh yes, yes sir I did that, I just hardly ever get a chance to use it," O'Rorden said and then asked anxiously, "was it OK sir?"

"Well let's put it this way, I've had my entertainment for the week, and more," Seamus said flippantly. "Come on then, let's go and see what's what."

The Garda were already there having secured the perimeter and were waiting for the detectives to arrive. An officer on the scene confirmed the pathologist had been called, as well as the Garda Technical Team for forensic examination. At the door of the church, they pulled on latex gloves and blue plastic overshoes. The door creaked open and the two of them surveyed the carnage.

A nun was lying splayed out on the floor, a pool of blood surrounding her head. Further up the aisle lay Father Cooney. He had obviously taken a severely damaging headshot, followed by several shots to the body. By the looks of it, he had almost completely bled out and the floor was covered in another spreading pool of the scarlet liquid.

"Who are these people? Do you know?" Seamus asked O'Rorden.

"Well he, I think, sir, is Father Cooney, this is his parish and she, if I am not mistaken, is the Mother Joan Margaret," explained O'Rorden.

"Who is she and why is she here do you think?" Seamus enquired.

"Well, I believe she was living with the Father, as his helper, companion so she was, he was getting on a bit you see, sir, I believe."

"Yes, yes I see." Seamus pondered the scene for a while and then said, "Seems like things got a little out of hand compared to Father O'Flaherty's murder, but it has a similar pattern."

"Well, they were both shot," O'Rorden observed.

"True, both the priests, but I don't think she was." Seamus indicated the Mother. "I'd say she was hit possibly with the barrel of the pistol, quite a few times judging by the amount of blood."

They took a look around but could see nothing which was particularly obvious or out of place. Seamus decided they should wait for the technical team and the pathologist who would no doubt reveal more information.

"Right," said Seamus thinking aloud. "We need to see if there were any eyewitnesses, and also we are going to need to find out if Father Cooney had a housekeeper and interview them. We also need to try and trace his movements and the nun's in the last 24 hours."

"Anything else, sir?" O'Rorden was writing it all down.

"That'll do for starters," Seamus said.

He left O'Rorden making some phone calls and talking to the officers on site. He decided to take a stroll around the churchyard. Breathing in the frosty air he looked at all the graves and wondered if Father Cooney and his Mother Margaret would also be buried here. A movement caught his eye, it was a flash of what looked like a face which suddenly appeared and disappeared behind a gravestone. He walked slowly and carefully closer to where he thought it had come from, keeping his eyes fixed on the spot. Rounding the stone, he suddenly came upon two figures with scared faces, a boy and a girl. At the sight of him, they took off towards the church gate.

"Hey," called Seamus after them, "stop, come here, it's alright."

He gave chase and arrived at the front of the church to find O'Rorden holding onto the two fugitives one in each hand. They were struggling to escape but it seemed they were held in a vice-like grip.

"Easy now, easy now," O'Rorden was saying to them.

"Well done, O'Rorden," Seamus told him coming up to them, he addressed the two young people. "It's alright, calm down, it's alright, we just want to ask you a few questions, you're not in any trouble now, just calm down."

They stopped struggling and stood looking at him with scared faces. They looked around perhaps eighteen years of age. A boy and a girl. Seamus could guess what they had probably been doing in the churchyard.

"Have you been here long?" he asked them.

They didn't speak or move.

"Come on, look, I'm not interested what you were doing here, I just need to know how long you've been here."

"We were here since before the priest went into the Church." The girl finally felt brave enough to break her silence.

"I guess you heard quite a bit then?" asked Seamus.

"Yes, yes we did, we heard what sounded like someone shooting, it was very loud it was." It was the girl again.

"Is that right?" asked Seamus. "Now, you didn't happen to see anything else, did you?"

"We saw the old nun go into the church and then, this woman came out and went out the gate." The boy had now regained his courage and was eager to also be included.

"OK that's really good, really helpful," said Seamus with appreciation. "So how about," he squatted down, "how about we take you somewhere to get something to eat, and drink. I bet you are hungry, and you tell us everything you heard and saw, how's that sound?"

The two of them nodded and told him there was a fast food place not far away.

"Listen, if my DS lets you go, do you promise not to run?" Seamus asked them.

"No, no we won't, we promise." Their initial fear had given way to excitement, the excitement of being involved in something potentially way beyond the normal humdrum existence of their world. They weren't going anywhere.

"OK." He nodded at O'Rorden who released them from his grip. They shook their wrists off gratefully rubbing them to restore the circulation.

"Come on then, show us where this fast food place is," Seamus said to them. He and O'Rorden lead the way to the car and headed for what was apparently Paddy's Diner.

* * *

Paddy's Diner turned out to be a 24-hour American style eatery which adjoined a fuel station about a couple of kilometres on the main road out of Ballygilly. Seamus and O'Rorden were sat in a booth opposite their two eyewitnesses. Maire Brown was a young eighteen-year-old girl, with mousy black hair and pretty eyes and mouth. She had the fresh-faced look of youth and clear white skin. Eion Nolan was also eighteen, tanned skin, thick black hair and the wisp of a budding moustache, he appeared to have had a fairly bad outbreak of acne.

The two of them had been in the graveyard at the back of the church carrying on a secret liaison which was apparently a frequent haunt of theirs. Seamus didn't enquire too closely as to what the liaison involved. They were both tucking into a Paddyburger special with a drink and fries. Seamus was nursing a coffee and O'Rorden a doughnut and a cup of tea. Paddy's establishment was apparently somewhat short on supplies of cake. The two young people had, by all accounts, been getting down to business when they heard a gunshot.

"What happened then?" asked Seamus.

"There was somebody shouting and then a shot like a gun, I know what it sounds like because my Da takes me shooting so he does, for ducks and stuff." It was Eoin.

"And then we heard five more shots I think it was. And then for a while, it went quiet." Maire took up the story.

"What did you do?" Seamus said.

"Well, we crept quietly around to the front of the church to try and get a view." It was Maire.

"Then we saw the nun go into the church. And then we heard somebody shouting again really loudly and then there was silence." It was Eoin.

"Didn't you think of calling the Garda?" O'Rorden put in.

The two of them shook their heads vigorously.

"Why not?" he enquired.

"We were scared," Maire told him honestly. "We didn't know what was going to happen and didn't want to get shot."

"Probably a wise move," Seamus told her. "What happened then?"

"The church door opened, and a woman came out. She was carrying a gun and and..." Eion said eagerly.

"She had blood on her face." Maire didn't want to be left out of the story. The front of the church was illuminated by the yellow light of a streetlamp which gave them a pretty clear view of the suspect it seems.

"What did she look like?" Seamus wanted to know.

There was silence while the young people thought for a while and then Eoin spoke.

"She was a bit taller than me I suppose, kind of slim but she had quite a nice figure"

"Trust you to notice that!" Maire nudged him.

"No, it's OK, this is important, any details you can tell give us are going to help us," Seamus reassured them.

"She had a black sort of hoodie thing on, but the hood was off. Black trousers and trainers," Maire said.

"Can you describe her face?" Seamus continued to probe.

"She was kind of pretty I suppose," Maire said after some consideration.

"Very pretty I thought," Eoin added earning himself another very sharp dig in the ribs. Maire evidently wasn't keen on her boyfriend admiring other females.

"Colour of her eyes?"

"I don't know, it was too dark," Maire replied to this.

"Me neither," said Eoin.

"Colour of her hair?" continued Seamus.

"Dark brown," said Maire.

"Blonde," said Eoin.

"No, it was dark brown!" she insisted.

"No, it was blonde I saw it clearly!" Eoin contradicted her.

"Brown!"

"Blonde!"

"Brown!!"

"It was blonde, Maire, I saw it!!!"

"No, it was NOT!!"

Voices were starting to be raised and some other evening diners were looking in their direction.

"Woah, woah, easy now, easy, let's not have civil war breaking out here," Seamus interjected. "Now was it brown or was it blonde?"

"I think it was brown but it's hard to tell," Maire told him calming down.

"Why is that?"

"It was the light, it's the orange light, it's hard to see proper colours in that light," Eoin explained.

"I see." Seamus thought for a moment. "Well, so what you are saying is it could be either, and you're not sure."

"Yes! That's it," the two youngsters spoke together happy a compromise had been found.

"What did the person do next?" Seamus asked them.

"She looked around for a bit and then went out the gate and down the road. We heard her get into a car and drive off." Maire replied.

"Did you get a look at the car?"

The two of them shook their heads. After a while, when they were sure she wasn't coming back, Maire had persuaded Eoin to look inside the church. He peeped in saw the dead nun and priest and then he came running back. They went to the nearest call box and phoned 999. They didn't use a mobile, so they couldn't be traced. Then they had hidden in the graveyard until the Garda arrived.

Seamus thanked them and praised them for their quick thinking. He explained they would need to give a formal statement of what they had seen, and he understood their reluctance to identify themselves before he had seen them in the graveyard.

"Well come on then, eat up, don't let it get cold," O'Rorden encouraged them.

They looked at him gratefully and tucked into their food, polishing it off in short order. O'Rorden took their addresses and details. O'Rorden and Seamus dropped them off home, they had to explain to each of set of parents how important their child's eye witness accounts were to the investigation but left each youngster to explain their graveyard activities. Those conversations would probably not too amicable thought Seamus.

He and O'Rorden returned to the site of the new murders.

The pathologist had completed his preliminary examinations and the team from the Garda Technical Bureau had by now set up and were conducting their usual thorough examination. The pathologist confirmed the Father had been shot through the back of the head, and by the position was probably kneeling when he was killed. He was then shot five further times in the body, but the pathologist said he would have already been dead.

The nun had been pistol-whipped and that would have quickly rendered her unconscious, she then bled to death. There were bruise marks on her throat indicating she had been choked but the pathologist didn't think this was how she died. He confirmed the time of death as around seven pm. Seamus thanked him and said the bodies would be shipped over for a post mortem as soon as forensics had completed their work.

"Are you trying to keep us busy or something?" Jim O'Grady asked Seamus as they stood looking at the crime scene.

"Don't look at me," complained Seamus.

"Ach trouble follows you around like a ghost, Seamus, so it does," Jim joked. He was always ribbing Seamus, they went back a long way working on many past crimes together. Jim had given Seamus many tips about forensics when he was just new to detective work.

"Have you found anything interesting, Jim?" Seamus changed the subject.

"Well, there's not a lot there, to be honest. The murderer was very careful not to leave us much at all. I think they certainly wore gloves for a start," said Jim.

"We know they had blood on their face and probably their clothes, we had two eyewitnesses in the graveyard," Seamus said.

"Did you now?" Jim raised an eyebrow. "Well, in that case, they may have discarded something, and we'll widen our search to the roads going out of the town."

"Good plan," Seamus agreed.

"I won't ask what they were doing in the graveyard."

"Don't." Seamus rolled his eyes.

"There is one thing," Jim carried on, "You know we found a long black hair in Father O'Flaherty's confessional and thought nothing of it."

"Yes?"

"We found a couple more in this one, we'll see if they match and if so then it's a bit too much of a coincidence."

"Yes indeed, that is interesting. Did you find any blonde hairs in there also by any chance?"

"No, no we didn't."

"Was it the same gun do you think, as Father O'Flaherty?"

"We'll check the ballistics and get back to you as soon as we can," Jim said. "That is assuming you don't conjure up any more crimes in the meantime." He was smiling.

"Thanks, Jim, your confidence in me is so reassuring," and with that parting shot, Seamus walked away.

"Anytime, Seamus, anytime." Jim laughed watching him go. In spite of their manner, the two had a great deal of respect for each other.

Seamus and O'Rorden discussed the next moves. The forensics were going to take some time and they couldn't interview anyone else until the next day. They had discovered Father Cooney had a housekeeper and put a Garda officer in to look after her and stay with her to make sure she didn't go anywhere.

They decided to go back to the station. Seamus would brief the team in the morning, they would now have to widen their enquiries and split their tasks between the two murders. There were a handful of officers local to Ballygilly and they would draft some of these in. Seamus would give an urgent press statement in the morning. Hopefully, they could confirm the murders were linked, but it seemed very likely they were.

Seamus was quiet on the way back the Ballysruth station. The suspect might have had blonde hair and Kerry hadn't been around in the afternoon. It worried him exceedingly.

Seamus phoned Brogan at midnight to apprise him of the news. He decided he had better tell him as soon as possible. If he didn't tell him until the morning, Brogan would complain. If he rang him this late, it was very likely Brogan would also moan about it. It was a no-win situation.

Seamus dialled, and Brogan picked up after only two rings, it was a good sign, he hopefully hadn't been asleep.

"Brogan?" came the familiar gruff voice at the other end of the line.

"It's DI Gallway, sir," Seamus began.

"I know it's you, Seamus, what the fuck do you want ringing me at this time of day?"

Seamus rolled his eyes.

"Sir, I am sorry for the late phone call, it's just I've got some not very good news."

"What the fuck is not very good news?" said Brogan testily. "It's either bad news or good news and whichever it is stop beating about the bush and spit it out."

Seamus grimaced, Brogan was more than unusually grumpy this evening.

He took a deep breath. "Sir, there's been another murder, in fact, two murders."

"Fuck me, you're fucking joking!" exclaimed Brogan. "When did this happen?"

"At seven pm this evening, sir, someone, we believe a woman, shot dead Father Cooney of Ballygilly parish in his church and beat his helper Mother Joan Margaret to death with a pistol."

"What the fuck is going on down there in your part of the world?" Brogan was off, "Fucking priests getting gunned down left right and centre as if there's not enough to do with this first murder we've now got another one. Christ all mighty, Seamus, I don't know what the world is coming to, so I don't."

Brogan was prone to hyperbole when he wasn't in a good mood and Seamus was used to it. He had obviously been having a particularly bad day and Seamus was catching the tail end of it.

"Well," said Brogan sounding calmer after his rant. "Give me the details, you might as well now you got me on the line."

Seamus neglected to point out it was exactly why he had phoned him, and instead filled him in on the plans for extending the investigation, the press conference, the eyewitnesses and said he would be following up some leads from this as soon as they had formal statements from them, and also interview the housekeeper.

"Hmmm," said Brogan after hearing this. "It seems you've got things underway alright. But with these extra murders, you are probably a bit light on resources. I'll get you two or three more detectives and some other officers. I can even get you a more experienced number two, you'll probably need one now."

"Thank you, sir, the resources will be useful. But I'm happy with O'Rorden and I don't need a replacement,"

Seamus told him. There was no way he was replacing O'Rorden and that was that.

"Well, fine, I see you're making a bit of a protegee out of him, there's nothing wrong with that, no there isn't. OK, have it your way, but I'll see you get the extra detectives and officers to support your investigations. They'll be on the way tomorrow."

"Thank you, sir, I'll look forward to it," Seamus said gratefully.

"It's OK, keep me posted, no doubt I'll be having a call from the bloody Archbishop tomorrow," Brogan complained. "And, Seamus, you should have told me you were short on resources, really, Seamus, you know if you need some help you only have to ask."

"Yes, sir," said Seamus hardly able to believe his ears. Brogan had disconnected, and so Seamus, unable to contradict him, was left reflecting on the very short memory his boss, at times, seemed to possess.

DAY 6

Seamus was up early and suffering from lack of sleep. Not only had it been a long night due to the recent murders, but he had also kept on turning things over and over in his mind. He kept coming back to Kerry, and the possibility she could end up being a suspect. He had never really thought she could be the murderer, but now there was some circumstantial evidence which pointed in her direction. It was important he found out the truth about her as soon as he could. Important for the case but important also for him, so important that if it turned out she was the murderer, he didn't know exactly how he was going cope with it.

Seamus had a shower, made himself presentable, got dressed and felt much better. No matter what, he was a professional and he had to be professional, regardless of his personal feelings. He made his way down to Kerry's parlour, wondering how he would feel when he saw her, how he would react. He need not have worried.

When he entered her dining room, Kerry jumped up from her chair. She had obviously been waiting for him. She flung herself at him and her arms snaked around him and without a second thought he kissed her. Long, hard and passionately. Almost as if he needed savour this as if it might be their last moments together. He was suddenly relaxed, at ease, he pushed the doubts aside, she couldn't be the murder, surely not.

"Hmmm, I missed you too," Kerry breathed putting her head on his chest. He brought his arm up protectively and held her close.

"Goodness," she laughed. "I should stay away more often."

"What happened last night?" he asked her, hoping for a good explanation.

"I went out for a bit, and then on the way back I broke down bloody car, I called Road Rescue, they came out, I came home, but you weren't here, Colleen said you'd had to go out." She pouted still leaning on his chest. She sounded evasive as if she didn't want to tell him everything she had done yesterday. He remembered a certain evasiveness about her before about Father O'Flaherty and it was also just after his murder.

"I had to I'm afraid, we intercepted a 999 call."

She looked up at him concerned. "Not bad I hope?" she asked.

"Father Cooney was murdered last night," he said watching her carefully.

"What!" She looked genuinely shocked, "Father Cooney? Dead?"

"Yes," he continued. "And Mother Joan Margaret was also, murdered."

"What?!" She pulled away and sat down. "How? How did it happen?"

"He was shot, and she was beaten to death," Seamus said.

"Shit, another murder, shit, shit!!" Kerry looked upset. Surely if she had just killed them, she couldn't be so upset. Unless she was a consummate actress. Seamus didn't think she was, but on the other hand, he couldn't discard it as a possibility.

"Two actually," Seamus said. "The murderer obviously doesn't do things by halves." He was trying to lighten the mood.

She seemed to be thinking for a moment, almost unseeing and then she rapidly shook herself out of it.

"Well, then you'll be needing your breakfast, you've got a lot of work to do." Kerry became abruptly business-like. She bustled around like a woman possessed, serving up his breakfast in double quick time and setting it down on the table. Seamus took his usual place and observed her with amusement.

"What's this? Are we trying to outdo McDonald's now?" Seamus said teasingly.

"McDonald's indeed!" she flashed her eyes at him, but she was smiling. "You've got a busy day and you'd better eat up and get going."

"Are you trying to get rid of me now, is that it?" he continued to tease her.

She sat down with a cup of tea opposite Seamus and looked at him her eyes suddenly soft.

"No, No, Seamus, I'm not, I would gladly spend the day in your company, but I know you've got more important things to deal with." She had suddenly become serious.

He smiled back at her in appreciation of the words, and then he fairly wolfed down his breakfast.

"And you were the one talking about serving it too quick!" she laughed.

"I didn't realise how hungry I was," he said with satisfaction drinking his coffee.

Draining the last drop, he rose from his chair.

"I best be going, sorry," he told her.

She stood, and he pulled her to him.

"I wish I could spend the day with you too," Seamus said before they kissed, a long kiss. He tried to hold onto the moment, wondering if this would be the last kiss they would have, wondering what he was going to find out today which might mean she came under the spotlight. Wondering how he would feel if it turned out to be the case.

* * *

Seamus arrived at the station and found everyone already gathered there and waiting. The news would have spread fast and there was a buzz of anticipation. The whole investigation had just ratcheted up a few notches. He nodded to O'Rorden and wasted no time in beginning.

"So here we are, day six of the investigation into the murder of Father O'Flaherty and if you don't know already, we now have another two murders on our books. Last night Father Cooney of Ballygilly parish was shot to death and his assistant, Mother Joan Margaret was battered to death with a pistol. I will go into the details of this more shortly and the actions we've now got to take but first a bit of news, which you might think is good or you might not. My boss and yours, DCS Brogan, has decided, in his infinite wisdom, that we are short on resources now we've got three murders instead of one and is sending us down some detectives and officers to beef up the team."

As he expected this announcement was not met with any enthusiasm by those present. They had come to regard the investigation as their own and since it was probably the most challenging police work they'd had for years, they were not happy to give it up. O'Rorden, in particular, was looking very downcast when he heard this and was probably expecting to be replaced. Seamus noted the glum faces and continued.

"OK, now just to be clear. First of all, O'Rorden will be remaining as my number two on this investigation no matter what happens." He noticed O'Rorden brightened up considerably on hearing this reassuring statement.

"Second of all, and I will be making this abundantly clear to anybody new coming on board. Nobody is getting replaced, nobody is getting side-lined, this is going to be a team effort and the new people, no matter who they are, are going to fit into our team, this team. I must admit I had my doubts when I first walked in here but all of you have pulled finger and done a creditable job so far, you've lived up to my expectations and beyond in some cases. We started this together and we're going to finish it together."

There was an unexpected burst of applause at this and Seamus smiled in spite of himself.

"Alright, alright, alright, let's calm down, shall we. Back to the business of the day, now we've got that out of the way. I'll go over the details of the murders. It appears the murders were carried out at 7:00 pm last night during confession. Although we don't know exactly what happened, it appears the murderer had entered the church, most likely after Father Cooney. It seems there was some kind of altercation or certainly shouting and then Father Cooney was shot once in the back of the head and then five more times in the body. We presume these extra shots were not intended to kill him since he would have already been dead after the first one."

Kathy O'Flynn put up her hand. Seamus nodded at her to speak. "How do we know about the argument sir? I take it there were maybe some witnesses."

"Yes, I was coming to that in a moment," said Seamus. "After the first murder, there was more shouting. We presume this was when the second victim Mother Joan Margaret was killed. She was beaten to death by repeated blows to the head. We also presume with the barrel of the gun."

"Why do you think they did that sir? Why not shoot her as well?" It was Paddy Doyle.

"Well for a start they had used up all the bullets in the gun at a guess. If it was a service revolver and perhaps they didn't have time to reload, maybe they were taken by surprise."

"Oh, yes I see, that's a good point," Doyle replied.

"OK, so as you might have gathered, we have some witnesses by some lucky chance"

"Well it was in church after all, sir," quipped O'Rorden

There were a few chuckles at this.

"Yes, O'Rorden, perhaps God was indeed watching last night. But in any case, a young couple were in the graveyard."

There was a little more laughter.

"Yes, alright, alright, we did not enquire what they were doing there, but I think all of us can guess. However, they managed to hear the murders being carried out and more importantly they saw the murderer. We have quite a good description. We are almost certain it is a woman, she has either brown or blonde hair. She was wearing black including a black hoodie and she was carrying a gun. Her face was bloody, no doubt from her attack on Mother Joan Margaret. So, this is a fantastic lead and O'Rorden and I are going back to get more details today and see if we can't get a better description. We are also going to interview the housekeeper, she may know something. We are also going to need another say four officers to make some house to house inquiries around the immediate area of the murder scene.

"Technical Bureau should finish today, and we'll get a report from the post mortem hopefully soon. The rest of you need to continue with the lines of inquiry we are already following up. I will make a statement to the press from Ballygilly church, they will probably already be there anyhow. Please keep it quiet about the eye witness account at this stage until we've had a chance to see if they've remembered any more details. If the new team members turn up, then let me know at once. OK, any questions?"

"Do you think it's the same person, sir, doing these murders?" asked Kathy O'Flynn.

"It seems likely yes, O'Flynn, although until we have the ballistics report we can't confirm it of course," answered Seamus.

"Thank you, sir."

There were no more questions, so they had a discussion about who was going to Ballygilly, and those officers selected went on ahead. A few minutes later, Seamus and O'Rorden made their way over to the murder scene.

"You can drive normally today," Seamus told him, not wanting a repeat performance of the previous night. Seamus reflected he had had fairground rides which were more sedate by comparison.

"OK sir, I'll just drive the usual speed."

"Thanks, O'Rorden, and my heart thanks you too, since it won't be in my mouth the whole way there." Seamus was genuinely relieved.

* * *

Their first port of call was the murder scene. The technical team was still on site, and Jim said they had a lot more to do. He spoke at length about the lack of understanding detectives apparently had for the painstaking work they did, and how two murders were doubling the load. They couldn't be expected to complete things in double quick time if Seamus actually wanted results, and on top of that, he said bitterly, some of them actually had managed to catch a couple of hours well-deserved kip in the van.

"With all these murders you keep finding, I've not seen my wife in days, my kids don't recognise me anymore and I don't even know the meaning of the word sex as far that's concerned, let alone be able to have any." Jim completed his pithy summary of the state of the world in general and his lot in life in particular. Seamus ignored it because he knew above all Jim was one of the most dedicated officers he knew and loved his occupation with a passion.

"I keep finding? I keep finding?" Seamus shot back. "You sound as if I rang up the murderer myself and asked them to come down and carry out the killings."

"Well." Jim grinned at him, laughing. "I maybe wouldn't go that far."

"Thanks," said Seamus. "Your continued faith in me is touching, so it is."

"When we've done in the church, we'll be conducting a thorough search along the roadsides." Jim became serious once again. "Killers often discard things, in my experience, particularly after a vicious attack like this and we don't want to miss anything. We should be done by the end of the day."

"OK thanks, keep the good work." Seamus clapped him on the back and headed back to the gate with O'Rorden.

"Tell it to my boss," Jim called after him, "maybe he'll give me the pay rise he's promised me for the last five fucking years."

Seamus waved a hand in acknowledgement smiling all the way.

"Does he always complain like this?" O'Rorden asked him.

"Oh, don't mind him," Seamus explained, "it's his way of getting through the day. He loves his job really, but some people can't let a day go by without moaning about something."

"I heard that!" It was Jim in the distance.

Seamus and O'Rorden chuckled as they reached the car.

"What now, sir?" O'Rorden said.

"Let's catch up with Maire and Eoin again and see if there's anything else we can get out of them. We'll need them to try and put together a photofit, but we can arrange it for later. We'll head back here then make a brief statement to the press and then we'll interview the housekeeper. Then we'll see where we go from there."

❋ ❋ ❋

The night hadn't elicited any further details from either of their eyewitnesses. Maire, in particular, looked somewhat chastened when she spoke to them. Seamus guessed she and her parents had had words. They spoke to her alone since she was over eighteen, but the parents were evidently not happy about the events of the night. Seamus assured them Maire's valuable input might be very helpful in assisting them to catch the murderer and it was really fortunate she had been in the graveyard that night. They seemed more mollified after this and Maire looked at him gratefully. She still thought the killer's hair colour was brown and was unclear on any other features. She agreed the woman was very pretty.

Eoin seemed quite blasé now about the whole affair, almost as if he had witnessed murders every day. His parents didn't seem bothered about his nocturnal habits and Seamus reflected the old standards of boys versus girls still seemed to apply in the provinces. They had not quite caught up to the modern world. In any case, his account was not any different to what he said last night, although he seemed very certain now the woman's hair was blonde.

They arranged both of them would be picked up at some point and asked to help make a photofit of the woman in question. Seamus decided they should get a photofit from each and then the artist could blend them together. He also cautioned them about talking to the press and asked if they would, if possible, please refrain.

"Do you think it will do any good?" O'Rorden asked him as they left Eoin's parent's house.

"Who knows. Journalists are sneaky bastards at the best of times, once they know we've got eyewitnesses they'll be trying to track them down and getting them to talk."

"Are you going to tell the press today, about them?" O'Rorden said.

"I don't know, it's a double-edged sword. Perhaps we will leave it until we've got a photofit. Just give a brief outline of what's happened," Seamus replied mulling over the options.

They arrived back at the murder scene and by then Seamus noticed some media people had gathered at the perimeter. He had made a phone call to the press office earlier and so this wasn't unexpected.

"Inspector, Inspector, can you give us some details about these latest murders?" The reporters were on him as soon as he opened the car door.

"How were they killed, Inspector? Is it true they were shot?"

"When did this happen?"

Seamus held up his hands to try and silence them. "If you just want to make your way over here, I will make a brief statement," he told them already feeling annoyed, as he always did when journalists became involved.

They followed him eagerly to outside the gate in the church and waited expectantly for him to speak. There were a couple of film crews, photographers and reporters. He chose to have the church in the background and kept O'Rorden by his side. Seamus wasn't immune to trying to keep the media happy, as much as he didn't want to talk to them at all.

"At approximately seven pm last night," he began, "Father Cooney was killed in the Ballygilly church."

"What was he doing there?" asked a young fresh-faced hack in the front.

"Ballygilly Church is the Father's church," said Seamus trying to exercise some patience, "and so I imagine he was there for confession or any of the other multitude of things a priest does in his church every day of the week. Going about his business as a priest, in his church!"

There was muffled laughter at this from a few people and officers who had heard it and his voice laced with sarcasm.

"Now if we can please leave the questions until the end, then it might make things a little smoother," Seamus went on. Nobody spoke so he continued his summary. "As I was saying, Father Cooney was killed, we think, at seven pm in his church."

"How do you know it was seven pm?" It was the same hack again, obviously, he was new at this and was trying to make a good impression.

"Ach will you let the man speak for God's sake," one of the other and older journalists piped up. "We haven't got all day."

"Yes, shut up and let him talk, we need to hear the story," another told the youngster.

Cowed by the members of his own profession, the young reporter subsided.

Seamus waited and when it was plain no further interruptions were likely to occur, he tried again, "Father Cooney was shot dead in his church last night. The pathologist has estimated the time of death to be seven pm. Father Cooney was shot once in the head and then five times in the body. The pathologist says he would have already been dead from the first shot, we don't know why the killer chose to shoot the body five more times.

"However, Mother Joan Margaret, who was apparently a companion to Father Cooney was also murdered we believe shortly after Father Cooney was killed. She was beaten to death in a particularly vicious, brutal and apparently frenzied attack. She was hit multiple times in the head we believe with the barrel of a pistol. The manner in which these attacks were carried out suggests perhaps something about the murderer's state of mind. These murders are obviously quite recent and we've nothing more to add at the moment.

"We are following up on some lines of inquiry and when we have more information, we will have a full press conference, probably in a couple of days. At this time, however, we would like to ask anyone who might have seen or heard anything to please contact Ballygilly or Ballysruth Garda station. The information will be treated in strictest confidence. Thank you. I'll take a few questions if you have them."

"Do you think it's the same person who killed Father O'Flaherty?" It was Jameson from the Irish Sun, the man seemed to get everywhere Seamus reflected irritated.

"We suspect it, but we cannot confirm at this time until we have completed our forensic examination."

"Are you sure it's not a sectarian killing, Inspector, that's two priests and now a nun." It was Jameson again.

"No, we don't believe it is, there is nothing to suggest it at this time."

"Do you think this is the work of the Masked Revenger?" It was the Irish Daily Star, they had coined the term.

"As I said before we do not have any information the killer was wearing a mask." Seamus was certain the headlines would read, 'Masked Revenger strikes again,' and smiled a wry smile at that.

"Should other priests be worried?" one of the network reporters asked.

"I can't say at this time," Seamus said. "It is our belief these were not necessarily random killings, it may be the murders were perhaps personal and the victims were possibly known to the killer. At least that is one of our lines of inquiry at the moment." Seamus wished he had not said it, as soon as the words left his mouth.

"How can you possibly say that? What are you not telling us?" Jameson was on him in a flash.

251

"It's all we have for now, we will let you have further information in due course."

"But, Inspector..." Jameson protested.

Seamus turned away and ducked under the perimeter tape, he and O'Rorden walked up towards the church and away from the reporters still vainly shouting questions.

"I am starting to see what you mean about the media," O'Rorden said.

"Yes, well I shouldn't have said the last bit," Seamus replied ruefully.

"I'm sure there's no harm done," O'Rorden tried to reassure him.

"I hope not, O'Rorden, I really hope not." Seamus didn't look convinced.

* * *

Diedre Flanagan was Father Cooney's housekeeper and maid. She looked to be no more than nineteen or twenty years old. She had blonde hair which hung limply to her shoulders and was a fresh-faced looking youthful girl, who was appealing in appearance. She had brown eyes and a thin pair of small but shapely lips. Unusually for a maid, she was wearing an off the shoulder white smock which revealed her shoulders. One of these had the edge of an obvious tattoo which probably continued down her back. She also wore a loose-fitting skirt and her legs and feet were bare apart from a pair of worn flip flops. It didn't seem she took particular care of her nails and those on her hands appeared chipped in places. Her eyes were a little wild and she seemed quite scared when Seamus and O'Rorden had arrived at the door.

There was a female Garda officer, Irene Connolly, in attendance, who had been there all night, to see she was kept safe. Just in case. Seamus had arranged it with O'Rorden.

"Don't be afraid," Seamus said gently, "we just want to ask you a few questions."

The girl nodded and beckoned them into the kitchen. It was quite warm and there was an Aga which obviously doubled as the heating and cooking facilities. It might account for her thin dress and no shoes at this time of year Seamus thought.

They sat down at the dining table and the girl sat opposite playing with her hair and biting her lip.

"You are Father Cooney's housekeeper? Would that be right?" Seamus asked her, keeping his voice soft.

"Yes, yes I am." Her accent was quite thick, not Irish, more Eastern European.

"How long have you been working for him?"

"About two years."

"And where are you from originally?" he asked kindly.

"I am from Poland, I am in this country for four years." She seemed a little more confident now it seemed the officers had no bad intentions towards her.

"It's OK, we are not here to enquire about your residency," he reassured her.

"I am legal, I had to come, my boyfriend he try to kill me, in Poland. I flee here, get asylum, then, my boyfriend, he follow me, he try to kill me again, he want to force me, to, to sex with him and to sex with his friends. I was working in Dublin, the police they catch him, he's in jail." It all came out in a rush, her story.

Seamus listened patiently.

"I understand, it sounds like you've had a terrible time," he said soothingly. "And how did you come to work here?"

"I got job, through church, I am good Catholic, I am good girl, Father Cooney he, he took me in."

"I see."

"Can you tell me? Is he, is he really dead, the Father?" she asked anxiously.

"I'm afraid so," said Seamus sympathetically thinking perhaps she must have somehow been attached to him or fond of him.

"Oh, God!" She sighed as if a weight had been taken from her shoulders, she sat up visibly less fearful. "Praise be to God, praise be to God." She made the sign of the cross several times on her chest. She seemed to be silently praying. Seamus noticed she was wearing a gold crucifix.

"You don't seem all really upset about it if I'm honest," Seamus observed.

Deidre looked at him as if deliberating something in her mind. As if she was not sure whether to tell them what it was or not.

"Did he do something to you?" Seamus asked her when she didn't speak.

"He, he... he made me to sex him! Sex him any time he wanted, in the day, in the night. He would call me, to his room, in other places, and I would have to, I would have to..." she stopped, and she began to cry, sobbing, it was obvious this had been weighing heavily on her conscience.

From the corner of an eye, Seamus noticed the muscles tighten in O'Rorden's face as he clenched his jaw. Seamus nodded to Connolly, the Garda officer, who came over and put her arm around Deidre to comfort her. Deidre put her head into the other's shoulder and cried it out. Seamus and

O'Rorden sat patiently waiting for her to feel able to speak again.

"So, he sexually assaulted you? Raped you? How often?" Seamus asked her when she seemed up to talking.

Connolly kept one arm about her to make her feel safe. Connolly's expression said it all, there was sadness and anger mingled all into one.

"Yes, many times, many, many times, for maybe one, one half years, maybe more, I don't remember," Deirdre said.

"You don't remember when it started?"

"No, no not really," she said helplessly. "Just one day, it just happened, and then..." she tailed off.

"And is it your real name? Deirdre Flanagan?" Seamus continued softly.

"No, no is name he gave me, he said to protect me. My name, Polish name, it's Anna, Anna Kowalski. He gave me name to hide me from boyfriend."

"Would you prefer to be called Anna?" Seamus enquired.

She nodded. "It's my name, nobody here knows, but it's my name."

"OK, Anna, we'll call you that just in here anyway between us three."

He noticed it put her at ease and she shot him a grateful look. Probably nobody had acknowledged her as a person, in her own right, in a long time, Seamus thought.

"I just need to ask you a little more about the Father, are you able to continue?" Seamus was careful, cautious, he could see she was harbouring a lot of pain.

"It's fine, I want to tell, I need to tell, I want to tell, everything," Deirdre, who was really known as Anna, asserted.

"What else did he do to you?" Seamus wanted to know.

255

"He, he also beat me, the first time when he want to sex me and then I say no. He said if I don't do, don't do this, he will punish me, then he will tell boyfriend, where I am, and boyfriend will kill me."

"And did he?" Seamus coaxed her.

"Yes, I cry, I say no please no, but then he punish me. He say I must do what God wants, I say God doesn't want that, but then he take his belt and he beat me, many times." Her eyes were once more wet remembering it.

"Where did he do that?" Seamus looked at O'Rorden and saw the other had balled up his right hand in a fist under the table. He put a hand on O'Rorden's arm as if to say he understood. O'Rorden gave him a weak smile of acknowledgement.

"Here, he beat me here in kitchen, he put me over table, bend me down, and take up my skirt, then he beat me. I cry, I cry so much, it was hurt, it was hurt very much." Tears started to her eyes and Connolly hugged her in tighter.

"And was it the only time?" Seamus said not expecting it would be.

"No, no, it was many times, every week or two weeks maybe at least once, and then after he beat me, he make sex to me." She buried her face in Connolly's jacket once more.

Seamus and O'Rorden looked at each other. It was obvious O'Rorden had never encountered something as graphic as this. But for Seamus, this was really one of many. Not that it made it any better. Not in the least. This type of abuse had been all too common, once, but to find it still going on in places like this, was more than just disappointing, it was criminal in his opinion.

Anna recovered herself after a while and turned back to face them.

"Did you know Mother Joan Margaret?" Seamus said lightly.

At the mention of Mother Margaret Anna's face clouded over, there was something in her eyes which could only be described as hate, unadulterated hate at that.

"She is bitch!" Anna fairly spat the words out.

"What did she do to you?" Seamus kept his eyes on her face, it was obviously something very bad.

"Is she dead too? I hear she is dead," Anna said anxiously once more.

"Yes, she is dead," confirmed Seamus.

"Good!" Anna said with satisfaction. "She is supposed to be nun? Woman of God?"

"I think so, yes," Seamus replied.

"She is not woman of God. She is woman of devil. She is devil. She is bitch, bitch from hell," Anna informed them in a voice filled with venom.

"Did she, do something to you, something bad?" Seamus needed her to tell them.

"She also beat me, she beat me for everything I do wrong, many times, many weeks, she beat me with this." Anna got up from the chair and opened a cupboard in the kitchen which anyone might ordinarily presume held brooms and the like. She produced from it a school cane and placed it on the table. The Garda officers looked at this with some aversion.

Anna had not finished, however. "And this." she placed a two-inch-wide leather strap with a split down the middle and a handle for holding it. It was obvious it served only one purpose.

"And also, this." A two-foot-long wooden paddle with a handle also found its way to the table.

"And this too." The paddle and strap were joined by a leather riding crop. Apparently, the broom cupboard was where Mother Margaret kept her discipline kit thought Seamus. It appeared to him Mother Margaret had more in common with Torquemada than the normal activities expected from a woman of the cloth.

O'Rorden was shaking his head sadly at this display. Connolly was looking grim.

"This, this is what she did, and Father, the Father too." Anna turned her back to them and lifted up her skirt. She wasn't wearing any underwear and the still present but fading bruises and welts across her buttocks were plain to see. She dropped the skirt and lifted the back of her smock. Her smooth back was similarly marked with more recent red welts probably made from the crop. She wore no bra.

There was a sharp intake of breath at these awful sights from the two other officers present. Seamus looked on with pain in his eyes. This was quite some of the worst abuse he had seen for a while.

Anna sat down and looked at them all with big eyes.

"Thank you," she said to them. "Thank for saving me"

Connolly's eyes teared up and she took Anna's hand and held it tight. Seamus saw that O'Rorden was only just holding it together.

"Anna," his voice was very gentle once again. "Is that what they made you do? Did they make you go without underwear? Like that?"

"Yes," she said. "All the time, they said was for, for easy access, for beat and for sex."

"Did Mother Margaret ever sexually assault you?" Seamus asked.

"No, she didn't touch me like that, but she watches, she watches Father do it many times, and others."

258

"Others?" Seamus tried not to show his surprise, was there no end to this?

"Yes," she continued. "Sometimes another priest came, or we went to his house also, and maybe one other I can't remember. They rape me too, beat me."

"Was it Father O'Flaherty? Was it his house?" queried Seamus wondering how deep this rabbit hole was going to get.

"The one who was killed, in the other church?" Anna said.

"Yes, that's right."

"Yes, I think so, I think it was him, I will know if I see photograph."

"OK, OK." Seamus was silent for a moment, Anna watching him, there was this incredibly thankful expression in her eyes. As if somehow, they were angels of some sort who had somehow rescued her from her awful existence.

"Look," Seamus said with some determination. "These things you have told us are very serious crimes, even though these people are dead it doesn't matter. These crimes need to be recorded. We are going to keep you safe. We will have a Garda Officer here twenty-four seven. We will need to bring you to the station soon to make a full statement of everything you've told us and anything else you can remember. In the meantime, we will arrange for a Garda medical officer to examine you, they can do it here, they will have to take pictures of your injuries, for evidence. Are you willing to do that?"

"Yes, yes, of course, I will do, whatever you need." She nodded willingly.

"Great, and we will need all of these things for evidence." Seamus pointed at the instruments on the table. "And anything else you can find. Can I also ask you to please don't

259

talk to any reporters, for your own safety as much as anything else?"

"Sure, sure I won't, I promise," she affirmed. "I stay here, inside, with this nice lady." She indicated Connolly who smiled.

"OK, so if you don't mind, we just need to ask you a couple more questions, is it OK?" Seamus said.

"Yes, yes is fine, I will help you if I can, I want to help," Anna assured him.

"Did you notice anything unusual yesterday afternoon, before Father Cooney was killed?" he asked her carefully. Although she definitely had a motive, he had no anticipation Anna could possibly be the killer herself. She was too scared and downtrodden for that, plus it was highly unlikely she had access to a firearm. Her whole demeanour spoke volumes about her innocence in this regard but she might still reveal some useful information.

Anna thought for a moment. "No, no I was just cleaning like I always do and Mother she was here. I didn't dare to speak, just clean, make dinner, I don't want her to beat me, then she go out too, she doesn't come back. I don't mind, I am happy. Then police they come, they tell me something happen to Father and the Mother. I wonder if they are dead, so many police come to the church, but I didn't know for sure."

"OK, but just think back, if there was anything at all, did you see anyone for example perhaps?" Seamus urged her hoping she still might give them something, a clue at least.

Anna screwed her face up and was obviously casting her mind back. Then she suddenly opened her eyes.

"Yes, yes I remember, Father had a visitor, a woman."

"What time was that?" said Seamus with some excitement.

"It was maybe five or something," she said recalling it.

"How long did they stay for?"

"Well, maybe one hour, at six they went I think. I open door for them, bring them to Father, then he ring bell, I show them out of house. Yes, at about six."

"Do you know what she came for, did you hear any conversation?" This was now becoming interesting.

"Well, no, no not really. I don't dare to listen. If I get caught listening then, you know," she shrugged indicating the things on the table. "He went into study, with her, they talked I think, I heard voices, he seemed pleased, to see her, like he knew her, they hug each other."

"I see, so they didn't have an argument or anything?" Seamus said.

"No, no argument, she just go, he hug her again, this was it."

"Can you describe this woman, what did she look like?"

"Yes, yes I see her very clearly, she has blonde hair like mine but more, very pretty, nice mouth, not like mine, mine is too thin I think." Anna laughed at this. "She has blue eyes, blue jeans I think, a pink blouse, a jacket, blue or black maybe, nice smile."

"Was she Irish?" Seamus was looking for confirmation, anything, because what he had just heard left a cold hard lump in his chest.

"Yes, Irish for sure."

"Thank you." This wasn't what Seamus had wanted to hear, not at all.

Seamus looked at O'Rorden. They both knew who had just been described. It was Kerry. However, there wasn't time to think about it now. Seamus had to take care of this girl in his charge. He would deal with the other issue later when he had had a chance to think.

261

"OK, Anna, you've been so very brave, all of us think you are incredibly brave," Seamus told her. O'Rorden and Connelly nodded in vigorous assent. "We will make the arrangements as I said, and we will see you very, very soon."

"Thank you, thank you, Inspector and officers, thank you, I owe you very much, I owe you for saving me from this terrible life. I thought one day I would just be dead, one day they just kill me, for sure, or otherwise maybe, I just kill myself." Anna shrugged, it seemed to her the only other logical end.

O'Rorden got up from his chair and spontaneously walked over to Anna. He took her in his arms, just like a child, like the daughter he never had. He couldn't believe the things he had heard. The cruelty, so bad, so severe it would drive such a young girl as this to contemplate suicide.

"I'm so sorry, Anna, so sorry for what they did." His eyes were wet and silent tears ran down his cheeks.

"Don't worry, officer, I will be fine now, thank you." Anna smiled when he released her.

"You will, I will personally make sure of that, and if you need anything you just ask for me." He pressed his card into her hand. She took it from him as if he had given her the greatest treasure on earth and cradled it to her breast.

Once outside the house, O'Rorden broke out into sobs, his shoulders were shaking. Seamus put his arm round him in sympathy. He had seen grown men cry before, it was part of the life of a detective.

"I'm sorry sir, I'm sorry, I've never seen the like, never in my life, that poor girl, those bastards, how could they do it, men and woman of God, how?" O'Rorden was choking on the words, hardly able to speak.

"I can't answer that, O'Rorden, I'm sorry, it's OK, this job gets to us all one way or another," Seamus said with feeling.

O'Rorden soon recovered and composed himself, blowing his nose into a handkerchief he produced from his pocket.

"Let's get the wheels in motion, O'Rorden, on the Medical Officer and a twenty-four-hour watch on Anna," Seamus said decisively, better to get into action than wallow he thought.

"Yes, sir," O'Rorden managed to reply weakly.

The spent a few minutes making phone calls. Irene Connolly had pronounced herself ready to stay there as long as needed and defend Anna from all comers. Seamus was impressed but sorted out a relief female Garda, so they could handle things between them. Having arranged everything to their satisfaction they headed for the car.

As they approached it, Seamus' phone buzzed loudly.

"Gallway," he answered wondering what else could have arrived to trouble his day.

"Sir, sir." It was Paddy O'Doyle who had remained behind at Ballysruth station.

"What is it?" Paddy sounded very agitated.

"You better get over here double-quick, sir, there's something going on in the field outside the station and I'm not sure what to do."

"On our way, sit tight," said Seamus clicking off the phone. He looked at O'Rorden.

"Blue light, sir?" asked O'Rorden hopefully having detected the urgency in Seamus' voice.

"Yes O'Rorden, blue light," he rolled his eyes. "Come then, do your worst."

* * *

263

Either Seamus was getting used to O'Rorden's hair raising driving or he had driven a bit better this time. Whichever it was Seamus wasn't quite as shaken up as their car screamed to a halt outside Ballysruth Garda station.

Quite a sight met their eyes on their arrival. There was quite a large flat green outside the front of the station. A quiet little spot where perhaps a person might sit and reflect on life. Not today, however. Two large articulated lorries were parked in the road and two very large prefab buildings had obviously been unloaded and were currently being bolted together.

"Well, will you look at that, sir!" O'Rorden said in wonder.

"I'm looking at it," Seamus confirmed. He had already formed a pretty good idea of who was behind it, but he jumped out of the car to talk to the artic drivers.

It didn't take long to ascertain from them these were prefabricated offices intended for the use of the Garda. They had evidently been ordered from Dublin and were now being put together and connected with all services. The drivers assured him this wouldn't take more than two or three hours and they'd be ready to use.

Thanking them Seamus walked back with O'Rorden to the station.

"Who do you think ordered these buildings, sir?" asked O'Rorden puzzled.

"Oh, that's no mystery, O'Rorden, not at all it isn't, just let me make a quick call," Seamus replied. He dialled Jack Brogan's number, while O'Rorden stood in earshot wondering what Seamus was at.

"Brogan," came the familiar terse tones on the other end of the line.

"Ah, sir, I was just ringing you about some unexpected deliveries," Seamus began.

"Ah, Seamus, yes, yes indeed you'll have got those new temporary offices I had sent down, will you not." Brogan sounded pleased.

"Well yes, sir, that's right. In fact, I wasn't quite expecting to return to the station and find someone putting up a bloody great high-rise right outside the front of it." Seamus was sarcastic.

"Ach come on, Seamus, you're exaggerating. High rise indeed, it's only a couple of prefabs so it is."

"Well, at least you could have told me they were coming," Seamus said trying to be more conciliatory.

"I could see you were short on office space, so I thought I'd help out, I thought you would be pleased." Brogan was starting to sound a little miffed.

"Sir, I appreciate it, yes indeed I do, although I was sort of getting used to the old station."

"Seamus, next you'll saying want to become a provincial Garda, you've obviously been down there too long already."

"It has its attractions." Seamus was thinking of Kerry at that moment.

"The new officers will be there shortly," Brogan continued.

"I hope you've sent me some decent people," Seamus said, knowing his boss of old.

"Of course, I have, what do you take me for? I'm sending you the best I've got," Brogan protested.

"That's what worries me," Seamus shot back.

"Ach, Seamus, will you have a little faith, I'm sure you'll be happy enough." Brogan tried to sound reassuring.

"As long as it's not the young idiot Brendan Duffy, from the last case I was on," Seamus pursued.

"Well, now I can't stay here all-day talking, Seamus, I've got a meeting to go to. I'll err, I'll catch you later, Seamus, that I will." Brogan seemed to suddenly be in a hurry to get off the line. The phone went dead.

Seamus stared at his phone in sudden suspicion. He shook his head, what will be, will be, he thought. He had enough to worry about without the addition of new personnel, especially Brendan Duffy, though God knows to be fair they were sorely needed.

* * *

Seamus was explaining to O'Rorden about the new offices after they got back to their desks. He was filling O'Rorden in on the vagaries of Brogan and the unpredictable things he was liable to do at any time. A number of the other team members had also returned from their enquiries and so the incident room was quite full.

O'Rorden and Seamus were discussing what to do with the new building when there was a sudden kerfuffle. The door of the incident room was slammed open and through it with a swagger came a young man, followed by several other members of the Garda. The cause of the disturbance was dressed in what appeared to be a fashionable sharp looking grey suit, pink shirt and purple tie. He had blonde spiky hair to which a large amount of mousse had obviously been applied. He was fresh-faced, clean shaven with blue eyes and couldn't have been more than about twenty-five. Black shiny pointed shoes completed his look and he surveyed the incident room as if he somehow owned it.

"Never fear, the professionals are here," Brendan Duffy said loudly with a smirk on his face. "We'll have this case solved in no time now we've got some real detectives on the case, namely moi, yours truly, DS Brendan Duffy, detective extraordinaire at your service."

This display of rank arrogance was not at all welcome judging by the looks on the faces of the occupants of the room. Behind him there were also some embarrassed expressions from the other newly arrived officers, it was evident this wasn't the foot they wanted to get off on.

"Brendan Duffy, is it?" Seamus spoke but he wasn't smiling in the least.

"At your service, DI Gallway, and ready to go into action. See I've got the gun to prove it, no priest shooting is going to get the better of me, I'm the sharpshooter around here." Duffy opened his jacket to reveal a holster and Garda issue handgun detectives always wore.

There was a sharp intake of breath from some of the officers, but not, as Duffy thought, through admiration. More in the sense of being unable to believe what they were hearing, it was beyond the pale in terms of conceited self-importance.

"Put the gun away, Duffy, I've no idea why you've pulled a stunt like that, and sit down, and it goes for the rest of you." He indicated the other officers in the room.

Duffy looked as if this wasn't the welcome he had been quite expecting and seemed minded to say so, but Seamus gave him such a quelling stare he sat down meekly in a chair along with everyone else. Seamus took a look around and recognised the two other new detectives as being from his department, Aileen Hughes and Iona Healy. He was pleased to see the team was now more balanced with the addition of two women and also, he knew them to be solid dependable officers. The same could not be said for Duffy. The new

Garda's he didn't know and there were four of them. He would get them all to introduce themselves shortly.

"Right, now you've arrived I might as well make a few things clear," Seamus informed the assembled company. "Firstly, I am happy to see some new faces and welcome additions to the team, for the most part anyway." He looked pointedly at Duffy who shifted uncomfortably in his chair.

Seamus carried on, "Now, I'm only going to say this once. I run this investigation is it clear? I say what goes on. We've got a great team here already doing a great fucking job and I don't want to hear anybody saying otherwise or they'll have me to deal with. We work together, or you don't work on this team. I want it understood the team we already have is a good team, and has been doing excellent work, I am very impressed with their efforts. Also, so nobody is in any doubt, DS O'Rorden here is my number two on this investigation and it will be staying that way."

Duffy rolled his eyes at this, but Seamus was still looking at him and he refrained from comment.

"To make this team more effective we are going to work as follows. Each detective will partner up with one of my existing team members. I know it's a bit unusual as they are Garda officers, but you can help each other. The detectives will bring their expertise in their area and the officers from here their local knowledge. You can learn from each other and that's a good thing."

Duffy made a scoffing sound, saw Seamus was turning to him again and tried to make out he had been coughing instead.

"We work together in this team, as a team, is that understood? I don't want any crap and I won't take it either. You respect each other, you work with each other and you help each other, and we get this job done. We've three murders currently under investigation and those of you who are new can bring fresh eyes. I don't want to hear any, and I do mean any, disrespect amongst this team, or anything else." He once again fixed his eyes on Duffy. "Don't come in here swinging the big dick and thinking you're the bee's knees because I will run your fucking arse right out of here and back to Dublin if you do. And I can assure you when you get there DCS Brogan is not going to be happy to see you. So, are we clear?"

The officers in the room signified their agreement and there was general approval all round at his words.

"Now, I haven't quite decided on what to do with the new monstrosity that's arrived outside the station, but rumour has it we will shift some of our operations over there." He looked around the room once more. "Although I've grown quite fond of this as an incident room, so we might keep our evidence base in here at least. I'll let you know shortly."

"In the meantime," he continued, "get to know each other and sort out partnering up, I will leave it to you. Duffy, you can come with me, I want a bit of a word."

If Duffy had thought being singled out was good, he was about to be disabused of the notion in short order. He followed Seamus out of the door and into the interview room. The look on his face told the others he thought he was moving up the hierarchy. The other new detectives glanced at each other because the expression on Seamus' face told a very different tale.

"I'm going to be straight with you, Duffy," Seamus began as the door closed behind them and he stood facing his junior.

"Well yes, sir, I'd like that, because don't mind telling you I really feel I should be your number two, sir, I mean I've got all the experience, what's he got? I've been to

269

detective school for starters and I'm pretty sure he hasn't, he's just a... just a..."

"Just a what?" Seamus looked at him his temper beginning to kindle, the impeding ire was showing in his eyes.

"Well, you know a provincial sergeant, I mean, sir, who is he anyway?" Duffy finished, his perceptiveness of the mood of others wasn't his strong point. In fact, it was fair to say in the universe of Duffy, there was only Duffy. He was by far the least popular detective with many of his colleagues who found his manner rude, arrogant and offensive. But Duffy had a thick skin.

"Sit down, DS Duffy, and stop talking," Seamus ordered him. Duffy did so but Seamus remained standing.

"I have no idea why DCS Brogan sent you here, but apparently in his infinite wisdom, he did. After the last case you almost completely fucked up for me, I personally asked DCS Brogan never to ask me to work with you again. But here we are, Duffy, here we fucking are." He paused.

Duffy said nothing, for once it seemed at least he was actually listening, he hadn't heard Seamus be quite so candid before.

"Here's how it's going to be. You are going to do your fucking job, you are going to stay out of trouble and you are going to work with whoever you have to work with, without complaining. Do I make myself clear?"

"Well, yes, sir, but...," Duffy began.

"No, Duffy, no buts, do I make myself clear?" Seamus spoke to him sternly.

"Yes, sir, completely, sir," Duffy subsided.

"Good, and just for the record, DS O'Rorden is a fine officer. He's one of the best I've worked with so far. He's an experienced officer and he's reliable as fuck, he's an asset to this investigation, which is more at the moment than I can say for you."

Duffy swallowed hard at this, home truths weren't something he was used to hearing.

"Don't fuck me around, Duffy, if you want to get on here, then I suggest you do the best job you can. And also keep that fucking gun in your holster, this is not Hawaii Five-Oh, have you got that?" Seamus asked him.

"Yes, sir, perfectly," Duffy said.

"I don't want to have to speak to you again, about anything like this again while you're here. If I do, you'll be out of here the next minute, is that clear?" When Seamus wanted to, he could be very straightforward and had a manner which commanded respect. Most of the time he never had to use it.

"Sir!" said Duffy, looking straight ahead not daring to look at Seamus at all.

"Good, I fucking well hope so, that's all."

And with those words Seamus left the room. Duffy stood there for many moments longer, he was somewhat bereft of words. Whether his DI's words had hit home, only time would tell.

* * *

When Seamus returned to the incident room, the rest of the officers appeared to be talking amicably amongst themselves and it looked like the pairing up was going well. He decided to go and check out the new offices leaving them for a few minutes longer.

The portacabins were actually quite spacious and had been kitted out with a number of desks, computers, lighting, heating and so forth. There was a large meeting table and whiteboards suitable for briefings. Having counted up the desks, he decided to move most of the team into this area once computers, networks and phone lines were installed. He would keep the big old school room for the evidence room nevertheless, although some of the current evidence might also be brought into here. Technicians were working overtime on connecting things up and it seemed Brogan had indeed pulled out all the stops.

While he was away, Duffy made his way back into the throng. He spied O'Rorden standing on his own drinking a cup of tea. Duffy sidled over to O'Rorden, watched by Kathy O'Flynn who surreptitiously moved within earshot.

"Number two hey, DS O'Rorden, that must be a pretty good position to be in," Duffy remarked casually.

"It's well enough thanks, so it is," said O'Rorden affably. He'd witnessed Duffy's little performance when he first turned up, so he'd already formed an opinion of the man. However, O'Rorden wasn't one to judge people too harshly, unless of course, they decided to try to cross him.

"So, how long have you been a detective then, DS O'Rorden?" Duffy threw in another question.

"Well, DI Gallway was kind enough to get me promoted." O'Rorden shrugged, he was a straightforward kind of guy and that was a fact. He waited though because Duffy was obviously looking for some kind of angle.

He wasn't wrong because Duffy's tone changed, to a much more aggressive challenging whine. "So not long then is it, because, O'Rorden, you see by rights I should be Gallway's number two, I've worked with him before, I've been to detective school, I've been doing this job longer than you, you're just a rookie."

"Is that a fact?" O'Rorden was unimpressed and put his empty cup on the table. O'Rorden might not cut an imposing figure but he had something else. A quiet presence and a self-assurance which went with long experience.

"Yes, that's fact, DS O'Rorden, so I suggest you watch your step because I'll be watching." What Duffy hoped to achieve by his statement is unclear, but it made little or no difference to O'Rorden's continued congenial expression. However, O'Rorden moved just a little bit closer to Duffy and his voice dropped ever so slightly.

"Well, now here's a word of advice, DS Duffy, we do things a little differently around here, when somebody wants to start getting a little cocky with us, we tend to go for the direct approach to deal with the problem, don't you see." O'Rorden's tone was incredibly pleasant but nevertheless behind it was a hint of steel which most people never really encountered.

"No, I don't see." Duffy was looking quite belligerent and started to square up to O'Rorden. Other officers in the room had begun to hear their conversation and had stopped talking.

O'Rorden didn't move and said a little more loudly than before, but so incredibly pleasantly, "Well let me put it this way, DS Duffy, if someone's going to give me lip, and if they're not inclined to stop, then they best be able to back it up."

"Are you threatening me?" Duffy was now bluster and bravado, but it was all an act.

"Threatening you, oh no, not threatening, I just want you to know that I'm not as stupid as you think I look, and I can take care of myself, so I can." O'Rorden smiled at Duffy amiably and with that, he walked off to see where his boss had gone to.

"I'm not scared of him." Duffy turned around and generally addressed the room, now he realised everyone was listening.

Kathy O'Flynn spoke up sounding very amused, "Is that so, DS Duffy? Well in your shoes I would be, O'Rorden was the Irish Garda Heavyweight Boxing champion five years in a row in his heyday. I wouldn't be wanting to mess with the likes of him, now that I would not."

There was general laughter at this information and Duffy looked suddenly very disconcerted. Duffy wasn't particularly viewed with any favour by the other team members, and he hadn't made a good first impression to those who didn't know him. Kathy O'Flynn was still laughing as she continued.

"And by the way, DS Duffy, nobody else wanted to work with you, so now you're working with me." She smiled at him sweetly.

DS Duffy received this news with what can only be described as a severe lack of enthusiasm.

* * *

O'Rorden found Seamus on his way back across from the new offices.

"Is everything alright, sir?" he asked Seamus.

"Yes, and no, O'Rorden," Seamus told him. "How are things going on in there?"

"Oh fine, fine," O'Rorden assured him. "Young Duffy seems to want to get a bit above himself, so he does, but apart from that it's all going well."

"Duffy," said Seamus with some irritation.

"I take it you've worked with him before?"

"Unfortunately, yes, he's very rash and so far, not proved himself a good detective. Last time he worked for me he fucked up something important. I don't know why Brogan sent him down here. Has he been causing trouble already?" Seamus asked, hoping for an excuse to send Duffy packing.

"Well," said O'Rorden. "He and I had a few words perhaps, but I put him straight on few things, so I did."

Seamus laughed. "I bet you did!" Seamus could imagine Duffy trying to get the better of O'Rorden and failing miserably.

"Anyway, we've paired him up with DS O'Flynn, she'll keep him out of trouble." O'Rorden was laughing too.

"Good plan," said Seamus "Good fucking plan!" Then he suddenly became serious.

"O'Rorden," he said.

O'Rorden caught his tone and stopped laughing. "Sir? What is it?"

He could see from Seamus' face he looked very troubled.

"You know what I've got to do now, don't you?"

"Yes, sir." O'Rorden instinctively picked up what Seamus was thinking. "It's Kerry O'Shea, isn't it?"

"Yes, yes, it is." Seamus didn't know how O'Rorden knew about these things, but somehow, he was well aware Kerry meant something to him and it went much deeper than a fling. He presumed there were probably few secrets in a small town like Ballysruth.

"I'm going to have to bring her in for questioning."

"I know." O'Rorden hated to see his boss looking quite so sad. It was his turn to put a hand on Seamus' shoulder as a friendly gesture of understanding. Seamus looked at him gratefully.

"God knows it's the last thing I want to do," Seamus said quietly.

"I know," O'Rorden said again. "It'll work out, sir, you'll see." He smiled reassuringly.

Seamus smiled back.

"Let's go back inside, you get the interview room ready and I will go and get her," Seamus said with sudden resolution. "Also, I am going to give Duffy something to do, to keep him out of trouble."

They headed back into the Garda station. O'Rorden went into the interview room and Seamus to the incident room.

"Alright everyone," Seamus said as he entered, there was an immediate hush. "I'm sure you've all got to know each now, so let's get down to some serious work, there are plenty of lines of inquiry already underway. Duffy and O'Flynn, I've got a particular job for you."

Duffy who had been scowling into a mug of tea procured for him by his partner brightened up at this announcement and eagerly came over to Seamus, followed by O'Flynn.

"What's it to be, sir?" Duffy asked. "Special assignment?"

"Yes, DS Duffy, it's a very important job, I want you and Sergeant O'Flynn to oversee the move to the new offices next door, see who you can get in there and who you can't."

"Oh, come on, sir, I'm here to do detective work not move offices around! This is just not fair!" protested Duffy.

"Well, if you can manage to do this properly then I might even let you loose on the case." Seamus was unmoved.

"Come on, DS Duffy, moaning about it isn't going to get it done, let's get cracking," Kathy O'Flynn said cheerfully.

Duffy realising complaining wasn't going to get him anywhere followed O'Flynn out.

"I want it on record I'm not happy with this, not at all, sir!" Duffy said over his shoulder.

"Noted, DS Duffy, noted." Seamus' voice was full of amusement, momentarily diverted from the unwelcome task ahead of him.

* * *

"You're back early," Kerry said in surprise at Seamus' sudden appearance in her kitchen.

"Yes," Seamus replied.

"Having the afternoon off?" She walked over to him as if to take him in her arms but something in his face made her stop. "What's the matter, Seamus?"

"Kerry," he started to say but he couldn't get the words out.

"There's something wrong, I can see it your face, Seamus." She started to look concerned.

"Come here," he said, "Sit down for a moment." He took her hand and led her to the table. She sat down in her chair and Seamus sat opposite. She looked at him expectantly. He sat there unable to speak.

"Seamus, for feck's sake would you stop this and tell me what's wrong!" The exasperation showed in her voice, but she was still half smiling.

"Kerry, I'm sorry," he said softly. "I've got to ask you to come to the station with me, I need to ask you some questions."

"Well, if that's all then I don't know why you've got such a long fa..." she trailed off looking at him as the significance of what he had said started to dawn on her. "Oh... I'm a suspect aren't I, that's it isn't it?"

"I'm sorry, Kerry, I don't want to have to do this." He looked very unhappy as he said it.

"You think I'm the murderer, is that it?" she said directly.

"It's not that I think you are, no," Seamus tried to explain.

"But you think I might be, is that it?" she pushed him.

"No, it's not that either, it's just there are some things I need to ask you, based on some things we've found out today," he said lamely.

"I see." Her lips pursed for a moment and then she said brightly, "well, if you must, you must, let's get it over with."

"Fine, let's go then." He stood up.

Kerry stood up too and then she held her hands out together in front of her.

"What are you doing?" he asked her.

"Aren't you going to cuff me?" Kerry asked her eyes dancing.

"I don't think it's necessary unless you want me to?" Seamus was feeling bad but hadn't lost his sense of humour.

"Well, in a different situation, you never know, I might say yes," she teased.

"Is that right?" He raised an eyebrow.

"Maybe." Kerry fluttered her eyes.

"Come here," he couldn't resist. He pulled her in and kissed her, God knows, he thought when he might get another opportunity. She returned his kiss with enthusiasm.

"I could keep you here for a long time like this," she purred her lips close to his.

"I know." He smiled, they kissed again and then when they had finished, said sadly, "we really have to go, I'm sorry."

"I'm not the murderer," she told him.

Seamus said nothing and just held tightly to her hand as they walked out to the car.

* * *

In the interview room, Seamus and O'Rorden sat opposite Kerry at the interview table. The recorder was rolling, and Seamus began, overcoming his reluctance to start.

"Kerry," he said to her. "Where were you on the afternoon of the murders of Father Cooney and Mother Margaret?"

"I told you," she replied, "I went for a drive and then my car broke down, I called out the breakdown and then I came home."

"Where did you go?" he continued.

"Just out." She was evasive.

"Kerry, please, that's not good enough, we need to know where you were, I need you to tell us."

"What if I don't want to tell you?"

"Then you are not helping yourself."

"Am I being accused of something?"

"No, but we need to rule out certain information we have."

"About me? Why don't you just tell me?"

"Because I want to hear it from you."

Kerry sat back and pursed her lips. Seamus looked at O'Rorden and O'Rorden looked at Seamus, this wasn't going well at all.

"Kerry," Seamus tried again gently. "We know you went to see Father Cooney."

"How?" she asked him. "Have you been spying on me or something?"

"Of course not! Why would you even think so? We have a witness who saw you." Her attitude was getting to Seamus, he couldn't understand why she was being like this, why couldn't she just cooperate.

"OK, but what of it?" she shot back.

"Ach come on now, Kerry. You went to see him about five pm, you left at six pm and then at seven pm Father Cooney was murdered, how do you think it looks?" Seamus was still trying to be reasonable.

"I knew it," she said her eyes flashing. "I knew it, you think I am the murderer."

"No!" said Seamus his voice showing his frustration. "That's not it at all, but the evidence shows you were in the vicinity before the murders took place, and we need to understand what it means, and you can help us do that."

"I told you, my car broke down," she protested.

"What time was that?" Seamus asked her.

"It was about eight thirty or something, as far as I remember," Kerry said after giving it some thought.

"So, what did you do between six pm and eight thirty pm?" Seamus enquired, not unreasonably.

"I just went for a drive," Kerry told him.

"Where did you go?"

"Just around, for a drive, you know," Kerry said vaguely.

Seamus sighed. Somehow, he had seen it going differently from this. He thought she would tell him everything she needed to know, eliminate herself from the inquiry and they would go back to the pub, kiss and make up. Instead, she was being evasive and refusing to answer his questions and he didn't know what to do, other than getting tough, and he didn't want to do that either.

"How well do you know Father Cooney?" Seamus thought he would try a different tack.

"He's an old friend," Kerry said.

"How long have you known him?"

"Oh, since I was about so high." She indicated what looked to be the height of a fairly small child.

"And would you say you and he, had a good relationship, as friends?"

"Yes, yes, and my mother knew him too, he was her priest I guess, she was a strongly religious woman. So, I guess he just became a friend because I saw a lot of him when I was growing up. My Ma went to his church." This tallied with Anna's description of Kerry and the Father greeting each other with a hug.

"And why did you go to see him on that day?"

"I wanted to ask him something, some advice of a personal nature," Kerry said.

"About what?" Seamus wanted to know.

"I told you, it was personal, I'd rather not discuss it."

"I see." But Seamus didn't see at all and he was less than happy with her responses.

"You met with him for about an hour and then, as you say you went for a drive?"

"I wasn't keeping track of time but if you say so, and yes, yes I did as I've already told you." Kerry looked at him daring him to push her harder.

"And you are not prepared to tell us where you drove to." Seamus made a statement.

"I don't see why I should have to, no." Kerry seemed somewhat adamant.

Seamus said he was suspending the interview and turned off the recorder.

"I'm sorry," he said to Kerry. "Will you please excuse us?"

"Be my guest, I don't imagine I am allowed to go anywhere at the moment anyway." Kerry was sarcastic.

"No," Seamus confirmed. "No, you're not, I'm sorry."

She made a face at him, folded her arms and sat there looking almost, for a moment, like a child who had been denied her way.

He ignored this with some difficulty, stood up and motioned to O'Rorden to come out of the interview room with him. They left Kerry with a Garda officer and went for a walk outside.

* * *

"Well, sir, that's a pickle and no mistake," O'Rorden said with feeling, he could see what his boss was going through, and he was holding back.

"I don't know what to do, O'Rorden, because, because..." Seamus tailed off.

"Because you've got feelings for her, sir, I know." O'Rorden's voice was full of understanding.

"What do you think I should do, O'Rorden?" Seamus sounded genuinely at a loss.

"Would you like me to question her instead, sir?" O'Rorden offered.

Seamus thought about this for a while as they paced back and forth and then said with decision.

"No, no I should be the one to do it, no matter how hard it is, but if you did question her how would you go about it?"

O'Rorden admired his senior's pluck and he said at once, "Ach well, sir, it's easy so it is. I'm a straight forward man, so I am. I would just lay all the cards on the table and see what she said then."

Seamus looked struck by this suggestion and nodded. "You're right, I'm just beating around the bush like she is, I should just go for it, tell her what we know and then see what she has to say."

"That's the spirit, sir." O'Rorden smiled.

"Come on." Seamus was now eager to return to the fray.

* * *

"Right," said Seamus to Kerry once they were sitting opposite once more and the recorder was running. "Let me tell you what we know and then perhaps you might be willing to answer the questions."

"I wish you would!" Kerry looked at him crossly.

"Here's what we know. We know you were let into Father Cooney's house at five pm by his housekeeper, we know you and he were obviously on good terms when you arrived because you embraced, and then again when you left at six pm. So, it doesn't appear to us any altercation took place from what we've heard from our witness."

She smiled at him a little triumphantly, but Seamus hadn't finished.

"However, we also know at approximately seven pm, Father Cooney was shot dead and then another five rounds were fired into his dead body by the killer. We also know Mother Joan Margaret was beaten to death with the pistol barrel shortly after that. We know the killer then left the church."

He paused, her expression was one of shock, almost as if she didn't know these details. Or was it because she was reliving the scene and actually was the killer. He pushed the thoughts aside and carried on.

"When the murderer left the church, they were seen fairly clearly by two witnesses who were hiding in the graveyard. They told us the killer was female and unlike last time the hoodie she had on was pulled down from her head. So, her head was particularly visible. We know from the description they gave us the killer most likely had blonde hair."

Seamus stopped then because finally, he saw the penny drop, it was all over Kerry's face. She finally understood why she was here and why she was being questioned. But was she the killer? Her face didn't show it either way.

When she didn't say anything, Seamus asked her again, "Kerry, please, please tell us where you went after you left Father Cooney."

Without warning, Kerry erupted and stood up with her hands on the table leaning forward.

"Why should I tell you anything, Seamus Gallway, you obviously think I'm the killer, that's why we are here isn't it? You think I killed them all don't you, so why should I tell you anything, go on then, do your worst, see if I care!" Her eyes were flashing with anger.

Seamus, who had been also holding himself in check, had had enough. He jumped to his feet and leant forward.

He shouted, "I never said I thought you were the murderer, but you are forcing me down that path by refusing to cooperate. You don't understand the next step is going to be searching your house, your car, forensics, is that what you want? Why won't you just answer the questions and stop being so bloody stubborn?"

It seemed a full-on blazing row was about to take place when O'Rorden intervened. Reaching over he turned off the recorder.

"Come on now, sit down the pair of you." His voice sounded as if he was talking to two squabbling children.

Seamus and Kerry looked at him in surprise but did as he asked.

"Sorry, sir," O'Rorden said apologetically to Seamus. "Sorry, I just had to..."

"It's OK, O'Rorden, you were right enough, that was unprofessional of me, I'm sorry."

"If you would just leave me and Kerry for a few moments, sir, just let me talk to her alone, maybe we can reach an understanding," O'Rorden said gently.

Kerry made a derisive noise. Seamus looked at O'Rorden and then he left the room. Kerry poked her tongue out at his retreating back. O'Rorden suppressed a giggle.

* * *

When Seamus had gone O'Rorden sat down again and spoke to Kerry.

"Kerry, we've known each other a long time, don't you know."

"That we have, Connor, that we have." She appeared to calm down at his soothing tones.

"Try to go a bit easier on DI Gallway."

"Easy on him?" she said bitterly. "How about he goes easier on me?"

"He is," said O'Rorden with honesty. "I've seen him in action with real suspects and believe me, he is going easy, easier than I've ever seen him so far."

Kerry digested this information for a moment before speaking.

"I want to, I want to but it's hard for me to do it and I don't know why."

"Hard for you to answer his questions?" he said softly.

"Yes, yes, it is," she replied.

"Why is that do you think?" He coaxed her a little more.

"Because... because." She paused as if she was trying to find the words. "Because I am angry he doesn't believe me, that he thinks I could be the killer, because it means so much to me if he thinks I'm guilty, it hurts me, it hurts me so much, it hurts me because I care about him, I care about him so fecking much, so I do." Her eyes were moist when she finished talking.

O'Rorden put his hand across the table and took hold of hers, showing he understood.

"And do you not think he feels the same now, Kerry, as you do?" O'Rorden smiled.

"Well, I don't know? I like to think he does, but he doesn't say it, I don't know what he's thinking because of this, this fecking murder inquiry. When he kisses me, I think I know, but then sometimes I think I just don't know him at all, like now." She dashed her hand across her eyes at this.

"Kerry," said O'Rorden, still gentle, taking her hand again. "Have no fear on that score."

"How? How do you know?" Her eyes were somehow hopeful.

"Because I've seen the way he looks at you, on those few occasions I've seen it. How he always makes sure he goes back for dinner. The anxiety he went through to bring you here and how he insisted on being the person to question you. He wouldn't even let *me* do it." O'Rorden was still smiling.

"Really?" Kerry seemed more cheerful on hearing this assessment of Seamus' feelings.

"He cares about you, Kerry, believe me, he does, whether he wants to say it, or not, so will you just cut the man some slack?"

"Do you think I'm the murderer, Connor?" Kerry asked him.

"Kerry O'Shea, I've known you a long time, I know you wouldn't hurt a fly."

"Thank you." She smiled back. "It means a lot."

"Now, Kerry O'Shea, will you stop being so difficult and just answer his questions?" O'Rorden chided her in a fatherly affectionate sort of way.

"I'll try," Kerry said with a tiny little pout, like a small girl who had to be coaxed to eat a particularly undesirable dinner.

"Fine, I'll go and fetch him back." O'Rorden let go of her hand and headed for the door.

Outside Seamus was waiting anxiously. He buttonholed O'Rorden as soon as he appeared.

"Well? What did she say? Will she cooperate?"

"Ach, sir, I think it'll all be fine now, so it will," O'Rorden assured him.

"What did you say? How did you change her mind?" Seamus wanted to know.

"Just things, things she needed to hear," O'Rorden said in a non-committal tone.

"What things?" Seamus looked at him with interest.

"Shall we go in now, sir?" O'Rorden gave him a wink, and with that Seamus had to be satisfied.

* * *

Seamus and O'Rorden entered the room. Kerry was sitting there, looking almost forlorn. Seamus desperately wanted to go over to her and take her in his arms, kiss away her fears, but he knew he could not. They had to get this over

287

with. He and O'Rorden took their places once more, started up the recording and began.

"Kerry, can you please tell me why you went to see Father Cooney?" Seamus asked her.

"Fine." She sighed. "There was something I wanted to ask him, something preying on my mind, I wanted to ask him what I should do about it."

"What was it?" Seamus said.

"It was something very personal, but not about me, about Liam, something happened to him a long time ago. I wanted to talk to someone about it, someone from the church, in confidence." Kerry stopped. Seamus realised happily this was far more than she had revealed before.

"Would you, could you, please tell us what it was about?" he pressed her gently.

"I can't, it's something Liam wouldn't want anyone to know, it's... please? Please don't make me tell you." Her eyes were pleading with him.

"OK, we'll leave it for now," Seamus conceded. "Why did you choose to go and see Father Cooney yesterday?"

She shrugged. "No reason really, for the day, I just knew I had a full staff on and it would be easy to get away, so I took the chance, it had been on my mind a bit I suppose."

"I see." Seamus was disappointed Kerry hadn't wanted to confide in him. Somehow it hurt him a little, but then, to be fair, neither had he shown her anything of his burgeoning feelings so why should she want to tell him?

"Was it helpful? Talking to him?" he asked her.

"Yes and no," she said, "I didn't feel my mind was any clearer if that's what you mean."

"OK." Seamus decided to move on from the topic, he could always pick it up later if it seemed important. "Where did you go after that?"

"I drove, to the coast, to my favourite spot, I like to go there to think, when I'm melancholy or needed to clear my head," she said.

Seamus immediately felt he wanted to know more about this special place, to go there, to be part of it with her. He pushed those thoughts aside.

"Where was it? Can you show us on a map?" he asked feeling as if they were getting somewhere.

O'Rorden disappeared and brought back a road map of Ireland. She showed them the location of Fado Cove. It was some distance from Ballygilly. More questions elicited the information about the time she had arrived at the cove, when she had left and where exactly she had broken down, and approximately what time. She also gave them the name of the breakdown company she had used. These locations and times were all noted down for further confirmation.

"Thank you, Kerry," Seamus said when they had finished. "That's very helpful."

"I'm trying Seamus, I really am," she said with a faint smile.

"I... we... appreciate it." He smiled. "I've still a few more questions."

"OK," she said. "Fire away."

He wanted to raise a sardonic eyebrow at Kerry's sudden willingness to cooperate but decided against it. He didn't want to ruin it.

"Did you know Mother Joan Margaret very well by any chance?" Seamus asked her.

"Not really," Kerry replied. "She used to run the old orphanage before it closed down. There were all sorts of stories about it, but I don't know if they were true or not."

"What sort of stories?" Seamus asked.

"Well, I heard she was a bit of disciplinarian, that sort of thing."

"So, you heard she beat the children in her care, is that it?" Seamus wanted to be clear.

"Yes, but those were different days to be sure, lots of that used to go on, things are different now," Kerry said blithely.

Seamus and O'Rorden glanced at each other on hearing this statement.

"So, you had no knowledge of her beating children?"

"No," she said flatly.

"Or Father Cooney?" He threw in watching her face.

"No, no of course not." She was emphatic.

"And do you have any knowledge of any abuse by other priests by any chance?" Seamus continued.

"No, no why should I?" Her answer was suddenly evasive, he could see it in her eyes. She knew something, but he did not know what. At this point, he declined to push her further. They had enough information to try and clear her from the inquiry, or not. He hoped it was the former.

"OK, Kerry, thank you, for your help so far." He smiled and formally terminated the interview turning off the recorder.

"So, is that it?" she asked.

"For now," Seamus reassured her.

"So, am I free to go then?" she said expectantly.

"No." Seamus shook his head. "I'm afraid you have to stay here a bit longer while we check your story."

"It's not a story, it's the truth!" She felt her hackles rising.

"It's just a manner of speaking." Seamus tried to placate her. "Garda talk that's all."

"Fine." She subsided. "So where am I supposed to stay in the meantime?"

"You're not going to like it," Seamus said

THE CONFESSIONAL KILLINGS

✻ ✻ ✻

"You are really expecting me to be locked in here?" Kerry asked him, looking around the small holding cell with an uncomfortable looking bed, small barred window, steel door, toilet and small basin.

"I'm sorry." Seamus looked genuinely apologetic. "It's procedure, I'm sorry."

"Procedure is it?" she threw back at him.

"Look," said Seamus. "If you promise me you won't try to leave then I won't lock the door."

"Oh no, why not just lock the door, treat me like a common criminal, let's go the whole hog why don't we, Seamus?" Kerry said with feeling.

"Kerry, please, I'm doing my best here. I don't want to do this to you, I swear, I've got no choice." He looked so wretched whilst he said this her heart melted at once and she couldn't be angry.

Kerry came up to him and put her arms around him.

"It's OK, but you're going to pay for this, Seamus Gallway, so you are." She looked up smiling into his face.

"Is that right?" He smiled back.

She kissed him and although he was a strong-minded man, this was not something he could resist from her, not today, not now. He had also been through a lot recently, they both had, he gave in to the impulse and kissed her back with passion.

"Would you like a cup of tea?" he asked her when their lips had finally parted.

"Now that would be nice." She smiled at him.

"I'll see if I can find some biscuits," he continued.

"Oh, the lap of luxury indeed," she teased.

"I'll bring it directly, in the meantime you can continue to dream up your Machiavellian schemes to get your revenge." He laughed.

"You have no idea!" she flashed back at him, laughing too.

* * *

Having procured the tea and some cake for Kerry, which O'Rorden thoughtfully provided from a secret supply he had, Seamus left her sipping the tea and went to see how the team was doing checking up on Kerry's movements. Because they had the locations and times, it would be easy to check if firstly what she said about her movements were true, and secondly whether or not she would have still had time to commit the murders. Usually, this would be an exciting time because they would feel they were perhaps close to a win, but not today.

The breakdown was remarkably easy. They traced it to a local firm and even managed to speak to the driver. He had it all on his records, which fortunately all legitimate breakdown companies had to keep. So that part of the story checked out extremely well. So far so good thought Seamus with relief.

What CCTV there was along the route she said she had taken, showed her car had indeed travelled there at the time she said. The trouble was the cove she had visited was small and not well frequented. There was no CCTV in the car park or nearby, so they couldn't confirm whether she had actually been there or not. This was a blow and meant the only other way was to see if there were any witnesses who might have seen her, and this would take time, plus where would they even begin?

Seamus and O'Rorden sat together going over the timings of what they knew about Kerry's journeys. Unfortunately, it did seem, at a pinch, she could have turned around and gone back to Ballygilly, carried out the murders and then by going a slightly different route end up breaking down exactly where she had done.

"But why, sir, why would she kill them? There's no motive we know of for it, none at all." O'Rorden said.

"I agree," said Seamus "but I am sure she is hiding something."

"Even so, sir," O'Rorden continued to argue. "You've said yourself looking at these timings it's very tight, it would have to run like clockwork, and yet we know it didn't look that way from the murder scene. It looked like as if the murderer had gone further than they intended. It doesn't look like they meant to kill Mother Margaret for a start."

"Sure, that's all true," Seamus agreed. "I guess though the only way we can really confirm it is to search her house and have forensics go over her car. If it shows up nothing, then I would say she's in the clear."

"She's not the murderer, sir," O'Rorden said earnestly. "I would stake my life on it."

"I believe you O'Rorden but it's not going to wash with DCS Brogan, we have to follow procedure." He sighed deeply contemplating the unpleasant task ahead. "I suppose I'll have to go and give her the bad news."

"Well, sir, I...," O'Rorden began but whatever he was about to say was interrupted by the arrival of Kathy O'Flynn looking quite breathless.

"Don't you have a home to go to, O'Flynn?" Seamus joked, "You always seem to be here."

"Well, sir, and if I had someone to go back to at night, then perhaps I might." She was looking at O'Rorden all the while she said this, and he looked somewhat alarmed. However, she glossed over it quickly and continued, "I've got an urgent delivery from the Tech team, sir, they say you'll want to see it."

"Thanks," Seamus said, "I'll check it over shortly, I've got something to do first."

"Sir, I really, really must advise you to check it now, so I must." Kathy O'Flynn seemed adamant.

Seamus looked at her. It was obvious she knew something, most probably about him and Kerry by the looks of it. She most likely also knew what the contents of the envelope contained. He began to think, with some irritation, there was nothing that wasn't common knowledge around the team or the town.

"Just tell me, O'Flynn, you obviously already know what it is," he said with resignation.

"Well, sir, the tech team conducted a roadside search all along the roads out of the Ballygilly," she began.

"Did they find something interesting?" He perked up a bit when he heard this news.

"Oh yes, sir, they certainly did that. It seems the killer had discarded some things onto the verge on the roadside. One of those items was this." O'Flynn opened the envelope and put a couple of photographs on the desk. Seamus stared at them in disbelief. It was a blonde wig, streaked with blood. The significance of this was just beginning to dawn on him but Kathy O'Flynn hadn't finished.

"That's not all, sir, by a long chalk. The blood on the wig matches that from Mother Margaret, and inside the wig were some black hairs which matched those found in Father Cooney's confessional and also the one in Father

O'Flaherty's. So, what do you think of that?" she finished triumphantly.

Seamus stood up as the import of this information finally dawned on him.

"So, it means the killer had dark hair not blonde. It means it's the same person that murdered Father O'Flaherty. And that means..."

"That Kerry O'Shea is innocent," O'Rorden finished it for him.

"Fuck, fuck, yes, good, yes, thank you O'Flynn thank you, you're a star so you are!" Seamus jumped up and unexpectedly gave Kathy O'Flynn a massive hug.

"Oops," he said, realising what he had done. "Sorry, O'Flynn, I got a bit carried away there, so I did." He looked embarrassed all of a sudden.

"No harm done, sir." She was laughing. "Go on, sir, go on and tell her the good news."

"Yes, right, good news, yes." Seamus fairly flew out of the office watched in surprise by the one or two of the other officers who were still there at this late hour.

"Well, would you look at that, Connor!" Kathy O'Flynn remarked.

"Ach, that's love for you that is," O'Rorden replied.

"Yes, it is now isn't it." O'Flynn looked O'Rorden in the eyes in a way he found incredibly disconcerting, he didn't know what to make of it.

* * *

Kerry jumped up as Seamus entered her cell. He had left the door open, as he promised, and she had stayed there exactly as she had also promised. He had been gone a long time and she had had a lot of time to think, mainly about Seamus. A large part of her days were taken up thinking about Seamus and in fact, she couldn't get him out her head most of the time. She wondered if it was the same for him, hoping it might be.

In a strange and twisted way, the murder of Father O'Flaherty had brought them together. She could be sorry for his murder, but she couldn't be sorry for the fact it brought Seamus into her orbit. Seamus seemed to be the man she'd always wanted, in her fairy tale dreams. To be sure he wasn't perfect, by any means, but he was close enough, of what she knew so far. The instant connection she had felt the morning she had looked into his eyes, and asked him what he wanted for breakfast, had never gone away. How romantic! Asking what he wanted for breakfast, she laughed at herself at the recollection.

"I'm glad to see you're in a good mood." Seamus came in just in time to hear the crack of laughter from her lips.

"Well I'm not in a bad mood," she teased him.

"You were laughing."

"I was thinking." Her eyes twinkled.

"About what?" He was interested.

"Never you mind what I was thinking of, DI Gallway." She looked at him slyly.

"Anyway, I've got good news." Seamus sat down on the bed next to her for a moment.

"Really?"

"Yes, evidence has come to light which proves you can't be the murderer and so you are no longer a suspect."

"And what evidence is that?" she enquired.

"I can't tell you, just yet, I'm sorry," he said lamely.

"Oh you! Seamus Gallway! I'm done with Garda officers and that's it!" She pouted at him, in a way he found exceptionally provocative.

"Are you now?" he said with a glint in his eye.

"No, no I'm not, especially not this one." She put a finger lightly on his lips.

"That's a relief," he joked.

"Oh you!" she said in exasperation.

"Shall we go?" asked Seamus getting up and holding a hand out to help her out.

"Yes, let's go," she said with resolution.

She stood facing him and then remembered something she had wanted to ask him.

"You know when you asked me about Mother Joan Margaret beating children, and then you asked me about Father Cooney. Why did you ask me that?" It had been bugging her in the back of her mind she realised now.

"I wanted to know if you had any knowledge of it," he explained.

"Knowledge of what?"

"Abuse by local priests." Seamus was matter of fact, he was so relieved he was past worrying.

"I told you I didn't, why? Do you have any?" She looked at him strangely.

"I'm not supposed to say," Seamus told her. "But OK, I'll tell you the truth, you deserve it after everything I put you through, there have been allegations, some serious allegations made against Father Cooney."

"What?" She was suddenly serious.

"Kerry, whatever you may know about him, it seems he wasn't the Godly man you might have thought I'm sorry." He looked at her and she could tell he was being totally honest.

"No, it's not true, it can't be true." Even so, something in her didn't want to believe it.

"I am afraid it is, Kerry, we have a recent statement detailing allegations of rape, cruelty and physical abuse by Father Cooney and also Mother Joan Margaret from the victim herself."

Tears suddenly clouded her eyes. She couldn't believe what she was hearing. Father Cooney, she had gone to him, to ask him about, Liam and Father O'Flaherty, and he had been doing that! She was distraught, disgusted, she didn't want it to be true.

"No, no it's not true, you're lying, you're lying, he was a good man!" She was raising her voice, looking at Seamus as if she couldn't even see him.

"I'm sorry, Kerry, but it is true, I'm not lying, he was a sexual predator and still continuing his crimes before his death and that's a fact," Seamus told her firmly.

"NO!! It's not, it's a fecking lie!" Her anger was at herself, at the betrayal of Father Cooney, he had told her to say nothing, it was all in the past. He had sat there listening to her tell him about Liam when he was an abuser himself. Her emotions boiled over. And in her fury, she lashed out.

The slap echoed around the cell walls and brought her to her senses. Seamus was aghast and in shock. She stared down at her hand, the hand she had used to slap him and felt instantly ashamed. She had just hit, hit the man she loved, across the face, for something he didn't even do. Seamus was still looking at her as if he could not believe what she had done.

Her hand flew up to her face, her eyes wide open.

"Oh my God! I'm sorry, I'm so sorry please forgive me, I didn't mean it, I didn't know what I was doing, Seamus, please forgive me, please, please, oh my God." Tears were running down her cheeks.

Seamus reached out to her.

"No!" she said pushing his hand away. "No! I'm a bitch, I am such a terrible bitch, you don't deserve it, you don't deserve me, God I'm so sorry."

"Kerry," he said gently.

Kerry looked once more at his face, turned and fled. She ran blindly down the corridor from the cells, pushing past O'Rorden who was coming to see how things were going, then out the front door of the station and down the street.

"Kerry, Kerry," Seamus called after her trying to pursue her. This was the last thing he had been expecting.

He almost collided with O'Rorden coming the other way. O'Rorden held onto him lightly.

"Sir, are you alright? What's the matter?" O'Rorden said concerned.

"Yes, yes, I'm OK, it's Kerry did you see her? She got a little upset. I told her about Father Cooney, the abuse," Seamus said anxiously.

"Ouch, sir." O'Rorden whistled seeing the red slap mark on his cheek.

"Yes, like I said, she got a little upset." Seamus rubbed his cheek, noticing it actually hurt.

"Shall we go after her?" O'Rorden asked him.

"No, it's OK, you wait here, I'll go," Seamus said and slid past O'Rorden making for the door.

Normally, O'Rorden would have listened to his senior but today he could see Seamus was in trouble. He followed on a little way behind him just in case.

* * *

Kerry reached the Baker's Arms and slammed through the front door. She headed for her kitchen, she needed time to think. What had she done? What the feck had she done? She still couldn't believe she had hit Seamus, and she still couldn't quite also believe the thought which crossed her mind in that same instance. The man she loved, that was the thought. There it was, her passionate caring heart finally exposing itself to her and she just did the stupidest thing she could possibly do. She hated herself right now.

When she entered the kitchen, Liam was there. He looked up and instantly seeing the state she was in went to her and took her in his arms.

"Ma!" he said with grave concern. "Ma! What's the matter, what have they done to you?"

He knew she had been taken to the station for questioning. She had left him a note, and in any case, it was hardly a thing one could keep quiet. He was angry enough at this. His mother was not a murderer. She burst into powerful sobs and he held her whilst she cried into his shoulder.

"Ma! Tell me, tell me what's happened, they questioned you, what's happened?"

Kerry found her voice, though a little muffled by speaking into his white smock. "Seamus... Seamus... he... I..." She couldn't get the words out.

Liam pushed her away from him and held her with his arms. "What has he done to you? What the fuck has he done?"

"He... he... I..." She struggled still trying to speak choking down the sobs.

Liam was nothing if not an impetuous youth. He always had been. He was also often quick to spark his hot temper. Today was no exception. Seeing his mother like that, he immediately assumed Seamus was the cause. He guarded his mother quite jealously in any case, so seeing her so distraught was too much for him to bear.

"Fuck it, I've had enough of this, I'm going to sort this out, you're not a fucking murderer, and he's going to fucking listen. I don't care if he's a Garda officer or not." He let go of her and pushed out of the room.

"Liam, Liam," she found her voice. "What are you doing? It's not like that, he didn't do anything, it was me! Liam!"

She heard Liam pounding up the stairs, muttering and cursing and then down again in short order. She went to the kitchen door.

"Liam!" she cried out again, but Liam had gone, the front door slammed shut.

Seamus had run full tilt to the pub and reached it in record time. He slowed down as he reached the gravel forecourt which was almost devoid of cars, it was well past last orders. He was making his way to the front door when it opened and shut with a bang. A familiar figure came out, it was Liam. Seamus was just about to walk forward and greet him when something made him stop, dead still.

"Don't come any fucking closer, DI fucking Gallway." Liam spoke with what seemed to him was a menacing voice.

Seamus wasn't impressed but he stopped in any case. Not because of anything Liam had said but because Liam was levelling a large service revolver at his chest.

"Now, now, Liam, what's got you all in a bother?" asked Seamus lightly.

"You fucking know what it is, Gallway, I don't know what you've done to my Ma but she's in there sobbing her heart out, so she is. I'm telling you to stay away from her," Liam continued.

"Well now that's a bit difficult you know, Liam, for a start all my clothes are in your pub," Seamus said not unreasonably.

"You think you're funny don't you, detective? Well, I don't think you're funny, so I don't. Coming here with your Dublin ways, beguiling my Ma! Accusing her of all sorts of things."

"Liam, you've got the wrong end of the stick there. Your mother's not accused of anything. And talking of Dublin ways, don't you live there yourself?" Seamus was trying to keep it light and wondering what to do.

"Shut up! You shut up!" Liam shouted. "I'm not having any of your bullshit. You've upset my Ma and that's enough for me. I want you out, get out of her life and mine."

"Well now," Seamus began, he held out his hands to the side to show he wasn't a threat and began to walk in small steps towards Liam. "I would love to oblige you there, Liam, I really would, but the fact is you've pulled a gun on a Garda officer and that's actually a criminal offence. So, you see I'm not going to be able to walk away from this, I'm sorry to tell you."

"You stop! Stop!" said Liam hysterically. "Or I'm going to shoot, you can send me to jail, I don't care. I don't fucking care, I'm warning you."

Seamus had fleetingly wondered about whether he could draw his own gun, but he discarded the idea, he couldn't do it fast enough. He stopped walking though, not because he was worried about Liam shooting him particularly, although there was a possibility of it he admitted to himself. However, it was actually because out of the corner of his eye he had noticed a shadow, a lightly moving shadow, hugging the wall of the pub, and that shadow was O'Rorden. Seamus realised he needed to keep Liam talking and Liam's attention on Seamus.

"Liam, come on now, you don't want to do anything hasty now, you don't want to end up in prison now, do you? You know if you kill a Garda officer it'll be a lifetime in jail. What will your Ma think then? I don't think she'll be happy, do you? So why don't you just give me the gun, put it down and it'll go so much easier on you, don't you think?"

The shadow was getting close, Liam hadn't seen it because he was looking at Seamus the whole time.

"I said shut up! I don't care about prison, I don't care. You've ruined my mother's life, ruined it. You think I won't use this, well I will, just you watch me." It seemed Liam was more trying to convince himself rather than Seamus of his deadly intent. Seamus very much doubted Liam would have the courage to pull the trigger, but nevertheless, he didn't want to chance it. Besides, O'Rorden was almost in distance with only just a few steps more and he could disarm Liam without danger.

"Liam, I hate to say this, but I think you're exaggerating just a little. I haven't done anything bad to your mother I promise. She's not a suspect, Liam, I promise you, she's not being charged with anything, we don't think she committed the murders, it's alright just put the gun down."

"I don't believe you, you're lying, you're fucking lying, you're going to take her and lock her up, I know you are, just like what you did to my Da! You'll lock her up just like him. Who the fuck are you trying to kid?" Tears were starting to run down Liam's face and it seemed the perfect time. O'Rorden made his move.

In his peripheral vision, Liam must have seen it. O'Rorden leaping for him from the darkness. It took him by surprise and very much later Liam would be able to say he hadn't meant to do it.

O'Rorden body slammed Liam with the full force of his not inconsiderable frame and in the struggle that followed the gun went off with a loud report. The two men went down on the ground but only one got up. Liam struggled to his feet before Seamus could move and sprinted away into the darkness. For a few heart stopping moments, O'Rorden lay seemingly lifeless and without moving at all.

Then to Seamus' considerable relief came a familiar voice. "I think I've been shot, sir, so I have."

"Fuck," said Seamus exclaiming loudly. He had half a mind to run after Liam, but Liam would be long gone, and he had an officer lying injured. And not just any officer, it was O'Rorden and somehow, he had become inordinately fond of O'Rorden.

Seamus ran over to O'Rorden and saw there was a tear in the left shoulder of his suit, which was turning somewhat scarlet with blood. Pulling off his jacket and his own shirt, he started to rapidly tear the shirt into strips. He wadded them up and pressed them to where he thought the wound would be to try and staunch the bleeding.

Just then, the door of the pub was flung open and Kerry came running out.

"What's going on? I thought I heard a bang," then she saw O'Rorden and Seamus holding a wad of torn up cotton to O'Rorden's shoulder. "Oh my God!"

"Kerry, come over here, take this and keep up the pressure I'll call for help," Seamus said urgently.

Kerry didn't hesitate but did as she was requested, everything else forgotten in the urgency of the moment.

Seamus pulled on his jacket again though he was now shirtless and took his phone from his pocket. He dialled the number of the station.

"Ballysruth Garda?" It was Kathy O'Flynn who answered.

"This is Gallway, we've got an officer down at the Baker's Arms, it's O'Rorden he's been shot by Liam O'Shea, get an ambulance here now..." he barked down the line. But he was talking to the air. Kathy O'Flynn had already left the building, the receiver stood dangling over the edge of the counter.

"How's he doing?" Seamus asked Kerry who was valiantly pushing down on the cotton pad.

"I'm feeling a bit faint sir, so I am." It was O'Rorden.

"Hang in there O'Rorden, help is on its way," Seamus told him and just as he spoke the sound of a siren could be heard getting closer. A moment later a squad car came flying round the bend blue lights flashing and siren wailing. The car didn't slow up for a minute as it careened into the car park and executed a perfect 360 handbrake stop spraying gravel out into the road. The car door was flung open with great force and Kathy O'Flynn came storming out of the driving seat. She didn't look right or left but ran over to O'Rorden and knelt down beside him. O'Rorden was lying with his eyes closed and his face had turned a pale shade of white.

"Connor, Connor, speak to me Connor, for God's sake Conner are you alright, say something," she cried out.

O'Rorden opened up one eye and rolled it in her direction.

"Ach will you keep it down, Kathy, you're too loud!" he said in some annoyance.

"Oh you big lug! What did you go and get yourself shot for?" Kathy said crossly at this and punched him on his right arm.

"Ow! What are you at, woman? Is it not enough I've been shot in me left arm, that you've got to damage me right arm too? Are you trying to cripple me or what?" came the response to this cavalier treatment.

"Oh God sorry, Connor, I'm so sorry, I really am, Connor," Kathy was immediately remorseful, she turned to Kerry. "Here let me do it, I'll do it."

Kerry allowed Kathy O'Flynn to replace her on the compression of Connor's wound, and then Kathy sat there fondly smiling down at O'Rorden dashing a few tears from her cheeks.

"Ach what are you crying for?" O'Rorden asked her.

"You had me worried sick," O'Flynn sniffed loudly. "I thought you might be dead."

"Well you can see I'm alive well enough and anyway, I didn't know you cared that much for me, Kathy, and that's a fact," O'Rorden said gruffly.

"That's because you were too busy with your nose in the wrong direction to see what's in front of you," O'Flynn complained.

"To be sure you're not making sense, Kathy, no you're not," and then he stopped as something seemed to dawn on him. "Oh! Oh, ooohhh, I see..."

"So now you get it, do you?" she remonstrated with him. "All these years I've waited for just one sign from you, one sign for the man who has my heart and what did I get?"

"Now just a moment there, what's all this about having my heart," interrupted O'Rorden. "Why didn't you say anything before that's what I want to know?"

By now the sound of several more sirens had been making themselves felt and several squad cars arrived plus an ambulance. Seamus turned around to meet the officers who were disembarking. He and Kerry had been listening to the exchange between O'Rorden and O'Flynn with growing amusement.

Before Seamus could do anything more, however, Brendan Duffy suddenly appeared in the car park completely out of breath as if he'd been running with his gun at the ready.

"Sorry sir, I just came over from the station sir. OK, where is he? Where is he?" he shouted loudly, "I've got this covered sir, so I have," he said taking up a position with his pistol in both hands as if he was about to engage in a gun battle at any moment. There was general laughter from the assembled officers and Duffy looked embarrassed.

"Put the gun away for fuck's sake, Duffy, this is not Miami Vice. The gunman is clean away by now in any case."

"Oh!" Duffy looked exceedingly disappointed and holstered his weapon. He tried to look nonchalant as if nothing had happened.

DS Hughes and DS Healy had by now also appeared. Seamus drew the three detectives aside and noted with satisfaction the ambulance crew were now attending to O'Rorden.

"Right, I'll overlook your little display for the moment, DS Duffy, and let's get down to business. Here's what happened. I arrived at the pub not long ago to be met by Liam O'Shea armed with a service revolver. We had some words and there was a standoff, I'll file a report on this tomorrow. However, O'Rorden had apparently followed me here and crept up behind Liam. O'Rorden attempted to disarm him and the gun went off injuring the DS. Liam

O'Shea disappeared. I don't think he's going to be around but just in case, I need you to get an armed support unit down here and have an armed officer at the pub at all times, for at least about forty eight hours, in case he tries to come back. Organise a search anyway and get a chopper down to help.

"As soon as I've got an address for him, we'll contact Dublin Garda to search his flat and tomorrow we will put out an alert to all units. Also, get forensics over here to see if we can find the bullet. Tape off the area where O'Rorden got shot. Have you got that? Healy, you can take the wheel on this if it's OK. We'll go over everything in the morning. In any case, if anything happens of note, then contact me straight away." Seamus finished talking and after a further brief exchange, the three detectives went off to get things underway.

O'Rorden was by now sitting on the back of the ambulance with his jacket off and Kathy O'Flynn in close attendance next to him.

"It's only a flesh wound after all, sir," said O'Rorden happily as Seamus approached them. "So, I should be fit for duty in the morning."

"You were lucky, O'Rorden." Seamus smiled at him. "And thanks, thanks for not listening to me for once, I owe you one."

"It was nothing, sir, really it wasn't," O'Rorden said modestly.

"No, O'Rorden, it was a lot, it was exceptional, and it was brave and courageous," Seamus told him seriously.

"Ach, sir, come on it's not all that now it's not," O'Rorden tried to demur.

"Don't listen to him, sir, we're all going to be so proud of him, so we are, especially me," O'Flynn put in.

"Ruined my new jacket though, so it did." O'Rorden held up the jacket from his new suit he loved so much and showed Seamus the rip where the bullet had gone through.

"Don't worry, O'Rorden, the Garda will stump up for a new one I'm sure, I will personally see to it."

"Thank you, sir, I appreciate it," O'Rorden said gratefully.

"Make sure he gets some rest," Seamus said to O'Flynn.

"Don't you worry about that, sir, I will be sure he does, so I will indeed," O'Flynn assured him.

"Oh Kathy, Kathy, Kathy, Kathy," said O'Rorden and put his good arm around her shoulders. She sank her head onto his chest with a sigh.

Seamus finally turned around to find Kerry. She had been standing on the periphery of it all with her arms folded patiently waiting for Seamus to finish what he had to do. She couldn't help admiring the way he just took control and could see why he was such a respected Garda officer. It simply made her heart swell all the more.

He stopped in front of her.

"Sorry," he said, "I had to sort everything out."

"It's OK," she replied. "It's my son who caused this after all."

"Let's go inside and talk." He smiled at her reassuringly.

"Yes," she meekly agreed and smiled a faintly back at him.

* * *

They sat once more in Kerry's parlour. She wouldn't allow him to speak until she had put a hot mug of coffee in front of him and a beef sandwich, because she insisted he must be hungry. He laughed but munched on it slowly and gratefully. She sat opposite him drinking her tea and eating a slice of brown toast laced with peanut butter. They didn't speak for a long time but looked into each other's eyes instead, and she felt as though she might melt with the way he made her feel.

"I'm sorry, Seamus, I'm so sorry about what I did," she said at length.

"You've nothing to apologise for," he said. "I should apologise to you."

"No! No, Seamus Gallway, I'm not having you take the blame, you were just doing your job, I was being a bitch," Kerry insisted.

"That's quite a slap you've got on you, I don't mind telling you," Seamus teased.

"Don't remind me," she said. "I am mortified, I am so ashamed, it was unforgivable, it's why I ran away, I hated myself."

"I've had worse," Seamus assured her.

"Really?" she was suddenly interested, then held her hand up. "No, don't tell me, I don't want to know."

"What made you hit me?" he enquired. "I mean it would be nice to know after all since I took the full force of the blow."

She sighed, "I didn't want to tell you, but I guess now it doesn't matter."

"I knew there was something," Seamus replied. "So, tell me now."

Finally, and with great relief, Kerry told him the story of Father O'Flaherty. She explained what had happened to Liam and how Father O'Flaherty had beaten him and then sodomised him. How she had gone to the Father and threatened to kill him if he ever did it again. She said she used to appear at his sermons and church, just to remind him of the fact she was there, in the background like an avenging angel.

The incident had started to weigh heavily on her conscience, once Father O'Flaherty was killed. She was afraid she would become a suspect and then Liam would. God knows it gave them both a motive. She was torn between protecting her son and wanting desperately to tell Seamus. So eventually she went to see her family friend, Father Cooney. She had no idea he was as bad, if not worse, than Father O'Flaherty. For all those years she had known him as a friend and confidant. She had even had many confessions with him when she was younger, about her sexual exploits and the like. Thinking back on it now, he always wanted to hear about those in great detail and he said this would allow her to purge it from her soul.

Her mother had been loving and kind to her, but when she was younger, she could be quite a handful. When her mother was vexed with her, she would go to see Father Cooney. Kerry remembered clearly how her mother told Kerry Father Cooney had advised her the Bible said not to spare the rod. Her mother did not and made liberal use of a wooden spoon on a few occasions. These also coincided with visits to Father Cooney. Kerry thought nothing of it at the time.

When Kerry grew up and got married though she never laid a hand on Liam. She had resolved she wouldn't treat her son the way she had been treated by her mother. Kerry got married quite young and her husband had been nice in the beginning, but it turned out he was involved in a paramilitary organisation. Now he was in prison for life for a bombing in Northern Ireland. They were divorced, and after endless questioning and investigation, Kerry was cleared of any connection with her husband's organisation of which she genuinely had no clue. He was also a bit of a drunk and had treated her quite badly. For Kerry though, that was all in the past.

However, when Seamus had told her Father Cooney was an abuser too, she had gone into shock. Many things began to add up in her mind. The worst thing was she had sat and told Father Cooney about what Father O'Flaherty had done to Liam not knowing Father Cooney was guilty of similar crimes himself. She had become upset, angry, at Seamus because it was from him she learned the truth. She hit out, in frustration and at her own gullibility, falling for Father Cooney's lies.

"You can't blame yourself," Seamus said when she had finished. "These people, particularly priests, go to great lengths to hide their crimes, usually it's only victims that know about it."

"Were they very bad? His crimes," Kerry asked him quietly. "You don't have to tell me if you can't."

"No," Seamus said to her, "I will tell you, you deserve to know."

He told her about what the Garda now knew, about Cooney's housekeeper Anna, and how she had been beaten and sexually abused at the hands of Father Cooney and Mother Margaret. Mother Margaret had beaten Anna badly and frequently, but the nun was also just as guilty even if she had not participated in the sexual abuse. Seamus explained how Father O'Flaherty was also involved. Kerry's eyes filled with tears when she heard this litany of horrific treatment meted out to Anna and her heart went out to the girl.

"I'd like to help her somehow," she said to Seamus.

"Well, maybe you can, I will let you know, we are getting statements from her at the moment and she is under Garda protection." Seamus explained about her boyfriend who was in prison and tried to kill her.

"So much to take in, so much," Kerry sighed.

"I'm sorry to press you for more, but we are going to need a picture of Liam and also his address in Dublin. I'm sorry, Kerry, but we have to find him if only for his own safety," Seamus told her.

"Oh, I want you to find him believe you me," said Kerry firmly. "I'll be having a lot to say to him when you do, so I will. Shooting a Garda officer, what on earth was he thinking? He'll be getting a piece of my mind and a big one at that."

"Well, I'll be sure to give you the opportunity, once we catch him." Seamus laughed gently. Then he asked, "Do you know where he could have got the gun?"

"I've no idea unless his Da gave it to him years back or he hid it somewhere. I don't know how; the anti-terror unit pulled my old place apart and didn't find any weapons, and then after my divorce, we took over this pub, there should certainly have been none here." Kerry was nonplussed.

"No matter," Seamus assured her. "We'll get to the bottom of it once we have him in custody."

Kerry found a recent photo of Liam and gave Seamus his address. Seamus phoned his counterparts in Dublin and asked them to visit Liam's flat to see if he was there and if not then to keep it under surveillance. He would sort out a search warrant in the morning with Brogan.

"I think it's time for both of us to get some shut-eye, don't you?" Seamus said finally.

Kerry nodded, hesitated, looking at Seamus with her eyes round and big.

"Seamus."

"Yes?"

"You can say no, but I don't want to be alone tonight." Seamus looked at her expression and she was particularly irresistible. In any case, he had been thinking the same thing.

"It's fine, why don't you come up with me? I would like that."

"There won't be any funny business I promise," she assured him.

"Oh well, I'm far too tired, at least tonight anyway," he said seriously. She smiled at the last part. It sounded promising.

"I might want a kiss or two though if it's allowed." She giggled as he led her up the stairs to his room.

"I can probably manage it." Seamus laughed.

"You look very sexy without a shirt in your suit."

"Is that right?"

"Oh yes!"

DAY 7

Seamus woke suddenly, just before his alarm, as he often did. He found himself unable to move. He was lying on his side and Kerry was spooned up into him from behind with her arms around him holding on tight. Not only that, they had both apparently gone to bed almost fully clothed. He reached over to the bedside table and quietly cancelled the alarm. Then gently and very slowly he eased himself out of her arms. She moaned softly but didn't wake. He sat up and picking up a towel from the back of a chair went into the bathroom, closing the door as silently as he could.

He surveyed his creased jacket and trousers with some distaste. Seamus liked to be neat and creases were an anathema to him. He could, for example, iron a shirt like a pro, something his mother had taught him early on in life. He removed and left the offending garments on the floor. They would have to be pressed most likely. Then he stepped into the shower. This was, to him, like a magic healing waterfall. The hot water on his face was refreshing, and when he stepped out again, he felt rejuvenated. Putting the towel around his waist he completed his toilette. He edged his beard with a razor and made sure everything looked tidy. Feeling ready once more to face the world Seamus went back into the bedroom.

Kerry was sitting cross-legged on the bed, her hair was tousled and eyes full of sleep, when she saw Seamus though she smiled.

"Oh my, oh my, Seamus Gallway." Her voice was full of appreciation. There was certainly something to appreciate. Seamus was well proportioned and well built, quite muscular but not overly so. He had some hair on his chest, as to be expected from a man in his thirties and he cut an attractive figure Kerry thought.

"You're awake," Seamus commented unnecessarily.

"Oh, I am, oh yes."

"I'm going to get dressed." He began to look in the wardrobe for another suit.

"What's the rush? Why don't you come over here for a minute and sit down?"

Seamus looked around and saw a playful glint in her eye.

"Oh no, oh no, we're not doing that!"

"Come on, Seamus, I just want to see what you look like without a towel on." Kerry had moved off the bed and was reaching out for a corner of his towel with the evident intention of pulling it off him.

"Oh no, no you don't." Seamus backed away behind the chair. "Not just now anyway!"

"Oh you!" Kerry pouted her best pout and sat down on the bed with her arms folded looking at him like a naughty child.

"Is that how you are proposing to get around me, is it?" Seamus' eyes were dancing.

"You're no fun!" she carried on pouting. "I only wanted to see if you've got a nice bum."

"All in good time, Kerry O'Shea, all in good time, I'll soon have a full team of officers champing at the bit over at the station and I need to get a move on."

She digested this information and laughed.

"Fine! But I will fix you, DI Gallway, just you wait so I will!"

"Is that a threat or a promise?" he teased.

"It's..." she stopped catching sight of herself in the bedroom mirror. A horrified expression spread over her face. "Oh my God! Look at the state of me! Why didn't you tell me? I look like I've been dragged through a hedge, and look at my clothes, they look as if I've rolled down a hill."

"Well, I thought you looked kind of cute, to be honest."

"Cute? Cute! I look like your feckin' worst nightmare," she protested.

"Well I wouldn't quite go so far, I have much worse nightmares than that." He was laughing.

"Oh you! You!" She jumped off the bed and started for the door. "I'm going to get changed and don't you dare go out without having breakfast!"

"I wouldn't dream of it." Seamus was still laughing.

"And stop laughing at me, Seamus Gallway, I mean it!"

He blew her a kiss, she poked her tongue out at him and hurried out of the room.

Seamus was able to dress now she was no longer there to distract him. He couldn't remember when a woman had made him laugh so much. He couldn't remember when a woman had made him feel so comfortable either. He did recall he had fallen asleep in her arms and she had made him feel so safe and loved. Loved, he turned the word over in his mind, it was a long, long time since he'd felt loved.

* * *

Kerry made breakfast, her heart all aflutter. Seamus did that to her, he made her behave like a little girl, who had been given the sweetest desert or the scummiest ice-cream. Her legs turned to jelly when she kissed him, and her heart did butterflies. It was extraordinary. She couldn't explain it, but Seamus made her feel like no other man had ever made her feel. And even better, she thought smiling, she was no longer a suspect. The contemplation of increasing her intimacy with Seamus inflamed her suddenly and she had to sternly force herself back to the task in hand.

Seamus arrived only a few seconds after she put down his plate of food and his coffee. She was hungry too and dished herself up some scrambled eggs on toast. Wondering if he always timed things this perfectly she sat down opposite him and began to eat.

"What are you going to do today?" she asked.

"Unfortunately, we are going to have to issue an arrest warrant for your son. And we will also have to search his flat."

"Go right ahead, the little toe rag, I hope you catch him as soon as possible." She smiled grimly.

"We'll do our best."

"Do you have to go up to Dublin then?" She was evidently hoping this wasn't the case from her expression.

"No, I'll have the Bureau take care of it unless they find something significant it's Liam himself we want."

"You don't think he is the murderer though, do you?"

"I don't know what to think, Kerry, but to be honest I don't think he has it in him, even though he could have had a motive against Father O'Flaherty."

"Oh good!" She breathed a sigh of relief. "Who do you think the murderer is then?"

"Well, now I don't know and that's the honest truth, we'll have to keep on digging."

"I'm glad you don't think it's me." She smiled.

"No half as glad as me."

Seamus finished his breakfast and waited for Kerry to finish hers in companionable silence.

"I like to see you eating with me," he observed.

"Do you?"

"Yes, but do you know what else I like more than that?"

"Tell me."

"I like you kissing me, and you know what, you've not done it today. You've been slacking on me, Kerry O'Shea!"

"Well you haven't kissed me either!" she shot back.

"I think then we need to remedy that."

"Oh you!" Kerry got up though and stood waiting for his kiss. Seamus obliged in short order.

✳ ✳ ✳

The daily meeting took place in the new meeting room in the prefab offices. It appeared O'Flynn and Duffy had actually managed to get the place into some sort of order. Seamus had to acknowledge the room was certainly bigger and roomier than the incident room in the old schoolhouse. His team had certainly grown, he was pleased to see, and he felt like now he could really get something done.

Duffy kept glancing round to see if O'Rorden was going to show up, which he had not done so far. He still seemed to entertain the notion he would be in the running for second in command. Seamus had already decided it would not be the case and would appoint either Aileen Hughes or Iona Healy. He was hoping, however, he wouldn't have to. He let the minutes tick on knowing he would have to begin shortly, his officers were all sitting shuffling papers and waiting expectantly.

Just as he had decided he couldn't wait any longer, the door at the far end of the portacabins opened and in walked the familiar figure of O'Rorden, closely followed by Kathy O'Flynn. The officers burst out into spontaneous applause at the sight of him and his colleagues jumped up to greet him. One person alone was evidently not happy at O'Rorden's successful return and that was Duffy whose disappointment was plain enough on his face. Seamus took note and filed away the thought that Duffy definitely still wasn't a team player.

"You made it, O'Rorden, I'm glad to see you," Seamus said when O'Rorden had managed to finish greeting his colleagues.

"Yes, Sir, that I did, I wouldn't have missed it for the world, now I wouldn't." O'Rorden smiled broadly.

Seamus shook his hand in a spontaneous gesture of friendship.

"How's the arm?"

"Oh, it's right enough, sir, right enough, it might be you'll have to take the wheel for a day or two though until it's healed up a bit."

Seamus wasn't particularly upset to hear this news, as it meant no more of O'Rorden's full tilt formula one style driving for a while.

"You don't look too put out by that, sir, now, not at all, was my driving that bad?" O'Rorden grinned.

"It's fantastic if you're the sort of person who likes going on the wheel of death at fairgrounds," joked Seamus.

"But I still got you there in one piece now, sir, did I not?"

The two men laughed and O'Rorden sat down waiting for the Seamus to begin.

"So, this is day seven of the investigations into the murders of Father O'Flaherty, Father Cooney and Mother Joan Margaret. And what a day we just had, as I'm sure you all know by now. First, though let me just congratulate O'Flynn and Duffy here on doing a fantastic job of getting these new offices ready for use. It might not have seemed like an important job at the time but with the expansion of the team having a proper place to work is essential so well done the pair of you. I'm impressed."

There were a few claps at this and Duffy seemed to have brightened up considerably. O'Flynn was sitting at the back smiling and keeping a weather eye on O'Rorden at the front. Seamus noted it, and he also remembered the exchanges between the two of them yesterday when O'Rorden got shot. He resolved to quiz O'Rorden about it later.

"Now, a lot has happened we need to go through so let's start with the priority things. You're all aware O'Rorden here was shot, I am certain though by accident in a struggle to disarm Liam O'Shea. And I need to thank O'Flynn also for her prompt action in responding to the emergency call, well done! That was some driving, maybe you can give O'Rorden some tips," he quipped.

A crack of laughter came from O'Flynn and O'Rorden took the joke in good part. He turned and gave O'Flynn a very affectionate look.

"Today we will be obtaining an arrest warrant for Liam and a search warrant too. I will contact Dublin to organise a search of his flat. I take it there's been no news of him since last night and nothing was turned up by the search."

Healy and Hughes confirmed the search had drawn a blank. Officers had been out until the early hours scouring roads and countryside, and a chopper was requisitioned for an aerial based sweep too. Nothing had been seen of Liam. Officers had also gone to Liam's flat but there had been no answer. A surveillance team had been assigned to watch the flat twenty-four seven. However, it seemed Liam had gone to ground.

"Later on, today I will make a statement to the press and circulate his details, once we have the warrant. I have an up to date photograph from his mother, who I might add is very anxious for his return, as she wants to have a few words with him."

There was general laughter at this, and those who knew Kerry probably felt for Liam once his mother was roused to ire. She was generally known placid and easy going but when her anger hit full spate, she could sometimes be a sight to behold.

"That's probably what's keeping him away," Paddy Doyle quipped from the back and everyone laughed again.

"On the subject of Kerry O'Shea, although she was helping us with our inquiries, as the saying goes, we have now eliminated her as a suspect. New evidence has come to light in the form of a wig discarded by the murderer of Father Cooney and Mother Joan Margaret. A blonde wig contained black hairs which match the DNA of similar ones found in Father Cooney's confessional and also Father O'Flaherty's. We should get the full report today also confirming a match on the ballistics meaning it definitely is the same person who killed all the victims. Kerry O'Shea did visit Father Cooney on the afternoon of the murder on a personal matter. We now know it was regarding her son

Liam who was abused by Father O'Flaherty when he was fifteen."

This was news to many of those present and there were some surprised glances at this revelation.

"Kerry O'Shea's movements checked out and as I say the wig is conclusive evidence she is not involved in the murders. What we do know is the murderer is female, and she has black hair. We are getting a photofit from the two eyewitnesses who saw her outside Father Cooney's church after the murder. Once we have it, we will also circulate it to the press.

"Onto the last thing for the moment. We are all aware Father O'Flaherty was a suspected abuser and we have the reports of allegations against him. We now have a further report as I said of abuse on Liam O'Shea, his mother will make a statement regarding this. However, we also have a victim in the form of Father Cooney's housekeeper who has made serious allegations of physical abuse, rape and sodomy against Father Cooney and Mother Joan Margaret."

There was a collective gasp at this news. Many locals obviously knew both these individuals and this intelligence was shocking.

"She is under twenty-four-hour protection for her own safety, she has an ex-boyfriend apparently in jail at the moment who tried to kill her. She has also assumed an alias for that very reason. We have had her examined by a Garda Medical Officer to ascertain the extent of her abuse injuries and record them. She is making a comprehensive statement and once it's all done, we will decide what exactly to do with the information. The perpetrators are obviously dead, but it doesn't invalidate the seriousness of the crimes. We also don't know at this stage if anyone else was involved. Right, before I go over the tasks for the day, does anyone have any questions?"

Seamus paused and there were a few clarifications to be made which were easily fielded and elicited little further discussion. Most of the officers present were taking in all this new information which had emerged in the last twenty-four hours. From one murder originally, it had developed into something much bigger and there was a lot to get to grips with.

"OK, some of what we need to get done today I've covered but to recap. An arrest warrant for Liam, a search warrant for Liam. Press statements once that's done which will be down to me. Photofits from the eyewitnesses if it hasn't been done and make sure we've got their statements. Full statements from the housekeeper if not already done or at least if not fully complete, we need all possible details recorded and on video.

"I also want someone to find out more about an orphanage Mother Joan Margaret used to run and was closed down. It was apparently in or near Ballygilly. We may get some leads on potential suspects from it. If she did anything like she did to the housekeeper, then she'll have left a lot of enemies behind her and that's for sure. Otherwise, any other ongoing lines of inquiry still in progress need to be completed. O'Rorden and I are also going to get in Mrs Flynt, Father O'Flaherty's housekeeper, for further questioning, she has a lot of explaining to do. Any more questions?"

There were none and the meeting broke up with the teams distributing the workload amongst themselves. Seamus ran his teams reasonably loosely. He liked to give them their head where he could and to take responsibility for dividing up the work themselves rather than trying to micromanage everything. This approach had proved to be extremely successful in the past and he saw no reason to change it. His team appreciated it too, it allowed them to invest themselves in the process. Seamus certainly got results and Brogan hardly ever interfered directly in the way Seamus ran his teams. A fact for which Seamus was very grateful.

"Well," he said to O'Rorden "Shall we go and get Mrs Flynt?"

"Oh yes!" O'Rorden was grim. "Oh yes indeed."

Whatever had previously been going on between O'Rorden and Mrs Flynt was now at an end that was certain. O'Rorden had been unable to stomach her lying and protecting her employer. For O'Rorden it was a bridge too far, he was ready to bring her to book.

✳ ✳ ✳

Mrs Flynt sat across from O'Rorden and Seamus for the third time. O'Rorden was looking at her in a way she found unnerving. Whatever had passed for affection between her and O'Rorden was certainly now absent from his demeanour. In fact, if she was honest, the look he gave her was quite cold and hard. She darted quick glances at his face and away again, unable to bear the intensity of his expression.

Seamus had allowed this the continue for a few moments without saying anything. He had noticed the change in O'Rorden's manner towards her himself. O'Rorden had fetched her, accompanied by a Garda officer, without demur. There was a certain hardness developing in O'Rorden which possibly was part of the makeup of all detectives once they have seen and heard what some of their fellow humans were capable of. Seamus hoped this would only become a small part of O'Rorden's big-hearted personality. He had grown to know the man who was his number two and he had liked what he saw. He hoped the essence of who O'Rorden was would always remain regardless of the nature of the cases he became involved in.

Putting these thoughts aside, Seamus turned on the recorder and began the interview.

"Do you know why you are here again, Mrs Flynt?"

"Well, not really that I don't. If it's about Father Cooney and Mother Joan Margaret, I don't know anything about their murders. You should be asking their housekeeper."

"We did, we have."

"Oh, well then I've no idea, Inspector, why you've got me here. I've already told you everything I know."

"You haven't." It was O'Rorden who spoke, unexpectedly.

"Now, Connor, you know that's not true I don't know anything else and that's a fact."

"Don't you Connor me! Those days are over, it's DS O'Rorden now you're talking to here. The only facts are that you are lying to us, that's a fact, and so it is!"

Mrs Flynt looked quite startled at O'Rorden's tone. She was obviously not used to having been spoken to like that by him and her eyes widened in shock.

"Mrs Flynt," Seamus took over. "I'm going to be telling you some facts because I'm tired of all this beating about the bush with you. Father Cooney was a sexual and physical abuser, we know it, we've evidence from a victim and we've seen the marks. Mother Joan Margaret was at the very least a physical abuser. We've heard it first hand from a victim, we've seen the punishment instruments she used, and we've also seen the marks."

Mrs Flynt was silent as if she was digesting this information.

"We also know the same victim was abused by Father O'Flaherty, we know the girl was brought to Father O'Flaherty's house and abused."

Mrs Flynt made as if to speak but Seamus held up his hand.

"We also know Father O'Flaherty beat and then sodomised Liam O'Shea when he was about fifteen years old for allegedly taking money from the collection. We already know about the multitude of complaints regarding sexual abuse and molestation filed against Father O'Flaherty. We also have a statement from Ronan Maguire regarding Father O'Flaherty's attempt to molest him."

Seamus had finished speaking and Mrs Flynt had now gone very, very quiet.

"That's quite a list isn't it, Mrs Flynt? That's a lot of allegations of abuse isn't it, Mrs Flynt? We also know the Bishop came to Father O'Flaherty's house and faked a burglary because he was looking for something of the Father's. So that says to us Father O'Flaherty had something to hide, in fact, he had a lot to hide, didn't he? And yet according to you, you know nothing about any of it. Apparently even after working in close proximity with him for thirty years, living in his house, you never saw or heard anything. That's slightly hard to believe isn't it, Mrs Flynt, and you'll be surprised to find we do not believe a word of it."

Seamus paused again for effect. Mrs Flynt had taken on the hunted look she had had before, the last time they had her in the interview room. Seamus didn't care, this time he was determined she was going to break.

"We suggest you start talking, Mrs Flynt," O'Rorden chipped in his voice sounding very hard.

"I don't know anything, I've told you, I don't know, I never saw anything...," she began to whine, and she started to cry.

"Stop this!" Seamus banged his hand on the table making her jump, but she went quiet and instead was starting to wring her hands together.

"These are very serious crimes that have been committed!" Seamus told her. "Very serious, crimes which would put these people in jail for a long time, if they didn't happen to be dead. But you know what, Mrs Flynt, and here's the problem. There is one person still alive who we believe knows all about it, and that's you. And if you are not going to cooperate then we are going to charge you as being an accessory to these crimes, we are going to take the house apart, search every inch of it, your room, all your belongings, we will get forensics in, the works. And then when do find out what you did, and what you know, and believe me we will find out, we are going to throw the book at you, Mrs Flynt. Is that what you want? Do you want to go to jail for the crimes of your employer? And you will go down for a very long time, we'll see to it. Is it how you want this to go?"

Which part of this finally got through neither of them knew, but Mrs Flynt burst out into a storm of tears and wailing the like of which they had never seen.

"No, no, noooo, please, please don't send me to jail! I can't take it, I'll never see my grandson again, please don't do this, I didn't mean it, I didn't want to lie to you, I didn't.

The Father told me I would go to Hell if I told anyone. I don't want to go to jail, please no, no, no, no, noooooo."

This performance certainly eclipsed anything they had witnessed on the day they relayed to her the fact Father O'Flaherty had been murdered. On that occasion, O'Rorden had been moved to go and put his arm around her. But this time no such impulse occurred to him at all. They waited patiently for the storm to subside. Seamus hoped he had finally broken through to her and would get to the truth.

At length, the tears and histrionics stopped, and Mrs Flynt sat sniffing quietly. Seamus had passed a box of tissues across the desk for her to wipe her eyes and blow her nose which she did, several times. Eventually, it appeared she felt recovered enough to speak.

"OK, fine, I can't do this anymore, tell me what you want to know, and I'll tell you everything, that I will." Her shoulders drooped in defeat and it seemed almost as if she had become ten years older in those last few moments.

What Mrs Flynt knew was everything and also nothing it seemed, in the end. It appears Father O'Flaherty did not involve her too directly in his sins although she had definitely been a witness to some of it. For example, she knew all about the beating of Liam O'Shea and had even been there to watch it carried out. At the time she had approved because she thought he deserved it. Once the beating was finished the Father had told her to go out for a walk. She had last seen Liam still bent over a table and the Father had explained he needed some time in that position to recover and repent his sins. She had not seen him sodomising Liam and was shocked to know of this.

There had definitely been other beatings of choir boys and girls, and each time the Father had explained it was for their own good. Sometimes she had found empty condom packets and used condoms, and the Father had passed these off as the youths in his charge being sinful and promised they would be punished if he found out who they were. She was satisfied with that. In fact, when she would see some hapless young girl or boy getting a taste of Father O'Flaherty's belt, later on, she thought perhaps they were the secret condom users. The Father hardly ever told her why they were being punished, apart from Liam, citing the sanctity of the confessional. He said God commanded him to do these things and God must always be obeyed.

There were other times when Father Cooney and Mother Joan Margaret, in particular, would come over for a visit. They would also usually have one or more young man or girl in tow, supposedly acting as servants or apostates returning to the faith. On these occasions, Mrs Flynt would prepare food for the guests and then be told to go out for a walk or have the night off. Usually, she would go to visit her sister in the next village. Sometimes she would return from a walk and pass the door to Father O'Flaherty's dining room which was always locked. She had sometimes heard muffled cries or the unmistakable thwack of leather on bare skin. But she hurried up to her room and shut the door not wanting to know more.

Father O'Flaherty, she said, had always been kind to her and good whatever else he had done. He would impress upon her the sanctity of God and the Church and her silence was Godly, and she would otherwise burn in Hell for all eternity if she revealed anything about the goings on in the house. So, for nearly thirty years Mrs Flynt had held her peace, a Godfearing woman in the most literal sense, expecting to be struck down should she breathe a word of what she knew.

Seamus asked her if there had been any other participants to these priest parties and she named two other local priests who had since passed away and occasionally the Bishop. Seamus and O'Rorden exchanged some significant glances at this. On the face of it, it wasn't enough evidence to implicate him, but it was another big indication he knew more than he had told them.

"What was the Bishop looking for?" Seamus demanded when Mrs Flynt had finished her very long confession about what she knew.

"It was something very private to the Father, he told me to guard it with my life and never allow anyone to know about it."

"Where is it?" Seamus said relentlessly.

"It's in my room, hidden away."

"Right, then we're going there now, and you are going to hand it over to us."

Seamus fixed her with an expression which dared her to refuse him.

She didn't, and they drove her back to Father O'Flaherty's house having now obtained everything they needed from her for the moment. On arrival, they accompanied her up to the top floor where there was a spacious apartment which was apparently hers. By the look on O'Rorden's face, he'd seen it a fair few times in the past. Mrs Flynt obviously wasn't quite the saintly woman she made herself out to be.

Against one wall of the sitting room of her apartment stood a large bureau with a pull-down top. She unlocked it with a key from her pocket and rolled up the lid. Inside there were several drawers but evidently, it held more than meets the eye. With a deft push on what appeared to be a piece of wood under the drawers, another secret drawer slid out. She reached inside and pulled out a thick sheaf of paper secured in one corner by a pink ribbon which held all the pages together. She handed it over the Seamus.

"There you are," she said quietly, her duty done.

The pages were handwritten evidently by Father O'Flaherty. At the top with a date was the title "My Confession." Each page was numbered in the top right-hand corner. The manuscript had been very neatly written with a fountain pen in a small well-formed script. There were well over one hundred pages or more. Seamus passed it to O'Rorden who gave a low whistle of surprise. They now understood why the Bishop had been looking for it.

"Did you read any of this?" Seamus asked her.

"Oh no, that I did not, I put it away directly, God strike me down if I'm lying."

"Considering the number of lies you've told us already I'm surprised you are still standing at all," O'Rorden remarked with some sarcasm.

"Connor, I never thought I'd hear you speak to me in such a tone." Her voice was full of wounded hurt.

"I never thought you'd lie to me the way you have and so comprehensively."

"Oh, Connor, surely you understand why I did it?"

"Frankly no, I don't, I absolutely don't, it was your duty, to tell the truth on a very important investigation and you failed. You have let me down and DI Gallway here, so you have."

Mrs Flynt's eyes welled up at this and she went up to Connor and touched his arm.

"Connor, Connor, can't we put this all behind us, won't you, come soon for some tea and crumpets, like you used to, can't you, Connor?" Her voice was soft and pleading.

"No, no we can't and thank you all the same, but I won't be taking you up on your invitation."

"Oh, Connor." Genuine looking tears fell down her face, on hearing her liaison with O'Rorden was evidently at an end.

"Thank you, Mrs Flynt," Seamus put in. "We'll be going now, we may need to ask you further questions and I expect the same honesty you've finally shown us today."

"Yes, Inspector," she said in a small voice.

"Goodbye, Mrs Flynt," said O'Rorden very pointedly.

The two of them walked away while Mrs Flynt went to her little table, sat on a chair and buried her head in her hands. As they closed the door she started to cry very loudly, and this became louder the further down the stairs they went until finally, they shut the front door on the noise behind them.

Seamus breathed a sigh of relief. "Thank God that's over."

"Yes, sir," said O'Rorden who had appeared completely unmoved by the recent performance. "Thank God indeed."

"Tea and crumpets? Is it what they're calling it now?" Seamus raised an eyebrow at O'Rorden.

"Don't ask, sir, please don't ask, I'll appreciate it if you can drop it, that I will," O'Rorden begged. Seamus burst out laughing.

His laughter subsided, and he continued, "I'll bet there's some interesting reading there, O'Rorden."

"Yes sir, something to keep anyone up at night with nightmares and that's for sure."

"I think I know just the person to read this." Seamus laughed again.

O'Rorden looked at him. "Duffy?"

"It'll keep him out of trouble!"

The two men continued chuckling over this, all the way to the car.

* * *

The blonde girl with her hair tied back in a long plait down her naked back was riding the slim young man lying on her bed. Moving slowly at first enjoying the feeling of him inside her, she started to pick up speed. Her eyes were almost closed, and her mouth formed an O of surprise. Her hands locked onto Liam's and she continued to move on top of him. He watched her body in admiration taking in her full breasts and lapping up the sensations in his loins which were slowly spreading up his spine.

"Liam, Oh, Liam, I always want you so much, I love to feel you inside of me," she breathed and her greeny blue eyes locked onto his dark ones.

"Mary, harder, go harder," he urged her.

She obliged moving faster and she pushed down to get him deeper into her. He thrust up as they met each time with a gasp, her breathing became ragged and deep. He reached up to cup her breasts in his hands playing with her nipples. She almost screamed at his touch.

"Oh, Liam, I love you doing that, I just love itttt..." Whatever else she was going to say was cut short by her sudden climax. She writhed on top of him, as the waves of her orgasm took over. When things had finally subsided, she slipped him out and lay down beside him. Liam kissed her.

"Did you not come?" she asked him anxiously snuggling in close.

"No but it's OK, but I'm fine," he assured her kissing her again.

"No, no it's not fine." She slid down to his loins and took him in her mouth.

"It's OK you don't have to," he protested.

"I want to."

He let her be, and her mouth began to do the work. He couldn't help thinking then of Diana and the last time in the library. She was so very good at it. The thought of it made him harder and Mary encouraged by this continued her efforts. It was working, he was getting close to finishing.

"Don't stop, Mary, don't stop."

Her head moved faster and then she slipped her hand over his shaft. She started to work him hard, with her hand, listening to his moans getting louder and louder. In his mind all he saw was Diana, her red lips curled around him in that little smile she always had, moving at precisely the pace he wanted, until he couldn't hold it anymore. He passed momentarily into the oblivion of letting go. Then, he could feel Mary cleaning him up with a tissue. Diana wouldn't have done that, she would have savoured it, he thought.

Then Mary was beside him and holding him gently, softly. Pulling him close to her as if she would never let him go.

"You know I love you, Liam," Mary whispered.

"Yes, yes I do," Liam replied.

But if she had hoped he would say it back, she was destined for disappointment, because Liam didn't know if he loved her at all. Although he felt something akin to love, he didn't really know what true love was. All the same, he pulled her in close and kissed her with passion and with that she had to be satisfied. It seems she was because her eyes closed, and she drifted off into the afterglow of sex.

Liam lay beside her, thinking. She was cradled in his arms. He had come to Mary because he didn't know where else to go. After the episode outside the pub, he had run. It was instinctive. He didn't know if O'Rorden was dead or alive at this point and he was also scared. Scared he was now possibly a murderer. It had been an accident. O'Rorden had come flying out of nowhere and his instinct was to fight back. The gun had gone off because his finger had still been on the trigger. He had simply got up and ran, with one objective being to get as far away as possible.

He was sensible enough to work out the place would soon be crawling with Garda and no doubt there would be a massive search. He had to put some distance between him and his mother's pub and then find a place to lay low for a while.

The first part was easy enough. Not too far from the town was a truck stop, where truckers would habitually take a break and get something to eat. He buttonholed a couple and found one who would take him to Dublin. The man was nice enough and talkative. He managed to keep things to safe topics like the Irish Rugby team's recent successful performances. Liam was also still carrying the gun but now it was tucked as safely as possible into his jeans and hidden under his jacket. This was not comfortable but for some reason, he didn't want the throw it away. It had been his father's. A memento he had hidden away for years, his mother certainly didn't know and would never have allowed him to keep it.

Once in Dublin, he headed for his flat, he wanted to pick up some clothes. He left his lights off, so nobody would know he was there, anticipating they might come after him in Dublin. He stuffed what he could into a bag and then the Garda had come and knocked on his door. He had hidden under the bed, hoping they wouldn't come in. They didn't, but he suspected they would be back.

When he looked out of the window onto the street, there was a car parked with two people in it, keeping watch. There was another way out, but it was tricky. On every landing was a window and if you went through the window you could, at a pinch somehow jump across onto the fire escape. If you missed, then it was three floors down and a trip to the hospital at the very best. At the very worst it would be the mortuary. He had no choice. He had judged it quite well and hit the fire escape thankfully without mishap. He was down it and gone in a flash.

The next thing was money. He went to the nearest ATM and drew out all the cash he could. Liam wasn't stupid, and they would be watching any withdrawals to pinpoint his location.

With these matters out of the way, he considered his options. There was Mistress Dana, but he thought it was a bad idea. She was already a little too needy at times. He could only handle her in small doses when he wanted really dirty sex. She certainly gave him that in spades. No, Mistress Dana wasn't a good choice, plus there was her lifestyle and her clients to consider.

His male university friends were also a bad idea, they could not keep their mouths shut. This was likely to be on the news, he knew that. They would most certainly give him away even if not on purpose.

Then he thought of Mary. Mary was ideal. Liam had had many casual girlfriends on and off, but Mary was always there. She came from a fairly strict Catholic upbringing and had rebelled once old enough and at university. She was funny, clever and also, he thought, quite chauvinistically, she had an amazing body. Sex with Mary was great. Mary also cared about him in a way he couldn't completely reciprocate. She loved him in fact. She would go to any lengths to protect him. Mary was his best bet.

When he turned up on her doorstep, Mary smiled, appreciatively, almost gratefully. She welcomed him into her arms and almost immediately into her bed. He told her something bad had happened and he needed her help. She told him she would help and gladly, no matter what. That was the kind of girl Mary was, loyal, caring, loving and kind. The thought he might be taking advantage never crossed Liam's mind.

Mary stirred, opening her eyes, looked at him lovingly and went back to sleep. He pulled her to him, tighter. Kissed her cheek. There was some sense of deep affection in him for her, he had known her a long time now and he kept coming back. She never asked questions, never complained. Didn't want to know if he'd seen some other girl. Maybe this was love he felt for her after all. He didn't know.

* * *

Liam was preparing food in Mary's small cubbyhole of a kitchen when he heard Mary calling him from the other room.

"Liam, Liam, come in here quick they are talking about you, on the News!"

Liam dropped the knife he was using in fright and put his head around the door. Mary was sitting on her small sofa in a loose-fitting robe evidently watching the midday news. There on the screen was his picture as large as life. They cut to a live shot of Seamus and O'Rorden standing outside a prefabricated building.

THE CONFESSIONAL KILLINGS

"Last night Liam O'Shea shot and wounded one of our officers outside the Baker's Arms in Ballysruth," Seamus was saying, "we have issued a warrant for his arrest under the Non-Fatal Offences against the Person Act 1997. We would like any members of the public who have any information on his whereabouts to contact us right away. We must emphasise we suspect Liam O'Shea is armed and he should not be approached under any circumstances. Although the officer in question was not badly hurt and has returned to active duty this in no way mitigates the seriousness of this offence. Liam O'Shea was holding another Garda officer at gunpoint with intent to shoot and was disarmed by the brave actions of DS O'Rorden here beside me who was then shot in the process of trying to apprehend him.

"The courage of DS O'Rorden has not gone unnoticed and I can confirm he will be nominated for the Scott Medal for Bravery. DS O'Rorden could have been killed but with no thought for his own life tackled Liam O'Shea and was spared by what we can perhaps term the grace of God. As many will be aware, we are currently investigating the murders of Father O'Flaherty, Father Cooney and Mother Joan Margaret. We would like to emphasise we are not seeking Liam O'Shea in connection with these murders at the moment. If you see Liam O'Shea please, do not approach him and contact the Garda right away, thank you."

Reporters were asking questions, but Mary muted the sound and turned to Liam, looking at him her eyes wide in awe.

"Oh, my God, Liam, when you said you'd done something bad I didn't realise you were a fugitive from justice." But she didn't seem at all upset, in fact, she almost seemed excited to discover it.

Liam came and sat down beside her. Her robe hung slightly open revealing the fact she had nothing on underneath, but he tried not to allow this to distract him.

"I guess I should tell you what happened but promise me, Mary, please promise me you won't give me away," he pleaded.

"Of course, I won't, Liam, I promise, but what did you do? I want to know everything."

Liam sighed and told her the truth from the beginning. He explained the circumstances leading up to the shooting and how he had been distraught seeing his mum come home crying from her interview with Seamus. He told her how he had become enraged because he remembered how his Dad had upset his mother when he was young. He just wanted to make them go away, he had done it without thinking, in a blind rage, got the gun and threatened Seamus. He told her how the gun had gone off by accident when O'Rorden had jumped him. How he had panicked.

"My goodness." Mary looked impressed. "Why can't you just go and explain it to them, that it was an accident though?"

"You saw what he was saying, they want to prosecute me, I could go to jail."

"You can't stay here forever though," she said reasonably although the prospect of having him all to herself for a long while was also appealing.

"I just need time to think, please, Mary, just let me stay for a bit at least."

"You can stay for as long as you want, Liam, you know that, I love you." She looked at him with adoration in her eyes. He looked back genuinely grateful.

"Are you sure you didn't kill those priests though?" she asked him thoughtfully.

340

"No, no I swear! I never touched them."

"Have you still got the gun?"

"Why?"

"I want to see it, show it to me."

"Why? Are you crazy?"

"No," she said shyly. "It just, makes me kind of horny."

"Oh."

He went and rummaged in his backpack and pulled out the gun and showed it to her.

"Can I touch it?" she asked him with some anticipation.

"Yes, but it's loaded, whatever you do don't touch the trigger or drop it either." His father had told him quite a bit about gun safety, so he was usually very cautious.

"I won't." She took the gun from him and held it gently. She ran her finger up the barrel and then several fingers feeling the hardness of the metal. Her eyes looked at him quite lasciviously now and she ran her tongue across the top of her lip. She put the gun up to her lips and ran her tongue gently up the side of the barrel.

The effect of this was not lost on Liam although he couldn't imagine why she found the gun so arousing. Her fingers and lips teasing the barrel made him start to get hard and he noticed she had now opened her robe even more. He looked at her body and unable to stand it took the gun from her and laid it gently aside. He lifted her up kissing her all the while, she wrapped her legs around him as he took her to bed.

Later on, as they lay together Liam said to her

"Why did the gun turn you on so much?"

"I don't know really, maybe it just made you seem manlier, like a cowboy, I've always had a thing for cowboys."

"Is that right?" He laughed.

"Yes." Mary sat up on one elbow and leaned over him.

"You know, you can't go out at all looking like that, we're going to have to change your looks."

"What! How?"

"Oh, I'm pretty good with the hair dye and the scissors," she told him. "We'll have you looking different in no time."

"You seem very into this all of a sudden."

"It's kind of exciting, and I'll do anything for you, Liam, that I will."

He pulled her down for a kiss. This level of devotion wasn't something he was used to. It was disconcerting. Mary was climbing on top of him.

"You're insatiable."

"I know." She smiled, and her fingers began to do their magic.

* * *

"Sir," protested O'Rorden to Seamus after the press statement was over. "A medal, sir? I was just doing my duty; any other officer would have done the same."

"No, I'd like to think that, O'Rorden, but experience has shown me differently. You had no idea if he was going to shoot me or not, he could have seen you at any time and you could have been dead. No, O'Rorden, this was definitely something beyond the call of duty. Plus, you didn't have a gun, because I hadn't managed to get you one yet and you approached him completely unarmed. Not many officers would have done what you did."

"But, sir." O'Rorden wasn't giving up so easily.

"How long have you been in the Garda, O'Rorden?"

"All my life, sir, give or take."

"I bet in all the time of long service you've done a lot of things which have gone unrecognised."

"I know, sir, but..."

"This time it won't, credit where it's due, O'Rorden, it's what I believe and DCS Brogan believes the same, so he's putting you forward whether you want it or not. And if you get your medal, you'll receive it with the gratitude it deserves and wear it proudly. So just take it, O'Rorden, and stop whinging about it."

"I don't know what to say, sir, really I don't." O'Rorden was subdued.

"Ach you big lug, just take the medal if you get it and stop being so modest." Kathy O'Flynn had been listening in on this conversation and gave O'Rorden an affectionate punch on his good arm.

"Ow, Kathy, how many times must I ask you not to do that?" O'Rorden said aggrieved as she walked off.

Seamus had noticed O'Flynn seemed to be around O'Rorden a lot more lately. Almost like a protective mother hen.

"I'm beginning to suspect there's something going on between you and O'Flynn if I'm not mistaken."

"Well, sir, between you and me, and apparently the rest of the office, I can tell you that you are not mistaken," O'Rorden said shyly.

"Well, well, well! Tea and crumpets still going strong then is it?"

"It's tea and muffins, sir, Kathy doesn't like crumpets, for erm, obvious reasons." O'Rorden smiled a secret smile.

"Tea and muffins, is it now? Well indeed, muffins. Is that a fact!" Seamus' voice was loaded with unspoken innuendo.

O'Rorden blushed scarlet. Seamus inclined his head and gave O'Rorden a knowing look which only served to make O'Rorden's face go a deeper shade of red.

"Come on, O'Rorden, let's go and see what progress we've got." Seamus decided he'd probably teased him enough.

"Yes, sir!"

O'Rorden was more than happy to return to the business of the investigation and end Seamus' scrutiny of his burgeoning relationship with Kathy O'Flynn.

✷ ✷ ✷

Quite a few things on Seamus' morning briefing list had been accomplished. The arrest warrant for Liam had been issued and circulated to Garda stations nationwide. The Dublin branch of the bureau had received the search warrant for Liam's flat and should by now be conducting a search. Seamus didn't expect them to find anything but at the very least it was worth a shot.

An officer had obtained a statement from Kerry containing what she knew about Father O'Flaherty and his assault on Liam. The full statements were finally completed from Anna Kowalski, as well as the medical examinations and records. For the moment she was still under Garda protection, but Seamus had to think about her situation because they couldn't do that forever.

The photofit of the suspected killer was also complete as well as the statements from the eyewitnesses at Ballygilly. The photofit reminded Seamus of someone but he couldn't quite place it. The woman in the picture had blonde hair, it looked to be about shoulder length or longer, she had full bow lips and oval shaped eyes. In real life, she would probably be very pretty. She looked nothing like Kerry, however. They also had a version with black hair. There were aspects of this which seemed familiar to him. Seamus left it knowing it would come to him sooner or later.

Duffy was sitting at his desk leafing through some of the files of young people who had made allegations against Father O'Flaherty. The job compiling a list was almost completed and most of those who might be traceable were being followed up. Duffy didn't look so happy and O'Flynn was eyeing him with some distaste. She had made efforts with Duffy, but he just didn't seem to respond too well to these. Duffy had a chip on his shoulder and, as she told O'Rorden, she had no time for chips.

"Mind if I borrow young Duffy here for an important job?" Seamus asked O'Flynn.

"Be my guest, sir," she replied.

"Duffy!"

Duffy who had not been paying attention jumped.

"Sir?"

"I've got a job for you, Duffy, and it's very important."

Duffy puffed out his chest a bit at this and looked pleased. "Yes, sir."

Seamus thumped Father O'Flaherty's confession on the desk in front of Duffy. Duffy looked at it nonplussed.

"What is it, sir?" he asked suspiciously. So far Seamus had given him some really shit jobs in his opinion and he was dying to get out there and do some real police work. Something he was fond of telling anyone who would listen, but sadly nobody wanted to.

Seamus wasn't really singling Duffy out or being unkind. He didn't hold with bullying in the workplace or anywhere else. But Seamus wanted Duffy to realise being part of a team meant doing the dull work as well as the exciting work. Since Duffy was here to stay then he was determined to lick him into shape somehow.

"This, Duffy, is Father O'Flaherty's confession. In here, Duffy, are probably multiple crimes."

Duffy started to look interested.

"I want you to read it, Duffy, inwardly digest it and note down all of the incidents, names, dates, places if you have them. I want a catalogue of all of the abusive and criminal activity down to the last detail. Do you think you can do it?"

"Can I do that? Yes, sir, for sure just let me at it." Duffy smiled at finally being given something he hoped was worthy of his talent.

"Oh, and make sure you make a soft copy and at least three more hard copies. It's the only one we've got, and I don't want it going missing. Get the soft copy onto our confidential server OK."

"Sir, yes, sir!" Duffy jumped up and gave him a salute.

"Carry on then, Duffy, this is an important job and I mean it, make sure you do the best you can."

Seamus left Duffy smiling and he hoped this at least might start being the making of the man. Kathy O'Flynn nodded in approval as he went past her and back to his own desk. There were two envelopes which had appeared since the morning. The pathology and forensic reports were finally back on the Cooney murder.

"We've got the reports in, O'Rorden," he said starting to flip through them. O'Rorden was sitting at the desk across from his drinking a cup of tea and eating a slice of cake.

"Anything interesting, sir?"

"Well, the pathology confirms what we already know. The first bullet killed Father Cooney severing his spinal cord. The others were just overkill if you'll excuse the pun and appear to have been fired at random. Mother Joan Margaret was killed by several blows to the head from the pistol barrel. The pathologist estimates between ten to twenty blows of some considerable force."

O'Rorden whistled at this information.

"Yes, it certainly fits with what we would call a frenzied attack. The murderer obviously had it in for Mother Joan Margaret big time I would say. Anyway, apart from that and the DNA we already know about from the hair, the other news is the bullets match those from the Father O'Flaherty murder, so we definitely are looking at the same person doing both."

"And perhaps with the second murders, things got out of hand then, sir, is that it?"

"Now you're thinking like a detective, O'Rorden." Seamus smiled and then asked, "Is it cake you're eating there?"

"Yes, sir, it's very nice, it's homemade, would you like some?"

"No, I'm fine, thank you, but I've never seen anyone put away as much cake as you and that's the truth."

"Ach well, there's always time for cake, sir, so there is."

"So, it seems O'Rorden, so it seems."

O'Rorden popped another piece of cake into his mouth and smiled.

"Well O'Rorden, as it's a bit of slow day right now why don't you go and get yourself a replacement for the suit Liam O'Shea ruined, I'll sign off on the expense."

"Really, sir? I thought maybe you were joking."

"I don't joke about things like that, it was damaged in the line of duty and the Garda should buy you a new one, it's all there is to it."

"Well if you're sure?" O'Rorden looked pleased.

"Yes, go on with you. O'Flynn can drive you and help you pick out a nice one." Seamus said kindly.

O'Rorden needed no second bidding and collecting Kathy O'Flynn in short order he headed off to town.

Seamus sat back in his desk pondering where they went from here. Two potential suspects were now not suspects after all, though to be fair it was only the perfume which first implicated them and then it turned out to be very popular. That fact Kerry was no longer in the running for the murderer was a matter of some joy to him.

If Liam had been the murderer this would probably have broken her, so it was just as well it wasn't the case either. Liam was in enough hot water as it was, and he wondered exactly where Liam was and who he was with. Someone must be hiding him, but they had no idea who. The search might help with that, but it depended if he had left any clues of that nature. For example, if he had left a laptop then it would be a mine of information. Seamus thought it unlikely. Liam wasn't stupid. He could have easily slipped in and out of his flat between the shooting and sending a team round to check. If he had then probably he'd have taken anything like a laptop with him. Seamus would ask Kerry if she minded him searching Liam's room at the pub when he got back there later. It was most likely he had some stuff permanently there, such as the gun. However, once again Seamus wasn't optimistic about finding anything of much assistance.

He looked again at the photofit of the murderer, there was something nagging at the back of his brain about this. It wasn't really accurate enough to trigger a full-blown recollection of what he was trying to think of. He put it aside knowing sometime, somewhere it would come to him. He hoped they might have more luck with the children's home if they could find out anything about it and then if they could locate the records.

* * *

Another person who was mightily pissed at Liam's disappearance was Mistress Dana. She had certainly seen the news and wondered how he could have been such a fool. She also wondered why he didn't come to her? After all, she was in Dublin, and she bet he was too. She had tried calling and texting but to no avail. Of course, he probably had his mobile off, she finally reasoned, otherwise they could track him with it and geolocate him.

Nevertheless, he could have contacted her, she would have helped him. She bet he was with another woman and it made her feel very jealous. Something she had vowed never to be. She cared about Liam, actually, she cared very much now she realised. That was rare, she never cared for anyone, especially not a man, not since all the bad things had happened. She was very annoyed and had taken her frustration out on the client she was servicing. She had made particularly effective use of her riding crop and he was now standing in the corner with his nose to the wall. This was one of the things he apparently enjoyed.

All of her clients were not clergymen, not by a long chalk. Her discreet list of patrons was long and varied. They all willingly paid her very high fees and she had amassed a good deal of money as a result. She owned the house from which she plied her trade and a much more besides. It also helped one of her clients was also a very good tax accountant. He was happy to accept non-financial remuneration.

She was not breaking the law, however, and since, she did not overtly offer sex then the clients were not breaking the law either by paying for it, which they otherwise could have done. None of her clients would dare go public on their little peccadillos, especially the priests. It put her in a unique position and as a dominatrix, she always remained in control. She did relax her no sex rule sometimes, depending on the client and how she felt. Although it was a job to her, there was definitely also an element of sexual arousal, undertones of things now deeply ingrained in her psyche. Mistress Dana realised she could probably never live a normal life.

Shrugging off these thoughts, Mistress Dana sat on the bed and addressed her client.

"Right, turn around, I hope you've learned your lesson."

He turned to face her, his eyes glittering through the gimp mask he wore at his request. He was otherwise naked. She noticed he was sporting a massive erection.

"I hope you've not been playing with yourself," she told him sternly.

"No, Mistress."

"Good, and what are we going to do with that monstrosity?" she asked him.

"I don't know, Mistress."

"Well, I'll decide later, in the meantime I don't think you've really learned your lesson at all, get over here now."

He obeyed and stood in front of her.

She liked this particular client and tried hard to please him. He was an ordinary bloke who wanted to be dominated, not like those priests. The priests had particular needs, to be punished for the things they had done. As far as she could tell, this fellow had done nothing bad at all. However, the game was the game.

"You've been very naughty, you've not been punished enough by a long chalk, so I'm going to put you over my knee and give you a good spanking." Mistress Dana informed him brandishing a rather mean looking ivory hairbrush. Apparently, this was his favourite and she had allowed him to choose the implements before the session since she was feeling kind, and she had a soft spot for this particular client.

"Yes, Mistress," her client sounded very gratified to hear this.

"Go on then, get over my knee right now and let's see what you're made of."

Her client obeyed, settled himself comfortably and Mistress Dana got down to business.

* * *

By the end of the day, things had moved no further forward. The ballistics report had come back for Liam's gun and it did not match the bullets from the murder weapon. Having this in black and white was a relief to Seamus. There could be no doubt now they were looking for someone other than Liam regarding the murders at least.

The team working on the children's home was still out, so there was no news on that front. Duffy had his nose buried in Father O'Flaherty's confession and was writing copious notes by the looks of it. It was dinner time and Seamus realised he was hungry. He decided to go back to the pub to eat and then probably he should return to the office to see if there was any further news.

Kerry was pleased to see him when he arrived, and it was always something to look forward to.

"Is there any sign of Liam?" she asked him anxiously.

"I'm afraid not, sweetheart, he wasn't at his flat, but a team has been to search it. I will tell you the minute we find out anything about where he is."

"OK, I wasn't expecting you'd find him so quickly to be honest." She looked a little disappointed for a moment but then Seamus noticed a mischievous look steal into her expression. He quizzed her about it.

"And, what are you looking all so secretive about, Ms Kerry O'Shea?"

"Nothing." But her secret smile betrayed her.

"Oh, nothing is it, well let's see if I can't tease it out of you then."

Seamus gathered her into his arms, and she responded willingly. Their lips met, and they kissed, just as they kissed every day now but to Seamus, it always seemed better each time they did. Kerry was smiling at him when their lips parted.

"So? What are you smiling about?" he asked her with a twinkle in his eyes.

"You, I am smiling about you, now come on let's eat."

With that, he had to be satisfied. His attention was claimed by a roast chicken dinner. As this happened to be a favourite of his, he put his thoughts to one side and concentrated on the excellent fare. Enjoyment of food was something he learned from his Dad, who had often said to him to do 'less talking, and more eating'. Seamus found out this wasn't simply a ploy to keep him quiet as a child, but a way of helping him to see you can enjoy something more if you focus your whole attention on it. His father always said they were blessed with a good woman and good food, and as such, they should take time to appreciate it. His father was a simple man of simple pleasures. Seamus thought at times there was a lot to be said for it, in this modern complex world.

"How's the case?" Kerry broke into his reverie.

"It's OK, we've not got another suspect yet, but I guess you can say we've made a lot of progress in eliminating them."

"So, you haven't locked anyone else up yet?" she said pointedly, but her eyes were smiling.

"Only you." He laughed.

"Oh you!" She couldn't help laughing too.

"It's a difficult case, but I am sure we will make a breakthrough soon."

"That sounds like public relations."

"It is." He laughed again. "This is a tough nut to crack Kerry and no mistake."

"You'll do it I am sure you will." She was looking at him with the deep affection of someone who cared, someone who had every confidence in him because of how she felt about him.

He sighed changing the subject. He was a modest man and though he never doubted his own abilities, he didn't shout about them either. He was good at his job, he knew. But he felt embarrassed when others pointed it out, or rather, self-conscious.

"You know, you are a fantastic cook."

"Thank you." She smiled.

"I can cook too you know, you're going to have to let me cook for you someday."

"Is that so? A man who can cook, sounds promising."

"We all have hidden talents," he said quietly.

"Really? Tell me more, DI Gallway."

"Later, later, I probably should get back to the office just for a little while." He had polished off his meal and was feeling replete but also guilty other officers were probably still working. However, in reality, Seamus worked hard and did more than his fair share of hours on the job.

"Oh, should you now?" Kerry's dropped her voice a little lower and sexier. She rose from her seat and moved round to his side.

"Well, I was thinking I probably should."

"Were you, were you really? And what if I had other plans?" She was standing in front of him now, looking at him from under lidded eyes, in a way he found hard to resist.

"What plans might they be?" Seamus stood up too and moved in closer to her.

"Oh, well now that's for me to know and for you to find out."

"Is that right?" Their faces were now very close and lips nearly touching, their voices in a whisper.

Seamus wasn't sure how it happened but somehow in the blink of an eye, Kerry had handcuffed his left wrist to her right one. It took him by surprise.

"Kerry! What do you think you are doing?" he demanded.

"Oh, Di Gallway, I'm placing you under arrest."

"What? Hang on now, I'm the Garda officer here." He protested but only half-heartedly because she was now regarding him with the sexiest of expressions.

"I'm going to be taking you for some close questioning," she told him, "And I've got the key right here, so if you want to take these cuffs off, you're going to have to retrieve it, oh yes." With that, she dropped the key to the cuffs into her cleavage. She smiled but her meaning was unmistakable.

"How long have you been planning this?" He wanted to know, smiling back.

"Oh, not long, but I told you, you were going to pay, didn't I?"

He laughed out loud at this. "OK, you got me there, what happens now?"

"I'm taking you to my room for further interrogation."

"Lead the way, as you see I'm in your power," he tried to sound resigned but in reality, he was filled with sudden anticipation. The exigencies of the office and the case forgotten.

* * *

Kerry's room was all whites and creams, with splashes of colour. She eagerly dragged Seamus up the stairs and into her boudoir as if she could hardly wait another second longer. And the truth was she couldn't. She had been thinking about this moment for most of the day. About him, in her arms, in her bed, making love. There was no way he was returning to the office if she had anything to do with it, she thought with resolution. At least not tonight.

She locked the door behind them and he raised an eyebrow at her. It was a trick he had, but she found it incredibly sexy. She found him incredibly sexy too, almost unbearably so at times.

"What happens now?" he asked her, although he could very well guess.

"This."

She pulled him close and began to kiss him with unbridled passion. This was more, something more than he had ever previously felt from her. Perhaps, she had been holding something back, they both had. But now she was now unleashed. He liked it. He loved it. Her free hand

355

snaked under his shirt and the sheer electricity of her touch hit him, just as it had the time in the corridor before. Without hesitation, his own hand reached into her blouse running over her naked skin. It felt soft and also hot. So hot. She gasped at his touch, loving the feel of his hands on her. Delicious sensations were already coursing through her body, making her want him all the more.

Urgently, Kerry pulled him over to the bed. Her need overriding everything. They sat down awkwardly. She cursed under her breath at the handcuffs, which had been her stupid idea. Now she just wanted them off, so she could cut loose.

"Is this the interrogation then?" he teased.

"Part of it, but there is more, a lot, lot more."

Her voice was full of lust, lust for him, and the need she had and the anticipation that finally it would be fulfilled. They kissed again, more fervently. His free hand found its way up her back reaching for her bra. It came undone with a snap.

"Goodness, DI Gallway, it seems like you've had a bit of practice at that." She giggled.

"You don't want to know."

The keys to the cuffs had now dropped from her cleavage. He picked them up and hastily unlocked the handcuffs. Now she was free, Kerry kicked off her shoes and seeing it, Seamus did the same. The cuffs slid to the floor. With their hands now freely roaming over each other, she pulled him down onto the bed, Seamus kissing deeply all the while, their limbs entwining. There was no finesse about their lovemaking; this was full on, unbridled, lustful, joyful steaming sex. Seamus was frantically trying to remove her buttons anxious to get her naked and she was doing the same to his shirt.

"Oh, God!" Kerry said in frustration when they wouldn't undo fast enough. "Let me."

They both sat up and then simultaneously shed their clothing as quickly as they could, almost ripping it off themselves. Seamus could finally see her naked body and his eyes widened in admiration. Kerry was fairly slim and well proportioned, and age had kind to her. Her skin was still smooth and her breasts full, even a little pert. To him she was perfect.

"Go on," she coaxed him, putting his hands on them, "They're not all mine unfortunately, I had them done, I wanted nice breasts."

"I can vouch for the fact they are more than nice." He cupped them gently in his hands and ran his tongue over her nipples.

"Oh, Seamus," was all she said.

Her mouth was urgently reaching for his and he responded filled with desire. Once more they lay together, she enjoyed the firmness of his naked body against hers. Kerry moved her hands down to explore the roundness of his bottom. He moaned in response as she squeezed his buttock cheeks. Each had wanted this moment for so long and had been holding themselves back from it. Now, they could not get enough of each other. Their hands roamed each other's naked skin in a frantic effort to feel it all, take it all in.

Kerry could feel the hardness of Seamus now pressing against her thigh, and he was very hard indeed. She knew she was wet and feeling incredibly wanton.

"Take me, please, just take me," she whispered to Seamus, unable to bear it any longer.

He needed no second bidding and was inside her in moments, moving slowly but there was an urgency in his loins. It was just too much. He began to go faster, unable to curb himself, and then harder, as if to plumb the very depths of her.

"Oh God, Seamus, I have wanted you so much, I wanted you to feel you so much... you have no idea..." She was gasping now, with every thrust. He filled her completely, she felt as if the moment would simply devour her very soul.

"I wanted you too, Kerry, more than you can ever know..." he managed to say, swept away by the intensity of it all. Without warning she began to climax, her legs wrapped around his back pulling him to her tightly. He too could hold it no longer and his own explosive orgasm took over.

For a long while they lay like that, covered in sweat. Kerry holding him with all her might, as if she never wanted to let him go. Her cheek against his cheek, their breathing starting to slow and normalise. Their bodies eventually began to relax, until they gently eased around and lay side by side facing each other. Their arms and legs still wrapped around each other.

"That was delicious," she told him.

"Like a scrumptious apple pie?"

Kerry laughed at his food analogy, he was funny. It was one of the things she loved about him.

"Much, much more scrumptious than that," she said emphatically.

"I'm glad."

There was silence for a while and Kerry was just looking at him. He could see the love in her eyes, which had gone soft and incredibly blue. Then she spoke.

"I'm falling for you, Seamus, you do know it don't you?" Her voice was low, almost a whisper. Kerry was direct, she didn't believe in being ambiguous about her feelings, too many chances were lost with hesitation. This was a chance she definitely didn't want to lose.

"I know," Seamus said quietly, "I do know you are."

"I don't mind if you're not." Then she amended her statement, "at least not yet."

"So, you are going to start minding it soon?" he joked gently.

"Oh you!" She poked her tongue out.

"I'm not going anywhere," he said it sincerely, and she knew he didn't just mean his location.

Kerry didn't have to ask him if he loved her. She could see in his eyes, the affection, the unarticulated expression. She didn't want to push him. Not too hard. She could feel it, even if he wasn't ready to say it. Even if he didn't know it. She knew this had all happened so fast. One day soon, hopefully, he would be ready to say it.

"You know I wanted you from the first moment I saw you," Seamus smiled.

"Really?"

"Yes, I saw this beautiful, special, sexy, incredible woman."

"I bet you say that to all the girls."

"No, no I don't. You're different, Kerry, to anyone I've known, when I said you are special, you really are."

"Thank you. You're special too, a special kind of special."

She kissed him again, and he returned the kiss and it became a long slow deep moment of connection.

"Where did you get those handcuffs by the way?" Seamus asked her at length.

"Oh, Kathy O'Flynn was kind enough to lend me a pair." Kerry was laughing.

"Was she now, perhaps I should be having words with Sergeant O'Flynn."

D. R. BAILEY

"Come on now, Seamus, we women have to stick together, so we do."

"Great, so half the office will probably know about it by now."

"Oh no, I think Kathy will be very discreet. She might tell Connor though." She laughed.

"That's all I need." He rolled his eyes. "Now, are we finished with your erm, interrogation, or is there more?"

"Oh, DI Gallway, there's a lot more, a lot, lot more, it's going to take a long time, days, in fact, weeks even..." she said innocently.

"Is that so?" He kissed her again.

"Yes, it's so, in fact, I may never complete my investigation."

"And is this another part of your inquiry?" he asked as Kerry began to climb on top of him.

"Oh yes, I've got to cover all of the angles."

He smiled as she began to make love to him once more, beginning with a gentle rocking motion it startled a moan of pleasure from his lips.

"This time I'm in control." She breathed enjoying the feel of him.

"Be my guest," was all he said, but he was still smiling and already losing himself in the moment.

DAY 8

The day began like any other day, with Seamus waking before his alarm. But this day was different. Emotionally, physically. It was almost as if someone had painted the world in brighter colours, or at least it was how it felt. There had been something about Kerry from the moment she had entered his world, that morning which seemed so long ago but in reality, was only a matter of days. Was this how it happened, true love? The work of an instant? Perhaps it was something like fate.

Seamus wasn't given to pondering too deeply on life in general. Not because he wasn't a deep thinker, but because he wasn't prone to the self-sabotage like so many are. Seamus was brought up a Catholic but had learned more, he felt, from eastern philosophies like Buddhism. He was well read, in his spare time, and had studied many texts. Seamus tried to always embrace change and look for positive changes. If something was good, he let it be good. One thing he took from his eclectic philosophical reading was a saying attributed to Buddha "Every morning we are born again. What we do today matters most."

With Kerry, something sparked, crackled, snapped and popped. She was like the Yin to his Yang. He couldn't explain it but also found he didn't need to. If Kerry was indeed "The One" then he would be a fool to walk away from it. Many girls had been through his life it was fair to say, he wasn't proud of it but it was the reality. None of them except his first love had really meant anything to him except in passing. If sex was a form of meditation, then he would have excelled in that department. But today, here right now, lying with his eyes closed in Kerry's bed, he knew he was a gold medal winner. If this was to be, then somehow, they would work out the details. That was all it took.

He opened his brown eyes and turned his head to find her blue ones looking at him. She smiled, and he returned her smile.

"Hello you," she said to him.

"Hello," he replied.

"What were you thinking about just then? With your eyes closed and the smile playing on your lips, Seamus Gallway?"

"About you."

"Good things I hope?"

"Very good things."

"How good?"

"This good."

His lips met hers and his fingers came up to ruffle her tousled hair. They pulled each other close into a warm embrace. The embrace immediately became more passionate, as their bodies inflamed with desire. Wordlessly and almost without thought, they began to make love. Moving together slowly and then faster, with an unhurried urgency. They locked eyes as Seamus thrust himself deeply into her, both of them breathing deep and ragged. Then it was over, perhaps all too soon but in a wave of consuming pleasure and ending on a kiss.

"That was nice," Kerry said a little while after they just lay together quietly.

"Yes, it was more than nice though."

"Apple pie?"

"With custard."

"Mmm."

"But I'm going to have to get up, sweetheart."

Her eyes flew open wide.

"Did you just call me, sweetheart?"

"Yes, I did, because you are," he kissed her then, "my sweetheart."

She traced the outline of a heart on his forearm and kissed him gently.

"I'm sorry, but I really do have to get up and go to work."

"Oh well, there's always later," she said.

"You'll wear me out, Kerry O'Shea."

"I intend to."

With an effort, he got out of bed. His clothes were crumpled in a heap on the floor, a testament to the previous night's frenzied passion.

"Can I borrow a towel?"

"Sure, but you can shower here."

"Yes, but my clothes are in my room."

"Well, perhaps we need to change that."

"OK," he said without demur.

"You can sleep here, in fact, I want you to, in fact, you better had, Seamus Gallway, I'm not taking no for an answer."

"OK, OK. I surrender," he laughed.

"Really?" She was suddenly shy.

"Yes really, I would like it very much. But you should let me keep my room."

"Why?" she demanded. "So you can escape?"

"No." He was still laughing. "Because the Garda is paying for it and you may as well have the money."

"Oh, I see." Her face was thoughtful. "Good thinking, DI Gallway, I can see why you are a detective."

"Oh, you can, can you. Perhaps I should demonstrate it a bit more comprehensively then."

He looked as if he was about to get back into bed with her, and she squealed.

"Oh no, you don't. Go on with you now, go and get changed. I'll get up and sort out your breakfast. I've got to do that anyway for the other guests."

"Oh, yes, yes OK, you do your duty, Ms O'Shea."

He gathered up his clothes, wrapped a towel around his waist and headed for the door.

"I'll give you duty!"

"Oh, I hope so, I very much hope so, but later."

"Oh you!"

He left and shut the door behind him, and then popped his head back around it.

"What now?" she laughed.

"You better give those handcuffs back to Kathy then, or better still, I'll take them."

"Oh you!"

A pillow headed in his direction and harmlessly hit the closing door as he beat a hasty retreat.

* * *

Showered, trimmed and suited, Seamus presented himself in Kerry's parlour. She was busy making breakfast for several guests, but she smiled at him and he kissed her briefly.

"Do you want a hand? You look a bit busy," he enquired.

"No, no you sit down and besides you'll mess up your suit, and we don't want that."

"Ach no come on, here let me help you." He put his arms around her waist and hugged her.

"Is this what you call helping?"

He laughed and squeezed her tighter.

"Fine, then take these plates to those journalists out there in the dining room."

If the journalists were surprised to see Seamus serving their food, they didn't show it. He didn't get away lightly, however.

"Are you doing a bit of moonlighting there, Inspector?" said one.

"Ach you know, I like to keep busy, so I do."

"I would have thought you were busy enough. You could try catching the murderer instead, how about that?"

"There goes 'my be nice to the press week'." Seamus joked starting to leave with the tray of full plates.

"Hey, you can leave the food now you've brought it," the reporter complained.

"Never satisfied you lot." Seamus laid the plates on the table.

"We'll be satisfied when you catch the murderer."

"I'll be satisfied when your paper prints something approaching facts," Seamus retorted with a grin.

"Touché, Inspector, touché. Thanks for the breakfast though, very nice."

"I'll let Kerry know, she's the one who cooked it."

"Kerry now, is it? Perhaps there is something more we should know about this, Inspector, is there?"

But he was talking to the air, Seamus had already left the room.

When Seamus returned to the parlour his breakfast was waiting and he sat down to eat. Kerry put some fried eggs on toast on the other side of the table and joined him.

"What were you doing in there? I thought you were just delivering the breakfast?"

"I was just having some friendly banter with the journalists."

"Friendly. I thought it would be mutually exclusive as far as journalists are concerned."

"Well, I make an effort, now and again."

She giggled at his answer. They ate in silence exchanging shy smiles and glances. It was as if they were teenagers who had just lost their virginity to each other. In a way, it felt the same. Something they had both wanted so badly and two people who obviously had more than just a smouldering desire for each other. This went much deeper and the consummation of it had simply served to bring them closer.

"I'll need to look at Liam's room," said Seamus when he had finished eating. "If you don't mind? I meant to ask you last night but we both know what happened there."

"Really? Did something happen last night?" Her eyes were teasing.

"I was kidnapped."

"Oh, my goodness, you should file a report maybe."

"If I do it'll be an A-plus." He laughed.

"What! I expect nothing less than an A star or even a distinction."

"Is that a fact?"

"Yes, Seamus Gallway, yes, it is, and I'll be demonstrating some of the finer points of why that is later."

"I'll look forward to it."

Kerry slid the handcuffs over to him with the key in them.

"You'll be wanting these, to return them I expect."

"Are you sure you won't be needing them?"

"No, I think probably the suspect will come willingly next time."

"I think you are right."

Seamus finished his coffee and rose from his chair, they kissed, and it was different again. Somehow more loving, more lingering than before.

"Come on," she said, "I'll show you Liam's room."

* * *

In spite of the morning's distractions, Seamus managed to get to the Garda station on time. Everyone was already there beavering away when he entered the office.

"Morning everyone, morning," he said airily. The others turned to look in surprise. They weren't quite used to this level of cheerfulness from Seamus first thing.

"What?" he protested at their expressions. "You look as though you've seen a ghost, surely I'm not usually that bad."

There was a murmur of laughter at this, but nobody ventured a comment. He sauntered over to his desk. O'Rorden was there talking to O'Flynn.

"Well now you're looking like you're in a good mood today sir, so you are," O'Rorden remarked.

"That I am O'Rorden, that I am." He paused and extracted the handcuffs from his pocket, he handed them to

O'Flynn. "Kerry said thanks for these by the way and asked me to return them."

A laugh was surprised out of O'Flynn and also O'Rorden, the cause of Seamus' sunny disposition had now been revealed.

"Did they come in useful, sir?" asked O'Flynn suppressing a smirk.

"Let's just say they certainly escalated things, in a good way. A very good way in fact."

"I'm glad to hear it, sir." O'Flynn smiled at him.

"Right then," said Seamus. "Let's get down to business."

He called the office to order and they assembled for the morning briefing.

"OK, so this is day eight of the investigation into the murders of Father O'Flaherty, Father Cooney and Mother Joan Margaret. Which to be honest is getting to be a bit of a mouthful. Does anyone have a suggestion for a shorter name?"

Several were forthcoming.

"Priest murderers."

"The Father Killings."

"Priest shootings."

"Confessional Killings."

Seamus thought for a moment and then continued.

"Good suggestions all but I like Confessional Killings the best. It has a certain ring to it. So, let's use it. Day eight then of the investigation into the Confessional Killings."

There was a murmur of approval at this, and Duffy was particularly pleased since it was his idea Seamus had gone with.

"I don't need to tell you the pressure is now on us to come up with a credible suspect. I know it's not been that long but it's always about this time people start to ask questions. We are not miracle workers. We just have to work a bit smarter. So, first things first. I examined Liam O'Shea's bedroom at the Baker's Arms today but there was nothing of interest, unfortunately. Do we have a report back from the search of his flat?"

"Yes, sir, we do." It was Healy. "They searched it thoroughly and apart from a very small amount of cannabis hidden in a plastic bag in the toilet, there was nothing of real interest, certainly not anything to reveal his whereabouts. No electronic devices were found, and we think he must have taken these with him, assuming he has any. We assume the drugs were for personal use, sir."

"Thank you, Healy. We can deal with the drug issue at a later stage and the DPP can decide whether to prosecute or not. I guess it depends on what happens in the meantime. I can stress Liam is not a priority for us. The ballistics report on his gun did not match those of the murder weapon. We obviously want to get him, we need to have him in custody, but we need to focus on the murders more. Now one thing about Liam, do we have his mobile number?"

Nobody answered and so Seamus continued, "OK, well it's a bit of an oversight but given everything which has gone on in the last day or so, I'm hardly surprised it fell through the cracks. Not to worry then, I will get his mobile number from his mother later on and then one of the team can obtain his phone records. Maybe it will help us locate someone who might know where he is or even be sheltering him. Once we've got those records, we can have someone working on the task. Moving on from Liam, the next most important issue is the children's home, do we have anything more on this at all?"

Aileen Hughes stood up to talk. "Yes, sir, as a matter of fact, we have. We have discovered a children's home called the 'Faith, Hope and Charity Catholic Home for Orphaned Children' ran since its formation in the early nineteen hundred's and was closed down around ten years ago now."

"Judging by the activities of Mother Joan Margaret there wasn't much faith, hope or charity going on there I would say," quipped Seamus.

"No, sir, apparently not because there were a number of abuse allegations raised, in fact so many the church closed it down. We have a lot of these cases recorded sir, but like the O'Flaherty ones, they were passed over to the church for further action. I guess the action was to shut it down."

"So it couldn't be investigated more like," Seamus said in frustration. "There seems to be a pattern here and I've seen it many times before. Abuse is reported and somehow the church manages to suppress the investigation, stop any charges being brought and covers it up. This time I hope we can bring someone to book over the amount and level of abuse committed. It doesn't help they are dead but never mind. Anyway, where did you find all this information?"

"Oh, in the library, sir. They have very extensive archives. The librarian was most helpful, she showed us where everything was, and it was very well catalogued. There were a lot of news articles and so forth which we've copied. We have a big file of those if you want to look at them."

"The librarian, Diana was it?" Seamus asked.

"Yes sir, that's right, why do you know her?"

"No, not really, I went there to borrow a book, she seemed a bit well to do, to be a librarian. Expensive tastes."

"Oh yes, sir, I noticed that I wondered how she could afford her Gucci outfit and so on."

Seamus nodded. Being a woman Aileen Hughes would have certainly noticed those things.

"OK, well fair enough. See if you can find anything more about her, check her on the criminal records database, you never know. I don't think she is a likely suspect, but you never can tell. Anyway, do you know where the actual files for the children's home are? Did you locate those?"

"No, sir, we think they would have gone back to the church. Maybe the Bishop of the Diocese would know?"

Seamus and O'Rorden exchanged significant glances. It looked like they would be paying the Bishop another visit.

"Good work, Hughes. O'Rorden and I will talk to the Bishop and see if we can get him to give up his records."

"Good luck with it, sir, we've tried phoning the Catholic church in Dublin and no joy so far, they said if there were any records then they would be confidential, off limits so to speak."

"Did they now? Well I think we've got a little bit more leverage with the Bishop, so I think we might meet with more success. Thank you, Hughes. So now then, Duffy, how's it going with Father O'Flaherty's confession?"

Duffy stood up as if this was his big moment.

"Well, sir, I'm about two-thirds of the way through it. It's a long document. I don't mind telling you sir that I'm shocked, absolutely shocked by the things I've been reading in there. I was brought up a good Catholic, sir, but this priest, now he's definitely a piece of work if you don't mind me saying it, sir."

"Not at all, Duffy, no that's pretty much exactly what he is. But anything so far which stands out at all?"

"Well, I've catalogued the incidents, sir, he confessed to. It's mainly about him, sir, and it's already quite bad. Father Cooney was mentioned, sir, several times and Mother Joan Margaret. Mainly in connection with some mutual abuse.

There was a couple of other priests, I've written them down to check up on them."

"They are probably dead," Seamus said, "Does it mention the Bishop at all?"

"Well now, sir, that it does, quite a few times as a matter of fact. It doesn't say he did anything, but he was certainly aware of it. There are a number of passages where the Father describes how he went to get absolution from the Bishop, so the Bishop would have known. He also notes the Bishop came apparently strictly as an observer to maybe two or three of the parties they had."

"Does it now, does it indeed?" Seamus was very interested.

"Well I haven't completely compiled it all yet, but I'll know a definite count soon or the incidents and so forth."

"Good work, Duffy, keep it up."

"Sir, I realise these other priests are dead, but does it make the Bishop an accessory, can he be prosecuted?"

"Well, Duffy, that's a matter for the DPP but what we do have at the moment is leverage, and with leverage we can get something out of the Bishop he doesn't want to give us, like those records."

"Yes sir, thank you, sir." Duffy sat down.

OK," concluded Seamus. "Before we break up the meeting let's focus today on wrapping up lines of inquiry, tie up loose ends. We're at a bit of a standstill so we need to generate some new leads and quickly. O'Rorden and I will go and get those files from the Bishop, and then we will have plenty to be getting on with. Are there any questions?"

There were none and everyone got back to work. Seamus turned to O'Rorden.

"I forgot to ask if you managed to get your suit," he said kindly.

"Oh yes, sir, Kathy helped me pick out a nice one."

O'Rorden handed over the receipt for the suit. Seamus glanced at it.

"I hope it's not too much, sir?"

"Not in the least, put in a requisition for expenses and I'll sign it off right away."

"Yes sir, thank you."

"Let's go then shall we and see the mighty or not so mighty fucking Bishop."

O'Rorden smiled at that, partly because he hoped Seamus would wipe the floor with the Bishop like last time and partly because he was hoping for some more delicious cake.

*　*　*

They drew up outside the Bishop's mansion once again having left the office almost straight after the meeting. If the ancient priest, who answered the door to them, was surprised to see them again so soon, he didn't show it. In short order, they were once more waiting on the magnificent ornate landing in the same gilded chairs as before. The priest had disappeared into the Bishop's office. They didn't have to wait long, however, before the priest emerged and ushered them into the Bishop's sanctum. A second visit did nothing to diminish the overriding splendour of the view and the office itself, with its ornate scrollwork and painted ceilings.

The Bishop appeared to be in excellent spirits and health, he rose from his desk in a jovial manner and walked over to greet them without any trace of the evident stiffness and soreness he had last time.

"Ah Inspector, Inspector, Inspector, and the Detective Sergeant too, back so soon, so nice to see you, won't you take some tea?" he enquired shaking them warmly by the hand.

"Coffee for me and tea for DS O'Rorden here please." Seamus was mindful of his junior's appetite for the Bishop's cake.

"Certainly, certainly, certainly, and I'll make sure there is plenty of the cake DS O'Rorden obviously enjoyed last time," the Bishop assured him.

"It was very good indeed," put in O'Rorden.

"I have the most excellent cook, now that I do, now please do take a seat and I will join you in a moment."

The Bishop went over and rang the bell and instructed the priest to obtain the necessary refreshments, before returning to sit opposite them without any obvious discomfort.

Seamus was moved to remark upon this.

"Well, we're glad to see you are looking better now Bishop, you seemed a little off colour last time we were here."

"Ach no, no, no, I just had a touch of the gout, I get it from time to time. Probably I should cut back on the after-dinner port, so I should." The Bishop laughed out loud at his own joke. Seamus and O'Rorden also did so out of politeness. They had exchanged looks after the gout was mentioned which indicated neither of them believed this explanation. It had looked a lot more serious than a touch of gout to them. How he had recovered so quickly was also very odd.

The priest returned with the refreshments and placed a large silver tray on the table. O'Rorden was overjoyed to discover two plates of different types of cake as well as biscuits.

"Well, now, go on, go on, go on, have some tea and some cake by all means," the Bishop invited them still continuing his friendly façade.

"I'll be mother, shall I?" offered O'Rorden and poured out the beverages. Seamus felt it would be churlish not to drink the coffee this time and so he sampled it pronouncing it to be very good. The Bishop assured him it came from Peru and was only the finest of blends. O'Rorden who had started on the cake stated it was definitely one of the very best he had eaten. The Bishop apparently lapped up all this flattery with much satisfaction. Seamus noted everything the Bishop had or talked about was only of the finest this or that, and rather than impressing him, considerably lowered his opinion of certain Catholic clergymen in general who apparently set more store by material possessions than the spiritual realm they purported to represent.

"So, what can I do for you officers this time?" the Bishop enquired after they had made some small talk.

"We're here about the Faith, Hope and Charity Catholic Home for Orphaned Children," Seamus said.

"Oh, that old place, it was closed down years ago, terribly old fashioned and out of date." The Bishop was offhand and dismissive.

"We know it was closed down, Bishop, it's why we are here."

"Well, I can't imagine what you would want with a closed down children's home, no I can't." A wariness had crept into the Bishop's expression.

"Oh, you can't? Well now let me enlighten you."

Recognising the tone in his boss' voice O'Rorden knew Seamus was just priming his powder for a serious onslaught. He was on his second slice of cake and once again ready to enjoy the spectacle.

"Well, now I wish you would, because as I said, it's closed, and I can't imagine why the Garda would be investigating it, that I don't."

"It was closed because of allegations of systematic abuse, something of which I am certain you are aware, Bishop, because you probably had a hand in closing it."

"Well, yes, now I'll grant you there were a few cases, now I think about it, undesirable sorts of things and so forth."

"And isn't it true the orphanage was run by Mother Joan Margaret?" Seamus changed tack.

"Yes, yes, it's true, poor Mother Joan Margaret so cruelly murdered God rest her soul. Such a kind soul too, yes so she was."

"Really? That's what you think is it? Mother Joan Margaret was a kind soul?"

"Of course, of course, of course, a kinder woman you've never meet, she wouldn't hurt a fly, loved the children in her care so she did."

"Loved them so much she beat them, and abused them?"

"Well now, DI Gallway, those sound like serious allegations, I don't know where you heard such heinous things about the sainted Mother, that I don't." The Bishop was starting to look a bit flustered now.

"Sainted Mother my arse. We heard them from one of her victims who was systematically beaten with a cane, a riding crop, a paddle and a leather strap by Mother Joan Margaret on an almost daily basis. The same victim who was also raped and assaulted by Father Cooney and beaten as well. The same victim from whom we have full statements, medical evidence and is in our protective custody."

The Bishop paused to take this in. It was obvious he was calculating what to say next.

"Well, yes, well, this is terrible news indeed if it is indeed true. Mother Joan Margaret, well now, I never would have thought it. She seemed such a kindly woman, so she did. If only I had known, if I had for one moment suspected, Mother Joan Margaret..."

Seamus cut him short, "Oh come on now, Bishop. You can stop all this play acting and drop the pretence. You know it is true and we know it. Stop prevaricating. I'm sure you were fully aware of allegations made against the home she ran and against Mother Joan Margaret herself. We know there were numerous complaints which like those against Father O'Flaherty also mysteriously never got taken any further."

O'Rorden once again in awe of Seamus' masterly interrogation technique was sipping his tea and contentedly eating the Bishop's cake.

"OK, OK, OK." The Bishop held up his hands in defeat. "OK you got me there, I did know about them, so I did. But as you know I can't discuss these things however and that's really why perhaps I seemed a bit uncooperative. It reflects badly on all of us this type of thing. You understand why I was reluctant to talk about it candidly I am sure."

Seamus sighed at this blatantly disingenuous statement by the Bishop.

"Bishop, we just want the truth. Do you now admit you closed the home down because of these allegations?"

"Well, yes, yes it was certainly part of it, it was definitely a factor, but it was also because it was no longer fit for purpose, it needed a lot of work, and was getting run down, and so forth."

"OK, thank you, Bishop, so in that case, you won't mind releasing the files on all of the children who were cared for if that's a word one can even use under the circumstances, and handing them over to us."

The Bishop looked thunderstruck, the smile wiped completely off his face. Seamus had nicely manoeuvred him into a corner and he knew it.

"Files, oh files you say. Files, is that what you are talking about?" he managed to say.

"Files, Bishop, I think you know what they are, and I think you know there would be files on every single child in that orphanage and I am pretty certain you have them."

"Well, now files, of course and if those files exist, and of course we can't be sure they do, well now those are church property and there would be all sorts of authorisations, certain authorisations to release them to the Garda, we would need assurances as to use and so forth and in writing, and this could go all the way up to the Pope himself." He looked somewhat triumphant by the end of this, thinking he had produced a clinching argument.

"Bullshit," Seamus replied losing patience.

The Bishop looked taken aback.

"What? What did you say?"

"I said, Bishop, it is absolute bullshit. It's a crock of absolute shit and no mistake. Authorisations. Don't make me laugh. I am pretty sure you can make those authorisations and I am pretty sure you can hand them over. This is a murder investigation, not some petty crime show. The murder of three of your own clergy. Whatever type of person they were or were not, they were still killed unlawfully. There is still a murderer on the loose out there. We don't know if the person might kill again or not, do you want it on your conscience? One of those children could now be the murderer, do you not understand that, and we need those files."

O'Rorden has lost count of the slices of cake he had consumed but they were very quickly diminishing on the tray. He knew he had had at least three cups of tea, however. He noticed Seamus had hardly touched his coffee but thought it politic not to mention it to Seamus who was now in full flow.

If the Bishop was in the least fazed by this speech, he tried not to show it. Instead, he held his hands up once again.

"Inspector, Inspector, Inspector. You have a very inflated idea of my powers here as a Bishop. I am just a minion of the church, a servant of God, and the Pope. I can't just give you the files as much as I want to, you really must understand. It's just out of my hands so to speak and very much in the lap of God himself."

Seamus was annoyed, but he still had one more trump card and was now about to play it. He stood up and decided to take a turn about the room. This allowed the Bishop to think he had won, but it was not the case, not by a long chalk. Seamus went over to the fireplace and stood leaning on it, as the Bishop had done the last time they were here. Seamus knew he still had plenty left in the tank, as it were, as the Bishop was about to discover.

"Let me tell you something, Bishop. I want you to cast your mind back to our last conversation, and in that conversation, you admitted you had faked a burglary because you were looking for something of Father O'Flaherty's. Is that not correct?"

"I did say something of the sort, yes, now I recall but I don't know why you should choose to bring it up again, that I don't."

"I'll tell you why, Bishop, I will certainly be more than happy to enlighten you even. The fact is we have found what you were looking for. Father O'Flaherty's confession, wasn't that it? And we have it in our possession. Well, over a hundred pages of it in fact."

"I am so happy to hear it, and in that case, perhaps you can hand it over, it is after all church property and it's confidential, sacrosanct," the Bishop said eagerly, far too eagerly for Seamus' liking.

"It makes interesting reading, so it does, one of my detectives is almost two-thirds of the way through it, we've got hard copies, soft copies, you name it, and you'll be pleased to know you get several mentions in it." Seamus smiled at him sweetly.

The Bishop did not look happy, he also stood up and came to the centre of the room.

"This is outrageous, it is church property, I demand you return it at once and delete all the copies," he said raising his voice, but it sounded very much like desperation.

"You are not in a position to demand anything, Bishop, not in the least, and we won't be handing it over to you and that's a fact." Seamus moved away from the fireplace and stood facing the Bishop squarely but very calmly.

O'Rorden realised there was only one slice of cake left and eagerly stuffed it into his mouth before contemplating eating the biscuits. His eyes were riveted on the scene playing out in front of him.

"Let me tell you something, so you plainly understand it. We have evidence you knew about these crimes and they are crimes, Bishop, make no mistake. Sexual abuse, rape, physical assault. Knowing about them makes you an accessory. Being an accessory means we can charge you with the crimes as if you committed them yourself."

"You'll never get away with it, the church has lawyers, we'll sue you, we'll..."

"You'll what, Bishop? You'll what?" Seamus started to pace the room. "Here are the facts. You know it and we know it. The church will abandon you, put you out to grass, and because, regardless of what happens in the courts, one way or another these things will get known. It's funny how accidentally the press gets hold of things like this and I am sure Father O'Flaherty's full confession would be something the press would love to get their hands on."

"You wouldn't dare!"

"Try me, Bishop, just you try me. This is a cushy number you've got here, is it not? How would it be if your world was to fall apart all because of someone else's crimes? Wouldn't be so great now, would it? Instead of drinking the finest coffee from Peru, you'd be drinking value brand from Tesco."

"What it is you want from me exactly?" The Bishop's shoulder's drooped, he knew he had lost.

"I'll tell you, Bishop. I can't tell if the DPP will take any of this further or not, but let's just say you start cooperating with us, handing us over all those files to help with this case, then it could be seen as a positive light perhaps. We might be willing to leave it all up to the DPP. However, let's say you keep on with this bullshit and non-cooperation, let's say you don't hand over the files. Then like I told you every department has leaks, nothing is safe or sacrosanct either. We have the best security we can of course, but you can never be sure, what goes missing."

Seamus kept the jubilation out of his voice. He knew you should never crow over an enemy in defeat because that was when they were most dangerous. He kept a straight face looking directly at the Bishop. The Bishop flinched from his gaze and stood silently for a moment, calculating, weighing up his options.

"OK, fine, fine, fine." The Bishop seemed to recover himself in no time, acting as if nothing had just happened, accepting he'd lost this round. "I mean if it was that important, Inspector, you just had to make it clear, no need for all this argy-bargy. I am the last man to argue with the Garda, now that I'm not. Nobody wants any trouble, least of all me. I'll tell you what we'll do, we'll get the files ready for you and then in a couple of days you can come back and get them."

"We'll take them now if it's all the same to you," said Seamus meaningfully. "We wouldn't want them to mysteriously go missing, now would we? Or the odd pages being omitted?"

It was the Bishop's last play and he took it in good part.

"Oh well, well, well, have it your way then. I'll have my assistant take you down directly to the archive wing and you can have all the files you want, take your pick. In the meantime, do sit down and finish your coffee, Inspector, in fact, I'll get you a fresh cup, and more cake, I see your colleague has certainly a taste for it, yes indeed."

Seamus settled back satisfied with the outcome and allowed more refreshments to be served. The Bishop settled once again into small talk and all was well with the world. In fact, the Bishop was feeling so magnanimous he even arranged for his cook to provide an entire cake for O'Rorden to take away with him, since, as the Bishop said, he liked it so much. This was a great compliment to the cook he assured O'Rorden who would be delighted to find such an appreciative guest in the Bishops house. O'Rorden was certainly particularly pleased with this result.

Once they finished, the Bishop and his assistant took them down several corridors and a flight of stairs to reveal a large dungeon-like room, with very high ceilings, there were files galore in boxes and on shelves. He pointed out the children's home ones and wished them well.

A sudden phone call had him departing with alacrity. He excused himself on the pretext one of his priests who happened to be on his final journey, as he called it, needed the last rites. Whether this was true or not Seamus didn't know but was happy not to have the Bishop fussing all over them while they took his files. Judging the quantity of files to be large, Seamus called the office and got O'Flynn to organise a van and another car tout suite. They arrived shortly and started loading up all the files.

"How on earth did you get him to give these up?" O'Flynn asked in wonder.

"Oh, he was just masterly, Kathy, just masterly," O'Rorden told her.

"There was a bit of negotiation, in which we managed to get the upper hand this time," Seamus said.

"I'm impressed, sir, that I am."

Seamus and O'Rorden left the Bishop's residence once the files had safely left the premises with O'Rorden clutching a tin of his precious cake. He mused on whether perhaps he should share it with the office. Seamus noting the sadness in his voice at this thought told him to take it home and share it with Kathy.

"To the victor go the spoils, O'Rorden, to the victor go the spoils."

"Thank you, sir. You certainly were the victor today by a long chalk."

"Yes, O'Rorden, but I've also made an enemy if I'm not mistaken. Don't underestimate the Bishop, he's a sly dog. I'll have to be watching my back."

"Don't worry, sir, I've got your back too," O'Rorden assured him.

"Yes, thanks, O'Rorden, I appreciate it, I really do."

It came as a surprise to Seamus how much he felt at home here and with these pleasant people. In Dublin, you tended to hold the provincials in some sort of contempt. Consider them to be country bumpkins. But this was far from being the case. O'Rorden was sharp as a button, even if he couldn't make coffee. On balance, Seamus was prepared to make allowances for this deficiency.

"Did you see all those files, the ones we didn't take, sir?" O'Rorden asked him as they drove back the Ballysruth.

"Yes. God knows what incriminating crap is in them. It would take a month of Sundays to sift through it and more, and then most of the people in them are likely dead."

"You're probably right, but somehow I feel it's wrong nobody can even take a look."

"There's a lot of ills in this world, O'Rorden, I've learned to deal with one's I can actually do something about."

"That's a good philosophy, sir, so it is."

"Let's get some coffee on the way home, I think we've earned it."

O'Rorden couldn't help but agree with this admirable idea.

* * *

By the time they returned to the station, the files had preceded them, and the detectives and officers were already starting to sort through them and organise them into some semblance of order. From there, they could be catalogued and then the real work would begin. Sifting through each one, checking painstakingly whether the person was living or dead and then compiling a list of potential suspects. This could take a few days Seamus knew but he also figured this was the best chance they had. He wanted to be sure they caught the murderer before they decided to kill again.

"Alright listen up," Seamus said raising his voice. The room went quiet and everyone stopped what they were doing.

"I am sure you know this but these files are probably our number one chance of finding the murderer. Everything points to a motive of revenge. We can particularly tell this from the manner in which the last killings were carried out and also what we know about the abusive nature of the murder victims. Make no mistake, these people were grade one abusers, if you want to put a label on it. If there was a Doctorate for abusers, they would have one. Mother Joan Margaret, in particular, was evidently running a master class in handing out brutal punishments, subjecting her charges to extreme physical violence in the form of beatings with many different implements as far as we can tell. We can only guess at the accompanying psychological abuse and the resulting psychological harm which would have happened as a consequence.

"If she was abusing the housekeeper at Father Cooney's then we can safely surmise that she had done it many times before at the orphanage. We can only guess at the hellhole it was. And from this appalling environment, the murderer must have emerged, one person who has spent their life plotting to kill the people who abused her. We know she's a woman, so that eliminates any boys for a start. She is in those files, we just have to find her before she kills again. Anything you find, anything of significance, let me know right away. I'm counting on everyone here. We are going to do this. Have you got that?"

The officers who had been listening intently agreed with enthusiasm. Seamus had a way with him when he got going.

"See what I told you there, Kathy," O'Rorden said to O'Flynn within earshot of Seamus. "Winston Churchill, he's got nothing on DI Gallway here, so he hasn't."

"Ach will you cut that out now." But Seamus was smiling.

"True, sir, it is. You see, Kathy, and modest with it."

"He's right, sir, you inspire all of us," O'Flynn chipped in.

"You guys." Seamus blushed.

"What's next on the agenda then, sir?" O'Rorden asked him, changing the subject.

"I'm going to phone the DCS and bring him up to speed. Then I'll pop back to see Kerry and get the mobile number off her. In the meantime, if you wouldn't mind lending a hand here, and I'll get stuck into it too when I get back."

"Sure, sir, I will, but you know you could just text Kerry and..." he stopped because Kathy O'Flynn had dug him sharply in the ribs, he looked around at her. "What did you, oh, ohhhh righttt, well, of course, sir, I am sure it'll be easier to get the number in person and well look at that now, it's nearly lunchtime."

O'Flynn smiled at him and gave him a wink. He winked back. Seamus pretended not to notice.

"I'll be back soon," he said.

"No rush, sir, I am sure we can manage while you do what you've got to dooo..." O'Rorden tailed off noticing Seamus' raised eyebrow.

"Come on, Connor, leave the man be, let's get stuck into this job right here."

"Oh yes, right you are, Kathy, right you are."

Seamus shook his head and laughed. After a quick glance around at the hive of activity in the office, he left the building.

* * *

Seamus walked back to the pub and dialled Brogan's number on the way.

"Brogan," came the familiar gruff voice.

"It's DI Gallway here, sir."

"Ah, Seamus, now I was just wondering when I was going to get an update. I've got the Assistant Commissioner asking questions, wondering why we haven't caught the murderer yet."

"I was waiting for that." Seamus rolled his eyes. "It's eight days sir, come on, you know how complex this investigation has been."

"I know, I know that, Seamus, so I do. Don't worry I managed to fob him off for a few more days, but what is the situation down there, have you any more leads at all?" Brogan sounded anxious. The AC had most likely been buttonholing him more than he was letting on. It was typical of the higher-ups to demand results, even when they knew exactly how difficult these were to get.

"Sir, we are certainly hoping to get something from our latest breakthrough." Seamus was sounding positive.

"Breakthrough, yes that's what I like to hear, what exactly was it then, Seamus?"

"Sir, we have retrieved all of the files from the children's home run by Mother Joan Margaret and recently closed down."

"Is that right? And how did you manage to get hold of those?"

"Ah, sir, now that's a story, yes indeed." Seamus was smiling to himself recalling it.

"I like a good story, Seamus, so go on tell me what happened, I'm all ears, so I am."

"Well sir, it involves the Bishop."

"The Bishop is it? Now you're talking." Brogan was well aware of how many problems the Bishop had already caused the investigation.

Seamus related the events of their interview with the Bishop and how he had persuaded him to part with the files, which he originally claimed did not exist. Brogan was chuckling profusely on the other end of the line. He particularly liked the part where Seamus had used the confession to effectively coerce the Bishop into cooperating.

"Ach, Seamus, you've made my day. That's priceless. It's about time we got one over on the fucking clergy. I've had it the with the Archbishop bending my ear every other day and now I've really got something to send him running for cover with that confession, I'll have to take a proper look at it, so I will." Seamus had ensured his boss had already been sent a copy knowing Brogan would appreciate it and could use the ammunition.

"But, sir," Seamus asked. "What are we going to do about all this abuse we've discovered? They are serious crimes. I know some of the perpetrators are dead, but for fuck's sake the church shouldn't be allowed to get away with this, they've covered it up all this time."

"I know, Seamus, I know, and the fact is I don't have any idea at this moment. This type of stuff will probably go way above my pay grade before I can give you any kind of answer. But look at it this way, you've now got quite a lot of leverage over the Bishop and that's good, because don't be fooled, you'll have a made an enemy there for sure."

"I am aware of it, sir."

"The problem is, Seamus, people like the Bishop can be useful to us, particularly if we've got him where we want him. I don't pretend to like it, but that's the way it is I'm afraid."

"It's not right, sir, so it isn't," Seamus protested, his sense of justice was certainly nettled by their seeming powerlessness.

"Seamus, some things we can't do on our own, and sometimes we have to just leave them."

"I know, sir, but I'd like to take those bastards down some day if I could."

Brogan laughed a hollow laugh. "Well if you get the chance let me know, in the meantime, just carry on, Seamus, and get the murderer off the streets."

"I intend to, sir." Seamus disconnected the line.

Seamus had now reached the Baker's Arms and he put the phone back into his pocket. O'Rorden was right, it was lunch time and Kerry would most likely be in her kitchen no doubt involved in preparing it. The pub had a main kitchen as well as Kerry's kitchen, at times of high demand, Kerry had explained she had a chef to handle lunch and dinner service in the main kitchen. But when it was quiet, she did it herself. It was also because she loved to cook, so she would always prepare some of the meals, like her pies, in advance. Most often though, Seamus knew, Kerry did the breakfasts, particularly when there were not many guests. He hoped today was a day he might catch her alone, and his pulse quickened as he entered the pub. He headed for Kerry's parlour and private kitchen.

She was there, with her apron on, fiddling with something on the stove. A strand of her blond hair had come loose and hung down across the side of her face. She was looking intently at the contents of a saucepan. She was wearing a loose off the shoulder pink blouse, and blue jeans without shoes.

"Do you know how sexy you look in that apron?" he said after standing there quietly watching her for a few moments in appreciation.

Kerry looked up with a start and almost dropped the wooden spoon she was using to stir the white sauce she was preparing.

"Oh my God, Seamus, don't do that you made me jump, so you did!"

"Don't do what? Don't come back and surprise you?" He started to move towards her.

"Well, not that no, but well, yes don't make me jump."

"How about I make you do something else instead?" he enquired continuing to walk purposefully in her direction.

"Now, now, Seamus Gallway, I'll have you know I'm armed and dangerous!" Kerry brandished the wooden spoon at him.

"Is that right is it, dangerous, are you?" Seamus having reached the stove, calmly took the spoon out of her hand and put it back in the pot, he leaned across the hob, turned off the element, and moved the saucepan to one side.

"Seamus, what you are doing? It took me ages to make the sauce and now it's going to be ruined, I…"

His mouth came down on hers and he gathered her up in his arms kissing her deeply and with wild abandon. She flamed inside immediately, the sauce was forgotten.

"Well," she managed to say, "I suppose I can always make another one."

"Never mind about the sauce," he whispered his voice loaded with passion.

In one move he lifted her up and her legs wrapped around his waist. Still kissing her all the while, he positioned her on an empty part of her kitchen worktop. She didn't object as his hands moved swiftly down to her jeans and removed them in one quick manoeuvre, along with her panties. Her hands undid the buckle of his belt with unseemly haste and pushed his trousers and boxers down, revealing he was more than ready. She pulled him into her and then he was inside her. She was holding him close, her cheek against his cheek.

"Oh my God, Seamus, oh my God," was all she could manage as he began to thrust into her, hard and fast. It was guttural, visceral sex. Passionate but quick and it was over in a few moments, leaving the two of them gasping in mutual pleasure to the finale. If Kerry had hoped to finish quietly, there was no such luck, both of them were loud and voluble at the last.

They held each other panting, catching their breath, before kissing briefly and restoring their clothing to its rightful place.

"Well, Seamus Gallway, now that was a surprise indeed!" Her eyes danced.

"A good one I hope?" he raised an eyebrow.

"A very good one," she assured him. "But are you going to do this every lunchtime?"

"I can't promise every lunchtime." He laughed. "But probably now and then."

"Thank God for that, you'll wear me out otherwise with your surprises."

"I thought it was you who was going to wear me out."

"Oh you!"

391

He kissed her again softly and gently, and she kissed him back.

"Sorry, I just couldn't help it, sweetheart."

"I like it when you call me that," she said shyly

"Sweetheart." He smiled again.

"Well, now you are here, you might as well have some lunch, I expect you are hungry."

"Well, yes, I am a little."

"You sit down, and I'll get you something, then I'll have to redo the sauce you ruined."

"Oh, I ruined, is it now? Is it that how it's going to be is it?"

"Yes, you! I'm the woman and so I couldn't possibly have done it, go on, go and sit down." But she was laughing and so was he. He took his usual place at the table and looked at her lovingly. Her eyes met his softened by what she saw there.

"Incorrigible!" he said.

"Oh you!" Kerry poked out her tongue at him and started plating up his meal.

* * *

Seamus was whistling somewhat tunelessly when he returned from lunch. He had not been away long but was in a startlingly good mood. A fact which wasn't lost on the rest of his team. It earned him a few more curious and knowing looks. He was sure soon his romance with the owner of the Baker's Arms would be common knowledge if it wasn't already. He didn't care, now Kerry was no longer part of their inquiries, it didn't matter. For the first time in a long time, he didn't feel the need to conceal his feelings nor a relationship. Seamus was usually a private man, particularly where women were concerned. Kerry was proving different, different in every way. As the saying goes, he thought, 'Vive la difference.'

O'Rorden was sitting at his desk sorting through files. He looked up as Seamus approached.

"Well now, I'm thinking lunch at the pub certainly agreed with you, sir."

"Indeed, O'Rorden, indeed, it's probably almost as good as Tea and Muffins."

O'Rorden laughed at that, and the two of them grinned in an unspoken camaraderie which had built up between them. Seamus had gone from wondering at their first meeting if O'Rorden was all there upstairs to considering him indispensable. It was funny, he thought, how friendships were formed, and the most unlikely people bonded. O'Rorden had very possibly saved his life, something he would never forget.

"How are things going with the files?" Seamus asked.

"As you can see, sir, there's a lot of them, the orphanage was open for many years. We are picking out the females first of course, and then we can take away those who would be too old. But they aren't in any sort of order, so they aren't. We're just working our way through and it's going to take a while, sir."

"It doesn't matter how long it takes, O'Rorden, I just have a hunch the answer is in there, somewhere."

"Yes, sir."

"Great, I've got Liam's number, so I'll get one of the others onto getting the records and checking into them."

Seamus went over to Aileen Hughes. Aileen was a good officer, Seamus had worked with her before. She was tenacious and very meticulous. If anyone could ferret out an answer from the records, it would be her.

"Aileen, this is Liam's mobile number, can you please get his phone records for say the last six months sent over here and then see if you can't shortlist a few people who might be hiding him."

"Sure, sir, I'll get one of the team onto it," Aileen assured him.

Seamus went back to his desk, picked up a pile of files and joined his colleagues in the long process of sorting through them. Each one of these files, he thought, was a life. The photographs and information written in it a snapshot of what really happened. And who would know what had really happened except those who had lived it? He wondered how many of these children had been abused, harmed psychologically and were carrying the scars of that hateful time. The abusers had taken their childhoods away from them. They had been left with the shame, the guilt and probably hate for their abusers. It was impossible to fathom what these children had been through and understand how it affected them. The actions of the abusers had laid the seeds, the foundations for murder. Seamus could almost guarantee the murderer would kill again. His job was to make sure they didn't.

He wished at the same time he could get justice for all these children. Somehow, he didn't feel he was ever going to be able to. Abuse in the Catholic Church was bigger than him, it was rife, they had failed to control it from within. And the authorities too had failed to control it from without. That was the real tragedy. Nothing would really change. Brogan had said to fix the things you could and leave the things you couldn't. A pragmatic philosophy but not good enough for Seamus. One day there had to a reckoning, through the law, he just didn't know how.

* * *

Liam contemplated himself in the mirror in Mary's bathroom. She stood behind him peeling off the plastic gloves from the hair dye she had been using.

"Oh my God! Is that really me?"

"Yes, I don't think anyone will recognise you now, Liam, that they won't."

Mary had cropped Liam's hair very short and it was now bleached with blond spiky highlights. She had even done his eyebrows. He was clean shaven and had divested himself, reluctantly, of all his silver jewellery and piercings. He was naked from the waist down, having just rinsed and gelled his hair and Mary thought he looked rather handsome.

"I think it looks very sexy, Liam, I could certainly fancy you."

"Did you not fancy me before?" he demanded, turning around to face her and putting his arms around her.

"Of course, I did, but now, you are really smoking hot in my opinion."

"Is that right? Smoking hot you say?"

"Yes, in fact, I can't keep my hands off you, see?" She moved her hands to his behind and began to squeeze. Then again, her hands went around to his front where she discovered he was already hard. She kissed him then and guided his hand down to her loins.

"God you make me so wet all the time, Liam," she murmured.

His fingers began to move, and she moaned softly in response. Then, grabbing his hand, she pulled him from the bathroom into the bedroom. She lay back on the edge of the bed, and he knelt down in front of her and entered her roughly. She gasped with delight, just as she always did to feel him inside of her.

"Give it to me, please give it to me, Liam," she urged him breathlessly.

Liam obliged thrusting hard and her legs wrapped themselves around his back. It wasn't long before she climaxed easily and quickly and so did he. Soon after, they lay together on the bed, naked and holding each other close. Mary kissing him softly.

"Do you think anyone will recognise me like this?" he asked her.

"No, I don't think so no."

"Shall we go for a walk, in the park nearby or something?" Liam just wanted to get out.

He was already feeling cooped up. Mary was crowding him, even though he was very grateful to her. Apart from anything else, she liked an awful lot of sex, and he didn't know how he could keep up if this carried on. But Mary loved him, and he was a kind soul. He didn't want to hurt her feelings. He vacillated between thinking maybe he did love her and deciding he didn't. That alone probably meant he didn't love her at all.

On the other hand, he did care for her. And to be honest, he liked sex, and she gave him it without hesitation. It was as if it was on tap. A young man in university ought to be happy with this type of attention. Many of his friends didn't even have a girlfriend and were certainly not getting any action. He decided he shouldn't be ungrateful, nor look a gift horse in the mouth.

Liam wasn't prone to deep thinking, but he wasn't totally inconsiderate. He just had the streak of selfishness of many young men of his age. He also was fortunate in being desirable to many females of his acquaintance, and he had the gift of the gab. His mother told him he was full of the Irish Blarney. It was true, and it had proved to be the gateway to the bedrooms of very many girls, including Mary.

"I'll go for a walk with you, Liam, if you promise to come home and shag me senseless afterwards," Mary told him bluntly.

"OK," Liam replied easily.

It was an off the cuff response, without the enthusiasm one might expect from a lover. Mary noticed it, but Mary didn't mind, she took what she could get. She retained the eternal hope on which many one-sided relationships had endured and finally foundered. The hope that one day her love might somehow be returned, even though she knew, deep down, it probably wouldn't be the case.

Out in the fresh air, Liam felt he could finally breathe. They walked through the park and ate ice-cream together even though it was a cold autumn day. They sat on a bench arm in arm, sharing a coffee. All was peace in their world. If only every day could be like this with Liam, thought Mary. Liam smiled at her benignly wishing he was far, far away and none of this had ever happened.

* * *

The day had passed without further revelation or incident. Work was proceeding as expected on the children's home files but nothing of interest had so far come to light. Seamus wasn't surprised. He had left the office for dinner at a reasonable time and having consumed it was now lying together with Kerry in her bed. They had made passionate love once again, and although it sounded like a cliché it was true. There seemed to be a true passion between them, one of the enduring kinds. A passion of the heart and of the soul. The physical manifestation of this through sex was one thing, but the real passion went far deeper than that. It was simply the need for the presence of the other, and the completeness of being in their company. Being, at home. Seamus discovered another word which had not occurred to him before. Home, he felt at home, here with Kerry in her pub.

"You are a beautiful man," Kerry was saying to him, her blue eyes only centimetres away from his brown ones.

"I've never been called that before."

"But you are, you are beautiful, you have a beautiful soul, I can tell."

"Thank you." Seamus kissed her. He could take a compliment. He had learned the art with maturity. And Kerry's compliments warmed him inside.

"You're beautiful too, Kerry O'Shea, inside and out."

She kissed him back, holding him close, never wanting to let him go. Wondering if one day she would have to. But that day was not today. She pushed the fears to the back of her mind.

"You know, you said you wanted to help if you could," Seamus said after they had kissed.

"Yes?"

"Well, there is something you could do, it would be a real help."

"What's that?"

Seamus turned on his back, to be more comfortable, but still kept hold of her hand.

"Do you think you could use another member of staff?"

"Why? Are you looking for some extra work?" she teased.

"No, nothing like that. It's the girl, the housekeeper who was abused by Mother Joan Margaret and Father Cooney, we've got her under Garda protection, but it can't last forever. She has a boyfriend in jail and she's going under an assumed name. We can help her with a new identity but it doesn't help her with a place to live, and to work."

"You want me to have her here? Working for me?"

"Well, yes that was what I was suggesting, but if you don't like it or it makes you feel awkward, it's fine I'll come up with another solution."

"No, no, don't do that, of course, I will help, poor girl, I know from what you told me that she had a rough time."

"She has, a terrible time."

"Bring her here, there is a room she can use, and I can always use some more help in housekeeping, and so on. I would be happy to help her."

"Great". Seamus turned to face Kerry again. "I'll make some arrangements, get her over soonest."

"Good." Kerry smiled and then looked at him expectantly.

"What?" He raised an eyebrow.

"What are we going to do now?"

"Well, I was hoping for a little shuteye."

"Oh." Kerry pouted, and her face took on a disappointed expression.

"But, on the other hand, Kerry O'Shea, perhaps I had better pay you some more attention."

"Perhaps you better had, Seamus Gallway."

Her lips found his and her hand found its inevitable way to his nether regions.

"Incorrigible" he murmured.

"Yes."

DAY 10

D ay nine passed without incident and moved on
   into Day ten. This was the type of police work
   nobody saw thought Seamus. The painstaking
reading of files and information, sifting through, for just one
tiny clue which might provide the breakthrough they so
badly needed. He began the morning briefing.

"OK, so this is day ten of the investigation into the
Confessional Killings. I know day nine wasn't much to write
home about, so I just want to remind everyone of this. Police
work isn't just about the arrests, it's about everything which
goes into getting to that point. I am sure many of you know
what I am talking about. Behind the scenes, there is a huge
amount of time and effort put into detailed searches like the
one we are doing."

There were nods of agreement in the room. Nearly
everyone there had their share of what might be called
drudging work.

"We've had a lot of excitement in the past week or so, and
it's all been leading up to this. False trails, dead ends, we've
been there. Don't think there's not a lot of pressure on us to
succeed from the higher-ups in Dublin now, because there

is, but let's not allow it to deter us from doing a proper job. I know the answer has to be in those files, and we're going to find it. Call it a hunch, blind faith, whatever you want, and my boss has called it many things I can tell you, but it's what I think. OK?"

He received the vocal support he was hoping for and was happy because he felt they needed this pep talk. Seamus tried to be the person he had wanted his bosses to be when he was in the same position as his team. However, bosses in his experience were rarely empathetic, understanding, reasonable or anything else. Seamus didn't want to turn into one of those.

"Have we got any further forward on Liam's phone records?" he asked.

Aileen Hughes spoke up, she had been working with Paddy Doyle on this task.

"We're working our way through the phone numbers and text messages. It appears Liam was acquainted with a lot of females. That's putting it politely, sir, he was more than just acquainted with some of them as his text messages will testify."

"So, he's been putting about a bit?" put in Seamus, there were a few sniggers.

"If you want to call it that, then yes, sir. He appears to be intimately connected to several girls at any rate. So, we've been calling them up and asking them about him. So far, we've not turned up any likely suspects. All of the girls we talked to said they hadn't seen him since his last encounter and were obviously concerned about the reports on the news. His mobile is switched off, so we can't get a trace on it."

"Good work, Hughes and Doyle, keep at it."

"Yes sir, thank you, sir." Aileen sat down.

"How's the confession going, Duffy?" Seamus asked.

"Yes, sir, it's pretty much all there. I'm just doing a last pass through, I'll type up all the findings and then I'll let you have them."

"That's good, well done, you can join the teams on the files once you've done that."

"Yes, sir."

"Great," said Seamus. "Let's get to it then, you're doing great and I appreciate it, let's keep it up."

The meeting broke up and people returned to their desks and the files.

"Do you really think we'll find the murderer in these files, sir?" O'Rorden asked him.

"Have a little faith, O'Rorden, it might not seem like it but every little step, is one step closer to the truth."

"Thank you, sir, that's a good point that is. By the way, I am working my way through the book you borrowed for me."

"Are you finding it useful?"

"Absolutely, sir, there's a lot more to detective work than I thought."

"That there is, O'Rorden, but also never ignore your instinct. Sometimes you have to go with your hunches, and I've got a hunch about these files."

"That's good enough for me then, sir." O'Rorden smiled and Seamus was gratified in O'Rorden's seeming confidence. Seamus wished sometimes he had as much confidence in himself. When your neck was on the line, it wasn't always a pleasant place to be when playing hunches. But at the moment Seamus had nothing else.

A while later Seamus picked up a fat file. He was sipping a coffee Kathy O'Flynn had made him. This was at least passable, not like O'Rorden's witches brew. He had noticed the team seemed to fuss over him a bit and look out for him. Perhaps it was the sunnier disposition he had had since Kerry and he had become closer. He would be surprised to find out about the loyalty his officers had for him. The Ballysruth crew were particularly appreciative of the way he has stood by them and ensured they continued to be involved. In reality, there were several who vowed they would take a bullet for him, just as O'Rorden actually had.

There was a camaraderie he had rarely experienced before. In a bigger department, you tended to work with different people on different cases, and they came and went. You bonded for sure, and you had partners, colleagues and even friends, but this was different. It was more like a family. Seamus wondered what would happen to this 'family' once the investigation was over, and then he pushed the thought aside too because it brought up the question of Kerry. He was enjoying the 'now' of he and Kerry too much to think about the future. He didn't want to think about it either, it was becoming painful to even go there.

Trying to pull his mind back to the present, he flipped over the cover of the file. It was a girl; her name was Deirdre Flanagan. There was a photograph of Deirdre, in fact, several at different ages. She was a pretty looking child with dark hair, a bow mouth and oval eyes. In one of the photographs, she looked very striking, almost vivacious, as if it had been taken by a professional photographer. It seemed unusual for an orphanage. In the photo, she looked to be around fifteen or sixteen. She was smiling and looked beautifully natural, but also looking carefully there was a sadness in her eyes.

Seamus' pulse quickened at the sight of this photo because it was beginning to look familiar, very familiar to him in fact. He started to scan through the notes and straight away these read differently from the usual mundane facts to be found in the other files. At the front of the file there was an information sheet about her antecedents, and at the bottom of that sheet, there was a section for observations. Clearly written in the box, was only one line "This child has the mark of the devil." The signature on the bottom of the sheet was Mother Joan Margaret's.

For one heart-stopping moment, Seamus stared at it. Then rapidly he began to leaf through the rest of the file his excitement growing. It read like a diary of problems Mother Joan Margaret had had with Deirdre's behaviour.

There were entries such as 'Deirdre has been wilful once again. I have tried to get her even to cooperate with such simple things as brushing her hair, but she is defiant in the extreme. Unfortunately, Deidre has had to be punished. I don't like to use the strap on her, but it seems to be the only thing that gets her cooperation,' and 'Deirdre was given six strokes of the cane for disobedience once again. She was warned about not going into the boys dormitory but she was found there last night,' and 'I have had to punish Deirdre severely because she was discovered playing with herself in the bath,' and 'Deirdre has been sent to see Father Cooney to see if he can counsel her better than I can,' and 'Father Cooney says Deirdre has the devil in her and it must be beaten out of her.'

On and on, like a litany of justified abuse about a girl they had decided was 'the devil', in plain hand, the hand of Mother Joan Margaret.

"O'Rorden, O'Rorden, come over here and look at this."

Seamus' urgent tone of voice broke into O'Rorden's thoughts as he was sifting through yet another file, his tenth today. He dropped his file on the desk and quickly came over to look. It sounded as if his boss was onto something.

"Here, here, read this, look at this, tell me what you think." Seamus thrust Deirdre's file into his hands.

O'Rorden took it somewhat bemused but then immediately became wide-eyed.

"Have you ever seen anything like it?" asked Seamus.

"No, sir, no I haven't not in any of these files at all, that I have not. This is unbelievable, sir, unbelievable."

"Did you read the first line, in the first note?"

"This child has the mark of the devil," O'Rorden repeated slowly. "The mark of the devil, now who would ever write something like that?"

"Exactly O'Rorden, who would write something like that? This is no ordinary child, O'Rorden, this is a child Mother Joan Margaret had it in for, who she abused time and time again, using the devil as an excuse. And not only that, who does this picture remind you of?" Seamus was excited.

O'Rorden looked at the photograph of Deirdre at sixteen which Seamus had been so struck by.

"Well now I'm not sure sir, but it does look familiar, so it does."

"Doesn't it?" Seamus said decisively, and he placed the photograph on the desk and then laid the photofit of the murderer beside it.

"Well I never," said O'Rorden much struck by the resemblance.

"It doesn't end there." Seamus smiled at him.

"Does it not sir?"

"No, because I now know who these remind me of, I've been trying to think for ages but seeing the photograph finally brought it to mind." Seamus indicated the two pictures.

"Who would that be, sir?"

"Diana O'Malley at the library."

On hearing this significant pronouncement, O'Rorden picked up the two photographs and examined them more carefully.

"Now you come to mention it, sir, I can certainly see the resemblance."

"Yes, yes indeed, O'Rorden."

"But there is one thing puzzling me, sir."

"And what's that?"

"Why did Anna Kowalski use it for her false name, Deirdre Flanagan."

This had not occurred to Seamus in his excitement at the discovery but now he remembered Anna had used that name. It was too much of a coincidence and needed to be investigated.

"Good point and I don't know, why don't we go and ask her, I need to see her anyway," Seamus said with decision.

"What about Diana, sir, what will we do about her?"

"That's a good question, we are going to have to approach this very carefully. Anyway, let's get over to Ballygilly."

Seamus grabbed the file on Deirdre Flanagan and informed his team, who had become interested in the excited conversation at his desk, they were following up what might be a good lead. He and O'Rorden headed for the car.

* * *

In the car on the way to Ballygilly, they discussed the next moves. Seamus was driving because O'Rorden had not yet been pronounced fit to do so.

"Do you think Diana O'Malley and Deirdre Flanagan are the same person, sir?"

"I don't know, O'Rorden."

"Well do you think she could have had a sister?"

"It seems unlikely otherwise why were they both not in the orphanage?"

"Good point sir, yes." O'Rorden subsided.

"Maybe she changed her name," Seamus offered.

"Yes, she could have at that."

"We can find out anyway from the records office."

"Yes sir, that we could."

"We need to question her that's for sure, but we've got nothing to bring her into the station for and we can't arrest her, we've got no proof she's done anything."

"What if we try and question her at the library?" asked O'Rorden.

"We could try, but it's risky if she is who we think she is then she could run."

"We could put her under surveillance, sir, what about that?"

"Brogan wouldn't go for it, she's not done anything to warrant it. We can't just say she looks like the photofit or a photograph. No, we are going to have to think of another way."

"It's a difficult one is it not, sir?"

"Yes, we can't step too far out of line, because if she's got nothing to do with the murders then Brogan will have my arse, so he will."

"Hmmm."

They both relapsed into silence grappling with what appeared to be an insurmountable problem. Like the chicken and the egg, they couldn't make a move without alerting her, and they couldn't find out what they wanted to know about her without making a move.

They arrived at Ballygilly once again and Father Cooney's house. Anna Kowalski had been living there still under Garda protection. They had kept the church at bay by saying the house was subject to forensic examination. This meant Anna could be kept on as housekeeper whilst not alerting anyone as to the real reason. Irene Connolly, one of the Garda officers assigned to protect Anna, let them into the house. They had already phoned ahead so she knew they were coming.

It seemed Irene had formed a good relationship with Anna, and the two were on very good terms. Irene looked at her charge in a very motherly sort of way and smiled at her fondly.

"Hi Anna," Seamus said when they were sitting down in the living room of Father Cooney's house. A fairly large affair, with a big fireplace, in which a warming fire was burning.

"Hi," Anna said shyly but she seemed more confident now and was looking better.

"How have things been with you?"

"Is all good. Irene, she is so very good to me, like mother. She take care of me, keep me safe."

Connolly smiled at this, and it seemed as if indeed the girl had taken to her protector.

"We just need to ask you something, Anna, if that's OK?"

"Yes, yes is fine." Anna smiled. "I have answered many questions, many, many questions, but I feel good because I can finally tell everything, I am happy to tell everything."

"Well hopefully this one is easy, it's just we were wondering, do you know why the name Deirdre Flanagan was picked for you, as a false name?"

"Mmm, well I not really sure but it might be because the Mother she call me the devil, child of the devil. She say once there was another child like me, of the devil she said, and it was her name. But I am not the devil you know inspector, I am good girl, not devil."

"I am sure you are, Anna, I don't doubt it," Seamus told her gently. "Did she, tell you anything else about this Deirdre Flanagan?"

"Yes, yes she say Deirdre was bad girl, they must punish her many times, they beat her too, like they beat me, they said I am same as her, and they must beat me too."

"Did they, ever mention what happened to Deirdre by any chance?"

Anna thought for a moment and then said, "Yes, they said she was bad, she ran away, one day, they never see her again, they said they were glad because she was devil. And when I hear this, I wish I could run away too, like her, but I had nowhere to run."

"That's great, Anna, thank you, you've been very helpful."

"It's OK." Anna smiled another beautiful sunny smile and Seamus wondered how she could possibly ever be viewed as the devil's child.

"So, Anna, I've got some good news for you, I hope."

"Yes?" Her face perked up.

"Well I've found somewhere you can stay and also work. It's not far, in a pub, with someone I know, someone I know very well, how does that sound?"

"Oh, sounds good, so good!" Anna clapped her hands at this news.

"But what we are going to do is sort out a new identity for you, to protect you. Once we've arranged it then you can leave here, it shouldn't take more than a few days. Is that alright?"

"Yes, yes thank you."

"No, thank you, we are grateful to you for your cooperation and sorry for everything that has happened to you."

"You can't help it." Anna shrugged stoically. "Is life."

They said their goodbyes to Anna and O'Rorden gave her a big hug. Seamus thanked Irene for her good work protecting Anna and taking care of her and then they went on their way.

"You seem quite taken with Anna," Seamus observed on the drive back to Ballysruth.

"She's a lovely girl, sir, who's been through a lot, if I had a daughter, I would like a daughter like her, I don't know there's something about her."

"You never had children then, O'Rorden?" Seamus was curious, they'd never touched on this topic.

"No sir, alas not. I was married once when I was a lot younger, but my wife died, and I never really found anyone since."

"What, not anyone?" Seamus' eyebrow was raised.

"Not counting Mrs Flynt, sir, but look how that turned out."

"I am pretty sure you are missing someone out and I am beginning to suspect deliberately." Seamus quizzed him.

"Do you mean Kathy, sir? Well now Kathy, now that's an interesting question."

"How's that? I thought you two were..."

"Well yes, sir, we are in a manner of speaking, but I don't know where it's leading and that's a fact."

"O'Rorden," Seamus said sadly. "There is only one way it's leading and if you can't see it there's no hope for you."

"Well, now, sir, I am not really following you at all, that I'm not."

"Come on, everyone can see she is head over ears in love with you, what's the matter with you?"

"Really? Head over ears, well I never thought..." O'Rorden went very quiet as he mulled this over.

Seamus glanced at his junior and chuckled to himself. Love was a funny thing, you couldn't see it when it was under your nose. And on that note, he had to suddenly ponder very hard himself.

* * *

Liam was lying lazily on the sofa at Mary's watching her TV when her mobile rang. Mary was in the shower. He glanced at it and it was a withheld number. Without thinking he picked it up and answered it.

"Hello?" he said.

"Oh Hello, is Mary there please?" came a female voice.

"She's in the shower," he told her assuming it was one of her friends.

"Oh, well who am I speaking to?"

"I'm a friend of hers, who am I speaking to?" Something in her voice had made him suddenly suspicious and the next moment he knew the reason why.

"This is DS Aileen Hughes phoning from Ballysruth, we'd just like to ask her a couple of questions."

"Oh shit!" said Liam involuntarily, he stared at the phone and then he dropped it.

"Hello? Hello? Are you there?" He could hear the voice at the other end still speaking.

As if in a dream he retrieved it and said, "I err... I can't hear you very well... sorry... you'll have to phone back..." He cut off the call.

The next moment he was in the bathroom.

"Mary, Mary, get out the shower I've done something stupid, come on get out quick!"

Mary turned the shower off and stepped out of the bathtub putting a towel around her.

"What is it, Liam, what's the matter? Why are you looking so scared?"

"It's the Garda, they phoned you, I answered it, I wasn't thinking. Shit, fuck, oh fuck!"

"What!? What did you say to them?"

"I said hello and she asked who I was, and I said I was a friend, I said I couldn't hear and disconnected, they'll probably phone again, fuck, fuck, fuck."

Right on cue, her mobile started ringing again.

"Don't worry, Liam, I'll handle it, calm down." Mary took the phone from him and answered it.

"Hello?"

"Oh, yes sorry, did you call before?... DS Aileen Hughes? Oh, I see... Oh yes, well sorry my friend answered it, he's a bit simple I'm afraid, I was in the shower.... Problem with the line?... yes, this mobile is a bit dodgy."

There was a pause while Aileen was obviously speaking. Liam was looking at Mary with panic in his eyes. She put her finger to her lips and smiled.

"Liam O'Shea, did you say? Oh yes, I saw it on the news, terrible, really terrible. Well now, I've not seen him for a few days now, that I have not. He hasn't tried to contact me, no. Well no, not since the shooting anyway. He has been calling me a lot? You've got his phone records, and texts as well. Is

413

that right? Well, yes that is true, we are sort of fuck buddies if you like."

Liam made a face at her hearing this. She poked out her tongue at him.

"No, no he's not my boyfriend. I really don't know where he is no. Yes, I did speak to him a lot. Why did I see him so much? Well because he's good in the sack that's why. Who is it here at the moment? Well, that's yes it's another of my fuck buddies as a matter of fact. Yes, I have several, yes that's right. Well yes, I like a lot of sex officer, is it a crime? Oh, it's not, ok then.

"Why did he drop the phone and say shit? Well, you know he's got a girlfriend and he thought maybe it was her. Sure well, you know it is university girl and all that. Oh? You don't know. Well, it's how it is these days, yes feminism and all that. Yes, I am lucky I suppose, yes. What's his name? Well, it's George, George Harrison, yes. I know it's not an Irish name no, yes it's true it is the same as the famous singer, he's always getting lip about that, so he is."

There was another pause and Liam put a hand to his mouth trying not to laugh at this conversation.

"What's that you say, you want to send someone round to talk to me? Why do you have to do that? Can't we just do this over the phone? Oh, I see, you want to know more about Liam, I see, well OK, yes, I suppose do know him well, certainly parts of him very well anyway. When do you want to come round? Oh, soon is it, well sure I guess so. George Harrison? Well, I don't know he's got lectures to go to. Well OK, I'll see if I can persuade him to stay. OK, OK then, sure. Oh, the address?"

Mary told the officer the address and then said goodbye. She disconnected the phone and looked at him quite upset.

"Liam, you're going to have to go, they're coming round, I tried but they didn't believe me. Come on you need to go quickly."

"Fuck it, fuck it!" Liam was shoving his clothes and stuff into his backpack with haste.

"It's your own fault you silly boy, you shouldn't have answered the phone!"

"I know, I know, Mary, I'm an idiot, I was being so careful."

"Go on, Liam, I'm sorry, I will try not to tell them when they come but I won't be able to lie to them face to face. I'll try to keep them talking for as long as I can."

"George Harrison though, Mary, what were you thinking?"

"I wasn't thinking, OK, it was the first thing that came into my head."

Liam had finished packing and put on his jacket.

Mary grabbed hold of him and pulled him close, she kissed him tenderly and lingered as long as she could.

"Go on now, Liam, go on and stay safe, I love you. You're not just a fuck buddy, Liam, I love you so much." She looked him in the eyes, and he saw hers were welling up.

"I know," he said comprehensively affirming he understood. He kissed her one more time and then he was gone.

Mary went to the sofa and began to softly weep. She always knew this would probably happen, but it still hurt, especially after he had spent all this time with her. It seemed as if it would last forever, but nothing does she thought, nothing ever does. She dried her eyes and started to tidy the flat, deciding how to deal with the Garda officers when they came.

* * *

When Seamus and O'Rorden arrived back at the station, Aileen Hughes was waiting anxiously to see them.

"Sir, we've just had a weird phone call with a girl who was apparently, a 'fuck buddy' of Liam's, her words sir not mine," she told Seamus.

"Really? What happened?"

Hughes related the conversations, and how it was odd a male had answered the phone the first time and apparently dropped it and then Mary had answered it the second time.

"Her answers didn't ring true, sir, and also George Harrison? It sounded like a name she pulled out of the air to be honest, for a start it's not an Irish name and he was definitely Irish."

"Perhaps she is a Beatles fan." Seamus sounded amused. "And you've sent someone round to talk to her?"

"Yes, sir, a unit is on its way from GNBCI."

"Great, although if it was Liam then he will be long gone by now."

"I figured that, sir, but we can still try to find out if he was staying there."

"Sure, see what they can discover. If it's done anything it's flushed him out of his cover, so we might have another chance of catching him. Circulate his details again, and make sure his mobile is monitored in case he uses it."

"OK, sir, will do."

"Keep me posted, good work Hughes."

"Thank you, sir."

Seamus and O'Rorden went back to their desks.

"What now sir? What about Diana?"

"Yes, well I'm thinking let's do some digging up on her first and on Deirdre Flanagan. You take Diana and I'll take Flanagan."

"Right you are, sir."

Before he could sit down, Seamus' phone buzzed. It was Kerry. He motioned to O'Rorden it was an important call and went outside.

"Hi, sweetheart, how's my beautiful girl?" he answered the phone.

"Oh my God, I got a sweetheart and called your girl all in one sentence."

"Well now if all this affection is getting too much for you then you let me know," he joked.

"Oh no you don't, Seamus Gallway, I'm lapping it up, so I am, I'm like the cat with the cream and it's top class cream at that."

"So, to what do I owe the pleasure of your call then sweetness?"

"Well, I was just ringing to check if you were coming back for lunch, you know in case I was going to get another of your surprises."

"I would love to, Kerry, but things are kicking off a bit here at the moment, so I hope you won't mind not getting a surprise this time."

"Oh no, it's fine, it's fine, it's just," she dropped her voice lower and sexier. "When you are planning a surprise visit, I could make sure I'm wearing something a bit more appropriate and easy access if you get my drift."

"Oh, is that right, and what would that be then?" Seamus was interested.

"That's for me to know, and you to find out, an incentive for you to find out then isn't it?"

"I'll bear it in mind."

417

"You do that."

"I will."

"Go on then what's going on that's got your pants on fire then, apart from me that is?" She laughed.

"We think we found out where Liam was staying but we don't think he's there now."

"Oh? Can you tell me more?"

"Sure, we think he was staying with a girl called Mary and we're not sure what their relationship is exactly, she referred to him as her 'fuck buddy', sorry to be so crude."

"Oh dear God, I probably wish I'd not heard that, my little boy grown up and having fuck buddies, oh dear." But she was laughing.

"He's probably flown the coop by now, but maybe we'll have a better chance of locating him."

"Yes, yes let's hope so, that's two things I'll be talking to him about when I see him."

"Don't be so hard on him, he's what twenty years old now?"

"I know, I know, it's difficult to let go."

"Sure, I know, my mother always thought I never ate enough no matter I had clearly been looking after myself very well for years."

"Any other big news?" she enquired.

"I can't talk about it right now, but as soon as I can I'll tell you all about it."

"OK, well I hope I'll see you later?"

"You will, sweetheart, that you will."

"Bye." She disconnected.

Seamus smiled. It felt nice, he felt needed and it was a good feeling. He went back inside.

* * *

Liam bought a pay as you go SIM and put it into his phone. He knew they would trace him otherwise and he was now out in the open. At least he was disguised so they wouldn't recognise him. He sat in the park and dialled Diana's number.

"Who is this?" came the suspicious reply when she picked up the call.

"It's me, Liam."

"Liam, and how are you my little fugitive? Are you still on the run?"

"I need your help."

"Oh, I was wondering when you'd get around to calling me. Why did you wait for so long? Why didn't you ask for my help before?"

"I was staying at a friend's house," he said defensively.

"Liam, you could have stayed with me, why didn't you just call me baby, I could have looked after you?" She pitched her voice lower, stopped being angry as it wouldn't help. She was angry, but she would save it for later. At least now he wanted her and maybe this was her chance to have him for herself. She smiled, a little scheming smile.

"I don't know, I didn't want to trouble you, you've got your job and stuff, I..."

"Liam, stop it, honey, it's OK. Listen, I will help you. All you had to do is ask. So first you need to get yourself to a hotel, I'll give you the address, it's in a town not far from Ballysruth, you can get a train there to the station. I'll book a room and I'll meet you there, can you do that?" Her voice was a purr, like a cat gentling his mind, calming soothing, like she always did.

419

"Yes, sure yes."

"How will you stop being recognised, your face has been all over the papers?" she asked.

"Oh, well my friend helped me cut my hair and I've changed the colour of it. So, don't worry, you might not recognise me when you see me."

"It sounds fun." She laughed but her eyes were not smiling. A woman must have done it for him. Just as she thought. Part of her didn't want to know the truth, and part of her did. The other part wanted to see him again so badly and have him in her bed, and that was the part she always gave in to.

"Yeah, you'll laugh for sure."

Diana gave the hotel directions to Liam and then said, "Ok, baby, I will see you soon then, bye."

The phone clicked off. He breathed a sigh of relief. He had half expected the Spanish Inquisition about Mary, but now hopefully he wouldn't have to say anything. Diana would look after him, maybe he should have asked her sooner. Something in his head was telling him not to do this, but he wasn't listening.

Liam headed for the train station. At the library, Diana carefully locked up, put a sign on the door indicating a temporary closure due to her sick aunt. She got into her slick black car, gunned the motor and the engine purred into life. The car slid quietly and effortlessly down the road.

✳ ✳ ✳

"Have you found anything, O'Rorden?" asked Seamus who had completed his own rather quick investigation.

"No, sir, I can't find anything about Diana O'Malley. I have spoken to the council and they emailed her identification, but the passport is a fake. I've checked it with the passport office. There are plenty of Diana O'Malley's who have birth certificates, but I doubt any of them are her. We've checked the address she gave the council and it turns out to be an empty block of flats, there is a redirection on her mail to the post office."

"So, we don't know who she is, we don't know where she lives and we don't know anything about her at all. Plus, she's not our databases."

"No, sir."

"So, this woman who clearly exists doesn't exist. Yet she must have bank accounts and other ways of paying for things. She wears expensive clothes, and so on. So, she must pay for it all, but how?"

"I don't know, sir."

"No, neither do I. I've also checked into Deirdre Flanagan and there are no records other than the fact she has a birth certificate and what we have on file from the children's home. It's almost as if she disappeared."

"Or died maybe?"

"Maybe but I doubt it, no she's alive and I'm betting she and Diana are one in the same person. But we have to get hold of the person herself to verify that."

Seamus came to a decision.

"OK, here's what we will do, we will go to the library with two units and arrest her on suspicion of identity theft. That way we can get her in and try to break her down."

"And if we can't?"

"Then we let her go but hopefully we'll be able to run surveillance on her afterwards."

"OK, sir."

Seamus rounded up Duffy and O'Flynn, Healy and her counterpart. He figured it should be enough. They jumped into three cars and headed rapidly for the library. Seamus sent Duffy and O'Flynn around the back, and the four of them headed for the front door. The library was closed, and the car park was deserted.

"Damn!" Seamus banged his fist on the door in annoyance.

The sign on the door said Diana had gone to visit her sick aunt.

"Sick fucking aunt my arse," Seamus said crossly.

He called Duffy and O'Flynn back to the front.

"OK, we are just going to have to keep a discreet watch on this place twenty-four seven. Duffy and O'Flynn, you take the first watch, then we'll replace you in about two hours. Healy, arrange a rota, will you? Park a discreet distance away and keep this place under surveillance. If she comes back let us know right away. Do not engage, have you got that, do not engage, she may be armed and one person with a gun, Duffy, is not adequate backup."

Duffy didn't look too unhappy at this assignment, and in fact, recently he had seemed a lot more cheerful and was even exchanging a bit of banter with other people on the team.

"Come on, Duffy, looks like it's me and you for a couple of hours, you can keep me entertained." O'Flynn smiled at him.

The others laughed, said their goodbyes and returned to the office. Duffy and O'Flynn moved their car a fair distance away from the library so they wouldn't be too obvious and settled down to wait.

THE CONFESSIONAL KILLINGS

* * *

Liam arrived at the Callyhon Hotel in Drumkelly. It was an exclusive hotel in a smallish town only a few kilometres out of Ballysruth and was served by a train which travelled from Dublin to Cork. The hotel was in easy walking distance of the small station and was a quiet enough spot in a small valley overlooking green hills beyond. He found it remarkably easy to get into the room Diana had booked. He gave the name Diana had told him to give and the clerk on reception handed him the key without question as if they had been expecting him. The easy familiarity with which the clerk had treated him put suspicion in Liam's mind Diana was possibly a frequent visitor to these premises. Who could tell? She was full of dark secrets.

The room itself was a double with a king-size bed. It was spacious with a desk and casement window, a small table and chairs. Probably one of the best rooms they had he thought to himself. Diana had money, he knew that much, she didn't do cheap. The décor was fashionably retro eighteenth century and somewhat overly ornate. It had a large bathroom with a deep Victorian bath. Liam wondered exactly how many men Diana had had in this room. Then again, he couldn't really talk given his own track record with women. He also wasn't in a position to argue, unless he wanted to sleep on the streets, and it wasn't his style at all.

Diana said he could order anything he wanted from room service, so he flicked through the menu and asked for a burger with chips. After it arrived served in appropriate style accompanied by a couple of bottles of Harp, he consumed it and settled down on the bed to wait for Diana.

423

Closing his eyes, he thought of Mary and wondered if she was OK.

Liam awoke with a start to find Diana in the room, it was getting dark in the late afternoon. She was sitting on the bed watching him with a lazy smile playing on her lips. He noticed she was wearing just a red satin robe pulled around her curvaceous frame.

"Hello stranger," she said to him when he opened his eyes.

"Oh my God, Diana, Hi, when did you get here? I didn't hear a thing."

"You were dead to the world, my sweet, and so fast asleep I didn't like to wake you, darling." She smiled at him sweetly.

"God, phew, must have been those beers I had, I'm not used to it." There were now four empty bottles on the table, he'd asked for two more after the burger and they had gone to his head.

"Yes, I see you've been pushing the boat out."

"Sorry, it's been a stressful time, so it has." He pulled himself upright against the pillows.

"I'm sure it has, but you're here now and so am I." She smiled and then laughed. "I like your hair, it's certainly... different, I'll give you that."

"Yes, well I know but at least I'm not recognisable now." He gave a wry smile.

"Well, I definitely can say that for it."

She moved closer and her hands reached out starting to undo his shirt buttons.

"What are you doing?" he asked her, although he knew full well.

"You won't be needing these now will you, not for a while."

424

Liam sighed softly, Diana's sexual appetite was just as big as Mary's.

"Oh, now don't sigh like that, Liam, you didn't think I came here for nothing now did you?" She spoke to him as if he was a child, gently, soothingly all the while removing his clothes until he was naked.

"That's better," she said once this was accomplished and she was looking him over appreciatively. "Now we can have some fun."

Diana slid gracefully onto the bed and straddled Liam's thighs. Her robe fell open revealing her lily-white smooth naked skin. Her breasts were full and shapely, her waist tucking in and then out again giving way to curvaceous hips. To many, she might slightly resemble the famous model Bettie Page in some ways, certainly in build, although she did not style her hair in Bettie Page's fashion. She was beautiful in the classic sense and the sight of her naked flesh was not lost on Liam. In spite of himself, he began to become aroused.

"Mmm, that's definitely better," Diana murmured softly taking note and gently took him in her hand. He gasped at her touch unable to resist. He never could. A longing for her swept instantly into his loins as it always did and within a few moments Diana had engulfed him within. She began to ride him softly at first and then harder, and then even harder.

"Oh, Liam, you have no idea how much I've wanted you, I've missed you, Liam, I needed you... oh God, Fuck, Fuckkk!" A stream of invective, dirty words, issued from her mouth as she neared her climax. She couldn't prevent herself, it was the feeling Liam gave her, the closest she had ever come to love. He made her so horny and hot, all at the same time as wanting to take him in her arms and take care of him. By now she had fully let go and was almost pounding him into the bed, harder and faster, crying out with no thought for anything but these moments of pleasure. She climaxed very vocally, setting Liam off. He finished thrusting himself up inside of her hard as if he couldn't get enough of her, pulling her down onto him. She stayed there panting, resting her hands on his arms. Looking deeply into his eyes.

Her recovery was however swift once the pleasure was over, and within a few minutes she was smoothing out her hair while still straddling his frame. Diana always liked to look her best, no matter what was happening. It was part of her immaculate control mechanisms she had built up to protect herself.

"Did you enjoy it, my baby?" she asked him.

"Yes, yes I did, I really did." With Diana he could not help himself, she consumed him somehow no matter how many times he vowed not to go back there.

"You see, you could have had the pleasure of my company if you had phoned me a lot sooner, Liam, isn't that right?" The anger at this fact suddenly welled up inside her, but as always, she controlled it, channelled it, she had learned how with long experience.

"Yes, Diana, but I told you I didn't want to bother you," he said lamely like a child caught out on an excuse.

"I won't ask where you've been, but I'm upset you didn't call, I was worried."

Diana was beginning to sound more like his mother than his lover, it irritated him.

"I'm sorry," he said letting his annoyance show not knowing what else to say to appease her, he could tell she was unusually angry, and he felt it wasn't fair.

"Sorry? Sorry? Is that all you've got to say?"

Diana's control suddenly slipped, perhaps it was his defiant tone or her sudden anger at thinking where he had been overtaking her. Her hand came up without warning and slapped him, hard across the face. His eyes went wide in shock, and then she slapped him a second time.

"Diana, please, don't." He was taken by surprise, tears sprang to his eyes, suddenly he was back there, back in the room with Father O'Flaherty, how did it happen? He began to cry like a small child. "Don't, Diana, please don't hit me, please don't."

This was not the reaction she had been expecting. She was instantly contrite. She should have known better, after the last time she had slapped his face. It had been much the same though that time he had sulked for ages. She crumbled at his hurt and his tears. How could she have allowed herself to let go? To drop her mask? She was angry now, at herself.

"Liam, Liam, I'm sorry baby, so sorry." She slid from her position and moved up beside him to cradle his head. "I'm so sorry I was just so angry, I didn't know what I was doing."

Tears were also rolling down her own face, in recognition she had no control over her feelings about him. The famous ice queen had melted.

"It's OK," he finally managed. "It's OK, Diana, I probably deserved it, I..."

"No, no you didn't, I should never have done that, you're not a person who deserves it, particularly not from me, not ever again, I'm so sorry, Liam."

There was silence for a while punctuated only by occasional sniffs from Liam as he choked up his tears. Finally, he spoke in a whisper.

"It's just when you hit me like that, it reminded me, of something long ago, that happened, that's why I cried."

"What? What happened? Tell me, Liam, tell me, baby."

Liam talked then very softly and quietly. She listened to the tale of the beating by Father O'Flaherty with her anger rekindled. There were echoes inside of her, memories stirred up. She forcibly tried to push them away. But it was hard to do when it happened to someone you loved. After he had finished Diana kissed him gently.

"I am so sorry this happened to you, darling." She thought about it for a bit and then said, "perhaps he got what he deserved then, Liam."

"I didn't kill him," he replied.

"Of course, you didn't, Liam, of course, I never thought that."

"And I didn't say I wanted him dead either, not that I'm so upset if he is."

"No, neither am I baby, neither am I."

She lay down under the covers and pulled him in with her. He snuggled his head into her arms and she held him protectively dropping kisses on his face.

"It's OK, baby, nobody is ever going to hurt you again."

The words vaguely penetrated Liam's consciousness, he was falling asleep. He felt protected and safe, but something in his head was also telling him to be careful. Reminding him this same line was the one most often used by psychopaths in movies right before they killed their victim. He told himself not to be so stupid and drifted away.

Diana looked down fondly at his now blonde head and in her mind, a plan was forming.

* * *

The day finished without incident. The surveillance rota had been drawn up and pairs of officers were keeping the library under constant observation. However, Diana had not returned. This was frustrating, but Seamus knew it was also part of the job. Sometimes you had to have patience even when it was the last thing you really needed.

Aileen Hughes filled Seamus and O'Rorden in on the results of the interview officers in Dublin had had with Mary Casey, who was Liam's friend.

"Sir, Mary Casey was reluctant to talk to the officers at first but after a bit of pressure she admitted everything."

"What did she admit to?"

"She said it's true Liam had been staying there and she had been helping him to hide out. It turns out she is not exactly his 'fuck buddy' sir, but she's head over heels in love with the guy."

"That makes more sense, and is he in love with her did she say?" Seamus was curious.

"Sir, she gave the impression the feeling wasn't mutual."

"Ah, oh dear, unrequited love, it's the worst kind."

"Yes, sir, indeed. Well anyway, she let them look around the house without a warrant and they found a used pack of blonde hair dye and hair clippings which looked like it was his hair. She admitted she had cut his hair and dyed it blonde for him."

"Oh right, well that makes sense, I would do the same in his position," observed Seamus dispassionately.

"I'm not sure blonde would suit you though, sir, that I'm not. What do you think Aileen?" chipped in O'Rorden who had been listening in on the conversation.

"I don't know there, Connor, maybe a redhead might be better."

They all laughed at this banter and Seamus said, "OK, enough about my hair you two. I'll keep it as it is if you don't mind. So, is there anything else? What were they doing all the time in her flat? Or don't I want to know?"

"I think it's where the fuck buddy aspect comes in, sir," said Hughes with a smile.

"Yes well, moving swiftly on, I assume there was no George Harrison."

"No sir, she made it up. It was Liam answered the phone and panicked. She said she was sorry, but she loved him and would do anything for him."

"Sounds about right, we've heard it many times before. Anyway, good work on picking it up, DS Hughes, that's well done."

"Thank you, sir, do we want to do anything with her? I mean charge her or anything?"

"For harbouring a fugitive from justice, you mean? No, there's no point, it wouldn't achieve anything. She wouldn't be the first one to make a fool of herself for love and she won't be the last. We'll let that one go, we've got a bigger fish to catch than her or even Liam."

"Right, sir, thanks, well I'll get back to the files then."

"Thanks, DS Hughes."

Even though they had found the person who was now top of the suspect list, they had to complete their search of the files. They had to glean all the information they could and make sure nothing was missed. Seamus would not let them abandon it because their suspect might end up being a dud, it had happened before. They had to hedge their bets, even though, in this case, his money was on Diana.

✳ ✳ ✳

Seamus and Kerry were eating dinner as usual in her parlour later that night. Seamus couldn't tell her about Diana at the moment although he desperately wanted to share everything with her. This in itself was unusual, he had never been with a woman who made him feel this way. A woman who was like his best friend and not just a lover. With Kerry, it was both and more.

The first thing she had asked him about was Liam of course, as soon as he came back for dinner. He'd asked if they could eat first and then he'd give her all the news. He was hungry and low blood sugar clouded his thinking. She acquiesced though he could sense her impatience.

They were eating Teriyaki Salmon served with a delicious salad and slices of toast. Kerry watched him enjoying each mouthful with satisfaction. Feeding him was, for her, an act of love, and she was in love with him, she mused, admitting it to herself at last. He seemed to be lost in thought. With a sly smile on her face, she ran the inside of one of her bare feet up and down his calf. Seamus looked up at her and laughed.

"Is it that time already?" His eyebrow went up in the sexy way he had.

"Nearly, yes for sure, but I thought you might want to share what you were thinking, and you were going to tell me about Liam remember!"

"Sorry, am I too quiet for you now, is that it?"

"Well, silence can be golden but not too much of it, I prefer it when you're a bit chattier, to be honest, so I do."

"OK well, you've waited long enough, I have a bit more news about Liam, but you'll have to keep it to yourself."

"You found him, do you know where he is? Why didn't you tell me! Oh you! Seamus Gallway, tell me this instant!"

"Woah, woah, woah." He held up his hands and smiled. "That's three questions and the answer to the first two is no."

"OK, but why didn't you tell me? Right away! Seamus Gallway, sitting there eating your food and saying nothing... like a... like a..."

"Like a man who loves your cooking and shows it the proper appreciation by eating it in silence while savouring every mouthful, do you mean?" he finished it for her.

"Well, well, I do mean that of course," Kerry replied blushing at the compliment and feeling suddenly flustered. "Oh Seamus Gallway, you're always saying exactly the right thing to stop me getting annoyed with you!"

"Oh, annoyed with me now is it? Is it the stage we're at now?"

"Oh you! You are impossible! You are infuriating, you are..."

"What, Kerry O'Shea, I'm what?" Seamus had risen from his chair and pulled her up from hers into his arms. His lips covered her lips with a passionate kiss.

"What you are, Seamus Gallway, is a lucky man," she said when she could catch her breath.

"I know that already, I know how lucky I am to have you." He laughed.

"Well, and that's good, yes that's good." He had taken the wind out of her sails, he seemed to have a knack for it.

"Come here and sit down," Seamus said softly. He sat back on the bench and patted the seat beside him. Kerry obliged and gave him a sexy look from under her lashes.

"So, we got a bit more information about the girl he was staying with, but he's not there now. We had a team go over and interview her."

"Oh, really? Tell me more."

"Her name is Mary Casey and apparently he's been seeing a lot of her. She's head over heels in love with him but it seems he doesn't feel the same about her. So, he's not quite just a 'fuck buddy' as she first told us, it's a bit more than that, on her side at least. We know he's had a string of girls, we've got their numbers from his phone records and spoken to several of them. We wouldn't have discovered any of this if he hadn't answered her phone by mistake. Our officer got suspicious and rang back. When she spoke to Mary her answers didn't ring true. Anyway, Liam was long gone by the time the team arrived. We know he got her to cut his hair and dye it blonde. Other than that, we don't know where he is now I'm afraid."

"Oooh the little bugger, wait until I get hold of him! Leading the poor girl, a merry dance like that. I'll give him a few fleas in his ear, so I will," said Kerry with determination.

"Well, we've got to catch him first and interview him, before we let you loose on him. You know he could be facing some serious charges related to firearms, don't you?"

"Yes, yes I do," she was looking grave.

"We'll go as easy as we can on him, depending on what he's got to say about it all. But at the end of the day I've got to do my job, he shot one of my officers and he could have killed him."

"I know, I am so sorry about Connor, I feel terrible. I keep wondering where I went wrong."

"You didn't go wrong, you've done the best you could as his Ma, I am sure of that. Your reaction is very common. When their kids go off the rails the parents always blame themselves, it's only natural."

"Thanks," she smiled at him weakly. "Might he, might he go to prison?"

"We'll try not to get to that stage if we can avoid it," Seamus tried to reassure her.

"Let's not talk about Liam anymore," she said decisively and turning her face to his, she kissed him.

"What would you like to do instead?" He enquired the teasing note back in his voice.

"I think you know."

"Yes."

She stood up and took him by the hand.

"What about the dishes, shall we?"

"No, leave it, there are far more pressing matters we need to attend to."

"Is that right? And what might they be?"

"Come upstairs and I'll show you."

"Is that an invitation or a promise?"

"Both."

DAY 11

When Liam awoke, it was morning. He found he had slept like a log and felt quite refreshed. Diana was sitting at the desk in the room looking at her mobile. She was wearing her robe loosely tied around her. Her curvaceous body looked particularly attractive in this garment which clung to her skin.

"Hello, sleeping beauty." She smiled at him noticing he had opened his eyes.

"Hi, God I slept like a baby." He yawned sleepily.

"It's because you are my baby." Diana got up and moved to the bed and kissed him. "I've ordered some breakfast, it should be here in a moment."

"Fabulous, I'm starved."

There was a knock at the door just then and Diana let in the waiter who was pushing a trolley. Silver covers hid the contents of the plates. There was a pot of coffee and tea, plus accoutrements as well as toast, jam and butter. She pressed a generous sized Euro note into his hand which was gratefully received. Once the waiter had departed, Liam jumped out of bed, he threw on one of the hotel robes and took the covers off the plates. Delicious smells emanated from the cooked breakfasts underneath. He grabbed a plate and sat down at the small table in the room to eat.

"God this is good," he said with satisfaction. "So much nicer when you don't have to cook it yourself."

"Or pay for it." Diana brought her own plate and sat down opposite.

He looked up sharply at what sounded like a bit of a dig.

"I'm joking," she said in a reassuring tone. It was partly true, but the other part was a tiny reminder of who was now paying the piper.

Liam shrugged it off and focused on his food. Diana watched him whilst picking at her own food. She wasn't a big eater, but she knew Liam was, most young men of his age had a good appetite. She was calculating whether to talk to him now or not, about her plan. Liam finished his food and looked around for more and saw she had left a sizable portion. She was now delicately sipping her tea.

"Are you not going to eat that?" he asked hopefully.

"No."

"Do you mind if I do?"

"Go ahead, I haven't poisoned it."

He laughed exchanged plates and then started to consume the remains of her breakfast.

"Liam?"

"Yes?"

"What do you think you're going to do, I mean now you're a fugitive, what's your plan? Do you even have one?"

"I don't really know, what can I do? Maybe just have to lay low for a bit longer and figure it out."

"Yeah, sure you could do it but what if there's a better way?"

"And what might that be?" he asked interestedly. He had polished off her left-over portion and was now drinking a cup of coffee and eating a slice of toast.

"Well, what if, just say we could go away for a while, you and me?"

"And where would that be?"

His offhand manner was starting to irritate her. Diana was easily irritated lately it was true. Underneath the façade of her calm exterior lived a very volatile temperament. She controlled it well, for the most part, but recently there had been times when she couldn't. When it happened things had not gone well at all.

"I just thought, we could go away, I've got plenty of money, and I need a break, we can go somewhere, you and me where we can't be found, even perhaps, you never know, make a new life together."

"What about your business?"

"My business, well I can take a break from it, besides it's relocatable, and I don't really need to do it for a while."

"Well I don't know," he said genuinely sounding thoughtful.

"What don't you know? Whether you want to go away or whether it's something else. You're a wanted man, Liam, you could go to jail, don't you get that?"

"Diana, I mean look, I know I've done wrong but maybe I can fix it after all. Connor isn't dead now is he? I could get a good lawyer. I wanted to finish my degree too, and there are all my friends and..."

"It's OK, fine." She stopped him, there was hurt in her voice. "I get it, I've offered you a chance of a lifetime to make a new life, but you don't want it and we both know why that is, don't we?"

"Do we? I was just trying to explain."

D. R. BAILEY

"You don't want to go because you don't want it to be with me. That's it, isn't it?"

"No, Diana, no it's not it, please don't think that it's just a big step, there's a lot to consider..." he stopped. Diana had shut down he could see it in her eyes.

"It's OK, let's not talk about it now, we can talk about it later."

"Diana."

"Liam, I said no."

Diana went quiet and Liam felt terrible. The last thing he wanted was to upset her. Liam wanted to please everyone, it was his trouble. The trail of broken hearts he left behind him was partly due to his inability to say no or to express his true feelings. The truth was though he didn't love Diana or anyone. He loved being with her, having sex with her, he loved her company, like he loved many other girls in the same way, but he didn't have feelings for her. At the same time, he didn't want to hurt her, or any girl, and this is how he ended up hurting all of them more. This attitude would be fine with most girls, they usually got over it and chalked one up to bad decisions. But Diana wasn't anyone.

Liam got up and went over to her, put his arms around her and kissed her cheek.

"Diana, I'm sorry, I'm not trying to upset you, it's just a lot to take in."

"Sure, Liam, sure." But she didn't respond, her voice was cold.

"Come on, babe, let's go back to bed, you know you're so sexy in that outfit, God you make me horny just to look at you."

Ordinarily, this would have been enough to bring Diana round, she had such a soft spot for Liam. Just the sound of his voice and his touch would melt her. But not today. She was angry, fulminating anger burned inside her. The anger of rejection, of things from the past, of hurt, of all the people who should have loved her and didn't. Of the mother who had given her up. She stood up shrugging him off.

"Not now, Liam, I've got to go, I've got work."

"Fine." It was his turn to pout and he did, a little. Then he went back to bed and lay down idly reading a magazine he had found on the table.

Diana didn't speak, in fact, she had gone awfully quiet indeed. She went into the bathroom and had a shower. He could hear her moving about obviously getting ready. She sat at the desk and carefully and meticulously did her makeup.

"You're so good at makeup, it must have taken a lot of practice," Liam observed but there was no response.

"Fine then." Liam gave up and folded his arms also now annoyed. His impulse was to walk out, but where would he go? Somehow, he needed to bring Diana round so he could stay here a bit longer. He relaxed and went back to his magazine, she would get over it.

Diana completed her makeup, dressed back in the clothes she had worn last night. She had carefully hung them up, so they wouldn't crease. Ordinarily, she would have brought a change of clothes, but she had hurried down here as fast as she could. She put away her robe and her makeup in her rather large handbag. She went back into the bathroom and made sure she was looking her best. Then, she carefully adjusted the red wig she had been wearing when she came to the hotel. It hid her black hair from view and it was styled in a bob. She liked to become as anonymous as possible, particularly at this hotel. She had used it before and always paid cash. They had no idea who she was, and she wanted to keep it that way. Money talks and it had talked her way out of leaving any form of ID with the hotel either.

"It suits you that wig," said Liam trying to restart the conversation so that she didn't leave in a huff. "And I'm sorry for the way I was earlier."

"It's OK, Liam." The act of getting dressed had calmed Diana. The everyday exigencies of putting on makeup and getting ready was soothing, normal, putting back control. She felt better even though she was still on edge.

"I'm sorry, really, it just took me by surprise that's all."

Diana relented, came and sat on the end of the bed.

"It's fine, we can talk about it later."

"Sure, yes, for sure," he said eager to make amends. "I mean I appreciate it, it was a really good offer."

Her face clouded. It was the wrong thing to say and he knew it the moment the words left his mouth. She stood up, he could see anger flashing in her eyes.

"Good offer? That's what you call it? Good offer, Liam? This wasn't an offer, it was a proposal, to take you away, to be with you, to spend my life with you, Liam, and do you know why?" Diana had raised her voice.

"I, Diana, no I don't."

"Well, that says it all, Liam, because you don't know do you, you don't get it do you! You don't get it that I love you! There I've said it, Liam, I fucking love you, you stupid fucking idiot, now do you understand?" There were tears starting from her eyes, anger in her voice, but more, shame, hurt, and pain, the pain of love which wasn't returned.

"Oh my God, no I never realised, not you as well..." He froze because her expression had become suddenly hard. He hadn't meant to say that either, it was stupid. Why did he think of Mary just then? Why the hell did he say it?

"What did you say?" Her voice had turned to ice.

"I, nothing look it was nothing... the heat of the moment." He was genuinely afraid, in her eyes was something new, something he had never seen before.

"No, no you did, you did say something, something very significant actually, you said 'not you as well.' What did you mean by that, Liam? 'Not you as well'?"

"Look it's nothing, Diana, nothing, don't worry about it." He was wondering what to do, how was he going to get out of it.

"Not who, Liam? Not who?"

Liam remained silent.

"Tell me!" It was a command and she didn't exactly shout it, but it wasn't a voice you didn't disobey.

Liam thought for a moment and then decided his best course of action was to come clean, in fact, it probably was his only course of action if he was going to get out of this.

"OK, look, Diana, the truth is before I came here, I stayed with a friend, Mary her name is, but she's not exactly a friend, well she's a bit more than a friend."

"She's your lover, is that what she is?"

"Yes, in a manner of speaking, yes."

"In what manner of speaking?"

"Well you know I'm a young man at university, you know."

"I don't know, Liam, why don't you spell it out for me?" She was making him sweat, making him admit it. She wanted to hear it, from him. She had guessed at it but now she wanted to hear it. The self-flagellation of the betrayed lover, the age-old story.

"Look, Diana, OK look, I've just had, have, a few girls I see from time to time and Mary is one of those, you know, I can't help it, it's just how it is."

"And these are girls you sleep with?"

"Yes, sure they are."

"But you said Mary is one of those, and plainly she is not one of those, now, is she? She is more than one of those now, isn't she?"

"Well, yes OK, fair enough, it's a fair cop, she is in love with me. I can't help it, Diana, now can I?"

"And she told you that?"

"Yes, yes she did."

"More than once?"

"Well yes, but what's with all the questions, Diana, this is getting to sound like an interrogation."

"Shut up!" Her tone was abrupt, it brooked no dissent. "I am asking you these questions because I want to know, and you are going to answer them, Liam."

"Well, well OK, Diana, but I don't know why you have to be like that about it."

She ignored this.

"She told you she loves you, and did you tell her you love her?"

"No, no I didn't."

"Because you do, or you don't love her?"

"Diana, please come on."

"Because you do, or you don't love her, Liam?"

"I don't love her no, I don't."

"Just like you don't love me isn't that right?"

He hesitated at this, looking at her. In her eyes, there was a small amount of hope, just a little bit. But he knew he had to be honest, it was the only way. The only way perhaps to make her stop.

"I don't love you, Diana, no, I'm sorry." His voice had gone very soft, he almost whispered it. He felt he had to say it because he just wanted all of this to end. Something had gone very much awry and he didn't know what to do.

"You don't love her, but you went to her house, you stayed there, no doubt fucking her brains out like the little fucking man whore you are, taking advantage just so she could hide you that's it isn't it? Just like you fucking did with me, when she couldn't hide you anymore, that's fucking well right isn't it!" She was choking on the words, angry words, she had walked over and grabbed her handbag and was fumbling inside.

"No, Diana, no it wasn't like that it..."

"SHUT UP!"

His voice died in his throat, at her shout. But it wasn't that which made the colour drain from his face. It was the wicked looking the service revolver which was in her hand, and the gun was pointing at him.

"I said, shut up," Diana said in a normal tone.

He looked at her, and her eyes were hard as flint. He had never seen her look like that and now he was in fear. The fear somehow, he wasn't going to get out of this alive.

"You used me, all this time, knowing how much I care for you, how much I love you. But you don't care, Liam, do you? You just care about yourself." There was a rage inside her, a rage that overrode her common sense. It had happened before, and last time things had gone very wrong. But she couldn't stop it once again.

"No, Diana, it's not true, it's not I am really grateful for everything you've done for me, everything we've shared together."

"Grateful? I don't need grateful, I don't need it, Liam. I gave you love, I was ready to give you my heart, and that to me is everything, do you know how hard it is for me to do that? And you've thrown it in my face."

"No, Diana, no, I can't help it if I don't love you, I'm sorry but feelings are not something you can make happen, if they are just not there, surely you understand?" He wondered if he could keep her talking, long enough, perhaps she would put the gun down.

"You threw it in my face and Mary's face, and God knows how many other girls faces. You are just selfish bastard, a selfish little bastard, like all those other men, all the men I've ever known."

"Diana, I'm not selfish come on, that's not true, I'm just, I'm just a guy."

"Yes, Liam, that's the trouble, isn't it? I thought you were different, but you are not, you are just like the rest of them, not worthy of anything."

Diana looked as if she was going to waver, the gun barrel was hanging a bit lower and perhaps she would relent.

"Yes, you're right, I'm not worth it, you should just kick me out, out of your life, Diana, I'm a stupid selfish fool." He was gambling, gambling this might work.

It didn't.

"No! No, Liam, No! Even if you are all those things, I love you, I've always loved you and I always will love you. You can't go I won't let you."

She had raised the gun again.

"No, Diana, please, you don't want to do that."

"Yes, yes I do, Liam, I do, because I won't let someone else have you, Liam, if I can't have you, if you can't love me then nobody can have you." She was babbling now, some primaeval force had taken over, this was no longer her, she was no longer in charge, the demons had been let loose.

"No, Diana, listen to me, please listen to me, don't do this, don't do something you will regret." He was talking in desperation, his voice had become shrill, there was no telling what she might do, she was acting as if she was insane. He cast around for something, anything to try and distract her, try at least to get out of there.

On the bedside table was a heavy looking stone ornament of a dog. He could see it out of the corner of his eye. Perhaps if he could throw it.

"Why should I regret it? You don't love me, Liam, you don't deserve anything more. Why should I let you be loved by someone else, some other fucking little bitch?" Her eyes were shielded for just a second as she dashed her hand across to wipe away her tears.

In that second Liam made his move. The moment he flung the stone dog in her direction, he knew he had made a mistake.

Diana saw the object coming, and without a thought moved to one side, it passed on harmlessly by landing in the corner of the room. Flight or fight kicked into her already adrenaline-fueled psyche. She brought up the gun without a second thought and fired once and then twice.

"No!!!" She screamed and then saw Liam slump forward onto the bed. The noise had jerked her back to her senses, back to the present.

"Oh God, Liam, Liam, no Liam, what have I done?"

She laid the gun on the bed and ran to him. He was bleeding but she wasn't sure if he was dead. She felt for a pulse on his neck and he still had one. Survival instincts took over. In one swoop, she gathered up the gun, chucked it in her bag and after quickly glancing around to see she'd left nothing else, she left the room. She walked unhurriedly down to the lobby, putting away her demons, back in their box. There was a commotion upstairs probably from people who had heard the gunshots. She didn't look back, nor left or right. Nobody had seen her, there was still time. The clerk was there, he obviously had heard nothing. The hotel had thick walls and was an old building, it wasn't surprising.

"Call an ambulance, to my room, there's been an accident, do it now." She told the clerk and then before he could say any more, she was heading for the front door.

"Wait, what? Aren't you staying madam?" he called after her. But Diana was out of the door and gone.

The clerk picked up the phone and dialled 999. The next moment one of the housekeeper's came hurtling up to the desk.

"Someone's been shot in room 66... what shall we do?"

"Ambulance and Garda," said the clerk to the call taker.

✳ ✳ ✳

Seamus was just about to start the morning meeting when the call came in.

"So here we are again it's day eleven..." He got no further.

"Sir, sir, there's been a 999 call, units and ambulance on their way to the Callyhon Hotel in Drumkelly, a shooting I think, someone's been shot." Paddy Doyle had taken the referral which was phoned through to them.

"How far is it?" Seamus demanded.

"it's about five kilometres, sir."

"Right OK, meeting postponed, O'Rorden with me, O'Flynn and Duffy, Healy and Hayes, with your teams, come on, let's go!"

Eight officers ran for their cars and O'Flynn's car led the convoy at high speed through the country lanes, blue lights on and sirens screaming.

"O'Rorden, get on to the team in attendance and find out what's going on up there, and if we need an armed support unit."

Seamus was driving and working hard to keep up with O'Flynn who was going on ahead like the devil.

O'Rorden made a call and had a quick conversation, then disconnected.

"Sir, someone's been shot in a hotel room, it seems the perpetrator has left the scene. I think the victim is still alive though. An ambulance is in attendance and they will take them straight to the nearest casualty unit."

"How far is that?"

"Oh, it's not far sir, it's about ten kilometres give or take."

"Right, that's good and is there any other info?"

"No, sir."

"Not to worry, we'll find out when we get there what's what. Call up to have RTB come down and do the forensics. I don't think the armed team is necessary, they'll be long gone by now."

"OK, sir."

The cars all drew up in the hotel car park. The ambulance was there, and a trolley was being wheeled out towards it.

"Come on, O'Rorden," said Seamus.

They quickly left the car with the other officers and walked up to meet the trolley. Lying on the trolley with compression bandages and a drip was Liam. O'Rorden and Seamus exchanged glances.

"Check out the crime scene," Seamus told his team. "O'Rorden and I will talk to the ambulance crew."

The other officers headed into the hotel. Seamus and O'Rorden walked beside the ambulance crew.

"Can you tell us what happened?" Seamus asked one of the crew.

"He's been shot twice at fairly close range from what we can tell. One bullet went into his chest, but we think it didn't hit anything major. The other hit him in the arm, we think it hit an artery. One of the hotel staff was a first aider, she helped to control the bleeding, probably saved his life. He's lost a lot of blood."

"What's going to happen to him now?"

"We're taking him to Kilbannog hospital, he'll go straight into surgery, a team is standing by."

"OK."

"Sorry, are there any more questions because we've got to go."

"No, you go on, it's fine, don't worry."

O'Rorden and Seamus watched the ambulance draw away and pick up speed, blue lights going.

"Sir," said O'Rorden. "Kerry."

"Yes," said Seamus. "I know, but first we've got to do our job, he's going straight into surgery anyway."

"But sir, she would be worried sick, you should tell her." O'Rorden looked at him with an urgent expression.

Seamus sighed. Duty versus loyalty, this was the thin line Garda officers had to tread.

"OK, let's take ten minutes tops to look at what's gone on in here and then you and O'Flynn can come with me to pick her up."

"Shouldn't you just phone her, sir?"

"No, no I want to be there to tell her in person, and besides I want to take her to the hospital."

"OK, sir, if you say so." O'Rorden apparently wasn't convinced.

They went into the hotel and found Aileen Hughes, she had been questioning the clerk at the desk.

"What's the story?" Seamus asked her.

"Well, apparently a man, who we assume is the victim..."

"Liam O'Shea," Seamus interrupted.

"Right, Liam, well he checked in yesterday afternoon. He ordered dinner and some alcohol from room service. Later on, a woman arrived who had booked the room, and she went up and stayed the night. This morning they had breakfast in their room. Apparently then all of sudden she appeared and told the clerk to call an ambulance, she said there had been an accident. Then she left."

"Right, did you get a description of her?"

"Better than that, they've got CCTV in the lobby, so we'll go through it shortly. But apparently, she's a regular, and uses the room a lot."

"What colour was her hair?"

"He said it was red."

"Oh." Seamus thought about it, but it didn't mean anything, it could have been a wig.

"OK, you carry on and we'll quickly go up and take a look at the crime scene."

"OK, sir."

Seamus and O'Rorden went upstairs and arrived at room 66.

"Interesting number, sir," remarked O'Rorden. "It's just missing a six."

Seamus laughed, and they entered the room but remained at the door. Duffy and Healy were in there with overshoes and blue gloves examining the scene. The room looked expensive enough thought Seamus and noted the remains of the breakfast on the table. The bed had not so pristine white sheets and there was a blood-soaked stain where Liam must have been lying when he was shot. In one corner of the room, a stone dog ornament was mysteriously lying on the ground. Seamus looked at it somewhat puzzled but other than that, at first glance, there was nothing remarkable to be seen.

"Sir, the victim was on the bed when he was shot as you can see," Duffy told him.

"Yes, I figured as much."

"We've had a look around but can't really see any traces of the perpetrator."

"There might be hairs on the pillow, that sort of thing," Seamus said.

"True."

"Well, do what you can, RTB should be here soon, leave the detailed examination to them but make any notes of anything unusual. We will catch up later. O'Rorden and I will head off to the hospital to check up on Liam."

"OK, sir, will do."

"Right O'Rorden, you can stop champing at the bit, find O'Flynn and get her to drive us to the Baker's Arms, we'll pick up Kerry and go to the hospital."

"OK, sir," said O'Rorden with some relief at hearing this.

Within minutes they were heading for Kerry's pub and within short space of time pulled up outside of it. Seamus jumped out while O'Flynn kept the motor running on the pursuit car she was driving.

He went inside. Kerry was in her parlour and smiled when she saw him, running up to him at once.

"Seamus Gallway, is this another of your surprises? Isn't it a bit early?"

He took her in his arms and kissed her and then held her a little way away.

"Kerry."

She saw the serious expression in his eyes and at once became concerned.

"What is it, what has happened?"

450

"Get your things, you need to come with us."

"What? Where? Why?"

"It's Liam."

Kerry's face fell.

"What's happened, what is it?"

"We think he will be OK, but he's been shot."

Her face went completely white, Seamus held out his hands to steady her.

"What? What did you say?"

"He's been shot, he's been taken to hospital by ambulance and they'll be taking him into surgery by now."

"Oh my God, Oh my God." Tears started into her eyes.

"It's OK, it'll be OK." Seamus gathered her to him and held her tight for a moment, letting her breathe, letting it sink in. She pushed him away.

"What are we standing here for? Come on let's go, we've got to go!" But her mind wasn't working, it was as if she was in a dream, a very bad dream.

Seamus helped her, got her coat and scarf, told the staff she had to go out for an emergency. Then he bundled her into the back of the waiting Garda car with him.

"Let's go, O'Flynn, and don't spare the horses."

"Right you are, sir, better buckle up."

O'Flynn fired up the blues and twos. She let out the clutch and revved the accelerator. The car took off at high speed. O'Flynn then treated them to a masterly performance of precision high speed driving. She took every corner precisely, using the brakes and gears perfectly. They flew down country lanes at a breakneck pace, but Seamus never once felt unsafe. He noticed though O'Rorden hanging on to his handhold in the front and chuckled.

Seamus told Kerry briefly what had happened and there were tears, but for the most part, she was quiet. He put his arm around her and she rested her head on his shoulder.

Fields and hedges flashed by, as did other motorists, not once did O'Flynn really slow down. She kept up the incredible pace right up until they reached Kilbannog hospital, screeching to a halt at the front entrance of the Emergency wing.

They got out of the car and Seamus turned to O'Flynn.

"That was one of the finest pieces of driving I've ever witnessed, O'Flynn." He smiled. "You could do with some lessons from her, O'Rorden."

"Ach sir, Kathy could have been an instructor, so she could," O'Rorden said proudly ignoring Seamus' jibe.

"Is that right? Well full marks to you."

"Thank you, sir, I'd rather have stayed here though, I turned it down. Anyway, sir, you better go and see about Liam." She noticed Kerry standing anxiously at his side.

"Sure, thanks, come on, Kerry." The two of them walked into the hospital.

O'Rorden turned to O'Flynn. "You were fantastic there, Kathy, actually you could probably teach me a thing or two."

"I think I already have, Connor." O'Flynn's eyes twinkled.

"That you have, Kathy, that you have," O'Rorden agreed putting his arm around her.

"Oh, Connor." O'Flynn turned her face to him and they kissed.

Some hospital orderlies watching started to cheer.

"Ach go on with you, haven't ever seen two people make out before?" O'Flynn told them laughing.

"Pay them no mind, Kathy, pay them no mind," said O'Rorden and they kissed again forgetting she was in uniform and they were on duty.

* * *

Once into the hospital building Seamus and Kerry went up to the front desk. Showing his warrant card worked like magic and they were soon standing in front of a doctor.

"Hello, I'm Doctor Martin, I was on the admissions team when your son, is it? Mrs O'Shea? When he was admitted to hospital." A youngish man in a white coat had come to see them. He had the customary stethoscope around his neck.

"Yes, yes," Kerry said.

"Well, he's in surgery right now so I can't tell you any more until he's out. I can tell you it was touch and go, he had lost a lot of blood and only the quick actions of the hotel staff saved his life." The doctor was very frank.

At this Kerry started to cry.

"Ach, now don't fret yourself there, Mrs O'Shea, he's got the best team on it, they'll have him right soon enough, you'll see."

"How long is it likely to be?" Seamus asked him.

"Oh, I don't know at least two or three hours at the outside. It's a complex thing."

"OK, thanks, and I'm sorry to ask but I need them to keep any fragments of the bullet they find, for forensic evidence."

"I'll pass it on to theatre no worries, now you get yourselves a cup of tea and hang on in there. If there's any update in the meantime I'll let you know but otherwise we'll let you know as soon as he is out."

"Thank you," said Seamus. "Thank you very much."

"That's OK."

Doctor Martin left, and Seamus turned to Kerry. She was looking at him strangely.

"Are you OK?" he asked her.

"No," she said, "No I'm not."

"You heard the doctor, he'll pull through."

"It's not that." Her face seemed like a mask.

"Then what?"

"When did you find out it was Liam?" she demanded.

"We got to the hotel where he was shot, and they were bringing him out to the ambulance."

"And then what did you do?"

"I asked them about it and they said he would go straight ahead into surgery."

"And then what did you do?"

"I went in to check out the crime scene briefly and then I came straight to get you."

"So, you didn't think to phone me?" She was starting to cry.

"I did but I wanted to tell you in person," he insisted.

"So, instead you went into the hotel and checked out the crime scene?" Her voice was angry.

"Yes, it's my job! I was ten minutes tops in there, I had to, we've got to find the person who did this to Liam," he said defensively.

"You could have sent someone else to get me, you could have phoned me, you didn't, you didn't think of me at all, did you? All for your fecking job!" The bitter words came out from her lips in her anger.

"Kerry, you're being unreasonable I came as fast as I could, he was going into surgery you couldn't have seen him anyway."

"He's my son! My son!" she said loudly.

"Kerry." He moved towards her as if to hold her.

"Get away from me, get the feck away from me, leave me alone." Her voice was almost a scream.

"Kerry!"

But he was talking to her back. She stormed away from him and out of the hospital.

"Oh dear! It didn't go so well then sir." It was O'Rorden, he and O'Flynn had witnessed the whole thing, and were now standing beside Seamus. They looked at him sympathetically.

"Better get after her, sir," advised O'Flynn.

"No, no I wouldn't do that, sir, leave her be to calm down."

"Trust me, sir, much he knows. Get after her, it's what she needs."

"Kathy!" O'Rorden protested.

"Connor, I'm a woman so trust me I know."

O'Rorden subsided. Seamus looked from one to the other and came to a decision. He nodded at O'Flynn and went outside. Kerry was standing a little way away with her arms folded with her back to the entrance. Seamus walked up to her and she turned around.

"Kerry."

"I thought I told you to leave me alone." Her voice was harsh.

"I know but the thing is I can't."

"Why? Why can't you, why didn't you phone me?"

"Because I wanted to be there, there beside you when I told you."

"Why? Why couldn't you just get someone to come and get me?"

"Because it had to be me, it couldn't be anyone else." Seamus was starting to feel irritated at her attitude. Why couldn't she understand?

"Why? Why did it have to be you, what was so important it had to be you, Seamus?"

"Just because." He didn't want to say it.

"Because what?" Her angry tone got to him at last, he had had enough, the words he didn't want to speak were forced from his lips.

"Because I love you, you daft idiot, that's why!"

Kerry looked at him, her whole expression changed her mouth open.

"There, see now you've made me say it," he said indignantly.

"Oh Seamus, Seamus, Seamus, Seamus."

Kerry came up to him and buried her face in his chest. He held her tight while she bawled her eyes out. With one hand he began to gently stroke her hair. Her sobs lessened, and she lifted up her tear stained face to his, he kissed her gently and warmly. Her hands came up to embrace him. They stayed like that for some time. Finally, their lips parted, and Kerry hit him lightly on the chest with her hand.

"What was that for?"

"Because I'm cross with you, Seamus."

"What? I thought you just got through with being cross with me."

"Yes, but now I'm cross again because of you, because I've been a bitch to you, and now that's twice, and all you've been is nice to me, and it's not fair." Her voice was small, like a little girl.

"Wait a second, you are angry with me for being nice and it's my fault?"

"Yes!"

456

"How do you work that out?"

"Because I'm a woman!"

Seamus laughed at this. "A woman I happen to love." Then he kissed her deeply once more.

"So, was that our first fight?" he teased when they stopped kissing.

"Well, I did most of the fighting," Kerry said contritely.

"Yes indeed."

"Oh you!"

"That's better, shall we go and have a cup of tea?"

"OK."

"You can make it up to me later in case you are wondering."

"OH YOU!!" But Kerry was smiling.

Hand in hand they walked back to the hospital, peace once more restored, and even more than that Kerry was glowing inside. He had told her he loved her. It meant everything to her to hear it.

"I told you!" O'Flynn observed to O'Rorden as they watched them from the window.

"Ach Kathy, right again, as usual." O'Rorden laughed.

"Just as long as you remember it, we'll be fine." O'Flynn squeezed his hand which she was holding tight.

The two of them laughed again.

* * *

Once Diana had left the hotel, she walked swiftly out of the car park and down the road to her car. She never parked it near the building to avoid any CCTV they might have installed. It was part of her plan for an anonymous life. She eased herself into the seat of her black Jag and started it up.

The motor sprang silently into life. She swiftly drove away but not too fast, the last thing she needed was to be pulled over. Within a few minutes four Garda cars passed her going the other way, sirens blaring and lights blazing. They were travelling very fast and flashed by in seconds. Diana was secretly pleased, she hoped they would get there on time.

She hoped Liam wasn't dead. That had not been part of the plan at all. Her emotions had overcome her. She loved Liam, that part was true. Loved him so much she had shot him rather than give him up. She wondered if she was insane. How had it come to this? There was a madness which had overtaken her when she pulled the trigger. Love had made her crazy. But was it true love, or some mad possessive love, like a person might love a favourite pet? She didn't know. People said if you truly loved someone you could let them go, not shoot them. Stupid! Stupid! Stupid! What the fuck was she doing?

They say love has been the downfall of many a good man, but it could equally apply to women too. Love can be universally kind and at the same time cruel. Love can make a person irrational and do things they wouldn't normally do. Love had intervened in Diana's perfect life and now she knew for certain she had made a mistake. She thought about it and it was true, this crime of passion was likely to prove to be her undoing. In fact, shooting Liam was the stupidest thing she had done. The priests were one thing, those were planned murders and well executed for the most part. But this was different, they would go after her even harder for this, an innocent boy, gunned down in cold blood. She knew the net would close in on her sooner or later.

There would be trails, as hard as she had worked to hide herself, she could not hide them all. Eventually, the Garda would find them, and they would lead back to her. She had made a bad mistake, an error of judgement. She had fucked up, she thought bitterly. All of the care, the control, the painstaking work keeping herself out of prying eyes, and certainly outside of the law, all gone for nothing.

Putting these self-recriminations aside, she pondered instead where to go from here. Liam was no longer in her thoughts, he would be dead, or he wouldn't. She loved him, in her way, but she had lived so long shutting out the emotion of his death would just be one more thing to wall off. She didn't cry and almost didn't feel anything, not now, there were other things on her mind. She knew now she would have to act quickly, there was a lot to do.

Long ago she had put in place an exit strategy, it just meant it needed to go into action sooner than she had wanted it. Figuring out how close the Garda would be to finding her, she worked out she had at least a couple of days. A lot could be accomplished in that time, and it needed to be.

There was also one more notch she wanted to put on the handle of her gun. One final hurrah, and really, she would be saving the best until last. She turned her car onto the Dublin road and dialled up the Bishop on her hands-free. He answered in less than two rings, it was his personal mobile, a number he very rarely gave to anyone.

"Yes?" His voice was suspicious.

"Ah, Bishop, it's your very favourite Mistress calling you at last."

"Oh, well, yes that's good, I had been trying to get in touch."

"Yes, I know, well, Bishop, here I am, and you'll be pleased to know I've a gap in my schedule that's just come up."

"OK, that's good, excellent in fact, when would it be then?" His voice was anxious but eager. It can't have been that bad then, after all, the last session, thought Diana. He had tried to contact her, to arrange another, but she was preoccupied. Also, she wasn't sure she had really wanted to have him as a client, but she had changed her mind. Now it became imperative she see him, one more time.

"Great, well how about the day after tomorrow? Does it suit you? About 4:00 pm?"

"Yes, fine, will it be the usual place?"

"Oh yes, Bishop, it will, and I will be looking forward to it, I will be there waiting with a well-oiled strap."

"Oh, I see, well yes OK."

"Don't be late, or it'll be very much the worse for you, and, Bishop, I will leave the door open for you, you can just come right up, I am sure you know the way."

"Fine, thank you, thanks I will see you then."

"Make sure you're sitting comfortably for the next couple of days because you won't be when I've finished." She laughed and hung up the phone.

The Bishop was a prize worth having, a scalp worth taking, he had been involved in a huge amount of abuse, that was for sure. He knew about even more abuse and had done nothing to stop it. He needed to be taken down, he needed to pay, to be properly punished, and he was certainly going to do that, with his life.

She smiled then, at herself, plans were already taking shape in her head, and it would be a race, it would be her against the Garda. Could they catch her before she killed again? If not then she would be gone, for good. Diana was determined this was a race she was going to win.

THE CONFESSIONAL KILLINGS

✻ ✻ ✻

Seamus, Kerry, O'Rorden and O'Flynn were sitting in the hospital cafeteria passing what seemed to be an interminable time waiting in pleasant conversation. Empty cups of tea, coffee and plates which once held slices of cake and sandwiches were a testament to the time they had already spent there.

Seamus had his arm lightly around Kerry's shoulders as they lounged in an area containing sofas and tables. O'Flynn looked on approvingly at this state of affairs. She had grown particularly fond of Seamus in the time he'd been leading the inquiry and she'd know Kerry a long time. Kerry needed to be loved, she was sure of that, and she was also sure Seamus was the man to love her. Connor had been regaling them with amusing anecdotes from his policing career at Ballysruth.

"Ach, Kathy, you remember Widow Callaghan, now she was a character, so she was," O'Rorden was saying.

"She was indeed." Kathy smiled at the recollection.

"You know, sir, she once asked me to arrest the neighbour's cat?"

"What?" Seamus let out a crack of laughter at this.

"Yes, indeed. She calls me up and gets me down there, says it's really important. Well, she was always phoning us up for something or other, that's before she died, bless her soul. But anyway, so I went down there half expecting someone had been stealing her carrots again or something like that. But, no, she takes me into her kitchen and there's her cat, a ginger female it was I think, called 'Tinker', yes that's it.

"Anyway, I says to her 'Sure these are nice kittens, Mrs Callaghan, but what's the emergency?', and she goes 'It's this, Connor, for God's sakes man this is the emergency', and I go 'Well I'm not really following you there, Mrs Callaghan, are you sure you're not needing the vet now, if the animal is having problems', she says 'It's not my animal that's having problems, it's that bloody little bugger of a tom next door, he's impregnated my pussy', well, sir, now you can imagine that I was having trouble keeping a straight face there, what with being called out because the neighbour's cat has got her Tinker pregnant and the unfortunate innuendo to boot."

"So, what did you do?" Seamus was laughing and curious all at the same time.

"Well, sir, that's what I said to her, 'So what are you wanting me to do about it then, Mrs Callaghan?', and she goes 'Ach, Connor, is it not what I've been trying to tell you, I want to you arrest the cat from next door and throw it in the jailhouse', well, sir, you can imagine my face being asked to arrest a cat. It took me the best part of half an hour to explain to her the Garda can't go around arresting cats and throwing them in the cells, and even then, I don't think she was convinced. She finally says, 'Well alright then, Connor, but I am warning you if this happens again I will be taking this up with the Department of Justice, so I will', and I was 'Well yes, Mrs Callaghan, I think that's a good idea, you should definitely do it', I couldn't get out of there quick enough, sir, I'm telling you that now."

Everyone was laughing now, and Connor had pulled out a handkerchief and was wiping his eyes with mirth.

"I'm telling you, sir, we've got a right set of people in Ballysruth, and that's a fact," O'Flynn put in.

"It's a great story," Seamus agreed once he had managed to stop laughing. "I wouldn't have minded one of those kittens though."

"Is that right, sir? Do you have a fondness for cats then?" O'Rorden asked.

Kerry's attention had suddenly perked up on hearing this.

"Well, yes I do have a bit of soft spot for them, we always had cats when I was young, and I've always loved them. I love their streak of independence and yet underneath it all, they give you unconditional love, as long as you treat them well, which of course I always do." He smiled at Kerry when he said this last bit, the analogy wasn't lost on her and she gave a secret little smile.

"So, do you have a cat then, sir?" asked O'Flynn.

"Well, had is more appropriate. The last one was a beautiful little cat. A pretty little thing. She was a tortoiseshell and very fluffy with it. I had her quite a few years too. Unfortunately, one day she got seriously ill, I had to take her to the vet. It was a very sad day for me." His eyes were slightly moist as he told them this. "It was probably one of the worst days ever, if I'm honest. I had her cremated and scattered ashes in one of my favourite spots out in the hills around Limerick. I haven't had a cat since then, just you know, work and stuff."

O'Flynn looked at him sympathetically, he obviously had a soft heart underneath it all.

"Sorry to hear that, sir, I've got a cat myself, he's quite a tearaway, so he is," O'Flynn said laughing.

"I can vouch for that!" put in O'Rorden.

"Oh, he loves you really, Connor."

"Well, he's got a funny way of showing it."

"Ach Connor, he's a just a bit feisty that's all."

"You got that right!" said O'Rorden with some feeling.

Kerry had remained silent during this exchange, but her expression was extremely thoughtful.

Suddenly Doctor Martin, who had spoken to them earlier, appeared at the table. They all turned to him anxiously and expectantly.

"Mrs O'Shea." His expression was serious but not grave. She looked at him with hope in her eyes, eyes which already glistened with tears expecting to hear bad news. Her hand crept down under the table, she found Seamus' hand and gripped on tight. He glanced at her briefly and with concern.

"Your son Liam is out of surgery and he's going to be OK."

"Oh God, thank God!" Kerry burst into tears. It had been over four hours since they had last spoken to the doctor and even though they had whiled away the time in conversation, part of her mind had always been on this moment, part of her consciousness had been with her son in the operating theatre.

Doctor Martin waited patiently whilst Seamus comforted her, and until she could finally speak.

"Don't think the wounds were not serious, they were. A gunshot can do quite a lot of damage. The one in his chest, fortunately, passed right through him and missed every vital organ there is. We had to repair a small graze to the periphery of his lung, but it was comparatively minor. He was lucky, to be honest. The other shot went through his upper left arm and bicep. It had partially broken his humerus or upper arm bone, and we've had to reinforce it with a titanium rod, but it should repair OK. The main problem wasn't that, it was the brachial artery being nicked by the bullet. This is very close to the heart and he lost a fair amount of blood. He was life was definitely saved by the quick actions of the first aider on site, there is no doubt about that.

"Anyway, we obviously repaired the nick in the artery and replaced the lost blood so that was OK. He is in recovery now, but he would have potentially sustained a massive shock from the trauma of being shot, so he will need to be treated very carefully when he wakes up."

Dr Martin turned his gaze specifically to Seamus.

"I know what you are thinking, Inspector, you are going to want to question him about the shooting I am sure, but I can't allow it, at least not for 24 to 48 hours depending on how he is. He is going into the ICU unit and will be on all sorts of machines and monitoring. Even when he wakes up, he won't be in a state to be coherent and will be heavily drugged I am afraid."

"It's fine, Doctor," Seamus said at once. "His life and his recovery are more important, obviously, we want to question him but only when it's safe to do so."

Kerry smiled at him gratefully on hearing this, she had been half taking in what was being said and half cruising on automatic. The fact Liam was alive was good enough for now.

"I would like to place an armed guard outside his room if that's OK. I don't there is much chance of the shooter returning but I don't want to take any risks."

"That's no problem at all there, Inspector. Well, I am sure you will have a million questions and we can answer them all soon. In fact, you will be able to talk to the surgeon leading the operation at some point to get the full details. But if there's nothing else then I'll be off, and I'll come back and tell you when he in the ICU unit."

"That's fine," Kerry managed to speak. "But would you please tell the surgeon one thing."

"Sure, Mrs O'Shea, and what would that be?"

"Can you say thank you for saving my son's life."

"I'm sure he will be grateful to hear it, Mrs O'Shea, and you can, of course, tell him in person soon enough."

He took his leave and Kerry turned to Seamus.

"Seamus, Seamus, how did this happen? I don't understand? I don't understand."

Seamus pulled her close and she lay her head onto his chest with tears rolling down her cheeks.

"O'Flynn, can you organise a two-man armed unit to watch over Liam? O'Rorden, give the team onsite a ring and find out what the news is, then let me know. I'm going to stay here at least until I've seen Liam is in the ICU and doing OK."

"Right you are, sir," came the response, the easy atmosphere of the last few hours was gone, although there was palpable relief in the air that Liam was OK. It was very much back to business.

* * *

Diana had arrived back at her house in Dublin. The house lay in a quiet part of the city in a very well to do area. It was a little set back from the road with a walled frontage and gravel drive. There was ample space to park a car or more. It was a period detached residence and was worth over seven figures. She had bought the house as a wreck and had it restored. When she moved her business activities there nobody would have suspected a thing, and they still did not. The only people who knew of its whereabouts were her clients. The house was lavish enough but not overly so.

Diana had expensive tastes, but she didn't waste money either.

Bella greeted her as she opened the front door and entered the hall, Diana put down her bag and keys on the hall table.

"I am glad you are back, Mistress Dana, I was wondering where you were, I was getting worried." She looked at Diana anxiously.

"Oh Bella, oh my beautiful Bella." Diana took her housekeeper's hands and held them gently. Two pairs of green eyes looked at each other. Bella O'Keeffe was a redhead with long straight red hair. She was slim and lithe, with small breasts. She had full sensual lips and a small pert nose. She was almost the opposite of Diana in build, but without shoes, they were equally tall.

"Mistress?"

"Come, Bella, come with me, I have got some important things to tell you, darling."

She took Bella by the hand and they went into the living room. She sat Bella down on the sofa next to her and held on to her hand.

"Bella, I've... I've done some bad things; very bad things and I'm going to have to make a few changes to my lifestyle," Diana began.

Bella's face fell when she heard this pronouncement.

"No, no, Bella, no." Diana tucked her hand under Bella's chin and lifted up other's head gently. "You are going to be fine, I am not abandoning you, I would never do that, but I am going to have to go away for a while, maybe for a very long while, and there are things, I need you to do."

"Yes, Mistress, anything, I'll do anything." Bella's voice was quiet in the stillness and already filled with sadness.

"Listen to me carefully, Bella, and what I'm going to tell you."

"OK," the sad small little voice sounded so small in the vastness of the room. Bella lowered her eyes.

Diana explained she was going away, somewhere where the Garda wouldn't be able to get her. The Garda would be coming here soon, it was for certain and she and Bella were not to be there. She was booking the tickets in the morning and she would be leaving twenty-four hours or so after that. The house they were living in had been put into a trust. The trust was for Bella, and it meant it couldn't be touched. They would also go briefly into town and activate some bank accounts she had taken out for Bella to use. There would be enough money for Bella to get by for many months whilst everything died down. Bella was to take any of her precious things she needed and disappear, for a good long while. Diana had bought another very small cottage in the south of Ireland and that was where Bella was to go and stay there, living a blameless life.

When finally, everything had blown over and it was safe to return then Bella could come back to the house here. Diana had made sure she would be OK until then. There was another car, under wraps, in the garage, for Bella to use, it was in Bella's name, and she was to take it and drive to where she would be staying. All Bella needed to do was keep herself to herself and eventually, things would calm down and everything would be fine. Whatever happened, and if by some chance Diana was caught by the Garda, Bella was to do nothing. She must not reveal herself no matter what, Diana wanted Bella to be safe, safe from harm and all of this.

"Do you understand all of that, Bella?" Diana asked following her lengthy explanation.

"Yes, I think so."

"Good."

"But what have you done, Mistress, that you have to go away?"

"Bella, for your own good I am not going to tell you, you will find out soon enough. I am not a good person; I am not really a fit person at all."

"No, no don't say it, don't say it! It's not true, you are everything, you are everything to me." Bella blurted out, her eyes filled with tears.

"No, Bella, I am, I am a terrible person, you don't know me, the things I've done."

"No, I don't care, I don't care what you've done, it doesn't matter, it doesn't matter to me." Bella's voice was choked with feeling.

"Oh, come on, Bella, what is it? What's the matter, darling? Don't cry my sweet." Diana was surprised by this display of emotion from her. She wasn't used to seeing this so raw, not since she had rescued Bella.

Bella started to cry.

"Bella, Bella!" Diana tried to coax her and then she moved closer to Bella and her hands went up to wipe away her tears. She stroked Bella's hair softly and gently. Bella choked on a few sobs but managed to stop crying.

"What is it?" Diana's green eyes looked into Bella's with great concern.

"It's just that, when you said you had to go away, it's just I felt like my heart, my heart would break, and it is breaking, it is."

"What? No, I don't want you to feel like that, I don't want you to be hurt."

"I'm sorry, Mistress, but I can't help it, I can't help how I feel."

"What?" Diana's voice became softer still and she suddenly was beginning to understand.

"I'm sorry," Bella said, "I'm sorry, Mistress, I can't help it, it's just that I, I love you, I'm in love with you."

"What?" Lower still, softer still, it was dawning on Diana.

"I love you, Mistress, that's all, and if I don't tell you now then you'll never know, and I'll never get the chance again."

"That's all? How long? How long have you loved me, Bella?" Diana asked her, her voice almost a whisper. Her face now very close to Bella's face.

"All my life." The other said simply.

Diana did not know how it happened, nor did she care, but one minute her mouth was centimetres from Bella's mouth and the next their lips had met, and the next they kissed. It was, to Diana, a kiss like no other. Soft and gentle, teasing and warm, sensual and full of love and emotion. Their arms went around each other and wordlessly they embraced. The kiss became more passionate, the longing Bella had felt all these years became a flame. For Diana, the effect was electric. Suddenly desire was unleashed within her, a guttural response to something quite unknown. She had never expected this, but even after just one taste, she wanted more.

"Bella", she whispered when their lips parted.

"Mistress," breathed Bella and her eyes were smiling, smiling with a joy that Diana had never seen. It was the joy of real true love about to be fulfilled. Diana had never seen it because she had never known it, nor had she ever felt it, not like this, but now it hit her like a thunderbolt. If cupid had flown with his bow and fired an arrow into her heart it could not have been clearer. This moment was a moment she had waited all her life for, and now, today of all days and all times it had to happen. Life was indeed cruel. But the night was young. There was still time.

"Call me Diana from now on," said Diana, "not Mistress, I am not your Mistress anymore."

She stood up and took Bella's hand, then quietly but quickly led her upstairs.

✳ ✳ ✳

Seamus was just finishing another coffee when he spied the doctor returning yet again. Kerry was leaning on his arm very quietly and patiently; she had said very little since they had received the news about Liam. However, it had been good news, as good as it could probably get thought, Seamus. He recognised Kerry was in shock and he needed to be there for her.

As much as he was champing at the bit to get back to the investigation, it could wait a little longer. He had very competent officers on his team and they would be dealing with it for the moment. Besides, it was good for them, he didn't need to do everything himself. One day they would need to lead an investigation too and so doing the leg work was an important part of training for that day.

Doctor Martin stopped in front of them.

"Right," he said smiling. "Liam is up in the ICU now, so you can go up and see him. Just please don't be shocked. He will have tubes and the like coming out of everywhere, plus all kinds of machines beeping and making God knows what noises. But that's all normal. There will be a nurse there constantly. Just remember don't try to tax him at all, he needs to rest and recover, it's the best medicine he can have now. Above all, he doesn't need any stress whatsoever."

The doctor had obviously dealt with some very pushy Garda officers before, thought Seamus, since he seemed to really want to labour the points about letting Liam be. However, he nodded and assured the doctor they would respect these strictures.

"A protection team will be on their way soon," Seamus told him.

"Great, well OK then, I'll lead the way."

Kerry seemed just happy to follow along and let Seamus do the talking. It was a great comfort to her she wasn't bearing this load on her own, and Seamus was there for her to depend on. They saw O'Flynn and O'Rorden in the lobby and Seamus signalled they were going up to see Liam. The two of them followed a discreet distance behind.

Seamus was prepared for the ICU since, as a Garda officer, he'd seen many of such instances with victims of crimes. Kerry would perhaps not be so used to it and so it proved when they entered the ICU room where Liam was lying. She all but slumped against Seamus and he had to steady her gently.

"Oh, God. Oh, my God, Liam, Liam," she said softly, tears were once more running freely down her cheeks.

Seamus observed this with growing anger, anger at the person who had caused her this much pain, pain to the woman he loved, anger her son was so nearly taken from her, anger she would be hurt so much, anger at her tears of grief. He resolved this murderer would be caught no matter what the cost. The ICU nurse tending Liam came up to them.

"Hello, it's Mrs O'Shea, isn't it? Liam's Ma? Well now, don't you worry, Liam is doing very well, we're keeping a constant and very close eye on him. He's in good hands here I promise." She smiled reassuringly.

Kerry broke away from Seamus and approached the bed. One of Liam's hands was on top of the covers; the upper part of his hand was connected to a drip. As if by magic, the nurse produced a chair and set it down beside the bed. Kerry sank into it gratefully and her hand reached up and took hold of Liam's fingers.

"Liam..." she whispered, "I'm here, your Ma, I'm here with you now, Liam, I love you so much."

The fingers she held onto gave hers a gentle squeeze, and Liam's lips curved into a very faint smile.

Kerry buried her face in the covers of the bed and sobbed.

Seamus observing this decided he had better try to obtain some support for Kerry, to help her through this and keep her company. As much as he would like to, he knew he was needed by the team, and also, he realised getting Kerry to come home was probably going to be impossible, at least not tonight.

He quietly left the room and went to talk to O'Flynn and O'Rorden who were looking through the window with very concerned faces.

"Sir, the two-man protection team is on the way, it'll be here shortly. They'll cover this room in shifts and they are both fully armed," O'Flynn told him.

"Good, that's great for Liam, but now I'm worried about Kerry, I need someone to look after her for a while. Can you organise a woman Garda pronto, please? I need to get back to the investigation."

"Sure, sir, I'll get right on it."

"O'Rorden, how's it going?" Seamus asked him.

"Pretty well, sir, so far. They've managed to view the CCTV footage and they've got a good view of the murderer arriving and leaving, plus several other occasions. It seems she had quite a few men up there from time to time, so Liam wasn't the first. There is no footage of her car, she parked it quite some way away, unfortunately, probably to avoid the car park CCTV. Also, she always wore a wig. The hotel has no details for her, no ID, and she always paid in cash, but she always used the same room, number 66."

"Hmm, yes there is probably something about that number, but I am not sure what, it seems too much of a coincidence," mused Seamus.

"Anyway, sir, forensics have taken away quite a few hairs for examination and they think they are likely to match the ones from the other murders, plus they have the bullets. They checked the room for any kind of DNA or fingerprints. I mean there are several of course but it won't help us if she's not on our database. It seems she never brought much with her and never left anything either. It's not much help."

"Did they have any idea why there was a stone dog on the floor out of interest?"

"Erm, well not really, sir, although Jim said maybe it was thrown by Liam."

"That figures, he could have been trying to distract her or something, who knows. She's a clever one, this woman, whoever she is. Whoever the real Diana is."

"Oh yes, sir, that does remind me, the name she gave for the Hotel."

"What was it?"

"It was Deirdre Flanagan."

"Ah for fuck's sake, this woman is playing fucking games!" Seamus sounded off his frustration.

"At least we know we're on the right track though, sir."

"Yes, but which fucking track, that's the problem, she has outsmarted us each time in spite of her mistakes, and I've got to think perhaps her shooting Liam was a mistake. But anyway, there must be a chink in her armour, we've just got to find it and fast."

"What do you think will be her next move, sir?"

"That's just it I don't know, it could be anything but more than likely it's to kill someone else."

"Another priest?"

"Perhaps, but who?"

"It's the million dollar question I guess, sir, isn't it?"

"Yes, it is, O'Rorden, that it is, somehow we've got to put ourselves in her shoes, think like her, maybe it will help, anyway, think on, let's think on, I'll just go back and check on Kerry."

"Yes, yes of course, sir."

Seamus went back into the ICU unit, Kerry was still sitting by the bed staring at Liam and holding his hand.

"How are you doing?" he asked her gently, squatting down beside her and putting his hand on her shoulder.

"OK." She shrugged, and her face looked a picture of misery.

"I guess it's going to be useless to ask you to come home?"

"I'm not leaving Liam."

"I thought so, well I'm getting a female Garda officer to come and look after you, stay with you."

"I don't need anyone..." she started to say.

"Yes, you do, Kerry, you do." His voice was firm, brooking no opposition. "Apart from anything else I won't get any sleep otherwise and I have to go back, I have to get on with catching the person who did this."

"I know, and I'm sorry, I am so grateful really."

Kerry turned to him, and they embraced. He kissed her lightly.

"You'll be the death of me, Kerry O'Shea," he said laughing. "You and your son."

"Not funny!" she told him, but he saw her lips curl in a smile.

"I saw you, I saw that little smile, Mrs O'Shea."

"Oh you!"

They both laughed, it relieved the tension.

"At least come down and eat something, then once the protection team is here, and the Garda officer, I really will have to go."

"I know."

She allowed him to pull her up and after one small forlorn glance at her son, she went out of the room with him.

"Stay here, O'Rorden, until the protection officers arrive, I am just going to make sure Kerry eats, you can come down and do that as soon as they get here, then once the Garda officer is here, you, me and O'Flynn will need to go."

"Of course, sir, I'll see you shortly sir."

Seamus managed to get Kerry to consume a few morsels of food, in fact, she found she was quite hungry and made no complaint. He tried to keep her amused while they were eating and then just as they finished the protection team and the Garda female officer arrived. Introductions were made and O'Flynn went up with the protection team, and to get O'Rorden.

O'Rorden said he would rather eat with O'Flynn back at Ballysruth so they were set to leave.

Seamus gave Kerry one last long hug and a kiss.

"Try at least to get some sleep and make sure you eat. Phone me if anything happens or if you need anything and I'll call you tomorrow, and then come by later, OK?"

"OK," she replied in a sotto voice.

"Bye, bye, sweetheart, I love you, remember that."

"I love you too," was all she said.

She waved as Seamus walked away and then she and the Garda Officer headed back to the ICU.

* * *

Once they had arrived on the landing, at the top of the stairs, Diana opened the door to the punishment room and led Bella into it. However, there was no intention to use any of the instruments contained within, it just had the biggest bed. Bella shut the door behind her, her eyes were wide in anticipation.

"You are very beautiful; do you know that?" Diana said, "I don't know how I haven't noticed this before."

Bella shook her head, but she smiled a delighted smile. Diana thought how pretty she really was, especially when she smiled.

"Come here," Diana said softly.

She pulled Bella into a kiss, a kiss of passion and a kindling fire. A fire within both of them. Slowly she began to remove Bella's clothes, marvelling at her smooth and white skin. It was almost translucent in the way redheads have. Looking at Bella naked she was at once consumed with desire. Diana began to undress more quickly now, and Bella reached across to help. As Diana peeled off her clothes, Bella began to run her fingers over Diana's naked flesh. It did things Diana had never felt. It was different somehow more sensual and loving than any man she had been with, even Liam. They fell onto the bed, their bodies entwining.

Diana pushed herself up to the top of the bed and Bella lay down gently on top of her. She was light, but the feeling was good, he body pressing down into Diana's. Diana could feel herself getting moist and put her hand between Bella's legs, to feel her there. Diana's fingers felt wet as she began to explore, Bella gasped, her eyes opened wider, she pushed down against Diana's fingers. Bella moved her own hand to reciprocate the feeling and Diana let out a long sigh of pleasure at her touch. The two of them brought each other to climax easily and quickly, Bella buried her mouth in Diana's as they did so. They kissed then, deeply long and lovingly. Diana was happy, but Bella wasn't finished. She moved down Diana's stomach laying a moistened trail with her tongue and then she found Diana's sweet spot.

"Oh my God, Bella!" Diana arched her back, she had not before, been so completely moved by the act of sex. But really, it wasn't sex, and she knew it, this, finally, was making love.

It could have been another hour, or it could have been more, neither of them knew, nor cared about the time. They just made love, passionately, carefully, slowly and lovingly. Bella was a considerate and caring lover, a giving lover, all of the things Diana had wanted in a lover, that was Bella. Diana gave it back to Bella, in full, and more, using all the tricks of her long years just to make Bella happy, to make her satisfied. Bella never lost her smile, nor the ethereal glow when she looked into Diana's eyes. And finally, Diana knew and understood what it was to be truly loved.

As they lay together, at last, spent, exhausted, a few stray tears ran down Diana's cheek.

"Why are you crying, my love?" Bella asked her.

"Because," Diana whispered, "because I have only just found you, really found you, and now I have to go."

Bella spoke with moving sincerity, quietly and softly, "I've always been here, Diana, for you, always, it has always been you, I've loved you from the moment I ever laid eyes on you, from the day when you took me in, until this."

"I've been such a fool, you've been there all the time and I never knew, I never could see it."

"Sshhhh." Bella put one slim finger to Diana's lips. "Don't cry, don't cry, my darling, I will love you, no matter what you've done, no matter where you are, I will love you until I die."

It was a vow, one many lovers might have made, and probably would never keep, but Diana knew Bella meant it, meant every word. She knew Bella would keep it too. The love she had been seeking all these years was right here, in Bella, her faithful housekeeper who was really, so very much more than that. She had been a fool, a fool bound up in vengeance, in revenge. A fool looking for love in all the wrong places, with all the wrong people, including Liam. Bella could have healed her, her love would have mended her, mended what was broken. But now she had broken it beyond repair. She was going to pay a price one way or another.

"Bella, maybe, once I sort things out, you can come to me, wherever I am, how about that?" It was a lifeline perhaps, for Diana, for Bella, hope, hope which springs eternal.

"Yes! Yes, for sure!" Bella smiled and kissed Diana, so tenderly Diana could feel all her heart in the kiss, and all of her soul. Bella believed her, believed Diana could and would work miracles. But this time, Diana was not so sure.

What she would do is she would make sure Bella came to no harm, that was certain. If she had fucked up, then Bella wouldn't be a casualty of it. Not now and not ever. She pulled Bella close, feeling her slim body, and held her tight, never wanting to let her go.

DAY 12

Sleep had not come easy to Seamus, and all too soon it was morning. His eyes were heavy, and he felt so weary. He had gone to bed in Kerry's room. He thought of using his own but instead, he scrunched up the robe she had last worn and hugged it to him. He could smell her smell and feel her close. And that is how he had finally gone to sleep.

So many things were troubling him, going around in his head. But he also knew without any sleep he would be useless to his team and to the investigation. After they had arrived back at the office last night, he had had a short meeting and sent everyone away to get some rest. There was a busy time ahead. A very busy time. He had updated Brogan briefly also and promised to talk more fully the next day. Now the next day had arrived. He wished it had not and there were a few more hours left to rest. But it was no use, he heaved himself out of the bed and into the shower.

The shower was nice as usual, but without Kerry, the room felt empty. He dressed, made himself neat, presentable, all of the things he did every day. However, there was something missing, the kisses, the love and banter. All those things had become part of him, were all those things he sorely missed already when they were not there.

"Kerry," he said to the mirror, "Kerry, Kerry, Kerry. What have you done to me? You've made me fall in love with you and now look at me. Besotted! So, you are Seamus Gallway, besotted!"

He pointed at himself in the mirror as if he was scolding himself severely, but it just made him laugh. Just like Kerry made him laugh.

His phone rang.

"Kerry!" He could hardly keep the smile out of his voice.

"Hi." There was an answering smile in her tone.

"How are you? How's Liam?" he asked her anxiously.

"He's much the same. I managed to get some sleep, they gave me a bed to use in another room, they had one to spare."

"That was very kind of them, did you sleep OK?"

"No."

"Oh, I'm sorry."

"Well, it's your fault." He recognised the teasing note in her voice and smiled.

"What? How is it my fault?"

"Because I don't sleep well when you're not with me, and... because I love you." He imagined her standing there pouting like she did, saying this, looking so exceptionally cute, as she always did. A stray blonde hair would usually fall across the side of her face, in that sexy way, as it always did. He sighed thinking of it.

"So, it's my fault you are in love with me?"

"Yes, yes, it is, Seamus Gallway!"

Seamus laughed.

482

"Stop laughing it's not funny, you come into my life out of nowhere, make me fall in love with you, and then... and then..."

"Oh, so I made you fall in love with me now? Is that what you are saying is it?"

"Yes, you did, and don't you deny it! You with your cute looks and handsome smile and all the other things you are, how was I supposed to help it?"

"Other things?" he said with interest.

"Yes, other things, and I'm not telling you so there, but yes, other things."

"You know I'm going to have to find out later what those other things are don't you?"

"Oh you!"

"Well anyway, you wanted to stay there and not come home," he pointed out.

"Oh you! Why do you have to keep being so logical?"

"I guess it's the Garda in me." He laughed. "Anyway, for what it's worth I didn't sleep well either, I missed you."

"Did you?" Her voice went all soft on hearing this.

"Yes."

"How much did you miss me?"

"So much I had to sleep hugging your empty robe for comfort."

"Oh... that's a lot." She sounded pleased to hear it.

"Yes.... Happy now?"

"Yes."

"So, how's Liam?"

"As I said just now, he's much the same, still heavily sedated and so he hasn't spoken or anything. I thought I saw his eyes maybe flicker open slightly but I'm not sure. The doctors and nurses are all saying he's fine, he's stable. But he's not fine, not to me, my poor little boy lying there like that."

"Hang in there, Kerry, Liam will be OK, I am sure of it." Seamus was immediately comforting and solicitous.

"I know," she sighed. "I'll be able to talk to the surgeon today and he'll tell me more."

"OK, but I am afraid I've got to get on top of this investigation I'm sorry, but I will try to come by later, that's if you are staying." Seamus was hoping she wasn't.

"Well, I've got to come home and shower and change, I can't stay here all day, I'll start to stink for one thing."

Seamus laughed. "Well just ask the Garda Officer to bring you, any problems ring me, let me know when you get home, I'll pop back to see you."

"OK, that sounds fine."

"I love you, Kerry."

"I love you, Seamus Gallway."

Seamus disconnected the phone and went down for breakfast. Colleen was surprised to see him in the breakfast room and ushered him at once into Kerry's parlour. Kerry had already rung her to make sure he got his breakfast. He was very touched, she always seemed to be thinking of him, no matter what else was going on. He wasn't used to it, in fact, he'd never really experienced it before. After all these years, Seamus was suddenly finding out the meaning of true love.

This investigation had been an eye-opener in more ways than one. Maybe there was something in the water in Ballysruth, that's what they said wasn't it when a place had a magical effect on you. Something in the water. There was certainly something about this town at least, that was for sure. He had arrived with contempt for everything and everyone in it and now, in less than a couple of weeks, it was almost as if he had been bewitched.

He really didn't know what he was going to do once this investigation was over and he had wrapped it up. Brogan would want him back in Dublin and onto something else, somewhere else. It was the nature of his job. Well, he thought, he would just have to stay here for as long as he could. First, he would have to catch this murderer, then complete the case for the prosecution service, and then somehow grab a couple more weeks after that. He smiled to himself, he would work it out.

Colleen had brought a full Irish and a pot of coffee breaking into his reverie.

"Here you go, Inspector, looks like you'll be needing this."

"Thank you, Colleen, it looks and smells incredibly good," he said eyeing the spread with great appreciation.

"It's probably not as good as Kerry's but it will pass muster I am sure." She winked.

"I'm sure it's delicious and I am starved."

She smiled taking the compliment.

"I hope you can catch whoever shot Liam," Colleen said with a note of grave concern.

"We'll be doing our damnedest I can assure you of that."

"That's good enough for me, enjoy your breakfast."

Colleen swept out of the room and he put his attention onto his food, tucking into it gratefully. He took a long drink of the hot coffee and waited for the caffeine to kick in.

* * *

The morning meeting was full of suppressed excitement. Seamus could feel it in the air. This often happened when they knew they were getting close. Except, in this case, close wasn't close at all. They were nowhere nearer to actually getting any concrete information on Diana O'Malley, they had no idea where she lived, or how to find her.

"OK everyone, we are here at day twelve. I would like to say this is an exciting day but have to remind everyone of the fact we almost had another victim on our hands. We know now barring DNA confirmation the murderer is a person known as Diana O'Malley, also known as Deirdre Flanagan, and in fact, the latter is the name she was born with. We have her file here on my desk and anyone is welcome to look at it and see if they can find something we missed.

"Everything we can tell about her, and that's not much at all, is she is a troubled soul. Obviously very troubled to have shot three people from the clergy and almost killed someone who she was apparently having sexual relations with, at least that's our assumption. She has, by all accounts from her file, suffered horrific abuse mainly at the hands of Mother Joan Margaret and also most likely Father Cooney. It is a catalogue of abuse on someone Mother Joan Margaret in her own hand has designated 'Child of the Devil'. Now I'm not telling you this to absolve her in any way of her crimes or to negate the seriousness of what she has done. But you need to know who you are dealing with. This is a woman who is by all accounts unstable, trigger happy and likely to kill again. Her background is probably a mitigating factor but it's not for us to decide, it is for the courts. Neither is it our place to judge her in any way for what she has done, although God knows I am sure we all have some personal opinions about it. However, we have to put that aside, be professional, and that's our job. We need to find her, arrest her and to bring her to justice, whatever the law will decide happens to her after is not up to us.

"So, for the moment, Diana is our focus, we need to find this woman and we need to find her as fast as possible. I am saying that, particularly because it's very likely she may murder someone else. Given her state of mind and the fact she knows we are probably going to be getting closer, it just might push her to do something drastic. It's clear she must have had some kind of plan for killing these priests, and very possibly has compiled a hit list. Let's try to make sure nobody else dies. So, let's maybe put our heads together now and if anyone's got anything useful to add or any ideas, let's hear it."

"Sir, we questioned the hotel clerk quite extensively, but he didn't seem to know anything." It was Hughes. "She's a regular client we've seen all the footage on CCTV from the lobby and so on, and we know a number of different men visited her there on various occasions apart from Liam. The clerk never took any of their names or their ID either. He doesn't know who she is, as I said, or anything about her. So overall, we've got nothing other than a lot of video footage, we have copies of that."

"The clerk seems to have gone to a lot of trouble to not know anything," Seamus said with some acidity.

"I think there has been some greasing of the palm in that regard, sir. Although he's not going to admit to it."

"Oh, I'm sure there has been, one thing we know about Diana is she's not short of money. For a librarian, particularly, she has a lot of money. Expensive clothes and so on. So, we've got to assume her salary hasn't paid for all of that. We need to try to find out how she's funded her lifestyle. Also, why would she go to the trouble of coming down here and being a librarian? There's got to be a reason for that too.

"Let's get a bit smart about this, Hughes, get a team back to the hotel and question all the staff, maybe somebody heard something, saw something, anything, any sort of clue would be helpful. Duffy and O'Flynn I need you to obtain a search warrant and get into the library, take a team with you and take it apart if you have to, carefully mind. Find out what the hell she was doing in there all this time. Healy, contact the council again and Libraries Ireland, can you try to find out who hired her, and if anyone there knows anything about her.

"Right, that's all I can think of for the moment, but if anyone else has a bright idea, go right ahead and follow it up. We all need to pitch in. Remember we are a team, and now is when we need to pull our weight. If there is genuinely nothing you can do on the Diana investigation, then there's always wrapping up the filing. So, let's get to it."

"Sir." It was Duffy.

"Yes, Duffy?"

"Well, what about the confession and the report I am writing on it? Do I just abandon it?"

"By no means, Duffy, the work is important, you will have plenty of time to finish it up once we've got Diana in custody, but until then keep it on the backburner, unless of course, you've nothing else constructive to do."

"Right sir, thanks."

"Listen, everyone, we will have to complete wrapping up everything after we conclude this investigation. I don't leave loose ends. We finish what we started. Particularly these abuse cases, we're not leaving these open. I don't know what's going to happen to them, but at least we will have compiled the evidence. Got it?"

There was general assent and the meeting broke up.

"What are we going to do sir? You and me?" O'Rorden asked.

"Good question, O'Rorden, I've got to phone the DCS and then we need to make ourselves useful. One thing you could do is organise the new identity for Anna Kowalski. Get in touch with the Witness Security Program team and I am sure they will sort it out when you explain the circumstances. Find a name for her other than Deidre Flanagan."

They both laughed at this.

"OK sir, I'll get onto it."

Seamus headed outside and dialled Brogan's number.

"Brogan"

"Sir, it's DI Gallway."

"Ah, Seamus, how's it going on down there? What happened the boy, Liam, who got shot? Is he OK?" Brogan sounded genuinely concerned which was nice.

"Yes sir, he's fine but in the ICU right now. He was very lucky, it could have been a lot worse."

"Have you been able to interview him?"

"Not yet, sir, the doctors won't allow it and also he's not been fully conscious yet."

"OK but try and get to it as soon as you can, hopefully, he can shed some more light on things." Seamus could tell Brogan wanted to push him harder on this but was holding back, for which he was grateful. It indicated Brogan had some degree of confidence in him.

"Sure, sir, but we are now almost certain the murderer is Diana O'Malley who worked at Ballysruth library, we are focusing all our efforts on her, although she's managed to conceal so much about her identity and whereabouts, it's difficult."

"Do you want to release details about her, try and get some public feedback, that sort of thing?"

"I don't think I want to do it just now, sir, for a start it will alert her to the fact we don't have anything on her and it will give her a chance to run. I have a hunch she will be planning something and will be sticking around."

"A last hurrah you mean?"

"Something like that, sir."

"Well, OK but we don't want another priest getting shot, Seamus." There was a note of warning there and Seamus was well aware someone else could be murdered.

"We'll do our best to avoid it. I want 48 hours and if we are no further forward then we'll go public."

"OK, Seamus, it's your investigation." That was a bit of washing hands by the sounds of it. If it all turned to shit, then no doubt Brogan would throw Seamus to the lions. As much as he liked his boss, Seamus had no illusions Brogan would go down with the ship, not when he was so close to retiring.

"At least you can tell the AC we're onto something."

"Yes, that's a positive at least, it'll keep him off my back."

"How's the Archbishop, sir?" Seamus changed the subject to one he knew would get a reaction.

"Ach, well he's gone awfully quiet since I mentioned O'Flaherty's confession, thank God for that is all I can say." Brogan chuckled, the Archbishop was a big thorn in his side and Seamus knew it. Unfortunately, many of Seamus' cases had involved the church and had involved the Archbishop phoning Brogan and complaining on a regular basis about the investigations. Brogan would be happy to now have something concrete on the church.

"You mean you're missing his phone calls then, sir?"

"I would miss them like I'd miss being shot in the head if you'll excuse the bad taste." Brogan laughed.

"So, do you have any ideas about what we can do with the confession afterwards, sir? Duffy has been compiling a full report on it." Seamus thought he would chance it now Brogan was in a good mood.

"Yes, well I'm still thinking about it... oh look at the time Seamus, I've got a meeting sorry, keep me posted."

The phone disconnected leaving Seamus visibly annoyed. It seemed his Boss was determined to avoid the issue and he wasn't happy. He could see this conveniently getting swept under the carpet, it wasn't something he was prepared to tolerate. However, this was a battle for another day. He put the phone back into his pocket and headed back inside.

✻ ✻ ✻

Diana opened her eyes, sunlight was streaming in through the skylight. Usually, she had the blinds drawn on all the windows in this room, but last night, she had wanted to let the moonlight in. She lay in bed and looked at Bella. Bella was lying there quietly watching her. They had made love for most of the night until they were exhausted and had fallen asleep in each other's arms.

She smiled at Bella and leaned her head forward to kiss her. She marvelled at the softness of her lips. This girl who had spent all these years with her, faithfully keeping her house, minding her clients, cooking her the most exquisite meals, reading to her at night, doing everything and anything for her comfort and asking for nothing in return, actually loved her. It was hard to believe, but it was true, in every act of love last night Bella had shown it. Diana had never had a person give themselves to her so completely and want nothing in return. She had shed bitter tears in the middle of the night for the lost time, and things which could never be, and Bella had simply gently wiped her tears away and kissed away her pain. Bella was all that was good, and Diana was the opposite. An angel in love with the devil, that's how it seemed.

"Bella, you are an angel, do you know that," she whispered.

"No, no I'm not, I'm not an angel, I'm lustful, I'm sinful."

"Compared to me you are an angel." Diana laughed. "I was called a child of the devil."

"No, not the devil, you are not the devil, not to me," Bella said emphatically.

"Thank you." Diana kissed her again. "But why do you say you are sinful? You are not sinful, darling."

"My father, my priest, they told me, they said I was a sinner, they said I committed a mortal sin."

"Why, because you got pregnant?"

"Yes, but not just because of that, it's because of this." She kissed Diana again.

"Because you like girls? Did you always like them then?"

"Yes, that's why, I always did, I was in love with a girl at school. We were caught together kissing, in my room. My father was so angry, he called up the priest, and then he punished me in front of the priest and my mother, and the other girl."

Diana flushed with red raw anger when she heard this.

"Don't, don't be angry, it's in the past, the pain lasted only a few moments and then it was gone." Bella stroked Diana's face gently. "The priest made me come to confession. I went many times. He thundered at me, telling me I was a mortal sinner. I had to pray and pray and pray, but it didn't work, I still liked girls, I was just more careful afterwards. Then, I thought to please my father, I would try to be with a boy, and that's how I got pregnant. It didn't please my father though." She laughed at this, it was funny to her now, all those years back.

"So, he threw you out?"

"Yes, and it's how you found me, on the street, with nowhere to go, I was thinking of killing myself."

"Oh, Bella, Bella, no, no." Diana pulled her close and held her tight.

"You saved me, Diana, you saved me, and I loved you from that moment."

"But you couldn't say it." Diana understood.

"No, no because I was still carrying the mortal sin, in my heart, because of what the priest told me. But then, when you said you were going to go away, I had to speak out, I had to tell you, it was my only chance."

"It's not a sin, Bella, it never has been, it's just love, that's all it is, just love. Nothing more or nothing less. The church has a lot to answer for. I wish you had told me sooner."

"I'm sorry," Bella said softly. "I wish I had too."

"It's too late for that," Diana said with decision. "What's done is done, I am just glad you told me now, that's all because already I can feel you have started to heal me, in my heart, in spite of everything I have done."

Bella hugged her even tighter.

"I forgive you, Diana, for whatever it is you have done, I forgive you now and forever."

"But you don't know, you don't know what I've done."

"I don't care, it doesn't matter. My love for you is all that matters."

"See, I said you are an angel, my darling and you are, you're my angel."

Bella's answer was a kiss, a long loving lingering kiss.

"I know, we'll spend the day together, our last day, we've lots to do, and then you'll have to go, but let's have a beautiful day, don't cry." Diana smiled.

At the mention of the last day, Bella's eyes had filled with tears.

"There are also things I need you to do, things I need you to take with you," Diana told her.

"OK, then show me, tell me."

Bella jumped out of the bed all of a sudden and stood naked in the room while Diana openly admired her beauty. Bella noticed and did a little twirl.

"Sexy," murmured Diana.

"And how about now?" Bella went over to the basket near the dressing table and pulled out a cane. She swished it experimentally in the air a few times.

"Mmm, Mistress Bella is it? I can see it, you just need the leather corset and heels."

Bella laughed and tossed the cane aside.

"Maybe I should take over the business," she teased.

"No, Bella, no." Diana was serious. "Don't do that, it will change you, and you are so innocent, so sweet, so beautiful."

She held out her arms and Bella came running into them. They kissed.

"We'll see." Bella's eyes were sparkling with fun.

"Don't lose the beautiful essence that is you my darling, don't ever lose it."

"I won't," Bella said, "I promise you."

"OK, well then have a look at this."

Diana got out of the bed and went over to the fitted wardrobe along one side of the wall. She opened it. Inside

494

were all kinds of outfits she used for her role-playing and other instruments of discipline. But there was also a column of shelves containing a computer and a myriad of little black boxes.

"What's that?" Bella asked her eyes growing wider.

"Recording equipment, all the sessions I have done are on these hard drives in here."

"All of them? Why?"

"My insurance policy honey. Just in case. I need you to take these with you and hide them away, until I want them, if I ever do."

"OK."

"We'll pack them in a suitcase, I won't be needing them anymore."

"Have you done your last session?"

"Not quite, but I don't need to record it."

"Yes, OK."

"Now, you know I've got a very big jacuzzi bath?" Diana took Bella once more in her arms.

"Yes?"

"I think we should have a bath, you and me, together, don't you?"

"Oh yes."

They kissed again, the future was forgotten as they focused entirely on the present and each other.

* * *

The search warrant for the library was easily obtained. A member of Libraries Ireland had come down from the Head Office in Dublin to open it up especially, there was no backup librarian for Ballysruth. They obviously preferred it to having the Garda break through the doors, and the subsequent expense of replacing them. When they could get into the library, Duffy, O'Flynn and the team had gone to work searching through the place.

After two hours, the search team returned.

"Finished already?" Seamus said surprised.

"Yes, sir, we've been through the library from top to bottom and there was hardly anything of interest." It was Duffy.

"You said hardly anything, so you must have found something."

"We found this."

Duffy put a large fat file on the desk. It was a plain manila folder without anything written on the front. Seamus flicked through the first few pages. They were clippings of newspaper articles about abuse allegations.

"Is this it?" Seamus said.

"Not quite, sir, go a bit further in."

Seamus flicked on through the various pages and finally came to a picture of Father O'Flaherty. It had a big red cross through it. The next picture was Father Cooney with another red cross. The third one was Mother Joan Margaret with another red cross.

O'Rorden, who was looking over his shoulder, gave a low whistle.

"Are there any more pictures like this?" Seamus asked. "One's without red crosses."

"No, sir," Duffy replied.

"Well, that's something."

"But what I think we can tell from the file, sir, is a lot of the information came from the library."

"Now, that makes sense, why she became the librarian. Also, why the historical information was in such good order.

She needed to have it in good order to get the information from it."

"Yes, sir."

"But what is this file telling us? Other than she planned to kill three people and she accomplished her aim. At least it shows these were planned and premeditated, the prosecution service will love it."

"I don't know, sir."

"OK, well the two of you go through it and see if you can find out." Seamus tossed the file over the desk at Duffy and O'Flynn.

"Sir."

"Well done, Duffy and O'Flynn. One thing though, did you find anything of forensic value in there, hairs and such like?"

"No, sir, but we've got the tech team coming down to give it the once over."

"That's good, well done for that too, now you are thinking like detectives."

"Thanks, sir, the librarian handed the key over to us and we will return it once we've finished. We've sealed off the area and there's a Garda team keeping watch."

"Great, that's good work, study the file and see if you can find something more."

Duffy and O'Flynn retrieved the file and headed to their desks.

"We're not getting anywhere with this, O'Rorden." Seamus sounded disappointed.

"It does seem like it, sir."

"Doesn't this woman make any mistakes?"

"She seems to be pretty smart, sir, that she is."

"Yes, she is, unfortunately." Seamus sighed. This was probably one of the toughest cases he had ever dealt with.

Usually, there was something, even a small thing and you pulled the string and there it was, the evidence. With Diana, there was nothing, she had it sewn up tight. The only thing to do was to carry on looking.

* * *

At lunchtime, Seamus went back to the Baker's Arms to see Kerry. She had returned from the hospital to shower and change. When he entered her parlour, she flung herself into his arms. He was speechless for a while, mainly because she couldn't stop kissing him.

"I missed you, Seamus, I missed you so much," she told him eventually.

"You were only gone for 24 hours," he teased.

"Oh you! It's 24 hours too long."

"I know, I'm winding you up sweetheart, I missed you too."

"Sit down, have something to eat sweetie pie."

"Sweetie pie, is it? I like that." He kissed her.

They ate hungrily and silently, just looking into each other's eyes. Kerry was wearing a loose blouse with a skirt and sandals. Throughout the meal, she periodically brushed her bare leg up and down Seamus' leg. He said nothing, but she could see in his eyes this was having the desired effect. When they finished their meal, she asked without preamble.

"Do you want to go upstairs?"

"Why's that?" His eyes were dancing.

"I want to show you how much I missed you."

"Well then what are we waiting for?"

They practically ran up the stairs like teenagers and tumbled onto the bed. They had by now reached the ripping clothes off stage all relationships go through, and soon these were in a heap on the floor. Their lovemaking was almost frantic with desire, fast and furious. The two of them had what seemed an exceptional passion each for the other. In a very short while they were lying together holding each other close.

"I needed that," said Seamus unashamedly.

"So, did I," agreed Kerry smiling.

"I can't stay too long, I've got to get back to the investigation, such as it is."

"Oh, is it not going well?"

He told her briefly what he felt he could. The focus on Diana and they were almost certain now she was the killer.

"It makes sense to me," Kerry said. "Particularly about Liam, he was probably one of her lovers or she was one of his, I don't know which. He never told me much, but I knew there was someone he had a particular, let's say weakness for, I just didn't know who."

"So, you think this was a crime of passion? In his case?" Seamus looked serious.

"Very likely, it's obvious Liam hasn't fallen for anyone yet, but perhaps she had fallen for him and shot him out of unrequited love, I mean I'm just guessing, and it doesn't make me any less angry with her for doing it."

"I understand," said Seamus and then the teasing tone was back. "Don't you go getting any ideas now, Kerry O'Shea."

"I won't." She pouted. "Besides my love is requited so I don't need to shoot you now, do I?"

He laughed then, and he kissed her.

"I'll keep it in mind."

"You do that, Seamus Gallway." But her eyes were smiling.

"Are you wanting to go back to the hospital?"

"Yes, I would like to."

"OK, I'll organise it. And are you going to stay there?" He was hoping perhaps she wouldn't but expecting her to say yes.

"No!"

"Oh?"

"Oh you! You know I couldn't stand another night away from you so there!" The pout was back.

"I'm glad." He put a finger gently to her lips and she bit down on it playfully.

Their lips met again. Seamus felt the same about not being apart and wondered how it was going to be when he had another case and had to spend many nights away. He pushed the thought aside, that bridge was for crossing another day, not today.

"I'd best get back then." He started to get up. Her hand caught his and held him. He looked at her questioningly.

"Not so fast."

"Oh?"

"I haven't finished with you yet."

"Is that a fact?"

Seamus allowed her to pull him back down and let her roll him onto his back. Kerry smiled as she sat on his legs.

"Now let's take a bit slower this time, DI Gallway, shall we?"

* * *

Seamus had taken somewhat longer than he expected at the Baker's Arms due to the unexpected energy of his girlfriend. He stopped himself on that thought. Girlfriend? Things had indeed moved fast, but he found he didn't mind it. In fact, he liked it. That he must inform Kerry she was now his girlfriend was his very next thought. He smiled.

"Did you have a nice lunch?" O'Rorden asked him.

"Yes, and you can take that smirk off your face, so you can." Seamus laughed.

"I never said a thing, sir," O'Rorden protested.

"You didn't have to."

"Sir, the forensics are back from the Liam shooting and they confirm the DNA from hairs found on the bed are the same as those in the other killings." O'Rorden changed the topic of conversation quickly.

"So, Diana is definitely our murderer."

"Yes, sir, it seems so indeed."

"Good, that's something, and what about the bullets?"

"They also match."

"Perfect! So, we know we are going after the right person, we just need to find her somehow."

"I've also sorted the new identity for Anna and it'll be ready in a couple of days."

"That's fantastic, I've asked Kerry and she says she will take her on at the pub, so we can move Anna there very soon then."

"That is good news, sir, very good news indeed." O'Rorden was happy to hear Anna would now be settled.

"I wonder how the team is getting on at the hotel," mused Seamus. "It would be nice if we could get even one small clue on Diana, the thin end of the wedge so to speak."

"Shall I give them a ring..." O'Rorden started to say when Seamus' phone started vibrating.

Seamus looked at in surprise, picked up the call and put it onto speaker so O'Rorden could hear.

"Well, well, well, talk of the devil." It was Hughes.

"Hughes, how's it going over there?"

"Well, sir, something interesting has come up."

"What's that?"

"We were talking to the clerk at reception yet again and trying to impress upon him this is actually a murder investigation and he needed to tell us anything he could remember, anything at all, you know what I mean, sir."

"Yes, I do, a very reluctant witness that one. And then?"

"Well, sir, then he suddenly says, 'Oh would you maybe be interested in a suitcase we keep for her in storage?'"

"What! What the fuck!" He and O'Rorden looked at each other. O'Rorden was shaking his head.

"Well yes, sir, that's what I said or something like it," Hughes replied agreeing with her boss.

"How did he think we wouldn't be interested? What the fuck was going on in his head?"

"Again, sir, I told him pretty much the same thing."

"And he said?"

"Oh, he said something like, he had forgotten all about it because she hadn't asked for it in a while and he had just thought of it then." Hughes sounded very unconvinced by the explanation as she related it to them.

"Oh really? Who the fuck is he trying to kid? Just remembered it. Jesus Fucking Christ!"

"Yes, sir, exactly my thoughts, sir."

"So, do you have the suitcase?"

"We have it, sir."

"And have you opened it, found out what's in it?"

"We have, sir."

"And?"

"You need to see it for yourself, sir, I can't quite describe it over the phone."

Seamus raised an eyebrow at this.

"Right, I see, well, have you finished the interviews then? If so, bring it over here right away."

"Yes, we are pretty much done with the interviews, sir, so we'll be back shortly."

"I'll look forward to seeing the mystery contents, Hughes."

"Yes, sir, I think you most definitely will."

She hung up and Seamus turned to O'Rorden.

"What do you think of that?"

"So, we've a suitcase with Diana's stuff in it?"

"It seems so."

"Well, it will be interesting to see what's in it."

"It will, O'Rorden, it will."

"One thing though, sir, we were just talking about Aileen and the next minute she rings, how does that work?" O'Rorden looked perplexed.

"Well, now Buddha would say humans can demonstrate abilities which may surpass the normal capabilities of man. But the Catholic would say the Lord moves in mysterious ways. Whichever it is, it couldn't come at a better moment."

"And do you follow the Buddha, sir? His teachings?"

"I've read a lot, O'Rorden, let's leave it there for now, and a lot of it makes sense."

"Hmmm, interesting." O'Rorden looked thoughtful.

They did not have to wait long before Hughes and her team returned, bringing with them a large pull along suitcase. It was expensive and locked with a combination lock. It was one of the hard-shell types. Hughes put it on the table and spun the combination wheels.

"Wait a minute," said Seamus. "You opened this using the combination?"

"Yes, sir," Hughes said in a matter of fact tone.

"But how did you know it?" Seamus could not keep the surprise out of his voice.

"I didn't, sir, I worked it out."

"OK Hughes, just how did you do it? I'm starting to believe you've got superpowers. First, you ring me just after me and O'Rorden here were wondering how things were going on over at the hotel, and then you come back here and tell me you've opened the combination lock without even knowing what the number is."

Hughes laughed. "It's nothing like that, sir, though I wish I did have superpowers. I just like numbers, and I've studied a fair bit about the black arts. I'm a sucker for those paranormal novels I'm afraid."

"And what, these novels gave you some idea of maybe a magic spell or something?"

"Ach, sir, you are teasing me, so you are. No, not at all. It's just I made an educated guess I suppose. Diana was called the child of the devil. Now she must have known that. Her room number was 66 and I don't think this was a coincidence either. So, I figured, well what's the number a child of the devil would likely use."

"And it was?"

"six, six, six, sir."

"Yes, of course! I should have twigged it." Seamus smacked his forehead lightly in acknowledgement of his own lack of perspicacity.

"Well as I said, sir, it's partly because of my fictional preferences. To a paranormal enthusiast the six, six, six, is obvious, it's the devil's number."

"Fantastic, well done. So now the mystery is solved, let's see what's in the case," Seamus said eager to find out.

Some of the rest of the team had by now gathered round to witness this event. There was obviously something significant about the suitcase contents and they wanted to know what it was.

"OK, sir, so now for the big reveal!" Hughes said smiling.

"I see you are a reality show fan too," Seamus quipped sarcastically.

"Oh yes, sir, oh yes indeed."

Hughes lifted the lid and opened the suitcase flat on the table.

Everyone looked with growing astonishment. The suitcase, like most of that type, had two halves in which things could be packed. In the one side were a number of items of clothing. Putting on a pair of latex gloves Hughes took them out and carefully laid them down. There was a leather corset, several thongs and other types of underwear, a normal corset, a nurse's outfit and one or two other costumes. There was also a gimp mask, and some leather restraints, as well as a gag. In the other side, neatly stacked together were various implements. A wide leather strap, a paddle, a cane, a riding crop, several other smaller leather paddles, hairbrushes, wooden spoons and so forth.

"Well," said Seamus at last, "I think we know what she does for a living."

"Yes indeed, sir," O'Rorden replied. "Welcome to Diana's school for discipline by the looks of it."

Everybody laughed at this relieving the tension of the moment.

"The tech team is going to love us," laughed Seamus. "They'll have a field day with this one, there are months of joke material in there for Jim O'Grady."

There was more laughter at this. Anyone who knew Jim knew he loved ribbing the other Garda officers.

"Get them over here, Hughes, as soon as you can, they'll need to photograph this lot, take prints and so on. Best nobody else touches it. It'll need to be bagged up for evidence. Apart from that, we've got a new line of inquiry and I've got just the man to do it." Seamus grinned an almost mischievous looking grin.

The rest of them looked at him expectantly.

"Duffy, Duffy I've got another important job for you."

There was a ripple of suppressed laughter at this and Duffy who had been standing quietly saying nothing went bright red.

"Sir, what? Why me? Why does it have to be me all the time?"

"Duffy, come on now, this is a job you will love."

"No, I don't think so, sir, not by the sound of it."

"Come on, Duffy, you are going to delve into the dark world of domination and the dominatrix, what could be more exciting?"

"I am? Well, I can think of a lot more exciting things, to be honest, sir," he complained.

"Yes, well never mind, Duffy, here is what I want you to do. I want you to scan the internet and see if you can track down Diana somehow. She must be operating from somewhere, advertising from somewhere. We need to see if we can get a lead."

"But, but, sir."

"Ach, sir, I'll help him, so I will, nothing fazes me. Come on, Duffy."

O'Flynn had taken pity on him and stepped in. Duffy looked at her gratefully and the two of them headed off to his desk.

"Right, that's enough sightseeing, let's go to it," Seamus said to the rest of the team, they returned to their desks. All except Hughes who was waiting to see if her boss wanted anything else.

"So, Hughes, was there anything else you found out at all?"

"Well yes, sir, in some of the interviews with the staff. Some of them reported hearing strange noises from room 66."

"Strange noises?"

"Yes, they said it sounded like something being hit, repeatedly and you know like a swishing sound and then a smack sort of thing. And sometimes they thought they heard a man crying."

"Ah, yes I see. And what did they make of it?"

"Not much, sir, they are taught to be discreet, hear no evil, speak no evil, sort of thing. Also, Diana sometimes paid extra for the rooms on each side of 66 to be vacant, I am guessing for the privacy of certain clients."

"OK, so Diana obviously used the hotel for some of her clients, probably local around here, but I bet it wasn't her main place of work, so to speak. No, she must have somewhere else, probably where she also lives that she operates out of. I am sure she has earned a tidy sum from it too. Now we've just got to find it."

"Yes, sir," Hughes agreed.

"That's great work Hughes maybe get those staff interviews in order, we may need some of them as formal statements for the prosecution service. So, you can organise those too."

"OK, sir, I'll get onto it and the tech team."

"And, Hughes, if you have any more bright or even magical ideas, let me know."

"I'll be sure to do that, sir, I surely will."

Seamus turned to O'Rorden.

O'Rorden said, "Don't you think you should ease up on young Duffy there?"

"Ach he can take it."

"Yes, I know that, sir, but he's actually starting to pull his weight, so he is."

"I'm surprised to hear that from you, O'Rorden, he was after your job when he first came here, I soon disabused him of that notion."

"I know, sir, but he's starting to be one of the team now, maybe you can cut him some slack."

"Ach maybe." Seamus didn't look convinced. "He fucked me over big time on an investigation, he needs to prove himself. I'll think about it anyway."

Seamus sighed and continued, "You know, this case has more twists and turns than a rabbit hole."

"I would say it's more like a wormhole, sir."

"You're probably right at that, O'Rorden, indeed you are."

The day had gone by far too quickly for Diana and Bella. They had packed a lot into it but both of them knew it would be their last time seeing each other for a very long while. Diana was under no illusions she would spend many years in jail if caught but she didn't tell Bella. She didn't want her to know.

They had accomplished everything they needed to do. After a long luxurious soak in the bath, they had made love once more. Then Diana had given Bella some fake identification she had made. The advantage of Diana's profession was she knew a lot of people in positions who would subsequently owe her favours. Getting things like that was easy, in return for silence. It was an unspoken thing, she never actually had to bribe anyone, they just knew. They had also been to various financial institutions and sorted out Bella's money supply. Diana had been depositing cash into these accounts for months and it was untraceable. It was seeded across several accounts in different banks so as to not raise suspicion. Large regular cash deposits into one account would have done it, particularly with all the modern concerns about money laundering.

When Bella had found out how much money there was for her to spend, she was shocked. She vowed to be frugal. Diana told her not to stint herself. Bella cried. Nobody had ever been this kind to her in her whole short life. There was a trip to Diana's lawyer and accountant, and then it was time to pack. Bella packed her clothes and they put the computer and hard drives into a suitcase for her to take. All of the surveillance cameras and microphones were hidden in the walls and ceiling and Diana would just have to leave those. It didn't matter because the Garda wouldn't have the recordings.

Diana had also figured the tax authorities would potentially try to catch up with her for not paying enough tax for some years. However, they wouldn't be able to get her hands on her money and the house was legally tied up in a trust. Bella would have it eventually. The cottage in the south of Ireland was in Bella's name. They couldn't take that either. It would take them months to find it anyway, the land registry didn't do name searches as a matter of course. Bella would be safe. Diana would make sure there was no record of Bella's name in the house, and she wouldn't be revealing Bella's name either. Of course, Bella, had a doctor, bank account, etc. but it still wouldn't be easy to find. Diana knew even if Bella was somehow found, Bella wouldn't reveal anything. They packed or burned all correspondence in Bella's name and made a redirection for any post to a PO Box in a town nearby to her new home.

Having done all they could and loaded up the substantial four-wheel drive which was Bella's new car. There was nothing left to do but to say goodbye.

The two of them stood there for the last moments, in Diana's hallway, holding hands. Then suddenly Diana reached behind her neck and unclipped a silver necklace on the end of which was a very small heart. She fastened this around Bella's neck and smiled.

"This was my mother's, it's the only thing I have of hers. I kept it all those years, hidden away at the orphanage so the bitch who ran it couldn't take it away from me. When my mother gave it to me, I was very young, and she was still alive, she said she was giving me her heart, to carry with her always. This is the most precious thing I own. Now I am giving it to you, my darling Bella, to carry my heart with you always. From now on, you will always be in mine."

Bella's hand flew up to touch the heart on the chain and her eyes filled with tears.

"Don't cry anymore, Bella, sweet Bella, you've cried so much already."

"I can't help it, Diana, my love, my heart is breaking because I have to leave you."

"But I will always be with you, my darling, no matter where I am. I never realised it, but I think I do now. I think somewhere through my bitter and twisted head, and all the bitterness in my heart, I do love you, truly. I probably always have, I just didn't know it. I always wanted the best for you. Your love, your precious love is all that matters now in this world to me. And now I just want to keep you safe. So maybe one day, we can be together once again. I don't really know how but I can only hope."

Bella was choking on sobs and Diana took her face in her hands, she kissed Bella softly and gently, and then with passion. Bella's arms came up and around her and held her tight as if she would never let her go. The kiss went on and on, neither wanting to be the one to break away. Finally, their lips parted almost by mutual consent. Bella had dried her eyes.

"Go now, my sweet, go while I still can let you go," Diana told her.

Bella turned to leave, and they held hands until they reached the car. After one final kiss, Bella got into the driving seat and fired up the engine.

"Goodbye darling, safe journey, keep safe, keep safe for me," Diana said.

"I love you," said Bella simply through the open window.

"I love you too, Bella, my Bella." Diana's eyes filled with tears.

The car pulled away, down the drive and then it was gone. Diana waved until she could no longer see the car at all. Diana knew she wouldn't see Bella again, probably not for years. Bella was under strict instructions not to make contact, especially not by phone. She would just have to hope Bella would arrive safely, and she felt sure she would. She had done everything she could possibly do for the girl she now loved.

Diana turned and walked back into the house. She had one more night and a day to finish up her preparations to leave and get ready for the Bishop. She focused her mind on that, in an effort to forget the pain she now felt deep inside her heart.

It was getting towards the end of another long and apparently fruitless day. They knew who they were looking for. They were sure Diana was the murderer. But now they couldn't find her. Seamus went over to talk to Duffy and O'Flynn accompanied by O'Rorden.

"So, how's your search going for our lovely Dominatrix then?" Seamus asked with just the hint of a smirk on his face.

"Let's just say we've looked through a large quantity of material, sir, and found nothing as yet," O'Flynn answered trying to keep things serious.

"Material is it? That's an interesting word for it, O'Flynn."

"Sir, until we embarked upon this particular part of the investigation, I had no idea these types of doings, if I might refer to them as that, were so common. However, it seems alas they are. People get their kicks in all sorts of ways and this is apparently quite a popular one of those," O'Flynn said wryly.

"Indeed, so how far have you got, through the err, material?"

"Well sir, so far not that far. We've trawled across all kinds of sites personal and otherwise but we've yet to find anyone who even resembles Diana, let alone Diana herself, and definitely no Mistress Diana, sir."

"That's the common title is it, Mistress?" Seamus said with interest, not being entirely acquainted with the ins and outs of the BDSM scene.

"Yes, sir, apparently it's what they like to be called."

"Well maybe she's not calling herself Mistress Diana, maybe it's something else."

"We've thought of that too but not much luck there either."

"Well, keep at it, the two of you are doing a grand job by all accounts." Seamus grinned.

Duffy had been sitting all through this conversation looking more and more aggrieved. He hadn't wanted this job and it seemed to Seamus, noting his reactions to what they had seen so far, he had led a somewhat sheltered life. To say he was apparently shocked was no understatement. All in all, he definitely wasn't happy and that was plain to see. He would probably have welcomed a dose of measles with more enthusiasm.

"I don't see what's so funny, sir, that I don't," Duffy complained.

"Ach come on, Duffy, cheer up, life's too short to not to find humour even in the most serious situations," Seamus quizzed him kindly.

"Well yes, sir, that's as may be, but still."

"But still, Duffy, you're still here, still on my team, that tells you something, so keep on going, it's what police work it's ninety percent persistence and ten percent luck. So far, we're still waiting for the ten percent luck. Maybe you'll be the lucky one. Well in a way you are, you're getting an education, of sorts. Perhaps it's not what you would have wanted but anyway..." Seamus tailed off as he realised he couldn't keep a straight face for much longer.

"Sir." Duffy looked less than convinced and was suspicious his boss was gently pulling his leg, but he couldn't be sure.

Seamus tapped O'Rorden on the shoulder and the two of them walked away. O'Rorden was chuckling to himself.

"I thought you were the one told me to cut Duffy some slack," Seamus said when they got out of earshot.

"I know, sir, but I can't help it, it's too funny, his face, didn't you see, it was a picture." O'Rorden burst into fits of laughter and he laughed until tears were running down his face. Seamus couldn't help laughing too, he'd been trying not to for the last five minutes and now he had to let it out.

A few heads turned in surprise to see them laughing in the corner of the office, but Seamus and O'Rorden knew it a was a joke they couldn't share.

"We're getting nowhere fast, O'Rorden," Seamus said once they could finally speak.

"We need that ten percent, sir, that we do."

"Yes, and we need it fast."

"Any more ideas, sir?"

"Well there is one, but I doubt it will work."

"What's that?"

"We could try prayer."

"Oh, sir, stop it, stop it..." O'Rorden was off again.

✳ ✳ ✳

By dinner time, Seamus gave his team the option to get some sleep or carry on working if they wanted to. They were to a large degree reliant on Duffy and O'Flynn. In the morning Seamus would put everyone on it if they hadn't managed to come up with anything concrete. He left the office and headed back to Kerry to get something to eat himself.

Kerry's welcoming smile was something Seamus would never tire of, nor the way she came straight up and hugged him, followed by a kiss. There were the little things other past relationships had lacked. He had had passion, and a lot of sex, but real love, this was something new, and the nuances that came with it were refreshing and so very different.

"What are you thinking?" Kerry asked him across the dinner table.

"Now if that's not just like a woman," he joked.

"Oh you!"

"Actually, I was thinking about you."

"Really? And what about me, Seamus Gallway?"

"Well, it was more of an us thing probably."

"Hmmm?"

"I was thinking I would like you to be my girlfriend, that is if you don't mind, if you'd like to..." he got straight to the point but then tailed off self-consciously.

"If I want to?"

"Well, yes I mean I would like it if you would consider yourself my girlfriend, would you?" He was suddenly anxious as if he had been expecting a positive answer but now was not quite so certain.

"Oh Seamus, Seamus Gallway..." Her smile was wider now than ever before. "I've been thinking of myself as your girlfriend for days." She laughed.

"Is that a fact? And were you going to consult me about it?" He feigned indignation but was secretly pleased.

"No," she said simply. "I just waited for you to catch up with me and you have."

"Ach, you're definitely incorrigible, I'm going to have to step up my game with you, Kerry O'Shea."

Kerry just laughed and poked her tongue out provocatively.

"Just wait until after dinner, Ms O'Shea!"

"Is that a threat or a promise?"

"Both." He was glad to be able to give her the rejoinder, she had used on him the other day.

"Touché, Inspector, but I think that was my line."

"Ah well, like you said I'm catching up."

Both of them laughed at this and then the conversation turned to more serious topics.

"I've been back to the hospital today, Liam seems to be making progress but still not really conscious, the doctors say it could take a few more days and they are still sedating him to an extent. I talked to the surgeon and he said the operation wasn't simple, but it wasn't complex either. He said the gunshots themselves caused a shock to his system and even though neither were anywhere near to being fatal they've taken a big toll on him probably psychologically as much as anything. He may have to have some counselling afterwards for PTSD or something like it. But otherwise he is sure Liam will heal up OK, at least physically that is."

"Well now that's good, but a shame about the possible psychological damage," Seamus said, "I'm sorry he's had to go through this."

"I am too, but I've had a lot of time to think sitting there by his hospital bed. I have had to realise he's a big boy now, I can't protect him all my life no matter how much I want to. If he is going to run with the wrong people, then to that degree he's got to take some of the consequences. Perhaps it will teach him to keep it in his pants a bit more often."

"Harsh, but fair I guess," Seamus agreed.

"I am not one of those women who can't be logical," and then seeing Seamus smile at it she amended it, "well at least some of the time, and don't you say anything!"

His eyes were twinkling at her in a teasing way, he raised his eyebrow.

"Oh you! Stop it!"

Seamus laughed.

"I am sorry he can't speak, we could use some help from him right now," Seamus returned to the subject of Liam.

"Are things not going well then?"

"We know Diana is most certainly the murderer, we have all the forensic evidence to prove it, but we just can't find her."

"Oh dear, well if Liam does finally wake up and can talk then I'll call you right away."

"There's some other interesting things we've discovered about our Diana, but I can't tell you just yet."

"Oh, now I'm intrigued."

"You will be."

Kerry didn't press him, she knew he couldn't always share everything with her from his job, though he very much wanted to. She would just have to be patient. Instead, noting his plate was empty she smiled, got out her chair and took him gently by the hand.

"Come on then, boyfriend, time for bed," she told him.

DAY 13

Seamus was happy to wake up and find Kerry's blue eyes gazing into his brown ones. It was a great feeling, to be loved. He had spent years inuring himself to the idea of being alone. Accustoming himself to the thought he would never find 'the one'. Then out of nowhere came this woman who pulled the rug from under all his preconceptions, all the false notions about what love really is. The happiness of companionship, of being part of someone else, of belonging, had penetrated his consciousness.

He began to realise he didn't want to leave. This job might end but somehow, he needed to find a way to remain, with Kerry, right here. But he didn't know how. Was it a matter of faith, or hope, that somehow the right thing would happen? The Buddhist would say Karma dictated what happens in this life, the Catholic would tell you it was up to God. Seamus didn't know about his Karma and he preferred to believe he had some hand in his own destiny. At least he hoped so. His mother used to tell him, what will be, will be. Seamus didn't agree, not now, not about Kerry, she had become too important to leave it all to chance.

"You're thinking again," Kerry whispered, "you're always thinking, Seamus Gallway."

"That's what you get for having a detective for a boyfriend."

"Oh, is that right?"

"Yes, it is so."

"And what were you thinking there, sweetie?"

"I was thinking about you and me, and how I want to hold onto you and never let you go."

She snuggled closer and put her arms around him.

"Be my guest."

She kissed him sleepily.

"I'm not going anywhere, Seamus."

"Me neither."

She smiled and pulled him closer, enjoying the moment before the priorities of the day, and his murder inquiry impinged upon them once again.

✳ ✳ ✳

Diana sat at her very ample expensive dining table which doubled as a desk. She laid out the airline tickets she had printed and the passport. She was leaving tonight after the Bishop was dead. There were places in the world without extradition or with very difficult extradition agreements. She was going to one of those, but not directly, by a circuitous route which would be hard to trace. She had seeded most of her money away to offshore accounts, these would also be difficult to track.

She gathered up the paperwork and put it away into her hand luggage. Then, she walked over to her computer, put in a USB and rebooted it. It fired up into a secure erasure program. It didn't matter, everything she had was backed up into the cloud. She pressed enter and the software went to work. She didn't want to leave any discernible traces. Her laptop had gone with Bella, she would buy another one. If she was caught, she didn't want to give the Garda an easy ride. Her phone contained contact numbers for many clients and she didn't care about that. Bella had her number but was under strict instructions not to use it. It was the best Diana could do. Nothing was ever bulletproof.

Diana went upstairs to pack. A single suitcase with nice clothes and shoes. All the rest of her beautiful outfits would have to remain here, which was a shame. Diana loved clothes, nice things, she had promised herself all of that when she ran away from the orphanage. There she had nothing. Now she had everything. As she packed her essentials, she wondered why she hadn't simply just continued, in her existence leading the life of a successful dominatrix. Why did she have to kill?

It was a question she couldn't really answer. There was no answer barring the burning level of hate within her for the people she had murdered. It had overridden her reason and her common sense. It had become an obsession. In a way, the more she had immersed herself in the confessions of the priests who came to her for punishment, the more her hate had grown. It was like pouring petrol on a fire, and the fire had burned out of control.

She had become everything they had said she was, 'a demon', 'a child of the devil', an avenging angel with a gun. Except she did not see herself as an angel, she never had. Diana knew, deep down, she was fucked up, almost beyond repair. That is how she saw herself. The clothes, the immaculate makeup, the exterior image, these were the things which had kept her sane. It kept her feeling normal, like a human being. It kept the savage thoughts inside her under control, that and the regular beatings she doled out to her clients. To other dominatrix' it was all an act, a play for the client. To Diana, it was all too real. Every blow she landed was in payment for the blows she had herself received. Every stroke of the cane she delivered was payback to those people she had killed. Except she hadn't really killed them. They still lived, in her psyche driving her on in a never-ending spiral of hate.

Then came Bella. Like oil on a troubled sea, she calmed Diana. She treated Diana kindly, caring, loving. The last day when Bella had disclosed her love was almost as if a magical amulet had opened. Temporarily taking away her hate, soothing her pain. Diana felt sure given time, Bella could have healed her. But time had run out. There was no going back. Not anymore. Tonight would seal the deal when she claimed her fourth victim. The angel would strike, one last time and vengeance would be hers.

* * *

At the morning meeting, Seamus spoke. He was fresh, replete with a good breakfast and it was a new day. Begin each day with optimism, it was something he tried very hard to do.

"OK, so here we are it's day thirteen. Now for some that would be an unlucky number, but let's see if instead, it can be lucky for us. We've got to catch this woman somehow. We have got to find her. Bend your minds to this problem. Let's see if we can't crack this today. I don't believe we have time on our side, I think she is going to do something, to kill someone and we need to stop her. I'm not going to lie, I'm all out of ideas, so I'm relying on you, all of us together. How about it?"

"Sir," said Duffy. "We've been working hard on the dominatrix lead, but we'll keep at it, I promise you that!"

"Good, and if anyone else has any bright ideas on it let me know, in fact, some of you can pitch in on this now and help out Duffy and O'Flynn, it's the best lead we've got at the moment."

The meeting broke up, there wasn't much else to say.

"I'm glad to you see you feeling a bit more upbeat there, sir," said O'Rorden.

"Today is a new day, O'Rorden, we've got to remain cheerful and optimistic, at least at the start."

O'Rorden smiled.

"Well, let's hope we can keep it that way then, sir."

"I hope so too."

"Have you noticed something, sir?"

"About what?"

"Well, you've not been banging tables recently."

A laugh was surprised from Seamus at this statement.

"And what do you deduce from that?"

"It's this place, it must agree with you somehow, and of course the Baker's Arms." O'Rorden gave him a knowing look.

Seamus nodded slowly.

"I think you may be right."

A couple of hours passed during which there was a hive of activity on the computers, as detectives and officers trawled the internet for signs of Diana the dominatrix. Seamus whiled away the time going through Diana's orphanage file once again, and then her own dossier on the clergy. He found nothing new in either of these, but it simply endorsed the fact her upbringing had definitely damaged her in some way.

Although there are killers who murder for the sake of killing, psychopaths, in fact, he was sure Diana wasn't one of those. There was a reason for her crimes and a method in her madness. The very fact she had erased her existence from view pointed to a person who was very insecure and also who obviously didn't want to be found. He was curious as to when she had decided to commit the murders and how long she had been planning them. He suspected it was a long time, maybe even years.

It was a shame it had come to this. Here he was investigating a woman who had murdered three people who had themselves perpetrated horrific crimes on others. The abuse they had carried out would have scarred many victims for life. If only Diana had come forward instead and they could have brought these people to justice, the proper way, the right way. Now she would end up in jail, but really, who had put her there? Was it really just her crimes, or was the whole cycle begun years ago when Mother Joan Margaret meted out her first punishment to the 'devil child'? Seamus didn't really know but he felt life wasn't fair. He couldn't hate Diana, knowing what he knew, but she nevertheless had to face justice herself now. He had to do his job and bring her to book. He just wished she had never begun this in the first place.

"Sir, sir, I think we've got something." It was Hughes and she was sounding excited.

Seamus shelved his meandering thoughts and walked over to see what she was talking about.

"I think we've got her, sir, this is her."

And indeed, it was. But it wasn't Diana, so much as Mistress Dana. It was the billing on what appeared to be a very exclusive website for discerning clients with expensive tastes. There was a photograph of her in a leather corset and high heels. Over her eyes, she wore a mask, with feathers protruding from the sides, but even so, she was unmistakable. There were those full red lips in a supercilious smile and her white, white skin. The river of black hair hung down her back. She was sideways on and from one hand, with painted red nails, hung a leather strap.

"What's your pleasure? Mine is your pain, Mistress Dana. My command is your wish," Seamus read out the tag line.

There were sniggers from the other members of the team crowding round the screen.

"Mistress Dana gives bottom marks for naughty boys, and girls. Do you have a confession? Do you need to be punished for your sins? My lips are sealed. Confidentiality assured. Top quality discipline. Get the very best, six of the best in fact. You won't be sitting comfortably I can guarantee it. Call me for more details," O'Rorden chimed in reading some of the blurb.

"It also says the clergy are particularly welcome. Get absolution, the right way. Feel my hand of vengeance for your sins," Hughes noted amused.

"So how did you manage to find her then?" Seamus wanted to know.

"Well, sir, it's the numbers again."

"Of course."

"I started searching for six, six, six, and other combinations and the devil and so on, and then this came up, Mistress Dana. I didn't click on it at first but then I thought, that makes sense, take away the 'I' in Diana and what have you got left."

"Dana! God that's good, you've definitely got the gift."

"Thank you, sir."

"It's OK, credit where it's due, Hughes. Now, I take it there is a number to phone?"

"Yes sir, it's right here."

"Well then, all it needs is for one of us to ring it and keep her talking."

There was a significant pause and then Duffy spoke up.

"I'll do it, sir."

"Duffy? You want to do it? Really? I thought you weren't keen on this part of the investigation."

"Well sir, that's true, but you know, I've got to be professional, and I started this, so I should finish it."

"OK, Duffy, you're on. Well played. Let's use one of our spare mobiles and we will go over there to the meeting area."

Everyone came to the table and stood watching expectantly. Seamus placed the Garda mobile on the desk.

"What should I say by the way, sir?" Duffy asked.

"Oh, I don't know, Duffy, make it up as you go along, pretend to be a client, you know wanting some services."

"OK, sir, will do."

"Let's go then, Duffy."

Duffy put the phone onto speaker and dialled the number from the website.

It rang twice, and a woman answered. But it wasn't Diana.

"Mistress Dana's answering service? How can I help?"

"Oh! Oh, well I was expecting Mistress Dana," Duffy said.

"Yes, this is her answering service, Mistress Dana doesn't take direct phone calls. How can I help?"

"Well, it's like this, you see, I was wanting you know like to have a session with Mistress Dana, I really need to have some punishment you see," Duffy was warming to his theme, "and I thought Mistress Dana would be the one for me."

There were a few suppressed giggles around the table at this.

"Well," said the voice. "Now of course ordinarily Mistress Dana would certainly be happy to be of service but at the moment she's not taking any more clients."

"Ah but, but I rung up especially, and it's her I want, can't you maybe just persuade her to see me, like today if possible."

"I'm so sorry but we've got strict instructions not to pass any more clients on to her. I can offer you some other very good mistresses. There's Mistress Anita, she's an absolute bitch of a woman if it's what you are after, really into humiliation but she gives a good spanking too, so I'm told, mind you she is also a transvestite and you might not be into that. She has plenty of satisfied clients though to be fair. Or there is Mistress Caitlan, now she's got a mean hand with a riding crop and no mistake, or at least so I've heard. She's very beautiful too, but again if it's a real bitch you are after then she's the one. We've got plenty more on hand, so to speak, just so you know."

"Well, erm, well yes they sound very good, but you know it's just I've got a real hankering for Mistress Dana, I've heard she's the very best, and I only want the best."

"I am really so sorry, but I just can't help you at all. I can't go against the wishes of our mistresses, you know. Otherwise, God knows I would be the one ending up across her knee and I wouldn't want that." The woman on the other end laughed at her own joke.

"Is there no way you can ask her? I'll pay double," Duffy said in desperation.

"No, no I'm sorry, but no I can't, now is there anything else I can help you with. Are you sure Mistress Anita wouldn't be your type? She's a lot more of a bitch than Mistress Dana, well in fact than anyone I know, she has a lot of years' experience, I can vouch for that, and cheaper too."

"No, no thanks, I'll leave it then thanks."

"OK well if you change your mind you know where we are, we've got spankings galore just waiting if you want them."

"Thank you, I'll keep it in mind."

"Well bye then, thanks for calling."

Duffy disconnected the phone. The disappointment showed on his face.

"Fuck it!" said Seamus momentarily expressing his frustration. "It's like a card game where she holds all the fucking aces."

"I am sorry, sir, I tried, sir, really I did." Duffy was quite upset by his failure in front of everyone.

"Ach don't take it so hard, Duffy, we all heard you, you did your best under difficult circumstances. Well done," Seamus told him.

"Thank you, sir." Duffy smiled somewhat mollified by this praise. A couple of people gave Duffy a reassuring pat on the back.

"Right then, I am sure it's a waste of time but, Hughes, find out where that fucking answering service is and either go round there yourself, or if it's in Dublin, which it probably is, then organise a team to go and put a bit of pressure on them to get Diana's number. There's probably no point, but we will give a shot."

"Yes, sir, I will get onto it," Hughes told him.

"OK, so that line of inquiry is pretty much a dud," said Seamus. "We've got to think of something else. Get your thinking caps on people."

"Sir, I've just had a thought." It was O'Rorden.

"Yes?"

"We didn't check if there was CCTV in the car park outside the library."

"That's right we didn't, good and what's your thoughts on it exactly, O'Rorden?"

"Well, sir, she must park her car there, we could get the number and maybe it's registered to her address."

"Yes! Smart thinking, we should have thought of this before, OK get onto it pronto, that could be promising."

"Yes, sir, I'll be on that right away, so I will!"

The team split up and headed back to their desks, to either pitch in with the urgent tasks or have another think about how to find Diana. Either way thought Seamus, time was marching on, and if they didn't get somewhere soon then events would probably overtake them once again when Diana made her move.

✻ ✻ ✻

At around lunchtime Kerry phoned. Seamus gladly took her call.

"Hi sweetie, how's it going," came Kerry's melodious tones.

"It's all good, my sweetheart, though we thought we'd got a good lead which turned out to be another dud."

"Oh really? Well, I am sure you will crack it soon, my love." Her voice was loaded with encouragement.

"I wish I shared your confidence, but we are throwing everything at it and no mistake."

"Well, I'm just letting you know I've driven myself to the hospital, I don't want to keep disturbing your Garda, you are all so busy with finding Diana."

"Thanks, but if you needed a lift it wouldn't be a problem."

"No, no it's fine, really sweetie, anyway I've looked in on Liam and he's not so pale but still in no position to talk I am afraid. They say he's not in a coma but he's not fully conscious either. They say it's not unusual and they are keeping him very lightly sedated for another twenty-four hours and then they will see if they can get him fully awake."

"Oh well, that's good news, for you and also hopefully we might be able to get to speak to him."

"Yes, both. Anyway, my sweetie pie, I don't want you starving so Colleen will give you some lunch if you want to pop back home."

"OK, I will do that soon, thank you, thank you for thinking of me so much, and caring for me and well just so many things."

"I love you, Seamus, the rest is easy."

"I love you too, Kerry."

"I love you more."

"Is it a competition now?"

"No, you are supposed to say, I love you more, back."

"But it goes without saying."

"Oh you!"

"Alright, fine, I love you more."

"I love you more twice over!"

Seamus went off into a peal of laughter.

"Incorrigible."

"I'll see you later, sweetie."

"Bye, darling."

He clicked off the phone. O'Rorden was regarding him with some amusement. It was significant Seamus had not gone outside to take the call.

"What?" said Seamus. "Can't I talk to my girlfriend now?"

"I'm saying nothing, sir, that I'm not. So, she's your girlfriend now, sir, is that right?" O'Rorden smiled.

"Yes, and?" Seamus said defensively.

"Nothing, sir, I'm glad to hear it, so I am."

"I am too, O'Rorden, I am too."

* * *

After a hastily eaten lunch and having been roundly scolded by Colleen for not eating it slower, Seamus returned to the office. The staff at the Baker's Arms were already regarding him as part of the family and treating him with a large degree of familiarity and inclusiveness. Whether it was stated or not, it was obvious he and Kerry were an item, and everybody knew it.

The pub was a bit quieter since most of the press had gone on to other stories. The murders had a shelf life and since not much was happening of note since the last murder, their editors had pulled them out. Seamus was relieved to see the back of them for the moment.

Within a short space of time, Hughes came over to their desk.

"Sir, we've had a team go over to the answering service. It wasn't easy to locate them in the first place, but they were in Dublin just as you thought. They were very uncooperative, sir, to say the least. It took a lot of persuading to get them to talk. It was explained to them we only wanted to know about Mistress Dana and we weren't going to raid them or anything. Eventually, though they had to be threatened with a search warrant and aiding and abetting a murder. That got some results, but the results were not much help. Basically, they get paid by Diana, in cash, for their services. They don't have an address, nor do they ask for one."

"How does it work then?" asked Seamus.

"Well, sir, what happens is when a potential client phones in, they take the details and then send those in a message to Diana, or Mistress Dana as she is to them. The message goes to a mobile and also an email address. But the email is a Gmail, sir, and there's no way to locate her from that. We got the mobile number, it's a pay as you go, and it's switched off. I would suggest she uses it only for the message service. We can try to triangulate the location of the phone when it did last pick up messages, but it's going to take quite a bit of time. Anyway, sir, then she decides if she wants to contact the client and that's it. After, she contacts them directly and presumably by a different mobile. She comes by every month and gives the service their money, they put her details on their website and that's the end of it."

"Did they know much about her at all. Did they say anything?"

"Nothing we don't know, sir. She is well spoken, she is well dressed and always been very nice to them. They do get feedback and reviews from clients, of course, who are all anonymous, but they know she's a very well sought-after dominatrix, sir, and she provides a top-quality service apparently."

"Really? And what's the going rate for her services then? Did they say?" Seamus was curious now.

"Well, that's between her and the client they said, but at the very least they reckoned it's two hundred and fifty Euros an hour or more and can often cost up to one thousand or more, sir, for a session. It depends on what the client wants."

"Whew! Is that right? We must be in the wrong fucking business, Hughes."

O'Rorden laughed at this.

"Sir." Hughes smiled politely.

"OK, well let's have a think. Follow up on the triangulation and also see if you can get a list of numbers of the clients from the messages. If the phone provider has them, even the more recent ones. We can try to trace some of her clients, one of them will know the address."

"Yes, sir, I will give it a go. It will probably take a while."

"Take as long as you need, get some help on it too, if you need it. And well done, Hughes, good work."

"Thank you, sir."

Hughes went away to continue her investigations, rounding up a couple of the other officers to assist.

"You know, sir, people really appreciate you. You always say well done and you acknowledge their work, it's a rare quality in the Garda," O'Rorden told him after she had gone.

"Really? I just think it's the right thing to do."

"Well, it certainly is something the rest of the team are happy with, sir, it makes them feel valued, so it does."

"I do value them, O'Rorden, very much, we couldn't get this job done without all of us together."

"Well I just thought you should know, sir; your efforts don't go unnoticed by the people who work for you."

"Thanks, O'Rorden, that's good to hear."

Seamus was always surprised to hear positive things about himself from others. He should not have been, he was a good officer, but he was incredibly modest too. To him, it was just doing his job. He tried to focus on the positive when he could, in others and those who worked for him, and for the most part, it paid dividends. Other bosses he had had were always carping and complaining and pointing out faults. The teams under them were disgruntled and hated working for them. Seamus never wanted to be like that. He needed the team and they needed him, that's how he saw it.

* * *

Shortly after Hughes had gone, O'Rorden looked up from his desk. He'd been on his computer and on and off his phone for some time chasing up the CCTV for the library.

"Sir," he said. "I've managed to locate the CCTV feed for the library car park finally. It wasn't easy, you know lots of red tape, but I've got it."

"How's it looking?" Seamus asked.

"If you come over here, I can show you some of the footage."

Seamus went around to O'Rorden's desk and watched his screen. There was a black and white video of the car park, a black expensive looking jaguar drew up and parked. Diana got out and went to the library, presumably to open it.

"Great, well done, have you got the registration?"

"Yes, sir, I have."

"And have you traced it?"

"Yes, sir, I have."

"Come on, O'Rorden, don't keep me in suspense what happened?"

"You're not going to like it, sir."

"I had that feeling when I didn't catch an upbeat tone in your voice earlier, there was no, we've found her, hooray element at all, to be honest."

"It's because we haven't, sir, no."

"Right, so what have you found," Seamus said in tones of resignation.

"A mail service, a paid for address where the mail goes to, so it looks like a residential address."

"Don't tell me, she paid for it in cash, nobody knows who she is, and she collects the mail in person."

"That's pretty much it, sir, so it is."

"Checkmate, again! For God's sake!"

"I'm afraid so, sir."

"I'll tell you this, O'Rorden, I've got a high degree of respect for this woman, so I have. She has pretty much thought of everything. It's almost the perfect crime."

"Yes, sir." O'Rorden sounded very glum.

"Cheer up, O'Rorden, it's not your fault. We are dealing with an out of the ordinary criminal here. Somehow, we've got to be smarter than her. It is not possible she has nothing to connect her to where she lives. She must have something, something we have missed. Maybe she is using a different name."

"That could be it, sir."

"Yes, but what? It won't be something chosen at random, there will be some sort of connection to her past. Something which is not obvious, but it's there staring us in the face."

"Yes, I see, sir, yes indeed I do. Well, let me think on it."

"I will too, O'Rorden, I will too, and in the meantime get someone to go through all of the footage back to the first murder, maybe there is something more interesting on it."

"Yes, sir, will do."

VESPERS THREE

At four o'clock the Bishop's car drew up outside for his session. As he had been told he went to the front door and it opened on turning the handle. He shut the door quietly behind him and headed up the stairs.

Diana was waiting in the punishment room. She was dressed as usual in her favourite leather corset. She wore a black leather thong and high black stiletto heels. The shoes were open toe, so you could see her painted red nails. They were a favourite pair of hers and she was wearing them probably for the last time, these were some of the wardrobe she would have to leave behind. Her hands were beautifully manicured with red varnish as usual. She had taken extra care with her makeup, as she wanted to make this final session one of the best. With that in mind, various implements lay on the bed, including the strap she was so fond of using.

The Bishop knocked, the knock sounded quite confident. Diana walked over the door and opened it.

"Good afternoon, Bishop, how nice to see you again. I hope you are well?" she said politely ushering him in.

"Well yes, yes that I am, Mistress Dana, and well recovered and err, rested, you know ready for the fray as it were."

"That's good to hear, Bishop, very good indeed."

"Now, is there anything you have to tell me before we begin? Or shall we get straight to it?"

"No, no I think I pretty much covered it all last time, to be honest, so I did."

"But you perhaps feel you didn't get punished enough last time, is that it?"

"Yes, and no, I suppose," the Bishop said uneasily.

"Yes and no, what's the no?" A small smile played on her lips at hearing this.

"Well, to be honest mind, and it's a bit shameful to admit it but the thing is, the thing is..."

"Spit it out, Bishop, spit it out, I've heard it all before don't worry."

"The thing is I kind of liked it, somehow I enjoyed it, I can't understand it really, but I wanted to try it again."

Diana's laugh tinkled around the room and the Bishop looked extremely discomforted at that.

"Ah, Bishop, don't you worry, you and the majority of my clients enjoy a good belting, so they do. That's what they come here for, they want it, they crave it even, they can't get enough of it, or me."

538

"Oh, oh yes I see, well then I suppose it's not so bad then is it." He sounded relieved.

"Not at all, Bishop, not at all, and your punishment will serve two purposes. One to punish you for the things you've done and two to punish you for enjoying the punishment. Kills two birds with one stone don't you think?"

"Well now you put it that way, yes I see, that's very good, very good, I probably won't need to confess it to anyone then." The Bishop apparently had found a way to reconcile this new proclivity with his conscience.

"So, then, Bishop." Diana smiled at him sweetly. "Shall we begin?

"Yes, I suppose so yes."

"Hmmm, it seems you've forgotten the rules."

"No, no I haven't, I mean, Mistress, it's just I wasn't sure we had started."

"Oh, we've started, Bishop, we've well and truly started. Now get those clothes off like the naughty little boy that you are, come on, you know the drill and then get yourself bent over the horse over there."

The Bishop obeyed with what seemed like an unseemly amount of eagerness Diana thought. However, she continued to play along, there was plenty of time, before she revealed her true purpose.

"And that," she said, playfully smacking his naked bottom several times with her hand, "is for not following the rules."

"Thank you, Mistress," said the Bishop.

"Stop procrastinating and get over that horse now!" she ordered.

The Bishop obeyed and took up what was by now a familiar position to him before tightly gripping the legs.

Diana picked up the strap and walked around the front where he could see her. She held in in two hands stretching it out in front of her.

"You haven't had this yet have you, Bishop? My strap? You've not felt this across your arse now have you?"

"No, Mistress."

"Well, you are in for a treat now, Bishop, because this is something I am particularly good at."

Slowly and purposefully she walked around to stand behind him.

"Let's begin with six of the best, shall we? And see where that takes us."

"Very good, Mistress," said the Bishop sounding unusually excited at the prospect.

"Oh, it will be, Bishop, believe you me, it will be."

She lifted up the strap raising her arm high and brought it swiftly down across his buttocks with a crack.

"That's one," announced Diana, as the Bishop cried out in surprise.

✳ ✳ ✳

An hour had gone by or maybe more. The Bishop was still lying across the horse. Diana had allowed him to get up once to pee, but for the most part, he had stayed there. She ran her hand lightly across the naked flesh of his backside which was now tinged a rosy shade of red by the repeated use of her strap. She had prolonged this session, mixing humiliating scolding with six or a dozen strokes of the belt. She knew exactly how to make it hurt but not hurt enough he could not stand it. That part might come later, when she had finished toying with him, like a cat with her prey.

540

"Well now Bishop, I think it's time for the restraints, don't you?"

"Erm, well, Mistress, if you think so Mistress, but I had a lot of trouble walking after the last time Mistress."

"You mean after I used the strap on dildo, is that it?"

"Yes, Mistress."

"That, Bishop, was the point, and now it's another six for your insubordination."

"But I didn't do anything, Mistress."

"That's twelve."

"I..."

"Do you want to make that eighteen?"

Twelve more strokes were duly and carefully laid across his buttocks by Diana. The Bishop kept quiet, not wanting any more. Perhaps it wasn't quite so exciting after all.

After she was done, she laid the strap aside and went to her bedside table. From the drawer, she extracted several leather restraints and securely fastened both the Bishop's hands and his legs to the horse. He now couldn't move.

"Mistress, what are you doing? I can't move."

"Are you questioning me again?"

"No, Mistress."

"Good."

She went to the wardrobe and brought out a thick plastic sheet. She laid it out flat at the front of the horse. It covered quite an area.

"What, what are you doing, Mistress?" the Bishop was alarmed by this inexplicable action.

"I don't want a mess on my carpet." She told him in a matter of fact way.

"What, what do you mean?" The Bishop quite forgot the role play and was now severely unsettled.

"Well now, let's see, Bishop, let's see if you can guess who I really am?"

Diana brought a chair and placed in front of the horse, she sat down. The Bishop pulled his head up so he could see her even though quite uncomfortably.

"What, what do you mean who you really are?"

"Just so, Bishop, can you guess?"

"I, I have no idea."

"Well, Bishop, let me give you a clue, I'm very good with my strap and my cane am I not, would you not say so hmmm?"

"Yes, yes I suppose so but... "

"Where do you think I learned those skills?"

"I don't know, the internet? I don't know what game you are playing at, but I didn't ask for this, let me up at once."

"Oh, Bishop, not the internet, not at all, no I learned these first hand at the sharp end," she continued ignoring his pleas.

"I demand you stop this, stop this I've had enough! I tell you that's enough!"

It was as if he had not spoken.

"I learned these skills, Bishop, from a very good friend of yours, who used her strap on me several times a month, can you guess who it was?"

The Bishop had gone quiet, something was registering in his brain and that was also overlaid by fear.

"Nothing to say, Bishop, my lovely little Bishop? Well, I'll tell you then, and perhaps then you might remember. It was your friend, not mine, the Mother Joan Margaret."

She watched him carefully as what she said began to register and saw his eyes go wide at the mention of her name.

"Yes, the bitch who ran the house of torture they called an orphanage. She made my life a living hell, and do you know, Bishop, do you know what they called me? Her and Father Cooney, they called me the 'child of the devil'!"

"Noooooooo," the Bishop cried out whilst the room echoed with Diana's laughter.

When he had subsided, Diana went over to her dressing table once again and extracted a large service pistol. Then she returned to sit on the chair.

"Now then, Bishop, shall we play a little game you and I? Shall we?"

He said nothing, his eyes were wild staring at the gun.

"You know Father O'Flaherty and Father Cooney, they never really had much of a chance. I shot them dead almost right away. And of course, Mother Joan Margaret, well I had run out of bullets, so I had to beat her to death with the barrel. I think that was fitting, don't you? For all the beatings she doled out to me? But anyway, I'm a fair-minded girl, you didn't actually assault me, although you knew about it didn't you, you might even have watched it, and you knew about others, you saw the others. So probably you also do deserve to die, don't you think? I think so really, Bishop, I really do."

"No, no please, I've done nothing to you, I swear, please, let me go, I won't tell anyone I promise, I didn't do anything to you. Please, this isn't right, let me go, please let me go!" Self-preservation kicked in, the Bishop was babbling.

"Sshhh, hush now, Bishop, as I said I'm a fair-minded girl, so I am, and I am going to give you a sporting chance."

She opened the revolver and extracted five bullets. She showed the Bishop there was only one left in the chamber.

"Now then, see only one bullet, that's a one in six chance. I think those are good odds, better odds than I had at the hands of your clergy."

"Please, please no, please," the Bishop sobbed.

Diana wasn't listening. She snapped the revolver shut and spun the barrel with her hand. It came to a stop.

"Well, Bishop, what do you think it'll be, will your prayers be answered or will they not?"

Slowly she walked over to the Bishop and placed the end of the barrel against his temple.

"What do you think? Is it deal, or is it no deal?"

"Please, please stop!" he cried.

"Let's find out."

She pulled the trigger on the gun and there was an ominous click.

"Noooo, nooooo, noooooo." The Bishop was crying openly from relief as he thought he had been about to die.

"Stop it." Diana leaned down and slapped him across the face.

He shut up abruptly.

"Good, so now you survived that round, only another five to go, that's still very good odds though don't you think? I will spin the barrel each time, just to be fair."

"Five, five rounds?" he looked aghast.

"Yes, yes, we are going to do this little game, six times in all, we've done one turn already and so we've another five left. I like the number six, don't you?"

She found her timer and set it for sixty minutes.

"Next round in sixty minutes, Bishop, don't worry we've got all night to play."

"I've done nothing to you, please let me go, please I can pay you, I have a lot of money."

"When are you going to understand!" Diana lost her cool. "I don't want your money. Fuck your dirty money, I want you dead! And I want you to suffer and suffer you will, just like I had to for years while you stood by and did nothing. You are nothing but a bastard, a deceitful self-seeking bastard. So, take your punishment little man, because that's what you are going to get, and don't bother screaming, nobody can hear you."

Diana laid the revolver aside and went over to the bed. She picked up the strap.

"Time for a bit more of this," she said.

Taking up her position, she brought the strap down, hard, across his behind.

"You fucking bitch!!" screamed the Bishop as the leather bit into him once more.

"That's no way to talk to your mistress now, is it?" Diana was back in control. She had slipped a little there but it wasn't going to happen again. The gloves were truly off though, and the Bishop wasn't going to go down easily. But she didn't care. He was going to pay for all of the rest of her suffering. He would be her Jesus, and she would be the Devil. This would be his crucifixion, just with a gun instead of a cross. In a way, it seemed quite fitting.

She lifted up the strap ready to deliver more of what she viewed as retribution.

* * *

At around five pm, O'Rorden suddenly became very excited.

"Sir, sir, I've got it, I've got it, I've got it."

Seamus sat bolt upright. He had been trying to focus on the report he would need to write when this was over, thinking he might as well make a start. He had not got very far.

"What? What? Slow down, O'Rorden, what's that you are saying?"

"Sir, I've got it, I know where she lives!"

"How? How did you do it?" O'Rorden's excitement was infectious.

"Sir, I thought about what you said and she might use a different name. So, I tried a few, different ideas but then it came to me, like a... like a..."

"An epiphany?" put in Seamus.

"Yes, sir, that! Well, I thought, the one thing we never did, and it's my fault, sir, so it is, is we never actually looked properly at the birth certificate for Deirdre Flanagan."

"Don't blame yourself now, none of us thought of it, but how does it help us?"

"It helped a lot, sir, and I'll tell you just now. Well so I did it, I got a hold of a copy, I was lucky because they were just all off home too at the registry. Anyway, sir, anyway, the thing is the thing we never thought to look at, was to find out who were the mother and the father."

"And were they on there? And I still don't see..."

"Wait on, sir, wait on, it'll all be clear shortly. Yes, they were on there, but the father's name wasn't Flanagan, it was her mother's maiden name."

"So, what was the father's name?" Seamus still didn't really understand where this was leading.

"It was O'Rourke, sir, Joe O'Rourke."

"And?"

"So, I put two and two together sir, I put Deirdre together with O'Rourke, Deirdre O'Rourke and that's the name she's used, sir."

"What?"

546

"Yes, sir, so then I started searching by that name and lo and behold, I've got her, we've got the address, sir, for her utilities, and property tax, it's all there."

The penny finally dropped for Seamus and he suddenly looked elated.

"Well done! Well done, O'Rorden, and where is it?"

"It's here, sir, just here."

He pulled up Google maps and showed Seamus a suburb of Dublin, and the address of the house. The satellite view gave them a good idea of access.

"Right, good, I'll get onto Brogan and we'll arrange a raid on the house right away. You'll be coming with me. Give me a few minutes. Let the others know about this and then sit tight until I get back."

* * *

Seamus dialled Brogan his hands were shaking. This was it, the moment they had been working so hard for, and finally, it was here. The adrenaline was already kicking in.

"Brogan?"

"Sir, it's Seamus, sir, we've got the address for Diana O'Malley sir, we've cracked it." His own voice was cracking too, with the relief of it all, with the excitement of the moment, that special moment when you knew you almost had the criminal within your grasp.

"Great, it's great news, Seamus, what's your next move?"

"Sir, can you please get an Armed Support Unit ready to meet me at HQ. I will be coming up there shortly, with O'Rorden and probably two other detectives. I will need a firearm for O'Rorden, he's had the training before, but we never managed to get it sorted to get an actual weapon."

"Yes, yes, but it's going to take you an hour to get here, can we wait that long, Seamus?"

"Sir, I will be there shortly like I said."

"What the fuck are you going to do, Seamus, fly?"

"Just get them ready and don't let them move without me. This is my arrest, sir, I earned it and so have my team. Can you possibly also get a warrant?"

"OK, OK, OK, Seamus, I don't know what stunt you are about to pull, and frankly I don't want to know but I'll have the team ready don't you worry, and the warrant, just get here as quickly as you can."

"Don't worry, sir, I will, you've got my word on it, you can count on me."

"That's exactly what worries me," said Brogan.

Seamus disconnected and then dialled another number. He spoke for only a matter of minutes and then hung up the phone.

Returning to the office, he found everyone waiting expectantly.

"Sir, while you were away, Hughes here finally managed a triangulation on the mobile," O'Rorden said.

"And?" asked Seamus.

"Well, sir, it's not as accurate but it's the same area as the address O'Rorden found," Hughes butted in.

"Good, great work, so this is it, what we've been waiting for and we're going in. Now listen up, this whole thing is a team effort and I want to thank you every single one of you. Hopefully, we are going to get a result. I would bet money on the fact she is likely to be still there, at her house. I am going up to Dublin to make the arrest and I'll be taking O'Rorden, Hughes and Healy. I've only got room for four people. Duffy, you hold the fort here with O'Flynn."

"But, sir," protested Duffy.

"Duffy, next time, I'm sorry, you've worked hard, but so have they."

"OK, sir, fine," said Duffy trying to hide his disappointment.

"Right let's go, Hughes, you can drive."

They made their way rapidly out to the car and Hughes started it up.

"Where are we going, sir?" she asked him.

"Won't it take an hour to get to Dublin, sir?" O'Rorden chimed in.

"Just drive out on the Dublin road, I'll tell you when to stop," Seamus said mysteriously.

The others looked at each other but assumed their boss knew what he was doing.

In about five minutes they came to open fields.

"OK, pull over there and we'll park."

"OK, sir, but I still don't see," said Hughes doing as she was requested.

"Patience, Hughes, patience."

They parked the car on the verge and Seamus told her to lock it. He then led the way into the middle of a large field.

O'Rorden was just about to open his mouth again and ask what they were doing when there was the unmistakable sound of a helicopter and it was getting louder.

Seamus extracted his torch from his pocket and started to wave it around. The chopper now appeared in the sky above and started heading straight for them. A spotlight came on and picked them out. In a matter of minutes, it had landed a few metres away with the blades still running.

"Come on, let's go," yelled Seamus above the noise.

The four of them sprinted for the helicopter and were rapidly helped in by the crew. As soon as they were aboard and strapped in, it took off and made for Dublin.

"Well, sir, I wasn't expecting this!" O'Rorden said once he had his headset on.

"Ach well, O'Rorden, I had to call in a few favours but go ahead, enjoy the ride."

"This is better than anything, sir!" O'Rorden was looking out of the window like a kid in a sweetshop.

The other two detectives were grinning from ear to ear.

✳ ✳ ✳

Diana was having a smoke, calmly watching the Bishop. An hour was almost up. She had used a number of implements on him as the strap on its own had become a little boring. His rear end was showing the effects and was beginning to bruise a little. She didn't care. He deserved it, he was paying for the crimes of all of his subordinates. Besides, one way or another he would soon be dead.

The alarm rang, sixty minutes was up. The Bishop looked at it in some distress.

"No, no, no, no, no, please not again, no," he started to say.

Diana picked up the gun and stood in front of him.

"Ready for our little game, Bishop?" she said.

"No, please, you have to stop this, please stop it, you can't do this."

Diana spun the barrel.

"What it is going to be this time I wonder? Will it be second time lucky, or not?"

"No, please, no stop..."

It was to no avail. Remorselessly Diana placed the gun against his temple once more.

"On three, then shall we?" she said brightly.

"Nooooo."

"One... two... three..."

The Bishop closed his eyes tightly and she pulled the trigger. Once more the gun clicked.

"Oh dear! You win again."

"I hate you, you bitch, I hate you, I hope you burn in hell!" shouted the Bishop.

"Dear, dear, dear, we are getting upset, aren't we?"

She put the timer on for another sixty minutes.

"Fuck you! Fuck you, you devil, you are the child of the devil! They were right, you are the devil. So, you are!" the Bishop roared.

"I'm afraid you just earned yourself another hiding, Bishop, what a shame."

Diana picked up the cane.

"Remember this?" she asked him.

"Go to hell!"

"Oh, I will, but you will be there sooner than me, that's for sure."

There was a swish and a crack and the Bishop resumed screaming obscenities.

* * *

Within a few minutes, the chopper was over Dublin and very soon landing in the grounds of the HQ building. O'Rorden had not been able to refrain from some ooh's and aah's and pointing out the sights on the way. The others had regarded him with amusement and quite a lot of fondness too. Seamus thanked the crew whom he evidently knew quite well and then they headed for the rendezvous inside the building.

Brogan looked up in surprise when Seamus and his detectives walked through the door to the room where the ASU team were tooling up.

"Where did you spring from, Seamus? We only just spoke a few minutes ago."

"I told you I would be here soon," Seamus said laughing.

"Well, well I'm not going to ask you how you achieved it but now it's your show, Seamus, you can start as soon as you like."

The arrest team gathered together, now all ready and fully armed. Brogan had handed over a gun to O'Rorden warning him to be careful and telling him he had personally signed it out, so nothing had better go wrong. O'Rorden assured him it wouldn't.

"OK, so here's the deal," began Seamus, "I am leading this raid and we move only on my say so. We know the suspect is armed and potentially dangerous. Having said that I don't want any trigger-happy cowboys getting ahead of themselves. I don't want Diana O'Malley shot and I don't want her killed. Shoot only if your life or another officer's life is clearly in danger, have you got that?"

The team said they had, and Seamus continued.

"We go in quietly, and softly, no sirens OK, no blue lights. Everyone moves on my word only, got it? Right here's the address and let's have a quick look at the satellite image."

Having briefed the team, they piled into a black unmarked van and headed for Diana's house.

On arrival, the driver rolled the van very quietly up to the drive entrance.

As silently as possible, the team exited the vehicle. Then, with Seamus leading they crept silently up the drive. In whispers, he sent a two-man team to guard the back entrance. Then the rest of them headed for the front door.

A battering ram was brought up and Seamus was about the authorise its use when Hughes stepped in and stopped him. He looked at her questioningly but allowed her to go forward. Perhaps it was her sixth sense or just luck. Anyway, whichever it was, she put her hand up gently, put her fingers to her lips and tried the front door. To everyone's surprise, it opened. Seamus held his arms out in mute appreciation, confounded once again.

Then, quietly, they entered the house, guns at the ready, it was dark and there appeared to be nobody in, but there, in the silence, they heard muffled cries from upstairs. Leaving two armed officers downstairs, the rest of them softly made their way up, hardly making a sound.

The noises started to become louder and, in spite of the soundproofing Diana had installed, there were the unmistakable sounds of leather striking bare skin. In fact, the soundproofing had been put there mainly for the external walls and so internally, sounds could still be heard, particularly at night. Diana had never been worried, since only Bella was there to hear them.

As they neared the closed door from which the noises appeared to emanate Seamus called a halt and everybody listened.

"So, what do you think Bishop? Which do you prefer, the cane or the strap?" they could hear Diana saying.

"You can go and fuck yourself."

"Language, Bishop, language. Tut, tut, tut, another six for that."

The leather obviously found its mark again by the distinctive sound they heard right after she had spoken.

"You are a fucking bitch from hell, you are damned, do you hear me damned," shouted the Bishop.

Seamus looked at the faces of the officers in the darkness, quite a few of them were openly smirking. He motioned them to keep quiet, got out his phone, moved nearer to the door and started recording.

Smack after smack resounded through the wood, punctuated by Diana's calm voice and the Bishop swearing hysterically. After about five minutes of this, Seamus stopped recording and put his phone back in his pocket. He signalled everyone to get ready.

Two of the ASU team took up position to break through the door. Everyone nodded, they were set.

"GO! GO! GO!" shouted Seamus.

All hell broke loose, at that moment. The door was busted in bouncing back and slamming off the wall. The arrest team poured through the door with their guns at the ready.

"ARMED GARDA NOBODY MOVE!" came multiple shouts.

Seamus and the detectives followed the ASU in, to be greeted by the sight of the Bishop, naked, strapped to a vaulting horse and Diana standing behind him with a leather strap in her hand looking surprised.

When she saw Seamus, she smiled and remained quite calm and composed.

"Ah, Inspector, how lovely of you to drop in," she said drily.

At the same time though, Seamus noticed her eyes slide to the gun on the dresser as if she was considering making a move for it.

"Don't even think about it, Diana, these guys can shoot the eye out of a playing card at five hundred metres."

554

"I am sure they can, Inspector, I have no plans to try to escape from all these lovely officers and in any case, the gun is no use, it's only got one bullet in it, and it's probably not even near the firing pin."

"Get me out of this, never mind her!" yelled the Bishop suddenly recovering from the shock of seeing the room full of armed Garda.

Seamus swivelled his gaze to the Bishop and then became aware of the rest of the team, suppressing loud sniggers whilst still trying to keep their guns at the ready.

"In a moment, Bishop, in a moment. Just for a minute let nobody move."

Once again, he removed his phone from his pocket and began to video the scene.

"What the fuck are you doing, you idiot, can't you see I am suffering here, get me out of this now!"

"Just need to get this for evidence, Bishop, and then, of course, we will help you right away," Seamus told him continuing to sweep his phone around recording everything.

"You dolt, you idiot, you moron, you fucking troglodyte, just wait until I speak to your superior, you'll be back in the traffic division, you'll..."

Seamus completed his recording and put his phone back in his pocket.

"You'll what, Bishop? You'll what? I've got this all on video now, I've got plenty of witnesses, so you'll what?"

"Get me out of this now, I order you!" The Bishop was in no mood to be toyed with.

"In a moment, Bishop, if you please!" Seamus said somewhat forcefully.

He turned to Diana.

"Diana O'Malley, I am arresting you for the murders of Father O'Flaherty, Father Cooney and Mother Joan Margaret. In addition, I am arresting you for the attempted murder of Liam O'Shea. You are not obliged to say anything unless you wish to do so but anything you say may be taken down in writing and may be used in evidence. Do you understand?"

"Perfectly, Inspector."

"I have a warrant here if you want to read it, it's your right to do so."

"No, no that's fine, I'm sure it's all in order." She laughed lightly and continued, "So, I guess you will be wanting me to accompany you to the station?"

"Yes, that's right. You'll be coming to Ballysruth."

"Oh, what fun. Well, am I allowed a change of clothes?"

Seamus considered this and said, "Under the circumstances, I think it might be wise. DI Healy and DI Hughes, you will take Diana into custody and assist her to change. She is not to leave your sight, and please put some handcuffs on her, I don't want her escaping."

"Inspector, you kinky devil." Diana winked and held out her hands. Hughes put the handcuffs on Diana's wrists.

The rest of the team could not refrain from laughing at these exchanges. Diana was quite unlike most criminals they had arrested.

"You can take the cuffs off to change," Seamus said.

"So kind, Inspector." Diana was escorted from the room by the two female detectives to her walk-in closet in nearby to find some more suitable attire.

When they had gone Seamus told the waiting officers.

"OK, so I guess we can release the Bishop and call an ambulance to attend to him. Otherwise, O'Rorden, take the gun into evidence and any bullets, help secure the premises and call in the RTB."

In a few moments the glowering Bishop was released from his bonds and wrapped in a blanket, someone had also gathered up his clothes.

The Bishop's parting words to Seamus were that he hadn't heard the last of this. Seamus wished him well and reminded him videos were all too likely to get leaked if people weren't careful. The Bishop looked daggers at him before being taken away by the ambulance crew. The officers searched the rest of the house and secured it but found nobody else.

Seamus rang Brogan.

"Seamus, I've been waiting here on tenterhooks, so I have, how did it go?"

"We got her, sir, no casualties, no shots fired."

"Excellent news, well done, Seamus."

"We erm, found the Bishop at the same time."

"The Bishop? At her house? Tell me more."

Seamus explained the circumstances and had to stop several times because his boss was roaring with laughter on the other end of the line. Brogan was also very cheered to hear Seamus had video and audio recordings of the event.

"Good, good, you keep those under wraps for now, it might come in handy."

"I intend to, sir, although the Bishop knows we've got it."

"Oh, him, well don't you worry, when he's had a think about it all he won't want it becoming more public than necessary."

"No, sir, I am certain he won't at that."

"So, are you bringing her then, Seamus, to HQ?"

"No, sir, I'm taking her back to Ballysruth for the interview process."

"What? Why? We've got all the facilities here? What do you want to do that for?"

"Sir, a lot of people have worked long and hard on this from that station. We wouldn't even have the address at all or have made the arrest if it wasn't for O'Rorden's brainwave."

Seamus explained about Diana's name switch and the birth certificate.

"So, I owe it to all of them, this is their arrest as much it's mine, sir. They need to be allowed to take the win on it too."

"Yes, yes I see, well OK then have it your way, Seamus, but mind it's done right and tight, recorded and so forth, we need to sew this up properly for the prosecution service."

"Don't worry, sir, it will be."

"OK, well then keep me posted."

"Yes, sir."

Seamus went to find Hughes and Healy and discovered them amiably chatting and already on first name terms with Diana. She was now nicely dressed and discussing the merits of different perfumes while they waited for their orders. She was wearing her handcuffs again now she was changed.

"OK, DS Hughes and Healy, I see you are all getting acquainted," Seamus said wryly. "Get a squad car to drive you and take Diana back to Ballysruth. Both of you sit in the back either side of her."

"Ooh how cosy," said Diana. "I must say, Inspector, you've got a lovely pair of detectives here in Aileen and Iona, and they think a lot of you too, so they've told me."

Seamus blushed. "Right well, thank you, that's kind of them to say so, now off you go, get going, and make sure she gets something to eat when you get there."

"Yes, sir," said Hughes as they escorted Diana out. He noticed they were pulling a small suitcase.

"Healy, what the fuck is that?"

"Oh, sir, it's a change of clothing, for Diana, we thought you wouldn't mind."

"Fine, fine, take it." Seamus rolled his eyes.

"You know these handcuffs are rather plain, I've got much nicer ones in my wardrobe, with diamonds in them, and also some with padding, much more comfortable," Diana teased.

"We'll use the standard Garda issue ones if you don't mind," Seamus said.

"Ah well, as you wish. Au revoir then, Inspector, no doubt we'll be seeing a lot of each other, in coming days." Diana winked at him in her saucy way and then left the room with the two detectives escorting her.

"Everything's getting sorted here, sir." O'Rorden appeared suddenly at Seamus' elbow, he hadn't done it in a while and it made Seamus jump.

"Great, O'Rorden, well once the tech team is here, we'll head back. We'll have to come here again over the next couple of days to look the place over and so on. Plus, we have to interview Diana. God knows how that's going to go."

"But we got her, sir, we got her, surely that's the main thing."

"Yes, it is the main thing for now. And it's down to you, well done."

"No, sir, thank you, but it's down to us, all of us in the team, isn't that what you mean?"

"It is indeed, O'Rorden, it is indeed."

＊ ＊ ＊

Seamus finally arrived back in Ballysruth on a high. Another Garda driver had driven him and O'Rorden there. When they arrived at Ballysruth station he went to make sure Diana was safely in custody. She looked up as he opened the small viewing panel in the metal door.

"Come to say hello, Inspector?"

"Just making sure you are OK."

"Yes, yes, I am fine thanks, of course, it's not quite what I would say I'm used to, but I suppose it will have to do."

"You probably better get used to it, you'll be spending a long time in a jail cell."

"Alas you may be right, Inspector, but that's life." She shrugged in resignation without a trace of discomposure.

"Have they made sure you've eaten and so forth?"

"Yes, thanks, I believe they obtained some very nice pie from your good lady at the pub."

"And how did you know she was my good lady?" Seamus enquired.

"Ah, Inspector, news travels fast in Ballysruth didn't you know?"

"Right, well, I guess I'll wish you goodnight, the duty officer is there if you need anything."

"Room service included, I am so lucky," she quipped. "I'll be sure to let them know. But now off you go to your comfortable bed, Inspector, arresting suspects must be very tiring, and I am sure Kerry will be more than pleased to see you."

"Is everything a game to you, Diana?" he asked nettled by her sarcasm.

"Inspector, I've had to learn to find the humour in every situation, that's just how it is." She smiled.

She was unreadable, that was for sure. Seamus wondered how on earth the interviews were going to go, but that was for another day. For now, he was happy she was securely in custody on the other side of the door.

"Goodnight, Inspector, sweet dreams."

He snapped the panel shut. Her attitude got to him just a little. She was a murderer, he had to keep reminding himself of it.

When he returned to the office, O'Rorden was relating the events of the night to those who had waited specifically to hear the news. It probably was slightly embellished, but Seamus let it go.

He said goodnight to everyone and headed for the Baker's Arms. He had phoned Kerry earlier after the big arrest to tell her the good news. She had sounded relieved. He went to the parlour, to see if maybe there might be something to eat and she was sitting waiting for him, reading a book.

"You didn't have to wait up," he said but part of him was grateful and happy to see her.

"I couldn't sleep, I wanted to be with you so badly, are you hungry?"

"Yes, I am, ravenous as it goes."

"Sit down, I'll make you something nice."

"Thanks."

Over a hastily heated up dinner, Seamus told her all about the adventures of the night in as much detail as he could. He felt able to now reveal the fruitless searches leading up to Diana's ultimate discovery and arrest. Kerry sat there enthralled.

"I'm glad you finally got her, for your sake and for Liam's sake," she told him when he had finished.

"Me too," he agreed. "Thanks, by the way, for sending some food over for her, I am sure it might have stuck in your throat to do so."

D. R. BAILEY

"Oh no, I'm not like that. She's still a human being after all, even after what she's done. Besides, by all accounts, she's had a terrible childhood. I'm still angry about Liam, but I know it's not all her fault."

"You are truly an angel."

Her eyes danced.

"I can also be the devil too."

"Is that a fact?"

"Yes."

"Would you like me to show you?"

"Yes."

They made love, upstairs, slowly and passionately. Taking the time to explore each other's bodies, even though they had done so many times before by now. But each time was new and different. Familiar tastes and scents but also different. Kerry loved the hard muscular frame of Seamus and he equally loved her softness and womanly curves. Their lovemaking was now becoming more familiar and an understanding building of what each of them liked or wanted. Thus, it was more satisfying in many ways. As Seamus moved, on top her, thrusting slowly and then harder, Kerry moaned, and words of love and affection were exchanged in abundance. Their climaxes were sweet and just like apple pie and custard in the analogy Seamus was so fond of. Wholesome, satisfying and often mind-blowing. They lay together afterwards, cuddling close, whispering terms of endearment as lovers do.

"So, what happens now, now you've caught her?" Kerry asked him, lying on her back when the afterglow of sex had slightly dimmed.

"Well, we've got to interview her, hopefully, get a confession, get all the detail we can for the prosecution

562

service. It will take some time no doubt, it might involve several interviews, we don't know."

"So, it could take a while, and then?"

"Well, then we've got to write up all our reports, standard stuff, put together all the files for the prosecution service."

"That could take a while too, and then?" Kerry sounded pleased.

"Well, then there's a lot of other loose ends to tie up, other parts of the investigation to put to bed and file, and in case you are wondering, that could also take a while."

"And then?" her voice was anxious now.

"Well, once it's all done, I'm taking at least two weeks leave and I'll be spending it with you."

"That's nice, so that's at least a month or probably a little more?" she said hopefully.

"Yes, at least." Seamus laughed.

"And then?"

"Well and then we'll figure it out, and when I say we, I mean both of us."

"OK, that's good enough for me, I've got you for a while longer it's what I care about."

She rolled back and pulled him close again, kissed his lips softly.

"Oh, you've got me for a long time, Kerry O'Shea, don't be mistaking that, you might even be stuck with me, so you might."

"Well," she whispered. "And I won't be complaining about that either."

After which no more was said, because they were too busy endorsing their mutual understanding with more kisses.

DAY 14
ONWARDS

W hen Seamus stood up to speak at the morning meeting, there was a spontaneous cheer from all assembled. He was grinning for ear to ear and there were smiles all around. Seamus was a popular figure amongst the team and was acknowledged by most as a great boss to work for.

"Alright, alright, settle down," said Seamus after a few moments. "So, here we are day fourteen and what a day! Our luck finally came through and we've got our prime suspect in custody, she will be formally charged today. So, let's take a couple of minutes to enjoy the win. I'm not going to single anyone out in this meeting, although there have been many stellar efforts from individuals in this team. But that's just the point, we are a team, we stand or fall by what everyone does as part of it, and I am pleased to say we are here and still we are standing. This case was solved, and Diana O'Malley was caught because of the persistence and diligent efforts of everyone here. We've gone down some wrong turns on the way, that is for sure, but we made it, and I want to thank all of you for your fantastic work, well done."

Of course, he had to stop talking then, as he was drowned out by the appreciative response to these words. When the applause had died down once more, he continued.

"OK, so there's still a hell of a lot of work to do. We've now got to wrap this up and prepare a case for the prosecution service. We have to conduct interviews with Diana and I need the interview room set up with TV recording, not just audio, plus a live link into here so others can watch it. Also, I need to have another live link patched through to Dublin so the DCS can see the interviews if he wants to."

"Sir." It was O'Flynn. "I can sort it out right and tight, don't you worry. I'll have it done in the next twenty-four hours or less."

"Great, thank you, O'Flynn! Apart from that, I need all the forensics reports compiled and checked. I need DNA taken from Diana and fingerprints obviously which we can get confirmed as matches for the evidence we already have. All individual reports must be completed and filled in by every officer concerned regarding the actions they took or participated in. Every other inquiry, including the abuse inquiries, all the files for those, and so forth must be brought to a decent completion point. I want reports on those activities written so we make sure everything is filed right and tight. Any potential prosecutions or further investigations on those crimes need to be highlighted. We need to cross check and ensure we have all the right signed witness statements and so on. We know all this stuff, but it doesn't hurt to remind ourselves of it. Take the time you need to finish this job properly.

"Right, so let's get down into the detail a bit more and divide up the work. Oh and of course one important job we need to do is to organise a little wrap-up party, I think we all deserve a night of downtime."

Nobody demurred at the party idea, and in fact, it was greeted with much enthusiasm. Once tasks had been assigned and taken on board, the meeting broke up and everyone got busy. Seamus looked approvingly at the hive of activity now occurring in the office. This was what he wanted. Investigations which were not properly concluded sometimes failed, things got missed. In court, you would be unable to rectify mistakes, so the best solution was not to make any. He knew there would now be pressure to finish all this up quickly for the AC, to get on with the next case, and the next, but Seamus was prepared to resist it, and he hoped Brogan would certainly back him for the most part at least. This was after a major and probably high-profile case they had just solved, it deserved proper attention to detail at the close.

He phoned his boss to discuss how things were going to go from here on in.

"Brogan," came the familiar gruff tones.

"It's DI Gallway, sir, just wanting to keep you up to date."

"Ah, Seamus, well done by the way once again, you've done a fantastic job getting Diana, the AC is very pleased."

"Yes, thank you, sir, but it was a team effort and I've got a great team."

"Of course, of course."

"With this in mind, sir, and bearing with the difficulties of this investigation I was wondering if there was anything in the budget for perhaps just a bit of a party for the team, you know to celebrate the win."

There was silence for a few seconds and Seamus thought the answer was probably going to be no. Brogan was nothing if not tight-fisted where his budgets were concerned. However, when Brogan replied he was evidently in a generous frame of mind.

"Ach, yes, of course, Seamus, just let me know some idea of what you want to do and I'm sure we can accommodate your request, within reason of course."

"Thank you, sir," Seamus said gratefully and with some surprise, "The team will appreciate it." He resolved to speak to Kerry about possibly having a 'do' at the Baker's Arms.

"I know you think I'm a miserly old bastard, Seamus, but I am happy to give credit where it's due and spend some money if needed to show it. In fact, I might even come down there myself for a drink or two."

This was something indeed, thought Seamus. Although he usually didn't want his boss around, his boss plus his boss' expense account credit card would possibly mean more generosity than he had hoped for.

"Well, sir, it would be great, if you can, I was thinking perhaps we could have the celebration at the Baker's Arms sir, the local pub here."

"Whatever you think best, Seamus, isn't it the place run by that woman, what's her name..."

"Kerry O'Shea, sir."

"The one you're sweet on."

"Yes, sir, that's the one." Seamus did not elaborate, and Brogan did not seem inclined to enquire further.

"Anyway, when do you think you can start interviewing Diana and wrapping all this up?"

Seamus was waiting for this and anticipating a battle he went straight into it.

"Well, sir, O'Flynn is setting up the necessary live links in the next twenty-four hours including one to patch up to you if you want to watch them. And then we've got a lot of loose ends to tie up, prepare the case for the prosecution, tie up the other lines of inquiry, such as the abuse, make sure it's all properly filed, and so forth."

"Good, good, and that's all as it should be, so it might take a little while I gather from your tone, well it's fine, take the time you need."

Seamus was astounded. This wasn't at all like his boss to be quite so accommodating. He began to suspect an agenda but couldn't think what it might be. He was sure, if there was one, he would find out soon enough.

"Thank you, sir, there is one more thing."

"And what's that?"

"I will be requesting at least two to three weeks leave once everything is finished."

Another few moments of silence and then.

"Oh, will you now? And I suppose you'll be wanting me to approve it then?"

Seamus sighed, he knew it couldn't all be so easy.

"Yes, sir, I would appreciate it if you would."

"And where will you be proposing to spend this leave, Seamus?"

"In Ballysruth, sir."

"What?! What on earth for? Anyone would think you would be wanting to be shot of the place, so what's there to keep you so tied up to Ballysruth if I might ask, Seamus?"

Seamus took a deep breath, he might as well get it out in the open with Brogan.

"My girlfriend, sir, Kerry O'Shea."

"Girlfriend, oh girlfriend is it? That's what she is now. Well, it's news to me. Since when did you decide to go and get yourself a girlfriend in the back of beyond, Seamus?"

"Since I fell in love with her, sir, if you must know."

"Oh, love is it? Love is it now? Dear oh dear, Seamus, there must be something in the water down there obviously. What are we going to do with you, Seamus? You're one of my star detectives and you've gone and got yourself attached to someone living hundreds of miles away from Dublin."

"Sir, it's not hundreds of miles, it's an hour at the most," Seamus protested.

"Ach well, well I know. But you've gone and fallen in love, now that's a serious thing, it's not like a fling, no it isn't. Have you thought about this properly, Seamus, I mean, I certainly don't remember you asking if you could just waltz off down there and fall in love with the first woman you meet, you know there's a protocol for this sort of thing, Seamus, so there is. You can't just..."

Sir, with all due respect, I don't need to..." Seamus interrupted somewhat nettled by this banter. But Brogan cut him short laughing like a drain.

"Ach well now, Seamus, don't you go getting yourself all hot under the collar, I'm only pulling your leg, so I am. Of course, I'll approve your leave request, you just send it in. Sorry, but I couldn't resist it, Seamus. You've got a reputation for being a bachelor and no mistake, and now you've gone and fallen in love, I never would have thought it."

Seamus was gobsmacked. He really wasn't sure what was happening and now wondered if Brogan had been drinking. It was either that or Brogan had other plans, he'd never been quite this agreeable before.

"Thank you, sir, well I appreciate it, you had me going for a moment though sir, I'll admit that."

"Don't you worry, Seamus, and I'll definitely be coming down to meet this lady properly who's stolen the heart of DI Gallway, yes indeed."

"Of course, you'll be welcome to do so," Seamus answered, his own heart sinking.

"Don't you worry I won't regale her with any tales of your more embarrassing exploits."

"Thank you, sir, I appreciate it."

"It's no problem, Seamus, I'll leave that to your wedding."

"My wedding...!"

At which Brogan who was roaring with laughter said he had to go and disconnected the line.

Seamus was left staring speechlessly at the receiver. Although when he thought about it, the wedding idea wasn't quite so scary as it seemed, in fact someday he might even think it was a good idea himself. In any case, he had got what he wanted out of Brogan, and that was a bonus. Quite what Brogan was playing at, and he was absolutely certain there was something, would no doubt appear in the fullness of time. He shelved these thoughts for another day and returned to the business in hand.

✳ ✳ ✳

Seamus went to check on Diana. The door of the cell swung open and she was sitting on the bed.

"Ah, Inspector, how kind of you to come," she quipped.

"I just want to check you are going on OK and being looked after."

"It's very solicitous of you, considering what you must think of me."

"I don't think anything of you, Diana, for the record, and even if I did it's not relevant. I've done the job I am employed to do."

"What, bring me to justice you mean?"

"Something like that, yes."

"But, Inspector, you must have become a Garda officer for some reason, you must have thought you were ridding the world of criminals like me, isn't that right?"

"No, sorry to disabuse you of that notion, but it's not. I feel perhaps there is an element of that, but the reality is I chose this profession because I like solving problems."

"So, all this is just a game to you, is that it?"

"No, it's not a game, it's deadly serious but you asked my initial motivation and that's what it was."

"And now?" She smiled at him faintly, sardonically.

"It's my job, people commit crimes and it's my job to catch them."

"Hmmm, I am disappointed, I had expected a little more nobility perhaps."

"I try to do the right thing, Diana, and to do my job to the best of my ability."

"You are a man of simple tastes then."

Seamus laughed at this. "You could put it that way."

"Do you think you are doing the right thing, by me, by arresting me?" She seemed genuinely curious.

"What do you think? Why don't you tell me?" he threw the question back at her.

"Maybe I will, maybe I won't."

"OK, well is there anything you need we can do for you, other than letting you go that is?" Seamus changed the subject.

"Well, Inspector, it's not exactly exciting in here, you might, if you are inclined to be kind, get me something to read, from the library perhaps?"

"Well, I suppose there's nothing in the rules against it, what would you like?"

"Anything by Jane Austen would be fine."

"Jane Austen?" He raised an eyebrow.

"You were expecting perhaps the Marquis De Sade or Venus in Furs?" Her laughter tinkled around the cell. "Oh, Inspector, I am a girl of simple tastes in many ways, and like most people, I'm a sucker for romance, although I like to be read to, I'm guessing it's not offer though."

"I'll see what I can do." Seamus decided not to say anything about the being read to part.

"I am obliged to you."

"OK, well, no doubt we will be talking again soon."

"No doubt we will, Inspector." She smiled as he closed the door and got the duty officer to lock it.

Returning to the office, he called Healy over.

"Sir," she said arriving at his desk.

"Healy, it seems Diana would like a bit of reading matter, and I can't see anything against it. Perhaps you could go over and get her some Jane Austen's from the library, I assume we've still got the key?"

"Yes sir, Jane Austen though?"

"It's what she asked for." Seamus shrugged.

Healy went away to carry out this request.

"Should we be making her so cosy, sir?" Asked O'Rorden.

"Why what should we do, give her bread and water?"

"No, sir, it's just that, what she's done... well..." O'Rorden tailed off.

"We're not her adjudicators, O'Rorden, we're not here to judge her, and besides if she's comfortable she might be more cooperative did you think of that?"

"Well, when you put it that way..."

"Exactly. And, have we got those ID's for Anna yet?"

"I will chase it up, sir, but they should be here any day."

"Great, I would like to get her settled over with Kerry soonest."

"Right you are, sir."

O'Rorden returned to his paperwork and Seamus went to see how everyone was doing. It was nice not to feel the pressure of the last two weeks. However, where they went from here in terms of what Diana would or wouldn't say was going to be anybody's guess.

* * *

At the hospital, Kerry was at Liam's bedside for her daily visit. She was idly flicking through a magazine she had stolen from the waiting room. The doctors had told her he may or may not wake up more today, but they just didn't know. They had stopped sedating him and were allowing things to take their course.

"Ma." Liam's voice cut into her thoughts. She dropped the magazine in surprise and turned to see Liam regarding her with his dark eyes.

"Liam!" She couldn't keep the pleasure out of her voice at hearing him speak.

"Where am I?" he asked.

"You are in hospital, darling, you've been shot. The doctors saved your life."

"Oh, oh yes." He squeezed his eyes shut as the memories came flooding back. Diana, the argument, the gun, and now he was here, all because of his stupidity. His eyes flew open again.

"Ma! I'm sorry, Ma!"

"Liam no, you've nothing to be sorry about." Her eyes instantly filled with tears and she reached out to hold his hand.

"This is my fault, I shouldn't have gone with her, I shouldn't have upset her."

"No, Liam, no, you don't have to think about it now, you don't need to."

"But I've got to tell the Garda, I know where to find her, I know where she lives."

"Liam, it's OK, they've already arrested her and she's in custody."

"Oh! Oh, oh I see." He subsided and closed his eyes with the effort.

"Sshhh, Liam, shhh, my darling boy, don't trouble yourself, everything is going to be OK."

The soothing words she had said to him, so many times in the night after a nightmare after he had fallen down and cried when he was young, still calmed him.

"Thanks, Ma." He visibly relaxed.

After another half an hour during which Kerry sat and held his hand, he opened his eyes again.

"Ma."

"Yes?"

"I'm hungry."

She laughed, that was her Liam, the one she was used to.

"OK, I'll talk to the nurses and see what they can do."

✳ ✳ ✳

Later that night over dinner, she relayed the information to Seamus, Liam had started to recover. He took her hand.

"Thank God for that," he said with feeling.

"I'm so relieved, I can't tell you."

"No need to, I can see it in your face."

"He was worried, said it was all his fault."

"He's bound to, victims often do, but it's not. He was in the wrong place at the wrong time, unfortunately."

"Well, he did put himself in that place too," Kerry conceded.

"Yes, it's true, hopefully, we can talk to him soon then."

"I'll ask him tomorrow how he feels about being interviewed, whether he is ready to do that."

"Great."

"So, do you want some apple pie and custard?" she asked with interest.

"Have you got some made?" Seamus said hopefully.

"It's not the kind you eat." She smiled.

"Oh, well, that's just as good, if not better."

"That's the right answer!"

"Incorrigible!"

"Oh you!"

"Well then, where is this apple pie and custard taking place?"

"In our bed."

"Lead on then, lead on..."

Holding hands, they headed for the stairs.

"I'll make you some tomorrow though," she said as they walked up to the bedroom.

"It would be nice."

576

"As nice as this?" She paused outside the door and gave him a long and lingering kiss.

"Nothing could be as nice as that."

"Right again." She laughed her eyes dancing.

He shook his head in mock resignation and opened the bedroom door.

* * *

At the next morning meeting, O'Flynn confirmed everything was ready for the big interview with Diana. Straight after the meeting broke up, Seamus and O'Rorden waited in the interview room for Diana to be brought in. She arrived escorted by Healy who sat her down and exited the room. Seamus started the recording and gave the preamble.

"Diana," he said, "You are allowed a solicitor to be present, would you like one?"

"Not at this point, no."

"We're going to ask you some questions."

"Fire away, Inspector, fire away."

"Can you tell us about Father O'Flaherty, how you came to decide to kill him?"

"No."

"I see, OK, then what about Father Cooney and Mother Joan Margaret?"

"No."

Seamus looked frustrated and decided to try a different approach.

"What happened on the night of the murder of Father O'Flaherty, what did you do?"

"What do you think I did?"

"We know you shot him, but we'd like you to tell us about it in more detail."

"And what if I don't want to?"

"Well that's your right of course, but it's going to make this a very long and tedious process."

Diana simply smiled and said nothing.

"Why did you shoot Liam O'Shea?"

"Who says I did?"

"Come on, stop this, you are being ridiculous, we know you shot him, stop playing games."

Diana shrugged.

"I take it from your answer, you are not going to tell us."

There was no reply.

"Are you going to answer any of our questions?"

"Well, Inspector, it depends if you ask the right questions."

"And what are the right questions?"

"That's for me to know and you to find out."

She assumed a mocking expression as if she was playing with him, testing him somehow, making him sweat a little, seeing if he would break.

His temper was rising it's true, but he had also been here before with criminals and had learned the hard way that shouting at them didn't necessarily work. In fact, if he lost his temper she would have won.

Seamus terminated the interview, they were getting nowhere.

"We'll talk again," he told her.

"I'll look forward to it."

Healy removed her from the room and escorted her back to her cell.

"That went well," said O'Rorden his voice laden with disappointment and sarcasm.

"Let it go, O'Rorden, she's playing with us, testing us, she's trying to see if we will break before her."

"You didn't lose your temper though, sir."

"No, but I could have done easily enough," Seamus said ruefully.

"Probably best not to," mused O'Rorden.

"No."

"What will we do now, sir?"

"Leave her to stew today and let's take a trip up to Dublin and give her house the once over, maybe we can find something to trigger her a little from up there. We need to see what the forensics have come up with anyhow."

"Ok, sir, can I drive?"

"Are you fit, has the doctor said so?"

"Yes sir, it should be fine."

"You best not be lying, or I will set O'Flynn on you."

"I wouldn't dare, sir, it would be more than my life was worth, so it would."

Seamus laughed, and they left the interview room to get their things.

* * *

After a pleasant trip up to Dublin where they had swapped stories about their youth and cases they had worked on, they arrived at Diana's residence. They had stopped for lunch on the way at a pub in a small village and the food had been good, but Seamus said nothing was as good as Kerry's cooking. O'Rorden agreed, he'd certainly tasted a few meals from her pub and could vouch for the fact they were very tasty.

Diana's house was more imposing in the daylight. It was more of a mansion than a house judging by its size, and evidently had a few more rooms than they had seen on the raid. There were neatly kept flower beds and at the back of the house, a conservatory looked out onto a sizable patio and lawn area.

"This must be worth a bit," O'Rorden observed as they walked around it.

"Yes, I imagine so, the dominatrix business is obviously a lucrative one."

"I'll say."

They met up with Jim O'Grady to discuss what forensics had discovered so far.

"Well, well two gluttons for punishment," he observed smiling.

"How's it going, Jim? Have you found anything of interest?" Seamus asked him.

"Well, it's required quite a bit of discipline on the part of my team, we had to restrain ourselves a few times, in fact, Seamus..." Jim began

The other two groaned.

"Oh, there's plenty more where that came from."

"Spare us, Jim, spare us."

"Ach you two are no fun."

They all laughed.

"OK, well seriously then, what we've found is the gun matches all the bullets from the murders and attempted murder and is the murder weapon for sure. We've also got prints on it and they are Diana's obviously. We've got a positive match on the DNA sample taken from her once she was in custody against the black hairs we found at the crime scenes and obviously plenty of others we found here. We've spent a jolly time photographing all of her toys, and there were many, her outfits and so on. It appears her business activities were confined to the 'punishment room' and the rest of the house was used normally. We found her computer, but it was security erased and we can't recover anything from it."

"She's a clever girl that one," observed Seamus.

"Oh indeed, a very smart cookie. We've obviously got her personal phone and the message receiving phone and we are going through those. There are records of numbers, etc. but most of the texts were gone. It's unusual since the providers tend to keep them for quite some time. We'll pass all the information on to you once we're done."

"I doubt it in her case," Seamus said. "She probably had a friend or client who worked there, who would have deleted them for her."

"Yes, of course, I never thought of that. Well, we've looked through everything, different rooms. To be honest, there is lots of nice stuff in the rest of the house but nothing to connect her particularly to the crimes or anything else. We've found some files of her correspondence, etc. if you want to take these and examine them, but I suspect she didn't keep anything which might be incriminating."

"Yes, fine, we'll take those and anything else which might be of use."

"We found her passport and aeroplane tickets, they are all in the box with the other papers."

"Really? So, she was intending to run then obviously, we got her just in time by all accounts."

"Well yes indeed. But then we also found something very, very interesting in her punishment room."

"What was that?"

"The room was wired for sound and had several hidden cameras. In the wardrobe was a set of shelves where we believe a computer system and probably hard drives were placed. They're not there now though."

"So, she was recording her sessions, they would make for some fascinating viewing."

"Wouldn't it just? I am sure there are a lot of people who might be compromised."

"So where is all that stuff now? Where are the hard drives?"

"We've no idea, we've looked, don't think we haven't, but our conclusion is they have been taken somewhere else. They are definitely not hidden here."

"Not in the loft or..."

"No nothing like that."

"Fuck it!"

Jim regarded him sympathetically, it was annoying when you knew there was evidence, but it had simply disappeared.

"There was one other thing though, Seamus."

"What's that?" Seamus looked hopeful again, perhaps this was some good news.

"We found a few strands of red coloured hair in her bed in the punishment room, and also the bath. We also found black pubic hairs we presume are from Diana and also some red ones under the bedclothes. There was also another bedroom, or room which looked as if it had been occupied or used. The bed had the same red hairs in it, and there were a few on the carpet. Obviously, quite a bit had recently been taken from the room in terms of belongings. We ran a check on the red hairs which were usable but no DNA match or anything."

"Were they male or female would you say?"

"Judging from the DNA she's probably female although we can't really be sure."

"That's interesting, perhaps we can take a look at the room."

"Sure, be my guest, it's on the ground floor third on the left over there."

O'Rorden and Seamus made their way to the room Jim indicated. It was a spacious room with a double bed, built in wardrobes, a sofa and chairs, and a small table. There was also a small en-suite bathroom. It more resembled a small apartment than a room and had obviously been occupied and used. There were clothes and shoes in the wardrobe, though gaps where some had obviously been taken. The clothing and shoes were those a female would more likely wear. In the bathroom, there were more signs of use, and there were still some toiletries and other items left there.

"What do you make of it, O'Rorden?"

"I don't know, sir, it seems someone was living here, perhaps a housekeeper? Diana couldn't have kept house herself or possibly even wanted to."

"Yes, it seems a fair assessment. And where is the housekeeper now do you think?"

"I suppose we'll have to ask Diana?" O'Rorden sounded as if he didn't think much of his own suggestion.

"Do you think she's going to tell us?"

"Judging on her last performance I would not be optimistic at all, that I wouldn't."

"Me neither."

They examined the rest of the house for clues and spent a while looking over the stuff in her punishment room. It didn't really yield a lot more information. Besides that, it gave Jim O'Grady multiple opportunities for terrible puns such as 'this gives a whole new perspective on being strapped for cash' and 'no doubt Diana whipped a few people into shape in here.' There were only so many of these they could take, and they hurried off to inspect the rest of the establishment.

It had several rooms which were unused and just contained furniture. Overall it appeared Diana had used the dining room, the lounge, the kitchen and conservatory most. She also had another bedroom for her use and walk-in wardrobe. The bedroom did not seem to be well used either.

After they had seen enough, and too many more terrible jokes, they took their leave of Jim and drove back to Ballysruth.

"What do you think happened to those hard drives then, sir?" O'Rorden asked after they had been driving silently for a while.

"I don't know, what do you think?"

"Maybe the housekeeper has them."

"It's true, I hadn't thought of it."

"Is there any point in asking Diana?"

Seamus gave a sardonic laugh.

"I'll take that as a no then, sir."

"Let's get a coffee on the way, O'Rorden, and forget about it for a few minutes."

"I'm up for that, as long as it includes cake."

"It goes without saying where you are concerned..."

O'Rorden smiled happily at the fact that his boss understood, for O'Rorden, cake was an essential part of life.

* * *

In the evening over dinner, Seamus told Kerry a little more about Diana's background and her interesting professional activities. He felt it was now safe to do so, and it would soon come out anyway, plus it was too good not to share. Kerry was wide-eyed when he described the visit to Diana's house and Diana's punishment room.

"Punishment room, hmm, perhaps I should have one of those," she teased when he'd finished relating the details.

"And perhaps you shouldn't," retorted Seamus.

"You're probably right, I couldn't keep a straight face with all that going on." She was laughing.

"And I'm not really into that sort of thing to be fair," Seamus said emphatically, "though I am sure there are many who are judging by the amount of money she must have made to afford that house and her lifestyle."

"Well, maybe I am in the wrong business myself then, maybe I need to ask Diana how she does it."

"You will do no such thing, Kerry O'Shea." Seamus made a grab for her and then chased her round the kitchen laughing. She let him catch her in his arms and he kissed her.

"You might look good in a corset though," Seamus said.

"Oh you!" Kerry pretended to pout and then, "do you think so?"

"Well, maybe."

"Maybe I should let you take me to Ann Summers then."

"Is that right?"

"Yes, I think you should, now I think about it, I definitely feel it's a good idea."

He held her away from him and looked at her quizzically.

"Are you joking or serious?"

He had never had a girlfriend invite him to do something quite so blatant before. Not that he wasn't acquainted with the store, but nevertheless.

"Yes, I'm serious." She nodded vigorously, and he smiled.

"Well, maybe I will."

"Oh, you will, you've got me thinking about it now and I'm absolutely getting one, and you are going to choose it."

"OK, I guess it's a date then."

"Most certainly it is."

"Wow, assertive, Ms O'Shea."

"Must be Diana's influence."

They both laughed.

"Actually, I've got something important to ask you."

"What?"

"Well, I wanted to have a little celebration for the team, you know, and I was thinking…"

"That you could have it here," Kerry finished it for him. "But of course."

"Do you mean it?"

"Yes, why not, it's perfect, we'll hold a private function. I've got a room for that though it doesn't get used too often."

"The Garda will pay."

"Sounds fine, we can work out a budget."

"Great. And there's one more thing."

"What's that, sweetie?"

"Um well, Brogan will be coming down for the party."

"Your boss?"

"Yes."

"It sounds OK."

"Well, also I told him you are my girlfriend and he'll probably give you the third degree."

"Well, I am your girlfriend, aren't I? And I'm not afraid of him."

"No, I can see you are not, in fact, it's probably the other way around."

"Oh you!"

Kerry looked happy at the news he was so public about their relationship. It made her feel very secure and comfortable and he could see that. Funnily enough, Seamus felt the same way too. He took her hand.

"That's enough talking."

"Is it?"

"Yes, come on, it's time for bed."

She did not resist as he led her upstairs.

* * *

At the following morning meeting, Seamus announced the wrap-up party was on and would be held at the Baker's Arms. Healy, Hughes and O'Flynn volunteered to sort out the details. He went on to confirm the findings of the forensics so far at Diana's house and described their visit there yesterday. Diana's correspondence was taken on by team members to check it over and see if there was anything of interest or of use contained within it. Having dealt with the formalities, Seamus decided to have another go at Diana and see if they could get her to talk.

"Are you going to ask about the housekeeper?" said O'Rorden.

"I'm not sure, I might want to keep that ace up our sleeves, for now, it doesn't do to show your hand too early."

Diana was brought into the interview room, she sat down and regarded them with interest.

"Are you keeping well?" Seamus asked her.

"As well as can be expected, don't worry about me so much, Inspector, I know it's not the Merrion Hotel but it's comfortable enough."

Seamus started the recording.

"OK, Diana, let's see how we go today." He did not refer to yesterday's debacle and decided to ignore it as if it had never happened.

"Go ahead, Inspector." She looked at him with interest waiting to see what he would say.

"Tell me about the Bishop."

"What about him?"

"Why was he at your house?"

"I should think it was obvious from the position he was in."

"I see, well, OK but it wasn't the first time he'd been there was it?"

"No, he'd been before, this was the second time."

Seamus and O'Rorden looked at each other, it seemed on this topic she was willing to open up. Seamus decided to press home the advantage.

"So why did he come back?"

"He liked it apparently, so he said, he enjoyed it."

"He didn't seem to be enjoying it all when we turned up."

"Ah, well it's because he didn't like the game I was playing."

"And what game was that?"

"It was a form of Russian Roulette I suppose, you might call it."

"Perhaps you could explain it a bit more for us."

"Well Inspector, basically I took all the bullets out of the gun, except for one. I spun the barrel and then I held it to his head and pulled the trigger. If the gun didn't fire, then I put on a timer for sixty minutes and then we did it again."

"How many times did you do that?"

"Well, I had only managed two goes when you lot turned up so inconveniently. We had another four turns to go."

"So, your plan was for six attempts at killing him?"

"Yes."

"Why six?"

"I just like the number, Inspector. I like to do things in sixes. My clients always get six strokes or multiples thereof at a time, then I give them a break, give them another six strokes and so on."

"How did the Bishop take to this game of yours?"

"He didn't appreciate it I am afraid, he totally lost his sense of humour, a shame really."

"So, you were planning to murder him?"

"If you must put it like that then yes."

"And then?"

"I am sure you found the tickets and passport by now."

"Yes, we did, so you were leaving the country?"

"Alas you also put paid to that, so you did."

"What would have happened if the gun hadn't gone off after six rounds, would you have let the Bishop go?"

"Oh no, Inspector, I'd have shot him dead."

"I see, so you intended to kill him regardless."

"Yes of course."

"And did he know?"

"No of course not, it would have spoiled the surprise, assuming he made it through the six rounds."

"Why didn't you just shoot him right away?" He wanted to add like the others, but he didn't because he felt she might clam up and they were doing so well.

"It wouldn't have been as much fun, and besides I wanted him to suffer."

"So why did he come to see you in the first place, the first time?"

"He wanted to confess some things, he wanted to be punished."

"What things?"

"That would be telling now wouldn't it?"

"Fine, OK we will park it. So, then he confessed to you and you punished him."

"Oh yes, yes I most certainly did, and I enjoyed it too."

"No doubt. How did you punish him, the first time?"

"Well, I made him strip naked, you know most of my clients like that, plus it's much more humiliating for them and I like that. Then I gave him a good caning, a very good one in fact."

"How long did this session last?"

"Oh, I don't know, I didn't really keep track, could have been an hour or two."

"An hour or two, you were beating him all the time?"

"No, not really all the time, in batches, six or twelve strokes at a time. You know there's a skill and an art to this though you might not think so. You have to draw a fine line between pain and pleasure, understand how to make it last a good long time for the client, and for yourself of course." She smiled a sweet knowing smile.

"And how did he take it?"

"He took it quite well I suppose all things considered."

"Did you do anything else?"

"Yes, as a matter of fact, I did, I secured him to the horse and then I used my strap on."

"A strap on dildo I take it?"

"Yes."

"And how did he take that?"

"Quite well really although he wasn't keen on it at first." She laughed at her own sense of humour.

Seamus and O'Rorden were also having trouble not laughing by this point. Seamus continued while trying to keep a straight face.

"When was this?" Seamus was curious.

"Oh, it was a week or more ago I suppose."

Seamus and O'Rorden exchanged glances, they were thinking about their visit to the Bishop when he was having trouble walking, it was probably just after.

"Who arranged the second session with the Bishop?"

"I did, but to be fair he had been ringing to me to get another session."

"Were you not going to do one then?"

"Originally no."

"So, what changed your mind?"

"I don't like the Bishop and I wanted to kill him."

"Why don't you like him?"

"He's seen too much, and he has done too much, he did nothing about it and he abused his position."

"It would help if you would tell us a bit more about it."

"No."

"What not? Why won't you tell us?"

"It's a bit like a confessional, Inspector, you know, sacrosanct and all of that."

"Right, OK, I am not sure we view it quite the same way, but anyway we'll leave it for now. So, you arranged the session and you were going to kill him."

"Yes."

"But you were also punishing him?"

"Yes, you know like I said. When you go to confession you have to usually pay some sort of penance, say a few Hail Mary's and so forth. My methods were the same, but perhaps you might view them as a little more extreme. They were, nevertheless, very effective."

"So, you're saying the priests, in particular, felt somehow, they had paid a price for their sins after they had received punishment from you, as it were?"

"Now you are getting the idea, Inspector. That's exactly how it was. I personally thought it was a good system." She smiled. "They paid, I got paid too in cash and I got to enjoy administering a bit of pain to people who plainly deserved it. It was a win-win all round."

Seamus had to suppress a laugh at this plainly twisted logic.

"I see. So, getting back to the Bishop, how did you punish him this time?"

"Oh, I used my leather strap mainly, it's my favourite."

"Right, and presumably it was the six strokes at a time sort of deal."

"Now you're catching on."

"Why did you have to punish him if you were going to kill him?"

"I wanted to make him suffer."

"And did he?"

"Yes, I am pretty sure he did, you saw how unhappy he was when you arrived."

"Yes, yes I did."

"I was just getting started really though on the suffering part, I was on the point of ramping it up a little shall we say."

"Why was there a sheet of plastic on the floor? Do you normally have that when you are punishing clients?"

"No, not at all, it's just I didn't want to leave a mess on my carpet after I shot him."

"Yes, right I can see how that would be, and is there anything else you can tell me about the Bishop?"

"No, not just now."

"OK thank you for sharing all of that with us."

"You're welcome."

"So, can you now tell us about Father O'Flaherty?"

"No."

"Why not?"

"It's all a matter of timing."

"What do you mean timing?"

"There's a time and a place for everything, Inspector."

"I see," said Seamus not really seeing at all. "And this is not the time for it?"

"No."

"Can you give us a clue as to when the time for it will be?"

"You'll have to wait and see."

Seamus acknowledged to himself they were done for the moment.

"We will terminate this interview."

"As you wish." She inclined her head gracefully, almost as if she was a princess acknowledging her subjects.

The recording equipment was switched off.

"Thank you for the books inspector." Diana smiled at him.

"It's OK."

O'Flynn arrived and escorted her out.

"That was a bit better, sir," O'Rorden observed with satisfaction.

"Yes, it was, a small breakthrough but we've a long way to go."

"What are we going to do now, sir?"

"I think we'll go and see the Bishop."

"Really?" O'Rorden didn't look happy at all.

* * *

"Come on, O'Rorden, why the glum face?" Seamus asked as they drew up at the Bishop's house.

"Well, I don't think we'll be getting much of a welcome this time, sir, not after what just happened up in Dublin."

"And, I presume you think we won't get any tea."

"No, sir."

"Or cake."

"No, sir."

O'Rorden's face grew longer at the mention of the Bishop's cake which had by now assumed legendary status as far as he was concerned.

"Cheer up I'll buy you some cake afterwards in that case."

"Thanks, sir." It didn't appear this mollified O'Rorden very much at all.

It was not very long before they were being shown into the Bishop's office. A place which was becoming a little too familiar for Seamus' liking. He didn't like the Bishop either although he felt Diana's solution to her own enmity was rather extreme. He wondered how the Bishop would greet them, but regardless of that Seamus' goal was to attempt to get him to agree to make a statement. Given the Bishop's demeanour, after they had released him, he felt sure the Bishop must be champing at the bit to help put Diana in jail, and he surmised it wouldn't be too hard to accomplish his aim.

"Gentlemen, gentlemen, gentlemen." The Bishop got up from his desk and greeted them both like long lost relatives without a trace of irony.

To say Seamus found this behaviour quite extraordinary, was an understatement. He had encountered some divisive people in his time, and some who were very good at dissembling, but the Bishop beat them all hands down.

"Ah now, Detective Inspector Gallway and DS O'Rorden, you must allow me to serve you some of the delicious cake

594

you like so much, and of course tea I think it is for the Detective Sergeant and coffee for yourself, is it not?"

Seamus graciously accepted this and the ritual of ringing for the attendant, who then brought in a tray laden with goodies was repeated once more. O'Rorden, however, was evidently well satisfied with this state of affairs and began pouring the tea as soon as it was brought in. Putting a couple of slices of cake on his plate he took a mouthful with evident satisfaction.

"What can I do for you, Detective Inspector, what brings you here to my humble abode once again?"

Since 'humble' was the last adjective anyone might attribute to the Bishop's residence, Seamus could hardly believe his ears. However, he held his peace and sipped what the Bishop had described as the very best Columbian coffee which apparently money could buy.

"Bishop, I know we met in slightly difficult circumstances before..."

"Now, now, now, I must stop you right there, Inspector, indeed I must. It was very unfortunate, very unfortunate indeed, but we must move on from these circumstances you mentioned, tragic though they may be."

Seamus would not have exactly described them as having been particularly tragic but didn't want to argue.

"Bishop, whilst I understand your first impulse, is to put all of this behind you, we would very much urge you to give us a statement as to your account of the events of that night, leading up to the erm situation in which we found you."

"Ah, ah, ah well yes you see, Inspector, no I really can't remember much about it now I come to think of it, I don't think I would be very good at giving a statement about it at all, no indeed."

"Is that so? So, you have no recollection of being strapped to a vaulting horse, is that what you are saying?"

Perceiving another battle of wits about to unfold before him, O'Rorden proceeded to fortify himself with some further sustenance in the form of more slices of the Bishop's cake.

"To be honest none of those events are particularly clear to me at all," the Bishop told Seamus earnestly.

"You can't remember you went there on two separate occasions seeking out the services of a woman calling herself Mistress Dana whose profession is to administer various forms of punishment to her clients?"

"I wish I could help you there, Inspector, indeed I do, but as I said, I'm a little hazy on those details."

O'Rorden poured himself another cup of tea. As a spectator sport, interviews with the Bishop had so far rivalled some of the very best.

"You are telling me, Mistress Dana did not play a game of Russian Roulette with you, spinning the barrel of a pistol containing a single bullet which she then held to your head and then pulled the trigger? Is that what you are saying?" Seamus was becoming annoyed.

"I have absolutely no idea what you are talking about there, Inspector, that I don't, are you sure you or perhaps this Mistress Dana person are not hallucinating, a pistol, no, no I don't recall anything like it."

"Bishop!" Seamus sprung of his chair and began to pace the room like a caged lion. "We have a person in custody who has committed three murders, is also charged with attempted murder and has admitted to also conspiring to murder yourself. We want to secure a successful case for the prosecution, so they can get a conviction. A statement from yourself corroborating her story. would be invaluable, can you not see that? A story, by the way, revealing the full, and I do mean full details of what happened on that night!"

"Of course, I do completely understand, and I sympathise, Inspector, but I seem to have contracted some form of amnesia on the subject. It's such a shame."

"No doubt," said Seamus in a tone of bitter frustration. "You are going to tell me how you wish you could help but you just can't."

"Exactly, exactly, exactly, how did you guess? I couldn't have put it better myself."

"I am sure you could not, Bishop, since these have been your own words on two other occasions when we have come here to seek your cooperation on very important matters."

"That's quite a memory you have there, though, Inspector, I must admit, I only wish mine was half as good," said the Bishop with maddening affability.

"It is obviously in better condition than yours appears to be at this moment," retorted Seamus by now absolutely furious.

"As I said, Inspector, and as you yourself observe, your memory is so much better than mine, things fade with age, of course, indeed they do."

"How can you say it; how can you sit there and say it? I am sure you know perfectly well what happened and instead you are now once more interfering with the process of justice!"

"Dear oh dear, you must calm yourself now, Inspector, have some more of this delicious coffee," was the only response.

"I am trying to be calm, but you are making it very difficult!" Seamus said crossly.

"Well this is the passion you have for your job, I am full of admiration for it, so I am."

"Oh, for God's sake!" Seamus expostulated forgetting where he was.

"Don't worry, Inspector, I have been praying every day for my memory to return and I am sure God, in his infinite wisdom will prevail."

"No doubt, Bishop, no doubt." Seamus got his temper under control, he was getting nowhere like this.

In fact, he recognised the Bishop had him at somewhat of a stand. If the Bishop did not want to make a statement, he could not be forced to do so. He could not imagine the rationale behind it but obviously, there was one. At the end of the day they had enough on Diana to put her away for a life sentence, so if the Bishop wasn't going to be party to it then the Garda would just have to wear it. Sometimes you had to let things go.

Without further ado, Seamus sat down again and decided he might as well enjoy the coffee which was really very good indeed. Nothing more was said about the Bishop's evident predilection for being spanked, during which time the rest of the refreshments were consumed. Once he perceived O'Rorden had eaten and drunk his fill, Seamus got up to leave.

"Well, Bishop, thank you for your hospitality, we'll be on our way."

"Not at all, not all, so nice of you to drop in, please do come again, anytime, anytime at all, there's always cake aplenty for the Detective Sergeant here."

"We'll be sure to do that," replied Seamus secretly hoping he would never have to set foot in the Bishop's house again, in spite of O'Rorden's desire for more of the Bishop's cake.

They shook hands with the Bishop and the old priest escorted them downstairs to the front door.

"It wasn't very helpful of the Bishop was it, sir?" O'Rorden said as they drove back to Ballysruth.

"No, it bloody well wasn't," Seamus agreed frustrated by the whole outcome. "Diana's statement about the Bishop is not much use to the prosecution if the Bishop won't back it up!"

"Can't he just be put on the witness stand anyway and questioned under oath?"

"It's no good, he could say he can't remember and what judge is going to find him in contempt or accuse him of perjury? A man of the cloth, I don't see it happening at all."

"Ah, I see what you mean sir, but couldn't you have threatened him with the video recording?"

"Brogan wouldn't wear it and besides it would only need for it to be known we'd coerced him in some way and the defence would have a field day."

"Hmmm, it seems he got the better of us then."

"Yes, he did, it was a complete waste of time"

O'Rorden, however, wasn't about to be quite as pessimistic.

"Not quite, sir, though, at least we got some cake, and tea, and coffee too."

"How is it your life manages to revolve almost entirely around cake, O'Rorden?"

"I think sir, it's the other way around, it's the cake that revolves around my life."

"Yes, I think you are probably right."

Seamus chuckled, the Bishop's iniquities were temporarily forgotten.

* * *

The following day the documents arrived for Anna Kowalski. Seamus and O'Rorden drove over to Father Cooney's house to collect her. When they arrived, Anna was waiting with Irene Connolly. She was wearing clothing more appropriate for the weather which they subsequently discovered had been purchased for her by Irene. Anna had a fairly small suitcase with her containing the few possessions she had in the world. She treated Irene with the familiarity of a treasured aunt and Irene obviously reciprocated the sentiment. They had a slightly tearful farewell and Irene pressed her card into Anna's hand telling her to keep in touch. Anna promised she would.

She sat in the back of the car with great excitement talking to O'Rorden while Seamus wrapped up some loose ends with Irene. Irene confirmed all of the evidence had been taken away, the instruments of punishment, and so on. Seamus had previously sent a team over to the house to search it thoroughly, but no other evidence had been uncovered and certainly no written confessions. They would be able to hand the property back to the church. A new priest would soon be in residence.

On the drive to Ballysruth, Anna kept up a steady stream of chatter. Considering she had been confined to Father Cooney's house for so long it must have been refreshing to get out and see the fields and the sky. However, as they approached the Baker's Arms, Anna fell quiet. Seamus looked around to find her looking suddenly scared and apprehensive.

"Don't be afraid, Anna," he said to her. "You're going to love it here, Kerry is looking forward to meeting you."

"Kerry?"

"She's DI Gallway's girlfriend, Anna, and she owns the pub," O'Rorden helpfully explained.

"Oh! Oh, I see, then, in that case, she must be very nice lady."

"She most certainly is that, Anna," Seamus agreed.

Seamus and O'Rorden brought Anna to Kerry's parlour, where Kerry was waiting anxiously to meet her. As soon as she saw Anna she broke out into a big smile.

"Oh, but you are so beautiful, such a beautiful girl so you are," said Kerry taking Anna's hands in hers.

Anna smiled, and but her eyes immediately filled with tears.

"Oh, don't cry pet, don't cry." Kerry folded her into an embrace and Anna's shoulders shook for a little while and then finally she let out a big sigh. She pulled away and looked at Kerry wiping away her tears.

"Nobody has ever called me that, you are very kind lady, very kind."

"Now, now, you come and sit down, I'll give you something to eat and we'll have a nice little chat. Then I'll show you your room where you will be living now. How's that sound?"

"It sounds good," said Anna smiling broadly.

"We'll leave you to it for a while, we'll go and have a coffee in the bar," Seamus said.

"OK, sweetie." Kerry blew him a kiss.

After what seemed a suitable period Seamus and O'Rorden returned to find Anna and Kerry chatting away merrily.

"Hi sweetie, we're getting along famously here," Kerry told him.

"So I see, well we're going to have to go then I'm afraid, but before we do O'Rorden has Anna's new Identity papers."

"Anna, from now on you'll be called Fiona, Fiona Cunningham. I hope you like the name, I didn't really have much choice in it. You can't use Anna Kowalski anymore, I'm sorry. We don't want anyone to find you, ever, we want you to be safe. Here's your passport and so forth," said O'Rorden.

He laid the documents on the table.

"Oh, but Fiona is a lovely name," Kerry said immediately.

"Yes, yes I like it, Fiona, that is good," Anna said. "No more Anna Kowalski, goodbye to her, Anna Kowalski, she is dead."

"Anna, I mean Fiona, told me what's she's been through, I feel so sorry for you darling."

"Please don't be sorry, it's over now, I have new life, thanks to you and to the detectives. I never had such a chance before. Thank you."

"It's OK, darling, you can leave Fiona with me, Seamus, I'll look after her."

"I'm sure you will."

"We'll take you shopping to get some new clothes I think in the next day or two, you look as though you need them," Kerry said with decision.

She had obviously taken Anna, who was now Fiona, under her wing and all would be well.

Seamus and O'Rorden took their leave. Kerry gave Seamus a loving kiss goodbye whilst O'Rorden and Fiona looked on with approval.

"You love him very much, I can see," Fiona observed to Kerry after they had gone.

"Yes, yes I do, very, very much."

"He is good man."

"The best," Kerry replied smiling. "The very, very best."

THE CONFESSIONAL KILLINGS

* * *

The day of the party arrived. Preparations had been made and a press conference was planned for the morning. They were now at least in a position to announce they had Diana in custody and she had been charged.

Other than that, they had not made a lot of progress with Diana herself. For some reason, she wasn't talking, and Brogan was getting impatient. Or at least, his superiors were. Seamus could not understand it and he was becoming increasingly frustrated. Diana seemed happy enough in her cell, she had been given plenty of reading material, allowed changes of clothing, showers and so forth. The female officers, in particular, appeared to be looking after her very well. However, her refusal to open up about the murders was inexplicable and he wasn't sure what to do.

The morning meeting atmosphere was good, everyone was looking forward to the evening do.

"Right, so here we are again. Looks like things are starting to wrap up nicely for the most part. We've got the press conference today and then the party!"

There were a few cheers, whistles and catcalls at this.

"Alright settle down, settle down. I just want to say a few words about that. Firstly, I know some of us like a drink but let's not get out of hand tonight alright. We've built a good reputation in this town and also there may be press hanging around no doubt, so let's keep it clean and as professional as we can. Also, don't forget we've got a very important prisoner in the cells, I don't want her escaping due to negligence. We've got to maintain the duty rota and the duty officers have to remain sober, is that clear? Also, the DCS is coming down for the party, so I don't need to tell you what it means but I will anyway. It means behave yourselves! Also, he's paying the bill, so that's another reason to keep him sweet."

There were more cheers when they heard this news. Seamus didn't like to lecture, but also if he didn't say anything then people were liable to take liberties and he didn't want that. He knew as well as anyone that off duty Garda officers could get out of hand when they had had too many drinks. He'd been to several do's where this had happened and experienced the severe reprimands handed out to everyone afterwards. He didn't want this repeated at Ballysruth.

"OK, OK, now, is there anything else before we finish?"

"Sir, I just want to ask a question, sir, because I don't think it's fair."

"What? What's not fair? It's Nora Reid, isn't it?"

Officer Reid was new to the team and had only been recently assigned.

"Well sir, everyone else is getting a turn looking after Diana and I was promised I would be part of it, so I could get some makeup lessons..."

"What? What that's you're saying?" Seamus had a puzzled look on his face.

"Sir, everyone else is getting makeup lessons from Diana and I'm not, and it's just not fair, I should be on the rota, I..."

Hughes and Healy were frantically digging Nora in the ribs, but it was too late.

"What?! What the fuck is going on? Makeup lessons? Are we running a fucking circus here or is this a Garda station? Am I to understand the prisoner is spending her time doling out advice on cosmetics to all the officers at this station? I'm fucking speechless, absolutely fucking speechless." Seamus had finally lost his cool, and the irony of his last words were lost on him.

"What else is she doing? Maybe juggling workshops perhaps, or perhaps you would like me to arrange her to run a seminar on assertiveness or fifty things you can do in the bedroom with handcuffs. Un-fucking-believable that's what it is. I just can't believe this is what is going on behind my back from professional officers on my fucking team." If he had not banged the table for some weeks, he made up for it now, ferociously punctuating almost every word by thumping the top of it very hard.

The room had gone completely silent and the new officer Nora looked as if she was about to cry. Perhaps the easy familiarity and friendly team atmosphere had belied her into misunderstanding some things were better left unsaid. Those who knew Seamus were au fait with his temper, but they had not seen it for some time. Now it was back in full force. Seamus stopped and looked around, there were expressions of alarm and some of them even looked quite scared. He hadn't meant to do it, but his temper once again had got the better of him. It was one of the few vices that he had, and he now felt a surge of disappointment he had let it out once again. He took a deep breath and closed his eyes for a moment to calm down.

When he spoke again it was in more measured tones.

"OK, OK. Perhaps I was being a little hasty. I apologise for banging the table, and for, for losing my temper so comprehensively, it was unprofessional of me too."

This was quite a concession coming from him. He never usually apologised for his outbursts. Something must have changed, and it was probably something to do with Kerry and being in love.

"OK so, out of curiosity has anyone been reading her bedtime stories?" he said remembering what Diana had said then seeing several hands about to go up amended himself, "No, don't tell me, I don't want to know. Now, let's start again. Officer Reid, I sympathise with your complaint, but you must understand prisoners giving makeup lessons to staff is not the normal way we go about things.

"So, here's what I want from all of you. Please, whatever is going on here I am not going to tell you not to do it, but I don't want to know about it. Don't ever bring anything like that up at this meeting or any other meeting ever again. I trust you all to do your jobs professionally just as you have done. I'm not going to tell you not to do anything and as far as I am concerned none of what just passed ever happened. We will never speak about it again. Just be aware of one thing and one thing only, if any of you compromises this investigation in any way then I will make sure your arse is busted to the traffic division or worse. Have you got that?"

There were sighs of relief all around and everyone appeared to relax on hearing this.

"Great, because I want you to know, notwithstanding my little outburst just then. I think you're all great, in fact, more than great. You are fantastic, you've done a great job and never forget that I think very highly of each and every one of you. So, let's get to work and keep on wrapping this investigation up and tonight, well let's have some fun!"

Everyone cheered at this, and there were lots of smiles. The meeting broke up and O'Rorden came up to Seamus looking concerned.

"Something's eating at you, sir, what is it? This isn't like you."

"Well, O'Rorden, it is like me sometimes I'm afraid, but you are right, it's Diana, she's not cooperating and it's pissing me off now. I don't know what to do."

"Have you thought of asking her?"

"What? Well, I have, and she won't tell me."

"No sir, I don't mean in a formal interview, you know, just ask her, off the record."

"Well, no I haven't that's true."

Just then O'Flynn appeared at his elbow.

"Sir, sorry to interrupt, it's just we've got all the files sorted out we took from the church and I want to know what we should do with them. Are we to take them back to the Bishop's house?"

"O'Flynn, O'Rorden, you two come with me."

Seamus led them outside and away from the buildings. When he was satisfied, they were out of earshot of other people, he spoke.

"Right, I trust the pair of you completely, with my life, in fact, so what I'm going to ask you to do is to go no further than the two of you, have you got that?"

"Yes sir, we've got it," O'Flynn said immediately and O'Rorden agreed.

"OK so, listen to me carefully, these files are not to go back to the church, understood? Not under any circumstances at all. They are to disappear into our archives, archives only you two know the whereabouts of. I want these files available one day, this abuse stuff is going to get glossed over, I am sure of it. Well, I'm not risking our evidence gets lost. I hope you are both catching my drift."

"Loud and clear sir, we've got your back. Those files will be gone from sight, in the next 24 hours, don't you worry about that," O'Rorden said.

"If anyone asks about them you don't know anything about the files at all."

"What files?" O'Flynn said.

"Exactly! Well done, and thanks."

"Sir, you've done so much for us, we'll always be here for you."

"That's good to know."

They returned to the office. O'Flynn went to sort out the files and Seamus turned to O'Rorden.

"OK," he said. "Let's try it your way. You come with me though, just stand outside the cell with the door open. Let's see if we can't appeal to Diana's better nature."

"Does she have one?" asked O'Rorden.

"God knows, O'Rorden, God Knows."

Diana looked up from her book smiling as usual as they opened up her cell. Seamus went in and sat beside her on the bed, O'Rorden remained outside.

"To what do I owe this pleasure?" she asked him.

"Diana, I want to talk to you. How about we pretend, just for a moment I am not DI Gallway. Let's just talk as if we were friends or something like that, do you think you could do that?"

"I probably could, if it's what you want. But what about him?" She indicated O'Rorden.

"I trust him with my life. And, he's my witness that nothing untoward happened here, just in case."

"Don't worry I am not going to betray you, Seamus." She dropped the formality as he had asked.

"Thanks."

"OK, so friend to friend, what now?"

"I want to know why it is you won't talk."

"Don't you know?"

"No, I don't, otherwise I wouldn't be here, like this, asking you."

"Well, Seamus I am surprised. You see, I'm thinking of you. I know you probably won't believe me, but I know you and Kerry are an item. That's a shame because I think we could have made a great couple. If I hadn't been a murderer and you hadn't been a detective. But c'est la vie. Anyway, I figured you probably needed some time, to spend with her, so I'm trying to help you out, spinning things out for a while if you catch my drift. You see, Seamus, I'm not so black as I am painted, now am I?"

Seamus's face showed some surprise, this was not what he had expected her to say at all. To find she had an altruistic side was in some ways refreshing.

"Yes, well I've heard about the makeup lessons," he said wryly.

"Oh that!" she laughed, "Well, you know, us girls..."

"How do you know so much? About what goes on here, about me and Kerry, how do you know all that? I mean you are hardly one for socialising by all accounts."

"Oh, you would be surprised what happens in the library, so you would. The library is where people come to gossip. They don't just come there for books and in fact, the books are mostly just an excuse. People come, they talk, and they think I'm not listening. But I hear everything, you would be amazed at what I know about the people in this town. Who is sleeping with who and so on. It's been very entertaining."

"I see. But why do you want to help me out? I'm a Garda, I've arrested you and you'll most likely go to jail because of me."

"I don't hate you, Seamus. I actually like you, although you may not believe it. You did your job and I did mine. I just got caught. Those are the breaks, I'm afraid. You're a good officer, a good detective, you caught me after all and God knows I didn't make that easy, did I? I've got nothing against you, you've done nothing to me. Not really. Plus, you've been kind to me whilst I've been in custody, made sure I was looked after."

"OK, well thank you, I appreciate it, but, Diana, now I need you to talk. Otherwise, you'll end up in Dublin and it will be out of my hands. If you talk, I can keep you here a little longer, so how about it?"

She sat silently for a moment, considering it and considering him.

"OK, it's probably time anyway, ask me tomorrow, I'll tell you everything you want to know."

"Thank you, thank you, Diana."

"You're a good man, Seamus, tell Kerry she's a lucky girl."

Without warning, she leaned across and gently kissed his cheek rather like a long-lost friend would do. Then she smiled. Seamus blushed. It was nothing but somehow, she made him embarrassed.

Seamus got up to go.

"See you later, Inspector, enjoy your party."

"Thank you, Diana."

She nodded, the formality resumed once more. She picked up her book and resumed reading, as he shut the door.

"That went well," O'Rorden said.

"Let's hope she'll stick to her word."

"Perhaps she does have a better nature after all, sir."

"Perhaps she does at that."

* * *

The press conference for once started out as comparatively a breeze. The fact they had made an arrest made things easier and the biggest issue was resisting the insistence of the journalists in trying to get as much information on Diana as possible. They had to release some details about her and the press would dig and dig until they found out more. Once her profession was revealed however it simply degenerated into a bun fight.

"What did she do for a living?" It was the Irish Mirror who had started it.

"She was a librarian in Ballysruth."

"Come on, Detective Inspector, we've heard the rumours, isn't it true she had another profession on the side?"

"OK, she was also a professional Dominatrix."

"Did she wear a mask?"

"I have no idea."

"So, she was the Masked Revenger after all. Just revenge of a very different nature."

"Who were her clients?"

"We can't reveal that information."

"What did she use to punish her clients?"

"How much did she charge?"

"What did she wear?"

"Was she wearing her outfit when she was arrested?"

The questions then came thick and fast and pretty soon the fact she had committed any murders at all seemed to become a minor issue compared to her other activities. The next day headlines such as 'The Dominatrix Murders' and 'The Priest Punisher' would be seen on all the newsstands. Seamus' low opinion of the press would be confirmed and several officers on the investigation would be shaking their heads in disbelief. Seamus had given severe warnings against talking to the press and although their offices would be besieged for a while everyone would obey that stricture to the letter.

When the conference was over, Seamus fought his way through the throng shielded by O'Rorden, O'Flynn, Healy and Hughes.

"Jesus fucking Christ!" he said when they finally made it back to the office. "That's the worst I've seen it."

"It's the sensationalism of it all, sir, that's what it is," said Healy.

"I hope they'll go away soon."

"Ach don't worry they'll be tired of it soon enough, sir," O'Rorden said.

"I fucking hope so, I really do," Seamus replied. He wondered if the conference had been such a good idea, particularly on the same day as the party. He just hoped nobody got drunk and spilled anything they shouldn't do to the press.

*   *   *

As it was, he need not have worried. There were no journalists staying at the Baker's Arms, they'd had to go and stay elsewhere. Kerry informed Seamus she'd told them all she had no rooms, in spite of having several of them empty. He was impressed at this quick thinking and kissed her many times in appreciation. With some relief, the party went ahead without mishap.

The private room was sizable enough with a bar. Kerry had outdone herself with the food and there were delicious delicacies of all kinds on a very large buffet table. A local DJ had been hired for the occasion.

"Well done, sweetheart, this is fantastic, I was just expecting a few pies, crisps and beers," Seamus said.

"Oh you! Is that all you think I would be capable of?"

"No! It's about the limit of my own party skills though."

"Well, you are just going to have to up your game, Seamus Gallway."

"I can certainly see I will, compared to you."

Kerry had certainly done them proud and within a very generous budget supplied by Brogan which included an open bar up to a certain limit.

"So, are you going to be drinking tonight?" Kerry asked Seamus.

"I don't know, possibly not. I'm not at my best when I start on the alcohol."

"Well, I want you at your best, Seamus, for later."

"I'll stick to the ginger ale then."

She laughed. The party wasn't due to start for an hour and so she said to Seamus she wanted to show him something.

"What? We haven't been Ann Summers yet and I hope you haven't gone without me."

"No, nothing like that. It's something you'll like, a present."

"Oh, really? For me?"

"Yes, come on."

She took him to the parlour and unusually the door was shut. As she opened the door, two little ginger kittens spilled out of it.

"Quick catch them, catch them!" she said laughing.

Seamus gathered them up to his chest and took them into the parlour. He sat down while Kerry closed the doors and tickled their ears while they sat briefly in his lap.

"When did you get these?" Seamus asked.

"Oh well I've been planning it for a while, but they were only just ready yesterday to leave their mother. A friend of mine, her cat had kittens. Aren't they cute?"

"I love them, but how did you know?"

The kittens jumped down and started chasing each other around the floor. Seamus laughed at them with delight.

"After we spoke, at the hospital, I decided to get you a cat."

"But there are two."

"Well, that's one for me and one for you, also so they will play with each other."

"Are they girls or boys?" he asked.

"Both girls."

"Aww. What should we name them do you think?"

"Well, you can decide."

Chloe and Erin were duly named, and Kerry was duly kissed, many times, for bringing them into their lives.

"So, apart from the fact you know I like cats, why did you really buy them?"

"Well, I wanted to be sure you had three reasons to stay here and not just one."

"Oh you!" he said mimicking her favourite saying.

"Oh you! That's my line."

They laughed as Chloe tried to scale Seamus' leg.

"See, she likes you already."

* * *

The party having been highly anticipated went off very well. Brogan arrived, and Seamus asked him to say a few words before they kicked off the proceedings.

"Well," he began. "First I want to say few words about DI Gallway here. I've known him for a number of years and he is an exceptional officer, you've all been very lucky to have him leading this investigation and I'm sure you probably know that. But any investigating officer is only as good as his team, and I've got to say he has also assembled an exceptional team. You've all done a fantastic job, there is no mistake about that. Due to your efforts, we've got a murderer in jail and we're also wrapping up some other very important lines of inquiry. So well done, thank you all, and let's get this party started."

There was much applause at this and Seamus shook his bosses' hand and thanked him.

"Well, now, Seamus, get me a drink and then introduce me to this girlfriend I've heard so much about."

Seamus did as he was asked and left him talking to Kerry. The DJ struck up some tunes and soon the party was in full swing. Seamus stuck to his ginger ale, in spite of a few efforts to persuade him otherwise. As the evening wore on, certain people were noticeably spending more time with each other, and secret liaisons became not so secret. Seamus, Kerry and even Brogan were seen on the dance floor. And towards the end of the night, the slow numbers came up. Kerry and Seamus were suddenly there locked in a slow dance.

"So how was Brogan?" he asked her.

"Oh, he was very charming."

"Yes, no doubt, he can be all of that for sure when he wants to."

"He seems very nice."

"I am sure you charmed the pants off him anyway."

"Oh you!"

Seamus looked deep into her eyes.

"What would I have done without you, Kerry O'Shea, what if I had never found you?"

"It would have been a sad day then, for both of us."

"Yes, that's true."

"But you did find me, didn't you?"

"Yes, and I am glad, because I love you, Kerry, I love you so much."

"I love you too."

Their lips came together in a long slow kiss, as they danced around the floor oblivious to everyone and also to the fact everyone was watching.

Suddenly the room erupted in cheers. Kerry and Seamus looked up and discovered they were the centre of attention. The both laughed self-consciously. They kissed again to be met with more catcalls and cheers. Seamus waved at them smiling all the while.

As the evening drew to a close, Seamus went out for a breath of fresh air. He found Brogan looking up at the moon.

"It's a great night isn't it, Seamus, and that's a beautiful moon, great stars from here also without all the light pollution you get in Dublin, I can see why you like it."

"Yes, sir."

"That's a good lady you've got there, she's a gem, don't let this one go, Seamus, take my advice."

"Thank you, sir, I don't intend to."

"See that you don't, women like Kerry don't come along very often believe me, Seamus."

"I know, sir."

"I don't know what we'll do with you though if you want to continue this rural lifestyle of yours."

"Sir? Well, Dublin isn't so far now is it?"

"Oh, we'll figure it out, Seamus, don't you worry about it."

"Yes, sir."

"By the way, sorry to mention work but while I think of it. If you've finished with those files you took from the church, the Archbishop wants them back. He's been making a particular point of it in fact, a right pain in the arse."

"What files sir?"

Brogan looked at him, with a disbelieving expression on his face.

"Come on, Seamus, don't give me that nonsense."

"Well, I'm sorry to tell you, sir, but the files, they somehow got mislaid, sir, I don't know where they've gone, and I just have no idea how it happened, but there we are."

"Is that right? And is that what I'm to tell the Archbishop now is it?"

"More or less, that's the size of it."

Seamus expected an explosion but instead of being angry, Brogan started to laugh, and he laughed and laughed until he cried.

EVENSONG

Whoever conceals his transgressions will not prosper, but he who confesses and forsakes them will obtain mercy.
Proverbs 28:13

T he day after the party the team had a later start than normal. Seamus had given everyone an extra hour or so in bed to recover from hangovers and the previous night's celebration. Brogan had stayed at the Baker's Arms and he would also be watching Diana's interview on the big screen in the office with the other officers. Seamus had told him he thought this day would be the day. He had confidence Diana was going to talk. Brogan didn't ask him how he knew because he trusted Seamus' judgement.

Seamus went and got Diana from her cell himself.

"Are you ready, Diana?" he asked her as he opened the door.

She was sitting there looking as beautiful as any woman could do. He understood how she had held her clients in her thrall. She was immaculate, nicely dressed and her hair hung down her back in a French Plait. Hughes and Healy had helped her to do her hair, and for some reason, they had formed a bond with Diana. You could almost call them friends from different sides of the fence. Unusual for any Garda officer to do so but Seamus could perceive no harm in it. Seamus turned a blind eye to this and other things like the makeup lessons, as long as the investigation was conducted and completed correctly.

"Yes." She smiled.

"So, this is it?"

"Yes, Inspector, it is. Don't worry I won't let you down."

"Let's go."

The two of them headed for the interview room where O'Rorden was waiting. O'Rorden stood up as she came in and Seamus settled Diana in her place. Both officers sat opposite, and Seamus started the recording.

"Diana, are you ready to answer our questions?"

"Yes, yes I am."

"OK."

"Where would you like to start, Inspector?"

"Why don't we start, at the beginning, tell us about yourself, how you came to the point where you wanted to kill a priest."

"Oh, well. I would have to go back to when I was a child. I was a small girl. My mother, Shannon Flanagan, was a beautiful woman. She was the most loving woman a girl could ever have. She had the same jet-black hair as me, and the same eyes, in fact, my father always used to say I looked like her, just a younger edition."

Her eyes closed for a moment remembering, Seamus noticed small tear ease from one corner of her eyelid, he held his peace realising some of this was probably very emotional for her. It seemed though in a moment she recovered and simply continued.

"My mother used to tell me every day, I was special, beautiful and the strength of God was within me."

Her voice was happy almost buoyant at the recollection, her mother had obviously meant the world to her.

"My mother called me her Angel. It seems funny now, to think it. Me, an angel. She told me to trust in myself, that I was stronger than I thought, and even in the darkest times her love would see me through." She paused, smiling, thinking about her mother.

"What about your father?"

"Oh, him. Well, his name was Joe O'Rourke. They were never married. They pretended they were, but it was never legal. He never cared much for me, not so much as he cared for his drink. He drank his life away most likely, not that I care either."

Her face twisted into a small scowl at the thought of her father, he was evidently not held by her in much affection, something which was easily understood when she related the subsequent events.

"He didn't love my mother, I knew that much, otherwise, he wouldn't have hit her. And he did, when he was drunk. He would hit her and then when he was sober beg her forgiveness. My mother bore it, every part of it and she would protect me, he never touched me. She would have killed him first."

Her voice rose a little higher and she stopped collecting herself once again, Seamus thought perhaps she was almost reliving the painful memory. A couple of minutes went by and the two officers sat patiently waiting.

"So, it went on and on like that, day in day out, week in week out. But I always had my mother beside me, all those early years, to love me, to make my life full of fun and laughter, no matter what. But then came one terrible day, a day etched in my memory for all time."

Tears squeezed themselves out once again and she began to breathe harshly, as if she was about to sob her heart out.

"Take your time, it's OK," Seamus reassured her, letting her try to recover and when she seemed calmer asked, "So, what happened?"

"On that day, he, he... beat her so badly, with his fists and she somehow fell and hit her head. It was an accident of course, but as usual, he was drunk, out of his mind. She was bleeding but he wouldn't get the doctor. He was afraid the doctor would know that he did it. He was afraid he would get locked up, the bastard. So, instead, he ran away, he left the house in fear, the coward. He left me alone with her lying there dying on the bed. She just lay there, all the life oozing out of her, leaving her by degrees, I was losing her, and I couldn't do anything, except to watch her die. You can't imagine, how, how painful it was, watching your mother dying in your arms ... oh shit..."

At this point she really did break down, it seemed for a moment as if she would not, but she began to cry, deep and bitter tears, perhaps so many that she had locked away for all this time. In the viewing room there was not a dry eye either, several female officers in particular were seen dabbing their face with tissue. Seamus was hard to put to keep his own composure, as much as anything it was the way she told it, so visceral and raw, as if it had only happened yesterday.

Once more and at length she regained her composure. O'Rorden slid a box of tissues across the table and she took one gratefully.

"Sorry," she said to Seamus.

"It's OK, I understand, continue when you are ready."

Her breathing steadied and she began again, "I didn't know what to do. As my mother lay there on the bed, dying, she took off her necklace and put it around my neck. She said to me, this was her heart and she would always be with me, her heart would always be with me. I held on to her, I pleaded with her not to die, but she did die, she died the very next day. I prayed to God, but God didn't listen. He let my mother die. I prayed to him, to bring her back, like Jesus Christ, but he didn't. He didn't..."

She stopped for a moment, the tears were once again running down her face. She reached for another tissue. In the viewing room Healy noticed Hughes was openly and silently crying, her hand slipped into her colleague's for comfort and received a grateful smile.

"Take your time," Seamus said gently. He looked at O'Rorden and his number two's eyes were glistening.

Diana seemed to finally compose herself, and the clouds in her brow cleared. She started to brighten up a little.

"I was so very young, but I watched my father leave my mother there to die. And from that day I hated him, with a passion. You could say it was the day I learned the other side of love, and that was hate, pure hate. So, then I stayed there, with my mother, holding her, holding her dead body. I don't know how long it was, a day, two. I wouldn't leave her. Finally, someone came, I think it was a friend of hers. She saw my mother lying there and the Garda were called. Then I was taken away. I was torn out of my mother's dead arms, just like that, not even allowed to say goodbye to her... you have no idea... no idea at all how that... felt..."

Again, another bout of grief from Diana, at this fresh revelation. Hughes gripped Healy's hand even tighter as the story was almost too hard to bear.

Through the choked-up tears Diana continued in a ragged voice, "I screamed and cried for her, but nobody listened. They took me away, to this place, the hellhole they called the Faith, Hope and Charity Catholic Home for Orphaned Children. It wasn't a home, it was a prison, it was a torture house. I was handed over to Sister Joan Margaret, she was a sister then I think before she took it over. That one time was the only time she was nice to me. She held me close and called me a poor child. I cried, in her arms. Little knowing what was to come. That fucking bitch..."

Diana's face now twisted in anger, directed at the woman she had killed.

"And what was to come Diana?" asked Seamus.

In a voice full of venom, she almost spat out the words, twisting her hands together as she spoke, her voice rising with passion as she told this part of her story.

"The next day, I was called to the Mother's office. Mother Belinda. Mother Bitch Face is what I used to call her. She told me my own mother was taken by God and was with God now. I was angry, I shouted at her God was a liar, and my father had killed her, and he was a bastard, a bastard from hell. She told me not to blaspheme, not to tell such lies, not to swear. She brought a cross and put it in front of my face ordering me to ask for forgiveness for what I had said. I took that cross and smashed it on the stone floor. I said 'take that you fucking bitches!' That was the first time I got the belt."

She laughed then, breaking the tension. "I learned those words from my father, probably the only good thing he ever taught me. Imagine their faces hearing 'fuck' from a girl my age, they were properly shocked, so they were."

"So, then what happened?" Seamus prompted.

She was still laughing. "Oh, they grabbed me, remember I was a small child. The Sister put me across her knee and pulled down my pants, she held me down. The Mother took the belt they used and gave me a real hiding. I screamed and cried but it was no use. In the end, I had to stop, it hurt so bad, but I didn't care. At that moment I vowed to myself I would no longer turn to God because God had turned away from me. I decided to embrace the devil and that's how it began."

"And did you? Embrace the devil?"

Her demeanour seemed to have lightened relating this part, it might be imagined the beatings were the worst thing, but it seemed this was not so, in fact she even smiled as she carried on talking.

"Well no, not really, I'm not a Satanist if that's what you want to know. It was just symbolic. I turned against God because the nuns symbolised God and I hated them. I identified them with God. They called me the devil, and, in a way, they were right. I did everything to harass them, to break the rules. I destroyed things, artefacts, everything. They hated me. I became the target for Sister Joan Margaret's ire. I was beaten by her on a weekly basis, sometimes more than once. All through my life there until I became around fifteen or sixteen. You know after a while, the beating becomes nothing, it has no effect."

She was still smiling. "You can see where I learned some of my trade though, Inspector."

"Yes, yes, I can, I can see that. I'm sorry this happened to you."

"Don't be sorry, it's just life." She shrugged it off.

This was the remarkable thing about Diana, she could change in an instant like the wind. Seamus brought her back to the subject on hand.

"And then what happened?"

"Well, I hadn't really changed and perhaps she realised beating me did not help. So, she took me to Father Cooney. She said he would be able to exorcise my demons. Except he did not. He cursed me and thundered at me. Then assaulted me and he raped me. Now he was a real bastard too, so he was, that was something new to me at first, being raped like that, the bastard."

She spat the words out then, obviously Father Cooney was burnt into her psyche, because her brow became thunderous and her expression murderous.

"How many times did he rape you, Diana?" Seamus tried to lighten her mood, by trying to be a little matter of fact.

"He raped me almost weekly I suppose, and then afterwards he would beat me. He would strip me naked and touch all of my naked flesh. Run his hands all over me, clutching at my breasts and so on. Then he'd get all excited and rape me. He was a disgusting man. I hated him!"

Her mood did not change and in fact appeared to get darker as she continued, "He told me he could not help me, but he never tried, he never tried. He encouraged the Sister to beat me more and sometimes she came to watch him, watch him abusing me. He said this was what God wanted. Such fucking bullshit, fucking bullshit, God wanted it my fucking arse." Her voice was now a low growl almost feral thinking of Father Cooney.

"So, you were raped and physically abused multiple times over a number of years?" Seamus asked as lightly as he could.

She paused for a moment, recovering her poise, clearing her thoughts, once again. It seemed uncanny how quickly she could do this Seamus thought. Then she spoke in a much more normal tone, almost conversationally.

"Yes, yes until I formulated a plan. I resolved to run away. I stored up food, I stole money from the collection, I hid it all in a special place, with my mother's necklace. They didn't suspect a thing because I learned to put on a mask. To pretend, that I was obedient, penitent. I did it but sometimes the devil in me came out, earned me another beating. But for the most part, they thought perhaps they were winning, but they weren't. I was just very good at hiding it. One day, late at night, I took it all, the things I had stored away, put in a bag and I ran."

That part made her smile, as it would anyone who had escaped from such a hellhole. It was almost a relief to everyone listening to hear it.

"What did you do, where did you go?"

"Just anywhere," she shrugged, "it's a long story but some women eventually took me in. I found out they were prostitutes. They looked after me, fed me, clothed me. Ironic isn't it, a pariah of the church found solace in other pariahs."

"Did you become a prostitute yourself?"

She was calmer now, on more familiar ground coming into the present, where perhaps it was easier.

"No, not exactly. One of them was a Mistress. She used to give men, mainly men, beatings, so I became her assistant. She was very good to me, like my mother she was, she's dead now poor soul. I learned the trade. I also went to school, finally was able to educate myself properly. Then I realised I would be able to do this myself, on my own. I saved enough money and started up my own business. Then things continued from there. And of course, I also discovered priests, those supposed holier than thou men, were not exempt from such carnal desires and possibly the desire in many of them to be punished was more exaggerated."

"I see," said Seamus.

"Well you've seen my place, Inspector, I worked hard to get it, a lot of hours and a lot of beatings." She laughed. "Oh, you probably think a dominatrix has an easy life, but I can tell you that it takes it out of you, so it does."

"I never thought it for a moment," Seamus told her without any display of the irony he felt about it.

"Anyway, I suppose you build up some good arm muscles. I'm pretty good with both hands too I'll have you know." She winked at him in a saucy way.

"I am sure you are, Diana, but anyway perhaps you could tell us this." Seamus felt slightly embarrassed with this teasing and tried to bring the interview back to the point. "When did you decide you were going to murder Father O'Flaherty?"

She sighed a big sigh, as if this was quite a boring topic but nevertheless began to speak, "I decided many years ago the people who had made my life a living hell would have to die. Part of everything I have worked for was to fulfil the promise I made to myself. I wanted to avenge myself but also my mother. Somewhere in the back of my mind, was that if I could take some of God's servants, I would be paying him back." She laughed. "Of course, it was when I was younger, but now, I know that I did it for me and for the others that were abused by those bastards."

"I see. So, talk us through the murder of Father O'Flaherty, how did you prepare for it, carry it out?"

"Ah well, I got the job in the library to help me with my research. I wanted to find out whether these people had done anything to others, I wanted to find out more about them. I researched them thoroughly. Father O'Flaherty had abused me, at least once, Father Cooney took me to his house a few times and he and other priests raped me and then beat me. Such a bastard, such a fucking bastard."

"Would you be prepared to give us more accurate dates and times of some of these events?"

"Yes, yes I would, no problem at all with that, it's about time somebody knew the truth."

"Sorry, carry on."

She stopped again for a little while as if thinking about the murder or perhaps what she ought to say. In the end she said an awful lot, "I decided it was time for the Father to die. I can't really tell you why. I just felt ready. You might not think it, but it was a big step. To kill. I didn't do it lightly. I was able to get the gun easily enough through a client, and the ammunition. I chose a particular day for the killing and made sure I had dressed in plain clothing with a hoodie to shade my face. I had my hair tied up, so it wouldn't be so easy to tell if I was a man or a woman. I timed it for around confession. I had been observing the Father for a while, from my car, watching who went to confession and when."

Observing her now, Seamus could see this other side of her, which was cold and clinical. It was the hallmark of someone who had killed, they often had no problem relating the contents of their crime as if it was a trip to the supermarket. This part of her story was much less infused with passion, he supposed perhaps the shooting of the priest was in some way a catharsis for her, albeit a very drastic and catastrophic one for her victim. The emotion she had felt was probably already spent.

"The day I picked it was unlikely anyone else would come. Also, I knew his attendance was dwindling. I parked the car up the road, went into the church and sat in the pew. The Father came in and saw me. He asked me if I was OK and I didn't answer him, I couldn't speak. Then he went into the confessional. I nearly left at that point, lost my nerve. But then I decided no, Diana, you are going to do this. I went and sat in the stall. He asked me if I had anything to confess and I said yes. I told him I had killed a priest. He looked a bit concerned and he asked who? I said you. Then I held the gun on him. He started to ask me why. I called him a bastard and shot him dead with one shot. Then I stepped out and walked away. The stupid woman with her dog was at the gate, so I just walked past as fast as could, got in my car and drove away."

"How did you feel, after you had done it?" He wanted to know particularly because right now it was as if she did not feel anything.

As she answered this though, her face and voice took on an air of excitement almost as if she was back there just after the murder, "I was shaking. The adrenaline was pumping through me. It was like a high, a hit from a drug. I don't know. I am not going to say I didn't enjoy the moment, or that I'm not glad he was dead. But it wasn't as good as I had hoped. I didn't feel as if I had been vindicated."

"Did you regret it?" Again curious, to see if she had any kind of remorse.

"No, regret is too strong a word. He deserved it. He had done so many bad things, he deserved to die. That's how I felt."

It seemed she did not, from her answer.

"And Father Cooney and Mother Joan Margaret?"

"Well, it was much the same thing I suppose. I planned it in the same way. I observed them carefully. Plus, he was my real target. So, I carried it out the same way." The same matter of fact tone, without much emotion at all.

"But you didn't though, you shot him in the back of the head and then five times more."

There was now a tinge of regret in her voice, but Seamus suspected this was because she had lost control, not because she had killed.

"No, it didn't go the way I had planned it. Not at all. When I got into the confessional, I became angry, I became enraged. It wasn't enough to just kill him, I wanted him to know it was me. That I was taking my revenge. I forced him out of the confessional and he still didn't know me. So, I showed him a picture and then he knew. And then I wanted him to suffer I suppose, it's why I made him kneel down, and I shot him like that. Once you've killed one time, the second time is easier. They say that and it's true. And then once I had shot him I just lost control. I emptied the pistol into his body, the rage inside of me came out in those moments."

"And Mother Joan Margaret?"

The mention of the Mother was different. Once again Diana's face twisted into a scowl, her voice pitched much lower and vibrated with sudden emotion, "Well, it was just unfortunate, for her that is. I wasn't planning to kill her at the same time, it was possibly going to be another day, but she came into the church. I was still angry, in a rage. I saw her, and I snapped. I tried to shoot her, but I forgot the bullets were gone. She recognised me, and I wanted her to know I was the one who killed her. I wanted her to realise she died at my hands, the hands of the devil. I kept on hitting her, with the pistol, again and again."

Dian closed her eyes on this, as if even for her this mental image was too much too bear, as if she was ashamed of the way she had killed the woman. It had been incredibly brutal. Seamus didn't believe underneath it all Diana was such a vicious or hard person as perhaps she wanted them to think. In anger and passion people did terrible things, things they wouldn't believe they could do. This was possibly how Diana felt.

Opening her eyes again slowly Diana continued, "She went limp and I dropped her to the floor. I was holding her by her throat. Then I left. It's a shame those idiots were in the graveyard. I didn't see them, but I found out later on the news. I drove away and then I found I had her blood on me, I was disgusted by it, so I threw away the wig and the other stuff into the verge. Obviously, I didn't throw it far enough, your forensics boys are good though, very thorough."

"Did you wear the wig on purpose, to implicate someone else?"

"No, of course not, it was just a disguise. Anyway, after the eyewitnesses and the photofit, I became worried. I decided to lay low. I was surprised you had not twigged me from the photo."

It appeared to Seamus, from that answer, Diana had been simply lost in her own path of twisted tortured vengeance. It seemed, in a way, such shame.

"Did you plan to kill any other priests?"

"Well, originally I had thought of it, but after I had killed Father Cooney and Mother Joan Margaret, I think I had perhaps felt I had done enough."

"But you still wanted to kill the Bishop."

"Yes, well I've explained he was an exception."

"Quite," said Seamus secretly thinking exception was a very appropriate word, and then, "so why did you shoot Liam O'Shea?"

"It was a mistake. I never meant to do it." Her eyes clouded over, and they started to glisten. Obviously there had been some feelings there, for Liam.

"What was Liam to you?" He was asking this as much for Kerry as for the Garda, he knew.

"I loved him. At least I fancied myself in love with him. I knew he had a lot of other girls I suppose but I'm a very jealous person. I tried to block them out of my mind. But then he asked me for help when he was on the run. We had been lovers, on and off. We had sex, at my place mainly. He knew what I really did for a living. He knew I lead a double life at the library."

There were a few tears running down her cheek, it was plain he had meant something to her. She wiped them away with the back of her hand.

"Anyway, I met him at the hotel. I used it for some of my clients down here. No doubt you found my punishment kit. The night before I shot him, I arrived, and we slept together, made love. I asked him to run away with me, start a new life. He wouldn't, I got angry, I got so very angry. I didn't know what I was doing, I got the gun and even then, I wasn't meaning to shoot him. I wanted to scare him, I don't know, I was in a crazy frame of mind I suppose. Then he threw a stone dog at me and then I reacted. I shot him twice. Oh shit, oh shit, I'm sorry, I am so sorry I never meant to..."

The moment of the shooting had hit her with a jolt, it showed in her face. She had screwed up her eyes, trying hard to block it out, but for a few short seconds the scene of her shooting Liam replayed itself over and over in her mind. She waved a hand ineffectually to ward off the images. A sudden storm of grief overtook her, and she buried her head in her arms on the table sobbing hard.

This was difficult to watch for everyone concerned. On the one hand Liam was well known and liked amongst some of the officers' present and of course he was Kerry's son. On the other hand, here was a woman plainly distraught and suddenly wracked by guilt for what she had done.

They waited for her sobs to subside, which they eventually did. She sat up with a tear stained face and made no effort to wipe it clean. Her mascara had slightly run but she didn't seem to notice.

Very softly and gently Seamus said, "But then you left, you could have stayed. You could have made sure he didn't die."

"Yes, I know. But survival kicks in, Inspector. It's something you learn when you've had to do it all of your life. I simply ran, I know it's bad, I can't justify it to you. It's just what I am. Perhaps it shows I didn't really love him after all if I had then perhaps I would have stayed and faced up to the consequences." She looked distraught but also as if she had simply resigned herself to what would be. Most people couldn't understand how she walked away, but then most people were not Diana.

She paused for a moment, trying to finally overcome her emotions and then she spoke, with self-loathing and some bitterness.

"I know you think I am a callous bitch. I am sure you hate me for leaving Kerry's son." There was a part of Seamus thinking really it was Diana who hated herself for her selfish act.

"I am not here to judge you, Diana."

"Well, I probably am a callous bitch, to be honest. I wouldn't blame you if you thought that or hated me." Again, the tone of self-abnegation, as if she needed someone to hate her, to make her feel some guilt. Seamus wasn't going to play her game.

"We are not here to hate you or judge you, we are here to get the truth," Seamus said.

She looked at him, wanting him to say something bad to her, wanting him to judge her, to punish her at least with words, but he was having none of it. She sighed.

"I can see why Kerry loves you, Inspector," she said suddenly and frankly.

"I'm not a saint, Diana," he responded.

"You are pretty damn close, let me tell you." She smiled a weak smile.

He smiled back unable to stop himself.

She shrugged, leaned forward to the tissue box and began to wipe her face with a tissue.

"Well, Inspector, that's pretty much it then. The rest you know. That was fun now, wasn't it?" she said sardonically, deprecating her own recent emotional display.

"Thank you, Diana, thank you for telling us all of that, we'll want to get it all in a more detailed statement if you are willing to do so and sign it."

"Yes, yes I am."

"I have a couple more questions."

"OK."

"Was there anyone else living at your house?"

"I'm not going to answer that." Her eyes narrowed, this was dangerous ground.

He noticed but continued, just to see if he would get somewhere, "OK, well then let me put it to you another way, we know there was. We have evidence someone with red hair lived there. I imagine perhaps your housekeeper?"

"I said I am not going to answer that."

"Where is she now?" persisted Seamus.

Diana said nothing.

"We know you recorded your discipline sessions, where are the hard drives and the recordings."

"I have no idea."

"I think you do."

"You can think what you want." This wasn't in the script, she was plainly not happy with this line of questioning.

Seamus realised they had touched a nerve. He hesitated before pursuing it, it wasn't necessarily important. He decided to try once more.

"You know we could try to find her don't you, Diana, we know she was a woman. Why don't you just tell us?"

"No! This has nothing to do with her! She doesn't know anything, and you won't find her. Just leave her alone, leave her out of this, I've told you to what you want. Leave her the fuck alone. Just leave her alone, please, just do this for me, please." Her voice once again rose to a frantic pitch, and she had started to cry again, it was obvious to Seamus this person meant something to her, and in fact from her reaction she probably meant quite a lot. But it was also clear enough if he pushed her anymore it might destroy the rapport they had built up, for good.

"Diana, it's OK, it's OK, I won't ask you anymore, OK. We're letting it go, just keep telling us what we need to know, and we'll let it go."

After a few moments, Diana appeared once more to pull herself together. She sat up straight and looked at Seamus. It was as if nothing had just happened at all. She looked perfectly composed. Apart from her slightly ruined makeup one would be forgiven for thinking nothing whatsoever had occurred to ruffle her mental state.

Seamus decided it was time to terminate the interview. They had probably got what they needed for the moment.

"That's all, for now, Diana, we'll talk again when we need perhaps a bit more detail on what you've told us."

"OK, Inspector, as you wish." She smiled brightly.

Seamus ended off and shut off the recording equipment. He was about to stand up to escort her back to her cell when she decided to speak.

"Let me ask you something, Inspector. Off the record, just between us three here. Why couldn't you just have let me go? You could have walked away," said Diana bluntly.

"I couldn't do that, it's my job," said Seamus taken aback by the candid question.

"Why? These men, these priests you know what they've done, to me, to others, they are dirty, dirty men, perverts, the worst kind."

"You could have come forward instead and we would have prosecuted them. Why didn't you do that?" he countered.

She snorted. "Prosecuted? Prosecuted is that it? Don't make me laugh. And who would have believed me, and would they have received justice even if I had been believed? No, the church would have covered it up like they always do, interference in high places, but they wouldn't have paid. No fuck them. My way, they paid. They fucking well paid."

"Yes, they did pay, with their lives. Why did you have to kill them? You were beating the life out them anyway, on a regular basis they came to you for punishment, wasn't it enough for you? Why did you kill them, Diana?"

"Do you really want to know?" she asked.

"Yes, yes I do."

"I'd had enough, I didn't want them to live. They didn't deserve to live. It was too much, what they'd done. It wasn't enough. Sure, I caused them a lot of pain, but they deserved to die. To fucking die for what they did. And I didn't want anyone to do go through that again. Their role was to save souls and they ended up destroying them instead, like mine."

It was clear all of the recollections had powerfully affected her, the emotional undercurrents she had kept in check for so long were just beneath the surface waiting to escape.

"You should have let me go. You're on the wrong side, DI Gallway, you're on the wrong fucking side."

"No," said Seamus emphatically. "No, I am not. There is no place for vigilante justice. Not in my world. It's not what I joined the Garda for. For all its flaws we have a justice system and it works as well as it can. I have to adhere to that and to the law."

"Justice. Don't preach about justice to me, in your world maybe but in my world, they got their fucking justice, I gave it to them."

Seamus softened his look and waited. He watched her face, one minute it was like a miniature thunderstorm and the next a blue and cloudless sky. It happened almost as if by magic, her brow cleared. This was the disconcerting thing about her, the way she could simply flip from one mood to another. Seamus could tell it wasn't an act. The life Diana had lived, had moulded her, made her who she was. God knows what it had done to her psychologically. However, it wasn't his to ponder, it was his to do his duty. Some days reconciling duty was harder than others.

"We're not going to agree on this one, Diana," he replied quietly. "And where you are going to you will have a long time to reflect on the philosophical implications, among other things, of what you've done."

"You're a funny guy, Inspector, I'll give you that." She laughed. He grinned unable to help himself. He had certainly meant to be sardonic.

"Is there anything else?"

"I guess that's all, Inspector, for the moment."

Seamus stood up. He had formed a lot of respect for her, as a woman and also one with a lot of guts, even if she had killed two priests and a nun. He took her back to her cell with O'Rorden. Hughes and Healy were waiting to see her into it and settle her down. Seamus could tell they had both been crying. He left them all together and passed no comment.

As they headed for the office O'Rorden turned to him.

"I said at the beginning, sir, it's a bad business."

"Funny how I thought you would say that, a bad business," Seamus laughed.

"And it is, sir, it certainly is indeed" affirmed O'Rorden.

"Come on, O'Rorden, let get out of here and have a coffee."

"No need for that, sir, I can make one."

Seamus paused and looked at him purposefully.

"No," he said firmly "That you won't, O'Rorden, that you bloody won't."

ACKNOWLEDGEMENTS

Thank you for reading this book. Crime is one of my most favourite fictional subjects. I have tried to write the story I would want to read. I've enjoyed the journey immensely and hopefully you have too. As an indie author reviews are important to me. I hope you will consider leaving one if you enjoyed it. This is the first book in a series about DI Gallway and the characters I have created. I have already fallen in love with them and their lives, they continue live on in my head and will do so in the forthcoming series. They will definitely be back with more mysteries to solve next time.

I would like to thank my wonderful wife who has encouraged me to complete this novel. She sat and let me read it to her, and what could be a better compliment than that? She also contributed ideas to the story and characters. I am grateful for her support in so many other ways. She has gone through her own personal battles with her health and in spite of that has always been behind my ambitions to make it as a writer. Without this I couldn't have succeeded.

I also want to thank my daughter, for her encouragement, help and support. Wherever we are in the world we still manage to have our long and hilarious conversations.

Thank you also to our friend Sharon who has been so helpful and supportive through some very difficult and trying times. We are eternally grateful.

And to everyone else along the way who has brought their fun, love and laughter into our lives. They know who they are.

ABOUT THE AUTHOR

D.R. Bailey was raised in a family of bibliophiles. From an early age he developed eclectic tastes in fiction including; SciFi, Romance, Crime, and the Classics. Some of his favourite authors remain Gerald Durrell, Jane Austen, Peter James, Ellis Peters, and Isaac Asimov.

At the age of eleven he wrote his first fictional story about his toy teddy bear clan. Since then he has gone on to have some of his non-fiction article published in magazines and also a fictional crime series.

He has engaged in several different careers and says that these life experiences have all contributed greatly to his penchant for storytelling. Bailey has now penned his debut full length crime novel, which is a genre he is particularly fond of.

Made in the USA
Monee, IL
09 May 2020

30181260R00377